To

Second
Chance

By

Dodie Hamilton

With Love

Dodie

xx

Dedication:
To my husband, my own personal angel
And to family and friends throughout the world

Acknowledgements
Thanks to Josie and John Lewin, co-founders of Spirit
Knights Paranormal Investigation. To Pat and Lee Jay in
Spain for their endless kindness. And to Simon Richard
Woodward and Julie Whitton Dexter, who are always
there for me and who I do love most dearly

Prologue

'We therefore commit his body to the ground, earth to earth, ashes to ashes, dust to dust, in the sure and certain hope of the resurrection and life to come.'

An icy wind whipped the preacher's surplice high in the air, the words of committal lost in the howling storm. Adelia took shelter under the wings of a marble angel.

'And you can stop that,' she muttered rebuking tears. 'You will not be a hypocrite.'

Hostile eyes glared across the coffin. The Rourke family are out in force, Bobby's mother so heavily veiled she looks like a worker from a germ-warfare establishment. Adelia's presence at the interment is considered an affront and indeed who can blame them. It hardly makes sense to her. Is there a woman in the world who would willingly attend the funeral of the man who tried to kill her?

Bobby invited her via a letter from his lawyer: '*You swore you'd stay with me til I died. I need you to remember that promise and to hang on til I'm laid to rest. Then as far as I'm concerned you, and whoever is with you, can go to hell.*'

Now the US flag has been removed, squared away by white-gloved cadets, she can see the coffin. So small and plain! Surely a man who left such a hole behind would have a fancier coffin. A powerful man able to convince a shy English girl to follow him half way round the world should

- 1 -

have a hero's funeral, trumpets and brass bands, a Gothic casket and drapery of Arum lilies, not half a dozen people shivering about an open grave.

Captain Robert Rourke, DFC is a hero. As an American bomber pilot he flew with the RAF during the Blitz. Wounded and decorated he was One of the Few. He saved scores of lives and yet had wanted her life.

Well known in Fredericksburg his photograph is in all the papers. Handsome, smiling, a flying jacket hooked over one shoulder and a cigarette dangling from his lips, he seems to epitomise all that is brave and bold. But the box about to be lowered into the icy ground holds a shadow of the man. Bobby died a month ago yet long before that was consigned to a more communal grave. Amnesia buried him along with Adelia's daughter and at least one of the men standing beside her.

Snowflakes flew into her face tiny points of light glittering on her lashes, shielding her eyes she gazed across the cemetery, restless fingers toying with a business card in the pocket of her coat, the edge of the card so sharp it cut her finger.

Déjà vu! She's done this before. Yes, she has! She's worn another sable coat, pushed her hand into the pocket and cut her finger on a florist's card that carried a message, 'Go home, English whore, and take your bastard child with you.'

It was a snippet of the past, a chink of light no sooner lit than extinguished.

So much of life is hidden. So much mystery packed into a handful of years. Who was Bobby Rourke? Who are the men beside her, handsome men, Colonel Ash Hunter, US Army, medal ribbons on his coat, and Gabriel Templar, ex-

Marine and frontiersman in velvet jacket, boots and spurs, his hair tied back with twine?

Yesterday at the old house, at a reading of Bobby's Will, she was stripped of everything she owned, left nothing but a bouquet of roses and a wedding ring. It was then one of the men talked of wishes. He asked what she would choose if granted a wish. She'd smiled and said, 'I'd sooner not wish. From what I've heard my life was hazardous enough.'

'Maybe so, ma'am,' he'd replied, Southern drawl making honey of his words. 'But my, weren't you dazzling.'

Now, shivering in subzero temperatures, a marble angel beside her, one slender finger pointing skyward as though to indicate heaven alone held the answer, she knows what she would wish. I wish to remember my life. I want to know who I am and who I was. I want to understand Adelia Challoner and be dazzled.

Book One

Sentimental

Journey

Chapter One
Fur Coats and Roses

'Is there any news?'

'Uh-huh!' The Custom's officer yawned. 'Not since the last time you asked.'

Eyes gritty with fatigue Adelia gazed about the hangar. It was almost empty, a last handful of British women and children waiting collection.

Eight hours she's waited here, eight hours rooted to the Customs and Immigration desk searching beyond the barrier for the one person who could bring her and her daughter through the gates into a new life.

Hours tick away and the lines of men dwindle. One by one the women are reunited with their GI Joes, kisses are exchanged and weary children swung up on daddy's shoulder. Adelia waited for her saviour to arrive but he didn't come. Now she's left with fear in her belly and a hostile immigration fellow who chews on a hang-nail while covertly eyeing her breasts.

'Do you think we might have missed a call?'

He sighed. 'Lady, have you any idea how many of you *GI brides* passed through these gates today? How many screaming kids cluttering the building, woman bawling and crying, inquiries up and down the length and breadth of the USA driving everybody nuts?'

'But Bobby has to be here. He said he would be here. He promised!'

'Say, Max!' He called to a colleague. 'The lady says her guy has to be here, that he promised. Max, what happened to the last dame whose guy promised?'

'I don't know!' the colleague grinned, the interchange beginning to sound like a Music-Hall double act. 'What did happen?'

'She's back on the boat to Blighty and he's doing time for bigamy!'

Boom! Boom!

Good God! She turned away. This can't be happening, not after all the years of planning and dreaming how it would be when they got to America.

The night before they embarked Bobby phoned the hostel where Adelia and her three-year-old were staying. Drunk, his Southern drawl a boozy husk, he complained of pupils at the flying school. 'Don't know why I bother. Rich kids and their adorin' poppas, they don't know their asses from a hole in the ground!' He carried on complaining until the operator broke into their call. 'Say, Adelia,' he was suddenly urgent. 'It ain't too late to back out of this. I'd understand if you did. I wouldn't be offended or nothin'. I mean, you gotta have doubts. I know I have.'

Crouched on the stairs, one ear open for Sophie and the other for this man with their lives in his hand Adelia had doubts. Who wouldn't? They are taking a hell of a chance, the thought of leaving England and everything they know to live with a virtual stranger would frighten anyone.

'I didn't know you had doubts.'

'I don't!' he said. 'It's you I'm thinkin' of. It's a big thing you're doin', you and the babe comin' all this way and not knowin' a soul.'

'But I do know somebody,' she'd protested. 'I know you.'

For a time then he was silent, the telephone line popping and whistling, and then he said, 'that's just it, you don't know me.'

Alone in the New York reception centre and everything she lives for in a pushchair she has to admit it's true, she doesn't know him. Close her eyes and one image of Captain Robert E Rourke, DFC climbs above the rest, a man in a hospital bed, left leg in a sling and right arm about a nurse, a down-but-not-so-out American eagle.

July 20th, 1942 he arrived from a nearby airbase with a broken leg got while playing baseball. Allotted a broom-cupboard of a ward across from paediatrics where she worked he was confined to bed, his leg attached to a pulley.

Bobby hated that pulley and anyone whose job it was to crank it up and down. 'Chrissakes, not that again!' he'd cuss. 'What d'you think I am a friggin' washing line?' Adelia thought him a foul-mouthed brute. Later, after a bombing raid when her own life was so dramatically changed, she saw him in a different light, a man to follow to the end of the earth - or at least to Virginia, USA.

'Mummy?' Sophie stirred in the pushchair. 'I'm thirsty.'

'Have a drink, darling, and try to sleep. Daddy will be here soon.'

'My daddy!' Sophie smiled blue eyes glowing above a milky moustache.

'Whoo!' The Custom's officer whistled. 'Them eyes! Shirley Temple eat your heart out!' He picked up the toy monkey and began tweaking the miniature flying goggles. 'And who's this little guy some kinda Ace pilot?'

'It's a Bomber Command mascot.' Sophie's lip quivering Adelia retrieved the toy. 'Her daddy sent it last Christmas.'

'Is that what your guy does, flies a plane?'

'Actually he owns a flying school.'

'Does he, *actually*? Well, that's America for you. You can't keep a good man down! Them US flyboys and their snappy uniforms?' he laughed. 'I heard you gals were crazy for them. I'll bet there were tears when they pulled out. I'll bet there were more than a few counting the cost. It's what they did, them fliers, loved 'em and left 'em…not that a lady like you would know about that.'

Damn the man! Adelia ground her teeth. She knew why he felt able to be so familiar. Left high and dry here with no-one to care who or what was happening he sensed contempt on the part of her GI and acted accordingly.

'It don't seem right,' he leant on the counter. 'A beauty like you should've been first out the trap not hanging back with the dogs. No offence, but I wouldn't give most of the women passing through this gate a second glance. Talk about frumpy! And the kids? They ain't seen a bar of soap in years.'

'Really?' She looked away. 'Considering how very difficult things are at home I thought how well everyone looked.'

'I guess it depends what you're used to. You Britishers had it tough but come on! A bar of soap never emptied the bank!'

She gazed out of the window. Does anyone in this golden land know how tough it's been? First impressions of America are castles in the air piercing a cloudless sky and not a bomb-crater in sight.

It is the Land of Plenty. Though rationing is in force there's a profusion of food piled high in the commissary. And the men and women look so smart!

Back home echoes of the war are ever-present, whole streets demolished and people struggling to make a living. There is poverty and disease, queues for bread and the stench of cordite hanging in the air.

1946 her own personal war is ongoing. In the early days of the blitz she lived in London completing midwifery training at St Barts. Much like bedpans war was a condition one got used to. Thursday you might be cowering under the stairs in the nurse's home, ack-ack rattling overhead, Friday evening you'd be sharing a shandy with friends in a pub, and in the morning, hair bound by white linen and apron about your waist you stumble to work over sandbags.

London was a dangerous city at that time and many of her friends removed by worried parents to less perilous parts of the country. Adelia's parents died in 1934. Other than Aunt Maud in Suffolk there was no one to worry. January '42 Maud suffered a stroke. March of that year a gale blew off the sea taking the cottage roof and her with it. Adelia thought to return to St Barts but with commuting so difficult and the cottage to worry about she decided to stay local. 'It's safer.' A bomb dropped on a Suffolk pub and she was never safe again.

'Say, Miss?' The immigration chap waved a dollar bill. 'You must be hungry. Can I get you and the babe anything from the commissary?'

'Thank you, I've had a sandwich.'

'You sure? Maybe candy for the little 'un.'

'No thanks.'

He took offence. 'Suit yourself. I was only trying to help.'

Yes, she thought, watching him stroll away, there'll always be men like you offering help to girls like me and but for Bobby I might've had to accept.

In the early hours of August 2nd, 1942, a German Junkers 88 dumped incendiary bombs over Needham. The blast demolished a brewery and the adjoining Black Swan Pub. It was the weekend, the place packed with service men. There were casualties, Adelia among them. Admitted to St Faith's she was given a bed in the annexe next to the mortuary recovering consciousness to a massive bump on her head, August 1st and most of 2nd buried beneath the bump.

People tried to fill in the gaps. Nurses said she was seen in the park with a GI soldier: 'Tall, dark and handsome, and with the bluest eyes.' Then later in a restaurant: 'the Yank looking like he wanted to eat you up.' Doctors tried to help but without success. July 31st is clear in her mind, a late shift and the buzzer glowing over Bobby's door. She remembers knocking on the door and him calling, 'false alarm, honey! No need to come in!' Then bang, there's a blank wall and feelings of shame.

Three years on, the wall remains blank, there was no walk in the park, nor did she eat lunch in Luigi's with a GI soldier, yet someone must've feasted that day because come October '42 she knew she was pregnant.

~

A telephone on the Custom's desk rang.

'Seems your guy's made it after all! He's on his way over.'

'Thank God!' She combed her hair, winding the thick braid into a coronet and then powdered her nose, a slick of lipstick, a prayer and an indrawn breath.

A door clanged at the rear of the building. A stranger, a tall man in uniform marched into view, his long legs cutting the dusty air.

'Attenhut!' the Custom's chap jumped up in salute. 'Look out, lady! The Marines have landed.'

The stranger came to a halt at the desk. He stuck out his jaw. 'I've been axed to collect Mizz Challoner and her little gal.'

'Is thait right then, Dan'l Boone?' The Custom's man mocked the thick Southern drawl. 'And who *axed* you?'

'Captain Robert E Rourke. The front desk gave me this-here pass.'

The officer took his time perusing the paper before holding it out to be read. 'According to this you're to accompany the Sergeant to Richmond, Virginia, where you'll be met by members of the Rourke family.' He slapped it in her hand. 'That's it, lady, take or leave.'

'I see.'

'You okay with that? Happy to go with this man?'

'Certainly!' She offered her hand to the Marine. 'Thank you for coming to collect us. I know we haven't met but I'm sure we'll be fine.'

Her hand was enclosed in warm concrete. 'Sergeant Gabriel Howarth Templar, ma'am,' he bowed his head, 'United States Marine Corps.'

Paperwork dealt with she gathered their bits together and sick with relief stood gazing about the hangar at the last of the British émigrés who, like her, were awaiting collection.

'What will happen to these people?'

The Custom's chap shrugged. 'Depends what lies they've been told.'

'Lies?'

'Yeah lies. I see women like these every day of the week. They think marrying US citizens they'll be living in Bel-Aire with a swimming pool and a limousine. Truth is they've married Micky the Mope from Nebraska or Tommy Tune from Idaho, guys who never had nothing but snazzy uniforms and smooth mouths.'

'You are offensive.'

'You think so?' The suitcase was slammed shut, a brassiere strap hanging outside. 'Love was taken on the run in war-time, moon and June and all that romantic stuff. Now the war's over and guys who looked cute in uniform ain't cute any more. They're nine-to-five mechanics in greasy overalls and bookie's runners, fat guys in flowered shirts.'

'You make it sound like coming here was a mistake.'

'As far as most Americans are concerned the programme *is* a mistake. Sickly women and their snot-nosed kids, we got trouble enough of our own without importing more.' He pointed. 'What's under the buggy?'

Paper splitting and fur oozing out, she lifted the coat onto the counter.

'That's some coat you got there. What is it?'

'Sable.'

'Sable!'

'Yes, sable.'

He goggled. 'What the heck is it doing in a paper bag?'

'I hadn't anything else to put it in and the case was full.'

'Jeez! You'd think you could've found something better.'

Oh yes, the sable. It's lovely but impossible to wear. It makes everything else look dowdy. Her suit is second-hand treasure found in a pawn shop under the viaduct. A delicate shade of grey- the jacket nipped in at the waist with a lightly padded peplum over the hip, a calf-length wrap-around skirt and a white georgette blouse with pussy-cat bow, three inch black courts and a strip of swansdown over her blonde hair - she thought she was the cat's pyjamas.

That was in England. A glance at the office girls in New York Harbour reveals the true state of her wardrobe.

The officer eyed her. 'What's a girl like you doing on that old tug? A guy who can buy sable can afford air-line tickets.'

Adelia chose not to answer.

He grinned. 'I'm assuming it was an American that bought that coat for you to wear and not your daddy back home?'

'Knock it off!' the Marine bit.

Crimson faced, the officer whirled. 'What did you say?'

Gabriel Templar stood firm. 'I said knock it off. That's a lady you're talkin' to.'

'I don't care what she is. She's got to abide by the rules.'

'I don't care about rules. Mizz Challoner is here at the invitation of an American citizen and should be treated right.' The Marine shrugged. 'Of course, if you'd sooner take it up with the Captain go to it, though how he'd take it, him a hero and a decorated man and this his intended, is anybody's guess.'

'Regulations are regulations.'

'Regulations!' The drawl tightened. 'What regulations allow you to beat up on a woman? To shoot your mouth off amusin' yourself pullin' wings off little things? Tell me what regulation that is because I'd sure like to know.'

Woken by the deep voice Sophie sat up in the pushchair. 'Daddy?' she said questioningly.

'Well, look at you!' He crouched down. 'Ain't you the prettiest thing?' He held open his arms. 'You wanna come up?'

'Sophie's rather shy,' said Adelia. 'She doesn't go to strangers.'

He smiled. 'You shy, honey?'

Sophie jumped into his arms.

He straightened. 'I guess we're done here,' he said and with the coat draped about Adelia's shoulders - pushchair and suitcase under one arm and Sophie perched on the other - he marched them out of the Reception Centre into the sunshine. 'Welcome to America.'

Chapter Two
Near Miss

When the truck braked Adelia woke. 'Are we there yet?'

'We're just comin' outa the Capitol.'

'Is that near Fredericksburg?'

'It's a sight nearer than New York.'

They've been on the road forever. She scrubbed the window making a peephole in the condensation. A pale face swam into view, dark circles under the eyes and a deep ridge on her cheek. 'I've slept on something.'

'That's the seam of my pants. You slept with your head on my knee.'

'Oh, my God, did I really? You might have woken me!'

'I tried proppin' you up a couple of times but you kept slidin' down.' He glanced sideways. 'You may not look alike but you and your daughter have your ways. You both dribble in your sleep.'

'Dribble?' Through the gloom she saw a damp patch and snatching a hanky from her bag hovered over the bulging thigh.

'Don't worry about it,' he said. 'I've had worse on my pants.'

Mortified, she gazed through the window. What a horrible journey.

Why wasn't Bobby there? Short of sickness and death nothing should have kept him away. Leaving the Harbour aboard a beat up truck she asked if he was well. 'Same as always,' was the reply.

Other enquiries received the same non-answer.

'Have you known Bobby a long time?' she tried again.

'Him an' me grew up on the same stretch of land but can't say I know him.'

'You're neighbours?'

Stubble rasping, Gabriel Templar rubbed his hand across his chin. 'We have a place close by. I've been helpin' with that house of his.'

'Oh, the house!'

Summer of '45 Bobby bought a house in Fredericksburg, a Mill-house, pre-Civil War and still standing. He wrote; *'The minute I saw it I knew it was ours. There's the house, a cute kinda cottage and a tower linking the two. It's run-down but I can lick it into shape. I figured until we get used to one another you and Sophie should take the cottage and me the main house. Ma said we should move in with her. I said you'd sooner eat glass.'*

Excited by thoughts of the house she turned to Gabriel. 'Back home we had a flat above the baker's and a postage stamp garden. I grew bits and bobs, you know, digging for victory and all that, but I'd like enough space to grow vegetables and perhaps keep the odd chicken. Bobby said there are roses.'

'There's roses right enough.'

'Do you have a large garden?'

'We gotta fair spread. You hungry?'

'Coco, my monkey, is hungry,' said a voice from behind the seat.

'Hello sleepy head.' She pulled Sophie onto her lap.

Thumb in her mouth the child stared at the man. Adelia brushed Sophie's dark curls from her forehead. 'Sergeant Templar is taking us to daddy.'

'Mornin' Sophie.' The truck swung off the highway and onto a cinder track to a building where a neon-sign flickered. 'It don't look much but I hear they got a good breakfast goin' and a clean washroom.'

'Oh right.' Adelia checked her purse. Bobby has money. He says he's comfortably off. Thirty-two pounds, eleven shillings, and six pence ha'penny probably means nothing to him but it's all they have in the world.

When she looked up Gabriel Templar was watching.

'Is it all there?' he said, the tone and implication shocking.

'Oh not that!' she said. 'I was wondering if they'd take English money!'

'Put your purse away.' Callused palm abrasive, he helped her down from the truck. 'I ain't so broke I can't afford a bite to eat.'

~

By the time she'd emerged from the washroom, hair in a glossy plait and spirits buckled up for the last leg of the journey, Sophie was sharing a bowl of ice cream on the Sergeant's knee. Such a contrast, the big man and delicate child, her complexion milky pearls against sun-beaten skin, her nose a dainty button beside his profile and her curls as dusky hothouse grapes upon straw.

'Don't get any of that down your frock, Sophie Challoner!' Anxiety made Adelia sharp. 'That has to last until you're home.'

Gabriel polished Sophie's face with a handkerchief. 'She's okay.'

'You're very good with her.'

'She's a doll.'

'Have you children of your own?'

'Just me and Ma.'

'Really? One would think you'd been around children all of your life.'

'Back home I got a pen filled with young 'uns. Birds brought down by a storm, sick critters, lost and busted things, this little gal is no different.'

'Sophie's neither lost nor busted.'

'Uh-huh.' He gazed over the spoon. 'Seems to me, Mizz Challoner, you're both lost and busted.'

'Won't you call me Adelia?'

'No ma'am, I can't do that. But you can call me Gabe. Most folks do.'

Gabe? Watching her daughter lean against the man she felt an overwhelming desire to do the same, to off-load anxiety onto shoulders broader than her own.

'Did Bobby say why he couldn't collect us?'

'No he didn't. Jest axed me to run a message.'

'Run a message?' she echoed, piqued by the words. 'Perhaps he hoped you'd have time to do a little shopping. You know, pick up the odd bargain while popping along to collect a couple of nuisances?'

'That's a heck of a way to pop.'

'I don't see why,' she said. 'If a three-year-old can travel thousands of miles to see him surely he can drive a couple of hundred. You'd think after two years he'd be eager.'

He frowned. 'Two years?'

'Actually it's nearer three. We last met in November '43.'

He dropped the fork. 'You ain't seen one another since?'

'No.'

He repeated. 'You ain't seen each other in three years?'

'No.'

He sat twirling the fork. 'Why so long?'

Adelia spread her hands. 'I suppose it was a matter of waiting out the war. We…that is, Bobby and I, always talked of coming to Virginia but neither sure when. It was always at the end of the rainbow sort of thing. We wrote to one another, kept in touch. Then your government came up with this idea and what was only ever dreamed was suddenly a reality.'

He continued to play with the fork.

Silence deepened until she felt obliged to fill it. 'You don't approve.'

He rolled his shoulders.

'I can see why you might not. Three years is a long time to pursue a dream. No one knows that better than me.'

'Is that what you're doin' pursuin' a dream?'

'No, not at all! I assure you there is nothing remotely dreamlike about my situation. It's really quite prosaic.'

'Prosaic, huh?'

Adelia ignored his gaze. She'd always known the long wait could prove problematic but what could she do? This is not a sudden thing. It's not a lark! Necessity brought them to the USA, necessity and the promise of mutual care. And anyway what's it to this man? What can a tough Marine understand of her life? They're here because they're here! Devil take the reason!

'So who's chasin' a dream if it ain't you?' Gabriel Templar swapped a 'worry-bead fork' for a coffee spoon and is stirring a hole in a coffee cup.

Declining to answer she again checked her bag. Purse, visas, ration-books and all paper-work, she is forever checking. It's a habit from the blitz, a bit like clean underwear - one never knows when one is about to be blown skyward.

Nervously, she took out a compact and powdered her nose. It was a gift from Mr and Mrs James, the owners of the bakery, a message engraved on the back, '*for an angel with amnesia. Try not to forget us.*'

But for the James's win on the pools the Challoners wouldn't be here. Last Christmas they were gathered round the tree. Edna James gave Sophie a teddy-bear and a compact to Adelia. 'We've good news and bad,' she said. 'The good is that Eddie and I had a little win on the pools. The bad is for you. We're giving up the bakery and going to live near our daughter.'

Minutes later with prescient timing the phone rang. 'It's that bloody Yank!'

With that and nowhere to live and no job there seemed no reason to stay.

'I did it for the best,' the words were out before she could stop them.

'Best for who?' he said, a hole driven through the coffee cup and her defences.

'I was hurt in a bombing raid. There were complications.'

'What kinda complications?'

She didn't try to explain. It's not possible. You can't explain an inexplicable illness to a man who looks like he's never been sick in his life.

'Does Bobby Rourke know of these complications?'

'Yes! We have no secrets. We try to be honest with one another. He said I'd get help here, doctors in the USA more advanced.' She fought to apply a brake to her runaway mouth but the magnet in this man's eyes drew words out of her tongue. 'Bobby was kind to us during the war. I...we...wouldn't have managed without him.'

'Tell me about it.'

'Oh, I couldn't! I don't know you. Let's just say when I was ill it was he who kept me going.' Chilled by memories of that time she dragged the sable about her shoulders. 'He sent this coat.'

'And that made you feel better?'

'I knew you wouldn't understand.'

Jaw taut, he leant forward. 'I'm tryin' to understand.'

'I know the coat is ridiculous. I couldn't wear it back home. How could I, to what event, queuing for a miserly quarter of bacon at the butcher's or the bi-weekly jaunt to the Gas Works for coke? I know how it looks and how it will always look to creatures like the Customs' man at the

Harbour. But it wasn't at all like that. Bobby only ever tried to help.'

'There are other ways of helpin'. That coat should've been left on the beast that wore it. It's like the letters, a waste of time.'

'Why not letters? How else do you stay in touch?'

'You look one another in the eye!' He banged his fist on the table making Sophie jump. 'You touch! You speak! You find out what's real! Fur coats ain't real. They won't tell what you need to know.'

'I know all I need to know.' Letters and photographs scattering, she rummaged in her bag. 'I've information coming out of my ears!'

'Show me!'

'I know about the effort he made to get us here. I know about work done on the Mill house and the cottage and the money spent. It's all here. What would you like to see? What about this, the cottage before and after?'

Heart pounding, suddenly terribly afraid, she knelt on the bench beside him offering photographs and breathing in lemon cologne and observing a dab of fresh shaving soap on his chin.

'This is of the cottage before the refurbishment. See the roof open and rooks nesting in the attic? It was a mess. Now look at the newly plastered walls? All the work that has been done!'

He pushed those aside. 'I know about the cottage. Show me the rest.'

She passed a favourite, Bobby leaning against the wheel of a gigantic plane.

'This was taken at the flying club. He sent it last Christmas.'

Brow furrowed, Gabriel gazed at the photograph. It was an age before he handed it back and when he did his expression was closed down.

'That's a B17,' he said. 'You won't see too many of them in no flyin' club. They're heavy traffic. Civvy rookies couldn't handle 'em.'

'Is that so?' She tried steering the conversation to smoother waters. 'I know nothing about planes. Have you always been a soldier?'

'I'm not so much a soldier as a Marine.'

'There's a difference?'

'Yeah to a Marine and no, I ain't always been so. Before the Corps I was fightin' another war, plantin' them that did fight in tin boxes.'

'Angel Gabriel puts people in the ground,' said Sophie, her arm about his neck. 'He said that way they grow into butterflies and fly to Jesus.'

'Butterflies? You were an undertaker? Oh I see!'

She didn't see. Undertakers are old men in mildewed jackets that smell of formaldehyde. They're not a golden-haired Adonis smelling of fresh air and wood shavings.

'What kind of woman are you?'

'What?' She blinked.

Fist clenched, he leaned on the table. 'I want to know what kind of woman leaves her folks and all she knows to go Lord knows where, with Lord knows who, on the strength of a couple of letters, a photograph, and a mangy coat?'

'I don't know what you mean.'

'Yes, you do! You know exactly what I mean. You wanna take chances with your life fine,' he grated, accent thick as molasses. 'You're a grown woman. Take all the chances you like. But you can't make chance of a child's life. You gotta keep her safe.'

'I have kept her safe.'

'Yeah, until you got a taste for fur coats and roses! Why didn't you think about what you were doin' before you came?'

'I did think! I never stopped thinking!' Anxiety boiling over, she snapped at him. 'Gabriel Templar, if you've something to say then say it! I have the greatest respect for Bobby Rourke. He wouldn't have brought me here if things weren't right and I don't care for hints that suggest otherwise.'

'It ain't no hint. I'm sayin' nothin' you ain't said yourself. Three years is a long time. A lot can happen in three years.'

'Like what?'

'Nu-huh!' A lock snapped down. 'No, ma'am! It's not my place. Folks must do what they can with their lives.' Then Sophie, troubled by tension, huddled closer, and words leapt from him. 'But I'll tell you this! I'd walk through fire before I'd bring a child of mine into harm's way.'

'Harm's way...?' The words stuck in her throat. She stared down at the photograph, Bobby leaning against the plane, and Bobby with his cap tilted rakishly and Bobby smiling into the camera. Then her gaze slid to Gabriel Templar and to his hand curled protectively about Sophie's head.

She leapt to her feet. 'We've got to get out of here!'

'Where you gonna go?'

'I don't know!' She gazed wildly about the room.

'It's too late to go anywhere,' he said. 'You had nerve enough to come. Now you gotta have nerve enough to stay. Best take your daughter to the washroom. I'll settle up.'

~

Sophie was fretful in the washroom. By the time they were done Gabriel had left the diner.

'If you're looking for your man,' called the waitress, 'he's gone ahead.'

The sky was beginning to lighten and the air smoky with smell of morning.

Head down, Sophie in her arms and angry words ringing in her ears, she stumbled over potholes toward the truck.

Powerful headlights cut the air.

A motor roared to life, a long sleek shape idling out of the shadows.

Engine revving, the car pulled away in a lazy circle and then wheeling in a wide swerve turned back.

Adelia stood shading her eyes when with a shriek of tyres the car leapt forward.

A figure raced out of the light. Heaving the pushchair aside Gabriel snatched them away, the car passing so close Adelia saw her own terrified face reflected in the driver's dark glasses.

'Did you s...see that?' she stuttered. 'That maniac tried to kill us!'

'He wasn't tryin' to kill you, scare you more like.'

'Well, he did that all right! He made me lose my coat.'

'I'll go get it.'

'No! Leave the wretched thing! I don't want it!'

He returned with the coat and the pushchair. 'He reversed over the coat.'

'And you say he didn't mean to kill us?'

'He didn't mean to kill you. If'n he'd meant that you'd be dead now. The way you stood there like a petrified rabbit he could've drawn a bead on you any time he liked.'

'What was I supposed to do? I didn't know which way he was going. And stop shouting! You're upsetting Sophie.'

'It ain't me yellin' it's you. You're so wound up you don't know what you're doin'. Pass the baby to me. She's working herself into a real rage.'

'No!' Adelia's ears were filled with other voices from other people who had tried to take Sophie away, people who called her an unfit mother. 'No,' she whispered. 'You're not taking her.'

Gabriel dragged them into his arms. 'Hush up,' he whispered. 'Ain't nothin' gonna happen to you.'

Adelia couldn't fight him. His body was too warm and his arms too comforting. She could hear his heart pounding, then slowing down and steadying until it boomed in her ear like a bell tolling.

With the cab of the truck wrapped around them like a metal blanket and curtains of steam at the windows, she lay against him. Gabriel closed her hand over his heart. 'Go to sleep. Come mornin' this'll seem like a dream.'

Adelia needed no encouragement. Long before she slept a complication was working its busy way into memory, nibbling facts, cleaning a screen and neutralising trauma.

Come the morning it would be as he said, it would seem like a dream.

Chapter Three
Kindness and Consideration

She stared. 'It's not how I imagined.'

'I didn't think it would be.'

The Mill, Fredericksburg, was a sprawling arrangement of whitewashed buildings. A three-story house, a two-story cottage, a squat mill tower rising between like a stubby thumb, and all cobbled together by a sagging veranda.

While the main house was in need of some repair the cottage at least was freshly painted with bright shutters. Apart from an area of rose-borders the long hoped-for gardens, however, were choked with weeds and dangerous underfoot, rusted machinery parts left lying about.

A crumbling terrace led to a sappy duck-pond and tennis court. The rest was meadow grass and dense woodlands. 'We'll need a goat,' said Adelia.

'Or a couple of hand grenades.'

'How old is the Mill?'

'I don't know. It's always been here. The innards were gouged out years ago, and the fantail hooked to an emergency generator.'

As if to demonstrate his words a breeze sprang up fanning the willows and scattering petals.

'It sounds like someone's in pain.'

'Better get used to it if you're plannin' on stayin'.'

'I'm not planning on leaving.'

'You were earlier.'

If it came to a choice of disappointments, the Mill or the man beside her, then the man would win hands down. Yesterday Gabriel Templar was a gift from God, the uniform wrapped about his stalwart body celestial armor. Now he's of the Dark-Side, battening down the hatches, putting space between him and worrisome females, kindness and chivalry folded away on metallic wings.

Memories of the journey from the Harbor are fractured. Adelia has a vague recollection of an immigration officer's bold eyes, and of breakfast at a Diner and arguing about Bobby, and…and?

'Did a car nearly run us down?'

'You don't recall?'

'Of course I do! I was just thinking about it, wondering why people drive fast cars if they can't handle them.'

Gabriel's frown told her he wasn't fooled. He seemed to know that she was sniffing the air trying to siphon back time. It's been this way since '42, bouts of recurring amnesia, memories mislaid. In England, after a seizure, if she was quick enough data might be retrieved via Sophie or Edna James, even then it was safe to assume time had been lost and seconds, minutes…hours…sucked back to unite with the Greater Loss.

Doctors said there was nothing to be done she would have to learn to live with it. She learned, but in so doing walked a high wire, body and soul teetering on a shadowy line between past and future, a child's umbrella the only aid to balance.

Now having seen the drawn blinds, and felt the well-spring of regret rising from the ground, she wondered if Bobby didn't walk a high wire of his own.

'The blinds are drawn.'

'They're always drawn.'

'I wonder why.'

She reached out stroking a downy rose. The border area was full of roses. It was quieter now the breeze had dropped, quiet but not calmer. There was nothing calm about the Old Mill. Too many blinkered eyes.

'Have we neighbors?'

'There's my Ma within calling distance and another old place back-aways, a home for spiders and such. Apart from that there's nothing and nobody for miles. Do you drive?'

'Afraid not.'

'You got keys?'

'God no! I assumed Bobby would be meeting us.'

Cursing under her breath, she swung Sophie up on her hip and stomped round the back and up the steps rapping on the door. 'Bobby, it's me!'

No reply, her voice echoing and a magpie skimming the willows. Reluctant to disturb a place where all was blinkered eyes she reached out and pushed.

The door swung back.

'Oh!' She sank down on the step. They are here! They actually made it!

Head throbbing, she fumbled for pills.

Gabriel knelt beside her. 'Are they for the complications?'

'You might say so.'

'Does he know?'

'Of course he knows! Why wouldn't he know? And will you please stop doing that! I told you last night we have no secrets!'

Adelia hated this man thinking her a cold hearted bitch. She yearned to tell the truth, that she isn't here in Virginia for fur coats and roses but rather because she feared she was going insane.

Gabriel was gazing at the ground, long tanned fingers tracing a broken tile. There were rose petals in his hair. She reached out to brush them and he shied away.

'So sorry, Sergeant Templar.' She scrambled to her feet. 'Thank you for your help. We mustn't keep you.'

Released by her words he was in the truck and gone, the sun going behind a cloud.

~

The Mill was an uneven place. There was an interconnecting hall, a door to the main house on the right, a gated tower in the centre, and the cottage door to the left. She tried the cottage door but it was locked.

The main door partly ajar they tiptoed in. A battered armchair leant against a wall. Adelia sighed. 'We'll sit and wait. Daddy won't be long.'

She sat with Sophie on her knee. It was warm in the hall and dark and musty-smelling, any daylight filtered through heavy green blinds.

A mirror hung on a facing wall reflecting a window. Birds flew back and forth outside, their shadowy shapes caught in the tarnished glass.

Adelia closed her eyes.

A clock tolled the quarter.

Briefly, a dark shape blurred the mirror.

'Daddy!' Sophie ran to the gate.

'Come away!' Adelia sprang to her feet. 'It's dangerous.'

Sophie burst into tears. 'I want my daddy and I want to go toilet!'

They tried the main house shuffling through a series of rooms that though comfortably furnished were dusty and neglected. There was a games room, but what a mess, plates of half-eaten food and beer bottles strewn about, and a billiard table used as skittle alley - bottles for skittles and baize badly torn.

They searched for a lavatory, following their noses to where flies buzzed and broken glass crunched under the buggy wheels. It stank in there, vomit on the floor, and dried faeces on the seat.

Adelia tried opening a window but everything was locked and cords on the blinds double-knotted. Needs must, she held Sophie over the pan, perched, pulled the chain and slammed the door taking refuge in what looked like a flower-room.

What a contrast! It was tidy in there, beer bottles in a crate and a bin for empties.

A telephone rang making her jump.

'Hello?' She hooked it off the wall.

'Hi honey. It's me, Bobby.'

'Daddy!' Sophie made a grab for the phone. Adelia wrested it away.

'Where are you?'

'Stuck in this god-forsaken rat-hole.'

'Is that the flying school?'

'Yeah, for my sins.'

'Are you coming home?'

'Of course I'm coming home! I can't wait to see you. We got a heap of catchin' up to do. But listen, honey, I'm on a pay phone and so I'll keep it brief. You got an icebox full of food and you got logs. If there's anything else you need there's cash in the log basket. The rest we'll sort out when I get back.'

Adelia was furious. 'And when exactly will that be? Are we to be alone much longer because if we are I'll find your miserable friend and get him to drive us back to New York so we can catch the next boat out of here!'

'If by miserable you mean Gabe Templar he's no friend of mine.'

'So I gathered.'

'Why, has he been sayin' somethin'?'

'Only that you *axed* him to collect us from the Harbour.'

Bobby guffawed. 'Yeah, that sounds like Gabe.'

'If he's not your friend what is he?'

'A bum I hire now and then.'

'I don't believe what I'm hearing.'

'I had to use him! How else were you to get here? Oh, come on, honey, don't start on me. I've been out of my mind with worry. You're my family. You're precious to me. Don't you think if I could've had it another way it would have been so?'

'I don't know what to think,' said Adelia. 'Awful day! But I shouldn't criticise Sergeant Templar. He was sweet to Sophie and civil to me. *And* he all about saved our lives!'

'What do you mean save your lives?'

'Someone tried to run us down.'

'Run you down? Jesus H Christ! Where was that?'

'I don't know exactly, a cafe on the road. He pulled us away from the car.'

'Well, bully for Gabe! I'll nab along later to that wooden shack of his and lay a couple of bucks on him.'

'Please don't do any such thing! He'll be offended.'

'Offended?' He snorted. 'Him and his ma are always short of readies.'

Too weary to argue she sighed. 'I can't get into the cottage.'

'So where are you exactly?'

'At the far end of the house, in the flower room.'

There was a crash, Bobby dropping the phone. Then he began yelling, 'what you doin' in the main house. Didn't I say the cottage was yours and the house mine? Didn't I say we was to treat one another with respect and anticipate feelins? Invading my space ain't respectful. Chrissakes, is this how it's gonna be, a guy having no privacy?'

'Don't you dare speak to me like that, Bobby Rourke! Have you any idea of the day I've had? Any notion of how it feels to struggle with luggage and visas and overbearing officials, and be met by complete strangers, and feel awkward and foolish and so damned weary, and not a bit of help from the man who swore he'd be waiting to meet us?'

'This is all wrong!' He was shouting. 'It wasn't supposed to be like this! It was supposed to be wonderful. You were supposed to be happy. I was supposed to be at the quay, a big bouquet in my arms and a bigger smile on my face.'

'Then why weren't you? Why am I left fretting about what might have gone wrong? Why send someone you didn't like to pick us up, a man you call a bum! And why now we are here are you yelling at me?'

'I know I'm yelling and I'm sorry. I had guys over from the club the other night and they left a mess. Go back to the cottage. It's the only place fit for you. There's a key top of the door ledge. I'll be home soon as I can. Okay?'

'If you say so.'

'Just one thing? Did Templar say anything?'

'Like what?'

'I don't know, maybe that his family and mine don't exactly see eye-to-eye?'

'Sergeant Templar is a man of few words. Should he have said something?'

'Nope, not a goddamn thing.'

Click! The line was dead.

~

Midnight and Adelia sat looking out of the window. Two rooms and a kitchen down, two and a bathroom up, the cottage is no bigger than the flat in Needham yet it is comfortable and cleaner than the main house. The kitchen is functional, a stove occupying the back wall. There's a sink, a pantry and an enormous ice-box crammed with lobster tails, salmon, and quails eggs! Absurd food, nothing suitable for Sophie! Not that it mattered. Most of it was off, the electricity having failed. There was a basket on the side with fresh milk and bread and eggs. There was a box of matches which is as well, a storm lamp the only source of light.

One step forward, one back, is how Adelia got through the rest of the day. Regret after regret piled up in her head and yet here and there were moments of hope, like the doll's house.

A carved model of a black-and-white Tudor house it sat in the corner.

'Mummy!' Sophie squealed. 'Look!' There was a doll, a label tied about its delicate wrist; *'For Sophie, Welcome to America.'*

Best of all were the beds. Golden coloured wood, flowers and fruit carved about the bedposts, they were beautiful pieces of furniture. A date was carved into the wooden canopies, December 23rd, 1945, the day she agreed to come to Virginia.

Fresh linen on the beds and the scent on lavender in the air, it took all of her willpower not to lie down, pull the blanket over her head, and pray to sleep forever.

She lit a fire in the small sitting room. The grate was choked with torn up papers and the remains of a photograph album and wasn't giving off heat.

She took a poker raking the mass and as she did a half-charred photograph slid onto the mat. She picked it up, a US soldier - light flashing from the cruciform medal hanging about his neck - gazed at her from under the sharp peak of his cap.

There was a message on the back, Bobby's hand; *'Ash Hunter at the MOH presentation: a hero in everyone's opinion, especially his own.'*

She used to dislike Bobby, thought him rude and arrogant, and yet when she was in trouble he was the one that helped her. She got nothing from colleagues at St Faiths. They saw her amnesia a lie. 'So you're pregnant?' they would say. 'So what? Have the guts to own up. Don't try covering it up with this amnesia rubbish!'

Bobby found the flat above the bakery and for a few weeks in '43 they were happy. Then he was transferred to another base until February '44 when there were two long months of silence. She thought him killed and grieved for him. Then April 1st - a clue if ever there was one - an airmail postmarked Washington dropped through the door. *'It's me, Bobby Rourke, the bad penny. Sorry about the delay. Me and a bike had an argument with a wall. Tell me you're still my girl, 'cos if you're not, me and the bike will find another wall.'*

Then the barrage of mail began. Every day brought a letter and in every letter a proposal of marriage until last Christmas when the phone rang in the shop.

He rang to see if the sable coat had arrived. With Edna James and the bakery going he couldn't have timed it better. 'Thank you,' she'd replied. 'It is lovely.'

He'd laughed. 'Plenty more where that came from, honey. All you got to do is book two seats aboard the Queen Mary.' Sad and unhappy, she asked what he wanted for Christmas. He replied, 'same as last year.' A moment's hesitation and she threw in their lot. 'Well then, Captain Rourke. It seems Santa has granted your wish.'

For a time then there was silence on the other end of the phone.

'Oh, dear,' she'd said. 'Wasn't I supposed to say yes? Was this only ever a game?'

Now they're here, and the game, if there is a game, has rules only Bobby Rourke seems to understand.

She stared at the charred photograph. Something about the soldier, something in the eyes, penetrating, unforgiving, like those of Gabriel Templar. And burnt in the grate?

What's wrong with you, Bobby, she thought? Why destroy photographs? They must have been important at one time.

Gabriel Templar's voice echoed in her ear: 'What's the use of letters and photographs? They don't tell you what's real.'

It's cold in the cottage. She clutched the sable about her shoulders pushing her hands into the pockets.

'Ouch!'

There was something sharp in the lining.

She pulled it out. It was a business card, a florist's shop called Forget-Me-Knot with an address in Fredericksburg.

There was a message scribbled on the back. She carried the card to the lamp.

It read, '*Go home, English whore, and take your bastard with you.*'

Chapter Four
Bogeyman

A new bed and host of new anxieties brought a restless
night, Adelia caught up in a serial-nightmare. It's always the
same, a soldier lies dying in a ditch, blood seeping through
his battle-dress. His buddy, a man with intense blue eyes,
will try carrying him to safety. 'Forget about it, you fool,'
the dying man will gasp. 'I'm beyond saving.' Stubborn, his
friend hoists him on his back, the dream ending with the
soldier dying. 'I know why you're doing this,' he'll sigh.
'You don't want to leave me like you left Adelia.'

She woke with her own name on her lips and the belief
she dreamt of Sophie's father. It is said that the eyes are the
windows of the soul. If that's true then the blue-eyed man
looks at the world through bulletproof glass.

The electricity is back! Nightmares notwithstanding, she
tied a makeshift apron about her waist and bucket in hand
did battle with the house. As she worked she wondered
why Bobby didn't pick them up. He said it was because of
the flying school. Perhaps he has financial problems.

During the war she fought to keep her head above
water. Everyone was in the same boat, no point in
complaining. If money came under discussion it was Bobby
brought it about. 'If you need cash you've only got to ask.'

She didn't ask, she paid her own way working night shift in the Annex. But then she was asked to leave but not because she was pregnant! Pregnant and unwed made her a target for gossip but didn't negate her expertise as a nurse. It was the idea of amnesia they didn't trust, people, nurses, doctors, seeing her illness as a vicious animal ready to slip a leash.

The baker's wife was disgusted: 'and you with all those qualifications! I'd like to give 'em a piece of my mind.' Edna James didn't care for St Faith's. She wasn't a fan of Bobby Rourke either. 'Why do you want to live among strangers? Why not stay here and marry a nice English Tommy?'

A question Adelia is still unable to answer.

~

A pick-up was pulling into the drive. Gabriel Templar had brought his mother with him. Strong of face and raw-boned, she stood almost as tall as her son. 'I've brung my mother May to meet you.'

'How do you do, Mrs. Templar?' Adelia offered her hand.

There was hesitation and then the same strong grip. 'I'm well, thank yer.'

Gabriel was out of uniform in denim jeans and shirt.

Adelia attempted a joke. 'Not soldiering or planting today?'

'I'm not due back at Quantico yet. As for plantin', around these parts we aim to do our dyin' and buryin' after ten.'

'How very civilized.'

'Ain't it,' he said a smile flickering. Silence stretched between them, his gaze searching her face, asking if she was well and she unable to reply.

May Templar coughed. 'How's the baby settlin' in?'

'Sophie's fine. She's upstairs playing with a new doll.'

'Like it, does she?' said Gabriel.

'It was you made it!' said Adelia, unexpected joy filling her heart.

Color rising he nodded.

'And the doll's house too?'

'It weren't all me. Ma did the drapes and clothes for the doll.'

'Sophie is overwhelmed. She won't let the doll out of sight. I admire your patience, Sergeant. It must have taken an age to carve.'

Mother and son exchanged a quivering look, silent words passing between them, all trace of a smile snuffed out.

Unwilling to tread on invisible toes, Adelia steered them toward the cottage to find Sophie shuffling downstairs, baggy pajamas floating about her middle and blue eyes wide and curious.

'Mummy? Have you seen rubber ducky?'

'Not today, I haven't.'

Sophie gazed at the visitors. 'Are you my nana?' she said.

May Templar stepped forward. 'Honey, I wish I could say I was.'

Immediately and eternally smitten, Sophie sidled forward. 'I've got baby rabbits on my pajamas. What have you got on yours?'

Face suffused in rosy pleasure, May crouched down. 'Don't know about rabbits. I might have a bit of lace about the collar.'

'We've got a big bath upstairs. Have you got a bath?'

'We got a tin tub.'

'Does Angel Gabriel bathe in it?'

'Some of him gets wet. Most times he kinda pokes out both ends.'

Sophie took May's hand. 'Come see me and my dolly take our bath.'

'Sure, I will, if that's okay with your Momma.'

'I think it a lovely idea.'

Sophie lifted up her arms. 'You'll carry me, won't you? Then after my bath we can look for my rubber ducky.'

Heart aching, Adelia watched them. Why couldn't we have had this yesterday, a kindly woman with open arms for Sophie and a man with open arms for me? 'I didn't expect to see you today, Sergeant.'

'I brung Ma along so you could get acquainted.'

'That was kind.'

He shrugged. 'She's lonely and so are you.'

'There's a lot of it about.'

Silence stretched. 'He didn't show last night?'

She didn't reply.

'Are you thinkin' of quittin'?'

'You talk as if I have a choice.'

'We all have choices.'

Unnerved by his presence she began pulling at the wisteria, dead-heading blossom, the sun hot on the back of her neck.

'You oughta wear a hat an' dungarees.'

'I don't have a hat or dungarees.'

'They got 'em in the store. I could run you.'

Adelia thought of the phone-call and of Bobby's fury when this man's name was mentioned. 'Kind of you to offer but better not.'

She felt rather than saw his eyes narrow.

'Spoke to you then, did he?'

'We've communicated.'

Out of the corner of her eye she saw him nod. 'I'll bet.'

Above them a window was flung open, May's head appearing. 'You want I should give the baby breakfast? Scrambled eggs, maybe?'

'That would be fine.'

The window closed.

'What about your breakfast?' he said.

'I ate already. Can I offer you a cup of tea, Sergeant Templar?'

'I got business in town but Ma will keep you company.'

Adelia was irritated. 'I'm pleased to meet your mother but I am not an invalid. I really can manage on my own. I'm a lot tougher than I look.'

His gaze flickered over her slender form. 'Uh-huh.'

The window above was flung open, May's head emerging. 'If you want to get goin', son, I can bide with Mizz Delia a while.'

'It seems I'm not the only one being managed.'

'She's always been like that.' Gabriel Templar strode off down the path. 'I'll be a child to my mother when I'm fifty.'

~

Sophie was talking to May. 'There was a bogey-man in my room last night, Mrs May.'

'Was he a nice bogey-man?'

'He was lovely. He gave me a chocolate biscuit.'

May laughed. 'Young 'uns! When Gabe was her age he reckoned there was a ghost in the privy. It was years before he stopped frettin' about it. Later he said there were a million such in the house across the woods.'

'Sophie has a vivid imagination. I think it's in her genes.'

'Would that be her Ma's genes or her Pa's?'

'Sophie's father and I lost touch years ago.'

May's nod seemed to suggest the information already known.

Adelia had questions of her own. 'Your son has a way with wood.'

'I'll say. Ain't no finer carpenter in all of Virginia.'

'And yet he's a Marine.'

'Huh!' May snapped her arms. 'That seems to be up fur question.'

'He's thinking of leaving?'

'Seems so.'

'What will he do?'

'What he does now when needed, bury the dear departed. It ain't what I want fur him but he's made up his mind.'

'You'd prefer he stay in the Marines.'

'I never wanted him to join. I never knew a minute's peace while he was away. My sister Belle lost both her boys. She's just about destroyed.'

'It's been a difficult time.'

'You can say that again.'

May began clearing the table, slapping plates together, her mouth screwed up. 'Back in the twenties we had a wood-yard in Alabama. We muddled through then my man took to drinkin'. We got into debt and moved here to Granma's. Gabe got a job makin' coffins.'

'That's how he came to know about wood.'

'Uh-huh, apprentice to old man Smith. He lost a lot of schoolin'. Got behind, you might say. He never was one for learnin', happier with critters in the field. It weren't my fault. You can't earn and learn. But he had it hard, some kid with too much to say givin' him a bad time.'

'Bullies are everywhere.'

'Not so much now they ain't! One look at the uniform and they shut their mouths. It's the same with gals! He never had luck afore. Now they're comin' out the walls. It's true I had worries while he was away but the Corps did him good. Made him see what kind of man he is. His troubles didn't end with schoolin' and nasty-mouthed kids, but the less said about that the better.'

'You are proud of him.'

'None prouder! A woman couldn't ask for more. Good man and a good son.' May glanced sideways. 'Any woman takes up with him is lucky.'

'I'm sure.'

'Real lucky!' May threw pots in the sink water splashing. 'But she'll need to wake up to what's goin' on! Stand up for herself and not knuckle down to bullies that pick and pry and slander a man's name.'

Bemused by the turn of the conversation Adelia could only nod.

Sophie broke the tension. 'I'm going to call my dolly Delia.'

'Oh, no, sweetheart!' Adelia grimaced. 'There are prettier names.'

Sophie held up the doll. 'She looks like you, mummy.'

Adelia gazed at the doll, the hair in a silky plait and the curved eyelids and long narrow hands. 'Perhaps she does.'

'Gabe worked from a picture the Captain gave,' said May.

'Is that so? I must say his skill adds a touch of beauty I'm more than happy to own.'

'No, ma'am,' May shook her head. 'It's as he sees it, nothin' added and nothin' taken away.' She was silent for a time but soon back to the subject of wood and other people's failing to respect her beloved boy.

'It was Gabe did the beds you and your gal is sleepin' in. Home on breaks from the Corps he put hisself to a lot of trouble on your behalf.'

'Yes,' said Adelia humbly. 'I'm beginning to understand that.'

'If I'd as many dimes fur the hours put into them beds I'd be a wealthy woman. Hour after hour tryin' to get 'em right. But that's Gabe. Anythin' he puts his hand to is gonna be good. He's strong on patience. He learned early there are situations in life as can only be met with patience.'

Adelia was having a hard time. Why didn't you tell me about this, Bobby? Did you think I'd feel less of you for needing help?

May coughed behind her hand. 'Seein' as we're talkin' about work you might remind your man he ain't paid for the last lot of Maple.'

'Oh, dear.'

'I ain't wishing to press but my boy has to buy wood afore he can make doll's houses and the likes. If'n he owes he can't get.'

Adelia took a five pound note from her purse. 'Will this cover it?'

'British money?'

'Quite above board I assure you. You can change it at most banks.'

'But does it leave you flat?'

Noting how May's fingers edged toward the note Adelia closed her purse. 'I have enough and Bobby will reimburse me should I need it.'

May pocketed the fiver. 'He won't miss it. His Pa, Bucky, made a heap of money before departin' this world. Hope you didn't mind me sayin'. Gabe won't mention it, too proud. He needs a wife and kids to make him see a debt is a debt. A good gal would suit me too.' She looked up sharply. 'You met your Ma-in-law yet, Ruby Iolanthe?'

'Ruby Iolanthe?'

'Ruby Iolanthe Cropper as was.'

'Not yet. You're acquainted with Mrs Rourke?'

'Ain't a body in Fredericksburg not acquainted with her.'

Still on the subject of bogeymen Sophie again came to the rescue. 'He came when I was asleep,' she was playing with the buckle on May's dungarees. 'Coco hid under the bed-clothes but I wasn't afraid.'

'An' what did the bogeyman say?'

'Fee fi fo fum I smell the blood of Englishman. Be he alive, or be he dead, I'll grind his bones to make my bread.'

'Sophie!'

'He did, mummy,' said Sophie, swinging her foot, a sign she fibbed.

'She sure got a parcel of words. You like this when you was three?'

'Sophie has a retentive memory. It helps no end with reading. I'm certain my education was more of an uphill slog.'

'No, you're bright. I see it in your face, you're bright and beautiful like the hymn.' May began to sing. 'All things bright an' beautiful, all creeturs great an' small. All things wise and...'

Sophie joined in, and then spurred by the notion of creatures, 'have you got a dog, Mrs May?'

'I have. I got horses too, least my boy has.'

'Can I see them?'

'I don't see why not. It sure would be nice to have a little 'un about.' May gazed at Adelia. 'She could stay fur a bite. I'd bring her back afore dark. It'll give you a clear hand here.' Then seeing Adelia hesitate she said, 'I guess not. You don't know me or my boy.'

'Yes, I do,' said Adelia. 'You have been kind to us. I know all I need to know. And I'm happy to have Sophie to spend time with you.'

~

She woke that night to the creaking of floorboards and swung her legs over the side of the bed. A mirror covered the far wall. A sleepy-eyed woman gazed back, nightdress rumpled and hair tangled about her shoulders. She was dreaming of the children's ward in St Faith's, a line of cots and the sour smell of nappies.

In the dream she carried Coco, Sophie's toy monkey. Then Coco became a live monkey. People were pointing and laughing. A man took photographs. 'Hold still!' he said. 'I can get another shot.'

Knowing people were laughing the monkey burrowed his head against her breast, its little hands covering its ears. 'Don't take any more!' Adelia begged. 'Can't you see he's afraid?' The man laughed. 'He's a clown. It's his job to make people laugh.' It was a horrible dream and all through Glen Miller's *Moonlight Serenade* playing.

They used to play that record on a wind-up in the nurse's home. Gossip says it was a favorite in the Twilight Lounge bar at the Black Swan. The pub was popular during the war, a couple of bar stools, a rolled back carpet and polished shoes disturbing the dust, it was a place to share a kiss before dying.

It's where she danced with a GI.

Adelia has never stopped thinking of Sophie's father. She had a ring clenched in her fist when dragged from the fire. Since then she's had it made smaller and wears it all the time though why she doesn't know unless it's a hope the giver had more than a one-night stand in mind.

'I mean, a ring suggests serious intention, doesn't it?'

Smothered smiles and barely concealed incredulity whenever she was discussed, life was difficult after the bomb. The things people said! And the people that said them! Not as you'd imagine some sour old maid in lisle stockings. It was colleagues who dished the dirt. 'Amnesia? Tell us another one do!'

A twenty-four hour abyss governed her life. She couldn't sleep for wondering who he might be. She'd walk down the street, a soldier would wink and she'd think, Oh, is it you? There's no comfort in ignorance, no comfort either in knowing she gave treasure away so easily.

~

Wide awake now she took the lamp across the landing. There was a sweet smell in the air and chocolate about Sophie's mouth. Adelia wiped her mouth. She woke and was straight in with immediate brightness.

'Can I have a dog? Mrs May's dog is black and white with a curly tail.'

'Not if you eat chocolate in bed you can't.'

'The bogeyman gave it me.'

'Sophie ! It's one thing to eat in bed but quite another to fib about it.'

'He did! I'm not telling fibs!'

'Go to sleep. We'll talk about it in the morning.' Cross, Adelia went downstairs. She needs to speak to May, can't have the child coming home with a mouth full of chocolate and head full of nonsense.

In the kitchen trying to light a kerosene stove she again heard music.

It is the Glen Miller tune! It was *Moonlight Serenade*!

It's coming from the tower!

Bobby is home!

Skin prickling and lamp held high, she grabbed the sable and slinging it over her nightgown went into the hall. The stair gate was open, music echoing all about the house, the Mill tower acting as an amplifier.

Hiking up the coat she began to climb.

'Ugh!' There was dust on the stairs and spider's webs hanging in glutinous ribbons from wall to stair.

Something furry bumbled against her cheek. Shuddering, she raced up the steps. There was a glimmer of light under a door. She stood on tiptoe peering through the glass. She could see a table and a tray of plants.

Bobby, a lamp casting a halo over his head and giving him bat's wings for lashes, sat with an artist's brush in his hand working on a pot of lilies transferring pollen from one blossom to the next.

His hand was shaking, consequently every time he lifted the brush yellow dust drifted down staining the petals.

Such concentration, the brush clenched between nicotine-stained fingers, he might've been Laozi, ancient Chinese poet inscribing verse.

Seeing him like that her heart opened like the lilies. She raised her hand to knock on the glass but hesitated not wanting to startle him.

The record spun to a close the needle hiccupping. He wound the handle and with music filling the room took up the lamp and began to dance with an imaginary partner.

Round and round he went, shadow bobbing on the ceiling and light from the lamp changing focus on his face, from left, to right, left, right…left…and right.

Adelia stood transfixed. Her hand was poised to knock but then, like a pale periscope withdrew.

Carefully! Oh so carefully, she began the downward climb, retracing her steps, sable whispering behind her.

By the time she reached the bottom her legs were unable to support her.

She sank to the floor, and the moon a spotlight, sat staring through the open door. A centipede crept along the ground. How agile he was, every segment supported by peripatetic feet. We should all be like that, she thought. All those legs? Just think how quickly we could run away.

God knows how long she sat. But then God must have been watching because he sent an angel, a tall angel in faded denims and dusty boots.

'Sergeant Templar,' she whispered. 'What are you doing here?'

Down he came, his face the silver moon, stonily sad and relentlessly bright. 'I was waitin' to see if you was okay.'

'You were right. Three years is a long time.'

His shoulders moved in a faint shrug.

Trying to rise she stumbled. He reached out, the tips of his fingers on her shoulders, steadying. She leaned against him, cheek against his shirt and thumbs hooked through his belt.

Behind her eyes a lantern revolved, right, left, right, left, light and shade flickering. Bobby waltzed around the room, one moment a clean profile, the next a cobbled mass and a hole where his eye used to be.

'Poor Bobby,' she whispered. 'How unhappy he must be.'

Gabriel was silent. Time passed. The moon slid behind a cloud, a ticking clock displaced by the tick of his watch in her ear.

She released his belt. He draped the coat about her shoulders.

Turning, she set her foot on the stair.

Slowly, feet leaden, she climbed the stairs and pushed open the door. 'Hello Bobby.'

Chapter Five
Blinds

'My love for you...my love for you...my love for you...'

Bobby froze mid-turn, shadows dancing and the record player stuck in a groove.

With only courage to sustain her, Adelia crept into the room. 'Sorry to disturb you,' she whispered. 'I heard music and came to investigate.'

He gaped at her.

'It's all right,' she continued. 'Sophie's fine. I left her tucked up in bed. She was eating a biscuit. But then...' recollecting what had been said, bogeyman and biscuit, she trailed away, 'you know that.' For an awful moment she thought he might bolt. But he set down the lamp, lit a cigarette, and taking a drag exhaled noisily.

'It must've been a shock finding yours truly at the top of the stairs.'

'It was.'

'I can imagine.' It was the same drawl heard so many times on the phone but exaggerated, the vowels drawn out in self-mockery. 'No doubt you were hopin' for the former Bobby Rourke, tall, dark, and handsome with all his bits in situ.'

'If you'd only told me!'

'And what was I to say?'

'I don't know...a few words in a letter perhaps?'

'Ah yes, the letters! Jees!' he snorted. 'Talk about counterfeit. I've never struggled so hard to tell so many lies. And pitiful lies at that! Absolutely nothin' worth sellin' my soul for.'

'You could have said something.'

'What, like, guess who's hidin' in the bell-tower these days, the Quasimodo of Eighth Bomber Command?'

'That would have been an exaggeration.'

'Would it? Then how about, don't bother coming to Virginia, Dee, 'cos your old pal Bobby ain't the man he used to be? That rhymes nicely and is certainly without exaggeration. Anyway, I did try to tell you. I sent a telegram.'

'Yes you did, All Fools Day 1944. How appropriate. You certainly had me fooled. What happened to you?'

'You mean how did I get this?'

'Yes.'

He shrugged. 'It's nothin'. No darin' do, my dear, diddly-squat to add to the DFC.'

'What did happen?'

'I got pissed one night and rode into a wall.'

'Oh.'

'Yeah, Oh.'

'Were you...did you...were you hurt in any other way?'

'As a matter of fact I was. I got a nice little mess here.' He pulled aside his shirt, revealing a raw area of his stomach. 'I got that from a branch of a tree.'

'It looks sore!' Habits dying hard she stepped forward. 'Perhaps I can help.'

'Leave it be.' He closed up his shirt. 'I don't want no fussin'. I sort myself out. I've always sorted myself out. It's what I do.'

Adelia dropped her gaze. Scruffy and foul-smelling, he was a mess. The Suffolk Bobby would've died rather than appear so. Particular about his appearance, he was always first to wash and shave, brown curly hair neatly trimmed and uniform, of which he was incredibly proud, immaculately pressed.

Even with a leg in plaster he had style, dressing gown and cravat, Noel Coward would've been proud! Slim, athletic body, a fur-lined jacket over his shoulder and daredevil smile on his lips, the photograph he sent last Christmas defined his brand of throwaway elegance. Now stubble on his chin and RAF tie keeping up his pants he dares a different devil. As for his face it is a montage of past and present, the smooth beauty of the right mocking the left.

He smiled and his cheek unzipped. 'Got the picture?'

'I'm sorry. I don't mean to stare.'

'It's okay. Everybody stares.'

'Can nothing be done?'

'You mean a new face? Sweetheart, if anything could've been done, it would've been done. No, this is it, the new improved Baby Rourke.' He struck a pose. 'What do you think? Should I call Paramount and double for Bela Lugosi?'

She could only shake her head.

'I guess you prefer the old me.'

'I prefer the truth not phoney photographs.'

'It wasn't exactly a lie. I did fly a B17. Admittedly it was a one off. Eighth Bomber Command I mostly steered Lancasters about.'

'A B17? Yes, that's what Gabriel Templar said.'

'Holy Christ!' He started up out the chair. 'You showed that snapshot to Gabe Templar! Oh, for fuck's sake! What did you do that for?'

Exhausted, Adelia sat on a couch amid beer bottles, gardening magazines, and Sophie's rubber ducky. 'I did it in all innocence. I was talking about you at the time, bragging I seem to recall, saying what a wonderful man you were.'

'Braggin'? You won't have to do that again, nothin' to brag about.' He lit another cheroot and began to hum a tune, beating time with his foot. 'So what did big old Gabe say about it?'

'He said I wouldn't find B17s in a flying school. They weren't meant for rookies.'

'He's right. Even I had trouble swinging the bitch round. Did he laugh?' Adelia shook her head and he nodded. 'That's right, he wouldn't. This is the guy that rescues wounded critters from the roadside, Virginia's answer to St Francis.'

Adelia picked up the rubber duck. Despite shock and anger she couldn't help feeling sorry for the wounded critter sitting on the other side of the room, right hand holding on so tightly to the left the knuckles bled.

'I see you've located Sophie's rubber duck,' said Bobby. 'Since the whole of Virginia is shortly to know me for the lyin' bastard I am I might as well hold my hands up to the theft.'

'You visit her at night?'

'I do. I am the bogeyman. I scare little kids so I don't go out in daylight. Smoozin' about in the dark is better. I spent most of last night watchin' you. I have to hand it to you. You're pretty much perfection.' When she remained silent he moved closer, the stench of stale sweat rising. 'Not gonna pass out on me, are you? I can't have you forgettin' me, not after all I've been through.'

'No,' she clung to the rubber duck. She wouldn't forget. Of all the big bangs this has to be the biggest but she would not fall. Something kept her upright, maybe the knowledge of Sophie alone in the cottage or strength gained through Gabriel.

Unable to think she stared at the floor, what have I got myself into? Worse, what have I got my little girl into?

Bobby seemed to divine her thoughts and gestured toward the duck. 'At least we don't have to worry about her breakin' in on our happy reunion. She's pretty much whacked out after her visit with the Hillbillies.'

'You knew she was with May this afternoon?'

'I know everythin'. Up here in the belfry I am the eyes and ears of the world, or should I say the eye and ear of the world.'

'You have no sight in the left?'

'I have a hole for a left eye and a shrivelled flap for a left ear. Isn't that jolly!'

The shift back and forth from the banter of his days at the RAF base to the true Virginia drawl was hard to take. 'You haven't played fair, Bobby.'

'Played fair? Oh, here it comes, the British complaint; stiff upper lip and take on the chin but with the odd whimper thrown in.'

'But you didn't play fair!'

'You think I should've made a clean breast of it. Maybe I should, then again maybe I hoped I needn't take the risk, and that the situation was covered in our agreement, the richer-for-poorer sickness-and-in-health baloney.'

'Did we make such an agreement?'

'We would if we'd gotten married but that's out the window. There's not a snowflake's chance in hell of that happenin' now.' He took back the rubber duck. 'I didn't tell you because I was scared. I thought my ugly mug would put an end to it. I played dumb because you know what they sa...say.' His voice wobbled, the nonchalant mask momentarily slipping, 'ca...careless talk costs lives.'

'Sorry.' Adelia got to her feet. 'I have to get some sleep. I can't think.'

'Yes sure,' he cleared his throat. 'But before you go are you saying we have to be rubber-stamped signed on the dotted line before the better-or-worse condition comes into play? Don't single folk merit love unto death? Are we outside the pale, 'cos if so it don't give much hope to us maimed critters.'

'You have a right to be loved, Bobby, as I had a right to know the truth. You should have kept your promise.'

'In what way have I not kept my promise? Didn't I promise you and your daughter a home?'

'You did.'

'And have you got a home?'

'Yes.'

'Did I promise food and shelter and money for the clothes on your back?'

'You did.'

'And are you starving? Are you naked and out in the cold?'

She shook her head.

'Well, then.' He tossed the rubber duck on the sofa. 'If you got all of those things what does it matter if I look like original sin?'

'You needn't have lied,' she said with dignity. 'That's what matters. Sophie and I deserve better than lies.'

'Yes, Adelia Challoner, late of Suffolk, England, and Miss Sophie, Princess of My Heart, you did and you do.'

She shivered, drawing the coat closer.

He nodded. 'I see you're wearin' the National Debt. If you like that particular present I have more up my sleeve.' Skirting the room, clinging to shadows as though needy of cover, he rapped on the closet door. 'This here is the doorway to dreams! The mother lode! Aladdin's Cave!'

The door opened and clothes oozed out, silk and chiffon, cotton, velvets and wools all clinging together in a brilliantly coloured mass.

'What is all this?'

A hanger rattled and scarlet chiffon settled on the floor. Bobby gathered it up and began intoning a catalogue of shops and seasons. 'This is Bloomingdales spring of '44. Me and the woman haggled over the price. This jacket is Fifth Avenue same year. That coat was Saks, Thanksgiving. And there's that...a shop on Broadway...and that, Winter '45...and this.' He pulled out a gown of black velvet so gorgeous it made Adelia's eyes water, 'I got the day I landed Stateside. I had your name embroidered in the lining, Adelia Rourke. You see, I was wishing even then.'

She stepped back. The war-starved woman in need of a pair of stockings yearned to pull the clothes from the closet, to gather armfuls, to roll in them! But the woman that had come through so much balked at the price she'd have to pay.

Fighting the desire to snatch Sophie and run, she stuffed her hands into her pockets her fingers closing about a charred photograph.

She rubbed her finger against a sharp edge and focussing on pain sent a prayer into the night, not to God or to the man in the photograph, to Sophie's father!

'Whoever you are,' she prayed, 'and wherever you are, show me what to do. Please don't let me make the situation worse.'

Outside the birds were cheeping. Dawn was breaking. Pale light pushed through gaps in the blinds bringing the room, and the man, into focus. A finger of light touched Bobby's boot, a spider retreating into the shadows, he shuffled backward.

Pity filled her heart. 'You poor thing!'

With a howl he hunkered down his hands over his ears trying to shut out her words. 'Don't you pity me! Don't you fucking dare!'

'Hush!' She ran to him holding him tight.

'She called me a bogeyman.'

'You mustn't mind Sophie. Once she gets to know you she'll be fine.'

'She won't! She'll still call me bogeyman.'

'She loves you.'

'She doesn't love me. It's May Templar she loves.'

'It's the animals she loves, the idea of horses and dogs.'

'I'll get her a dog. And a pony! She can have a zoo if that's what she wants. She don't need to go beggin', not from them.' Tears dripping from the dark pit that once held an eye, he sobbed. 'Do you reckon she'll love me ugly as I am?'

'You are her hero.'

'Some hero, scufflin' about in the dark!' He twitched away fumbling for a cheroot. 'You mind me smokin'?'

'There are things I mind more,' she said, trying to be as diplomatic as the situation allowed. 'I don't care for cursing, little pitchers having big ears. And a wash-and-brush-up might be in order as would a visit to the tailor.'

'I'm not sure about tailors. I'm not good with people anymore.'

'We could go together.'

He fingered a slatted blind. 'Does that mean you'll stay?'

'I'll stay, but there must be no more lies.'

Released, the words came thick and fast. 'I never meant it to be this way, truly I didn't. Everythin' got out of control. I'd say to myself you got to tell her. You can't bring her here to live with a wreck. But I lost my nerve. It's like this house. I could hire all the men I needed but couldn't stand the thought of them lookin' at me. So when he was on furlough and offered I got Gabe to help.'

'He didn't laugh at you.'

'Maybe not, but there's plenty that do! I wanted to tell you. I was prayin' you'd come and prayin' you'd stay away. The Lord didn't know whether He was on His holy ass or

His elbow! I never thought you'd come. A woman like you, I figured another guy would move in. Then you said yes and I was scared because it wasn't a Yankee doodle-dandy you were sayin' yes to. It was a Dodo, an extinct bird.'

'If this was such a burden, why not say you didn't want us?'

'Because I did want you!' he cried. 'And still do! You and Sophie are my lifeline. If I had you comin' I had somethin' to live for.'

'Don't cry. We'll work it out.'

'Yeah if folks give us a chance,' he said, wiping his nose on his sleeve. 'I'm not so bad. There are guys worse than me. I could go see my tailor. Maybe give 'em a buzz beforehand let 'em know the way things are.'

'We'll be fine. As long as we stick together we'll be fine.'

He looked up. 'What about the man woman stuff? We gonna be fine with that?'

The air went from her lungs, hesitation saying more than words could tell.

'That's something we'll have to learn along the way. Please,' she said, teeth chattering. 'I can't talk anymore. I must rest.'

'Sure,' he draped the sable about her shoulders. 'Go get some sleep.'

She started down the stairs. 'There's one thing you can do for me.'

'Anythin'.'

'Get rid of the blinds.'

'Yeah, sure.' He watched as she stumbled away, her hair a tangled mass of light about her face. At the tower gate she looked back. 'Glad we had this little chat,' she said, voice raw. 'Now we can get on with it.'

'Roger control!' He saluted. 'Message received and understood!'

Alone again he gazed about the tower room. Jesus, he hates this room, every dark stinking inch of it. Alone and wretched, abandoned by the world, it represents everything loathsome in life, secrets and lies, spying and his ugly face.

Not wanting to stay longer than necessary he ran down stairs and stood for a while in the hall combing his fingers through his hair. She'd left the cottage door ajar, lamplight shining, a gentle invitation to enter. He wanted to go in. He ached to do it, to share breakfast with his family, to be normal, to be happy and stake a claim in the future. It was all he'd thought about through these terrible years.

Lifting his fist to rap on the door he caught the smell of sweat. He couldn't go anywhere stinking like that.

Back to the house he went the same cloying misery descending. Stumbling about in soupy gloom he barked his shin on a corner of the chesterfield.

'Goddamn blinds!' he muttered. All this crap! He reached up tugging at the cords but like his gut they were glued together with years of bile.

Cursing, he caught hold of a corner. Down it came clattering to the floor. Exposed to the light he covered his eyes. Then he leapt again hurling his body at the window. Sunlight crashed in, showering the hall with sparkling motes of dust. He leapt again, and again, pulling the blinds down, tearing them apart with his hand, stamping and smashing and kicking the bastard things from here to eternity.

When they were in tatters and every window bare, he made for the upper floors, running, panting, and weeping, his shadow scuttling ahead like a bogeyman.

Chapter Six
Ruby Iolanthe

Time dragged on. Adelia left the cottage door ajar but slammed the door to her heart.

Call it self-preservation yet if they are to have any kind of life there has to be continuity and that means doing away with a heart. Witness the mistakes made when following that tricky lump of gristle! Though likely as unreliable, her brain must be in charge, desperate mind, if you like, over fickle matter.

So when Bobby didn't make contact that night or indeed the next three days and nights she maintained the status quo. The tower gate open and music drifting from the tower, a car roaring in and out of the drive, she made no searches. If that's what he needed to do so be it. Sooner or later he will return to stake a claim. Sooner is okay. Later is better.

The following days were spent taking inventory of the Mill. Ears ever cocked for creaking floorboards, she retreated from her former self installing bullet-proof layers betwixt Adelia USA and the fragile fool of yesterday.

Alas, now and then the fool still broke through, witness earlier this morning when she was woken by Sophie calling, 'Angel Gabriel's here!'

The first instinct was to fling her arms about him. But *we* can't have that; not if *we* are to survive. Proposing a brisk good morning, she opened the window. She needn't have worried. He had erected barriers of his own. A brief nod and he was about his business clearing the ground of junk.

Clang! Another lock on another door!

'Where are you going, Sophie?'

'Sophie, what are you doing?'

The Mill brought new worries. So many hazards, lunch time Adelia turning her back and Sophie racing toward the crumbling garage.

Learning to drive is a must! Back in Suffolk she asked an ambulance driver for lessons. 'Sorry, love,' he said. 'Not with your medical history.'

Too bad! That was then. Now she's here and it's that or stay a prisoner. There's a jeep back of the garage, a beaten up thing it hardly matters if she were to dent the chrome. When Bobby surfaces she'll ask. It's certain he wouldn't want her anywhere near the sports car!

Fabulous car and British made according to the badge, she trailed her hand along the shiny bonnet.

'That belongs to daddy,' said Sophie.

'Ah yes, daddy.' Adelia hasn't tried explaining Bobby's plight. Sophie seems happy with her life. Sensitive to atmosphere, she no longer hankers for Nana Rourke believing the role amply filled by Mrs May.

May Templar is a Godsend but also a Trojan horse. But for her kindness they'd be on their way back to England. What she knows of their current situation is anybody's guess yet judging the cordon of silence drawn about the topic she knows enough.

Another day and a note poked under the door.

'The delivery van due today. If you need anything tell the guy. It's paid for.'

Adelia threw it and another plate of food in the bin. 'Much more of this, 'she muttered, 'and we'll need a pig as well as a goat.'

Secret notes and telephone calls, they might as well be back in Suffolk.

Every morning at eight, using food delivered the day before, she cooks breakfast for three. In the evening she makes dinner for three, the slops going in the bin. Used to wartime scarcity, she finds it hard as does the continued silence. Lies, evasion, what's been gained? She's unhappy, and if last night's drunken singing and vomiting in the outside loo is to go by - so is Bobby.

~

Late afternoon, having worked hard all day, she took a bath.

A pallid Ophelia she lay in rust-tinted water, her hair floating out like silver weeds. Relax, she told herself. Sophie's with May there's no need to worry.

Sounds came and went. Thoughts came and went.

A thought filtered through, a handsome thought, steely eyes staring from under a peaked cap, the photograph in her pocket along with the florist's card.

Trust the sable coat to be a harbinger of doom. But what an awful card! Who in America would do that, call her a whore!

The cottage door opened and shoes slapped the flagstones. Adelia hurried down to find Bobby's mother in the kitchen rifling through her handbag.

'You oughtn't to leave that lyin' about,' the woman didn't even blush. 'You never know who's prowlin'.'

'So it would seem! Good afternoon, Mrs Rourke. I'm sorry I wasn't down to meet you. I didn't hear you knock.'

'I don't knock. This is my son's house.' Mrs Rourke pulled out a chair. 'I ain't begged permission before. I ain't gonna start.'

'Of course not. I only meant…'

'I know what you meant.'

Adelia offered her hand and received a nasty wrench in return, multiple bangles clinking about a sinewy wrist. 'How do you do, Mrs Rourke.'

'As well as I can be under the circumstances. Where's the kiddie?'

'Sophie is visiting friends.'

'Friends? What friends have you got when you know nobody?'

'We do know somebody,' Adelia's spine prickled in recollection of another such conversation. 'We know you. I recognise you from your photographs.'

Mrs Rourke sniffed. 'I was a lot younger then, had less to worry about.' She frowned. 'It's the afternoon. What you doin' in a robe?'

'I took advantage of a moment alone to take a bath.'

'I come by early yesterday.'

'Really? Why didn't you say hello?'

'You was sloppin' out the privy and the kiddie was abed.'

'I would have woken her.'

'I do flowers at the Mission. I can't be hangin' about. Seven of a mornin' is for up and doin'. You won't find American children abed that time.'

'Possibly but Sophie's had to contend with the blitz. She needs sleep.'

'Oh yeah, the blitz. Get's blamed for a whole heap of things does the blitz. Idle folk lookin' for a handout and men and women doin' what the heck they like. The war's over. It's time folk stopped complainin'.'

'I didn't know I was complaining.'

'Some do it that long they don't know they're doin' it.'

Adelia filled the kettle. 'Would you care for a cup of tea?'

'Tea makes me bilious.' Mrs Rourke circled the kitchen, her gaze lingering on the Donald Duck cup and saucer in the sink. 'Been spendin' I see.'

'A couple of things needed.'

The kitchen was bright with sunshine, the radio played and a kettle sang on the hob. 'You sure made yourself welcome.'

'I thought since Bobby has gone to the trouble it would be wrong not to feel welcome, and of course you, Mrs Rourke, I'm sure you helped.'

'I did not. I said from the start I was havin' nothin' to do with it. Baby makin' trouble for hisself is up to him. No good lookin' to me for help.'

'You call him baby?'

'That's his mother's name for him.'

'How sweet,' muttered Adelia, anger taking over from disappointment. Then she bit her lip. Be careful, she admonished, this rigid broom handle with the purple perm is to be your mother-in-law. 'Coffee?'

'Is it fresh?'

'I can make fresh.'

A rumble of wheels outside, May and Sophie arriving! 'Excuse me.' Adelia went to the door. 'Hello darling. Been a good girl for Mrs May?'

'Good as gold, ain't you, sweetie? I was only sayin' to Sue at the store, you won't find a better behaved kiddie anywhere. She…oh, you got company.'

'Mrs Rourke's here. Won't you come in and have a cup?'

May shook her head. 'Thank yer, Delia, I'll be on my way.' She bent, a quick kiss and whispered word for Sophie and away striding to the truck.

Adelia didn't urge her to stay. The look on her face said it all.

Sophie stood inside the door. 'Look who's here!' said Adelia, brightly.

'So you're the one got folks runnin' around,' said Mrs Rourke. 'Kinda small for your age, ain't you? You don't say much. Come here, gal, let me look at you!'

Thumb in her mouth, Sophie turned. Mrs Rourke smacked her hand. 'Take that out your mouth! You don't know where it's been.'

Sophie's eyes filling with tears Adelia led her to the stairs. 'Go play with dolly, darling. I'll be up shortly.'

'Well,' Mrs Rourke sniffed. 'She didn't so much as offer me a kiss.'

Adelia spooned coffee into the grinder. She had to do something or she'd strangle the woman. How dare she slap

Sophie! And that voice! Grinding monotone, is she human? She can deliver blows without raising her voice!

'Did you hear what I said? She left without givin' me a kiss?'

'Did you want a kiss?'

'Cain't say I did, leastways, not 'til she's washed her face.'

'Maybe she's anxious, not knowing what to expect from her nana.'

'Now hold on a minute!' Mrs Rourke banged the table. 'Before you go any further there's a couple of things you need to get straight. Here in Virginia we're God fearin' folk. We don't hold with modern goin's on, men and woman actin' like beasts of the field. We don't hold with children born out of wedlock and all this fornicatin' before marriage. And we ain't hypocrites callin' one another by false names.'

'Are you saying you don't want to be called nana?'

'I'm sayin' we don't try passin' another man's kid onto some innocent feller.'

'Are you accusing me of saying Sophie is Bobby's child?'

'Well, ain't you?'

'I most certainly am not! It's true I don't broadcast my situation, it being nobody's business but my own, but neither do I lie about it! Damn cheek! I referred to you as nana because I hoped you might like to be thought so. And I refer to Bobby as her daddy because it's what he wants.'

'So you say.'

'So I say! Sophie is my daughter. I'm proud of her. She belongs to me and no one else, and I am deeply offended by you suggesting otherwise.'

Mrs Rourke popped a toffee into her mouth. 'I'm tellin' you as it is. Bobby ain't her daddy and she ain't my grandbabby and it's no use puffin' up your feathers. I believe in speakin' my mind. Honesty is best policy I find.'

'Fine!' Adelia snarled. 'Be happy with your darn policy but keep your voice down. A three-year-old understands loving kisses not you laying down the law.'

'Just makin' sure there's no misunderstandin'.'

'There is none. You've made yourself perfectly clear.'

'Somebody had to tell you. You needed to know what's acceptable. And quit with the cursin'. You're not in your own country now.'

Desperate to drown her out Adelia spun the handle on the grinder. Mrs Rourke carried on talking. Short with bandy legs and a mouth dragged down in runnels either side her nose she was still talking when grinding ceased.

'Now that Gabe is in the Marines he struts about like he owns the place. Marines? The country must be desperate to take on the likes of him, thievin' murderer that he is.'

'I like the Templars. I am sure they are thoroughly decent people. Sergeant Templar met us at the Harbour. He behaved like a gentleman.'

'Gabe Templar a gentleman?' Mrs Rourke snorted. 'You must have some queer men-folk in your country if that's how you recognise gentility. Why, that dummy can't even sign his name.'

'I have nothing to say on that score other than May Templar is kind to Sophie, which is more than can be said for you smacking her.'

'Children need chastisin'. It keeps them on the right way. "Spoil the rod spoil the child," Proverbs 22.15.'

'No!' Hands shaking and grounds spilling, Adelia spooned coffee into the jug. 'Don't quote your nasty brand of Christian rhetoric at me. You don't wish to be thought of as a grandmother fine! Stay away from Sophie, and though it pains me to say it, you being Bobby's mother, stay away from me.'

'You throwin' me out?'

'I'm asking you to leave.'

'So this is what I get for tryin' to do a good deed. But then ain't that always the way, the Lord stretches out a hand and He's turned away.'

'I don't know.' Adelia shook her head. 'I had hopes of you but you're not at all what I expected from Bobby's mother.'

'What did you expect?'

'The same I get from your son - kindness and consideration.'

'You think scrapin' shit off privy floors is kindness and consideration?'

Adelia made for the stairs. 'I must get dressed. Perhaps you'd see yourself out.'

Mrs Rourke was ahead of her. 'He's up there, ain't he?' She gestured to the tower, her bracelets rattling like jailer's keys. 'I see that car of his in the garage. You know about that car, don't ya, some piece of British junk he imported?'

'What Bobby chooses to drive is none of my business.'

'It should be. It's the wrong car for him. It's too powerful and will kill him one day for sure. So what does he do up them stairs?'

'He works with plants.'

'Plants my eye! He's up there drinkin' hisself stupid, though why he does is beyond me seein' as he weren't brought up that way.'

'He's unhappy.'

'His face is enough to make anyone unhappy. Talkin' of faces, Baby is right. You do put folks in mind of that foreign movie star except you're skinnier. That your own hair?'

'Last time I looked.'

'You use rouge on your lips?'

'When I can get it.'

Mrs Rourke took a mirror from her purse. 'I don't hold with women paintin' their faces. If the Lord meant us to have scarlet lips He'd have given 'em.' She nodded to Adelia's open-necked shirt. 'Same as if He'd wanted our bosoms hangin' out.'

'Is that so?'

'Yes, it is. Baby was brought up strong in the Lord. He was taught to walk the paths of righteousness, to honour his father and mother and not give way to the lure of the flesh. He was told to be wary of whited sepulchres, to recognise the false from the true. And if he did fall by the wayside he was made to pay. Like I said of your kiddie, 'spare the rod and spoil…''

'Oh be quiet!'

'What did you say to me?'

'I'm sorry but you have to go. I've had enough for one day.'

Mrs Rourke snapped her purse. 'You think you're somethin, don't you, with your platinum hair and hoity-toity mouth. You ain't so marvellous. Afore the war Baby had his pick, the Abercrombie girls from Richmond Park forever makin' goo-goo eyes. And that girl back East, father a judge, she was real taken with him. Scores of girls there were and all good American stock. He din't need to end up with a foreigner 'specially one that ain't right in the head.'

Adelia walked away but still she followed, every word meant to kill.

'I know about you,' she said. 'You're one step from the madhouse. It's you that needs Baby, not him needin' you. And it's you keepin' him in that tower.'

Liquorish breathed into Adelia's face, she stepped closer. 'Don't think you can come throwin' your weight around tellin' me what I can and can't do. He's my son. I know what's good for him.'

'You think calling him baby is good for him?'

'I've always called him that. He's used to it.'

'And telling him he's less than a man. Is he used to that?'

'I never said he was less a man.'

'Didn't you? I thought you did. But never mind!' Adelia took a broom to leaves in the hallway. 'We've had our conversation. You've said what you came to say. It's done. Now we can get on with our lives.'

Finally all out of words Mrs Rourke stared.

'Anything else?' Adelia stared back. 'No charitable advice on how to be accepted into a God-fearing society? No loving words from the Good Book, like ''come unto me all you who are heavily laden and I will give you peace?''

With the dragon gone, Adelia sank down on the stairs. 'You can come down now, Bobby,' she said. 'She's gone.'

He stood looking over the rail. 'Sorry about that.'

'It doesn't matter.'

'It does. You shouldn't have to listen to that shit.'

She shrugged. 'Honestly, it doesn't matter. I've heard it all before, maybe not the same words but certainly the same message.'

He sat on the step. 'She's always been like it, hard as the proverbial!'

'She has a way with words.'

'Yeah and her fists. You're not the first she's frightened away.'

'Let's hope I am the last.'

'What? You want more of the same because believe me there is more. Don't think because she walked away it's over. She'll be back.'

'And I shall be here.'

'How can you want to stay after that? Chrissakes, Delia look at me! Look at this place, the pack of trouble you've inherited! What is there to stay for?'

'I made a promise.'

'You made it not knowing the facts. No jury in the land would hold you to it.'

'Bobby, do you want us to stay? I mean truly want us, because I can't help wondering if your mother was right and it's me making you unhappy.'

'Ma blows it out of her arse.'

'Bobby!'

'No, but she does! What does she know of my feelings? What could she know about anything? She's never loved anyone. Not me, not Pa. She knows nothin' but what's dredged from the filth of her mind.'

'You didn't answer my question.'

'Why would I want you to go when all I think of is you?'

Adelia got to her feet. 'We'll stay but on one condition.'

'And what's that?'

'That we share a life. You have to join Sophie and me. You can't loiter on the outside. We have to try to be a family. It won't work any other way.'

'Okay, but it ain't gonna be easy. I've been too long with my own misery to change overnight.'

'I know that and I'll give you all the space you need. But please, Bobby, my illness, this awful thing is weighing me down. I'm depending on you for help. Please keep your promise about that. Sophie has to be made safe.'

'She will be. You can trust me on that.'

'Fine. So you'll come and have dinner with us this evening and, if you're up and about maybe breakfast in the morning?'

'Sure will.'

'And you'll let me know your plans?'

'Sure will.'

'And we'll grope our way along together.'

'Yeah, grope.'

~

Adelia could erect all the barriers she liked but couldn't shut out the past.

The blue-eyed man is ever-present, even reaching through sleep to invade the day. In the early hours of the morning she woke knowing she was not alone.

Every nerve in her body taut, she called, 'is that you, Bobby?'

Not a sound. Heart beating, conscious of the deal they made, she sat up.

'If it is you come in! Please don't hover!'

A presence did indeed hover at the end of the bed, although bestrode would better describe the stance.

The soldier-ghost, for what else could he be, was dressed in combat gear, a helmet on his head, rifle across his chest and camouflage stripes on his cheeks.

There was a moment of utter stillness, a girl and a soldier gazing at one another, and then the vision melted.

Only the blue eyes remained. They smiled and faded away.

She cried then, Sophie's father is dead. That was his ghost come to say goodbye. It has to be so. As with the ring she wears on her finger the dreams that have puzzled and comforted over the years are only dreams.

Chapter Seven
Colonel Bogey

Bobby was ill in the night. Adelia heard and went to see if she could help.

'It's okay,' face ashen, he leant against the door. 'It's leftover from my fracas with the wall. Go back to bed. I'll get over it.'

'Maybe you should see a doctor.'

'Nah! I've had my fill of them.'

'Is there anything I can do?'

'No, not unless you can wave a wand and turn back time.'

'Afraid not.'

Gently, but firmly he closed the door. 'Then forget about it, my dear Watson, and retire to your boudoir.'

Seven am next morning he was up and gunning the Morgan.

That car! She doesn't care for it, and by the spat witnessed a while back neither does Gabriel Templar. She saw them arguing, couldn't hear what was said yet the tension in Gabriel's shoulders suggested harsh words.

She asked Bobby what it was all about. He shrugged. 'Some crazy idea in that bozo's head 'bout how I tried runnin' someone down.'

'And did you?'

'Of course not! What the hell do you take me for, a murderer?'

That was weeks ago. Now he's on his way out again.

'Do you think you're well enough to go out?'

'I'm okay.'

'You could stay home with me and Sophie.'

'I've urgent biz at the club.'

'Well, drive carefully.'

'Yes ma'am!' He saluted. 'Thank you ma'am! '

'And the tailors?'

'We'll go another day.' He slid a pair of dark glasses over his nose. 'What will you do, go downtown with May?'

'I've the study curtains to measure and then a look at your bedroom. The wallpaper's dreadful. I don't know whose idea it was but it has to go.'

'It was Ma's idea.'

'Sorry.'

'Don't be sorry. It is nasty, makes me giddy just thinkin' at it. But in terms of doin' stuff, you do know the lady of the Mill don't have to do anything,' he said, irritation in his voice. 'We got women to do stuff like that.'

'It's fine. I like to do it.'

'As you please.' His fingers beat a restless rhythm on the wheel. 'Speaking of hired help, Templar's droppin' by to look at plans the architect sent, figurin' how much wood to fix the tower floors. I shan't be here but don't worry! He's as obsolete as the rest of us now so no need for extra tea and dainties on the lawn.'

'Just a minute!' she ran indoors, returning with a swatch of materials. 'Which do you prefer for the long sitting-room, the Prairie Gold or Seascape Blue?'

'Buggered if I know,' he said, pushing sunglasses back of his head and bringing the swatch of cloth up close. 'It's all the same to a blind man.'

'I thought we agreed to no cussing.'

'We did,' he grinned. 'I guess I'm a hopeless case. Toodle-oo, old girl! See you when I see you! *Per ardua ad astra* and all that!' With a wave of his hand he was gone, gravel spinning and klaxon horns sounding a defiant salute.

She breathed out. Four months have come and gone; sixteen suffocating weeks of polite behaviour, apart from the odd trip to town she spends her time perched on a stepladder a paintbrush in one hand and tape measure in the other. On the rare times Bobby is home he's in the greenhouse, a shadow behind glass.

When they lunch together Sophie chatters, Adelia picks at her food, and Bobby flicks ash. Most evenings are spent in stilted conversation.

'Something you'd you like to do?

'I don't know. What would you like to do?'

'You choose!'

'No you!'

Five minutes of that and to the relief of all they go their separate ways.

At night, fists clenched, she watches the bedroom door.

DIY fills a void. There are cushions to cover, curtains to make and pies to bake. She is the very model of a modern American housewife. Early morning is the best. Alone, she hacks through the woods, the mist making droplets on her hair. On return she heads for the vegetable garden.

Bobby hired men to dig the soil. Now she's planting and weeding.

During the war they had a plot back of the bakery. Every year she'd plant potatoes and every year slugs took first pickings. Here she has a fruit cage, an orchard and a chicken run. Future plans include hogs.

'Mummy!' Sophie ran down the passage. 'Has Daddy gone?'

'He had to go to town.'

'But he said we would go look for a dawg today!'

'Dog, darling, not dawg.'

Sophie has accepted Bobby readily enough. A disfigured bogeyman holds no fears for her. In the evening she sits beside him with the toy monkey in her lap. Coco is restored to favour and the doll relegated to second place. It happened the evening Bobby came to dinner. Not wanting to scare the child he wore an eye-patch. 'Hi, sweetie,' he said. 'Remember me, the bogeyman?'

When at length he quit the room Sophie fell upon Coco, kissing the crumpled face. Insightful child, she looked at the goggles and RAF badge on the monkey and saw what her mother did not: Bobby's sad opinion of himself.

'So, can we have a dawg?'

'We'll see. Sergeant Templar's coming today. You could talk to him.'

'He's not a Sergeant anymore, mummy. He's a man.'

Gabriel quit the Corps. It was so sudden it even took May by surprise.

They met on the High Street. 'It must be a relief having him home,' said Adelia.

May wasn't at all pleased. 'Don't know about relief,' she says. 'Seems to me he's got hisself out of one danger and smack dab into another.'

Sophie spends a deal of time with May. Bobby doesn't like it. Adelia doesn't care what he thinks. Sophie loves the Templar homestead and with all the building work at the Mill there aren't many places she can play in safety.

May Templar is sensible and kind, and as Adelia pointed out - daring Bobby to disagree – she is as a grandmother should be.

Ruby Rourke is as hostile as ever. A blood hound with a nose for discord, she surfaces on the heels of trouble and always creating more. For a month or two, poisonous florist's card notwithstanding, Adelia tried mending fences. Sophie didn't bother. Why bruise your heart when there are softer bosoms to hug? Bobby spars with his mother playing up to her bible-thumping habit. Adelia hates the teasing banter. She hears cruelty in their words and intimations of violence past and present.

Friday evening he surprised her by suggesting May might help. 'You need a woman to take a load off. It'll give you more time for yourself.'

'Would May want to do it?'

'I reckon so. Gabe bein' ex-officio will have left them short.'

'What am I to say to her?'

'You don't need to say anythin'. I'll talk to her.'

May was a long time responding. Then one sunny morning the phone rang.

'That you, Delia?'

'Oh splendid, you're on the phone now.'

'I don't know about splendid. Up and down answerin' the blessed bell, I'm fair worn out. Now listen, our sow's dropped her litter. Tell Sophie if she wants she can give me a hand. And if you want a hand with that barn of a place I don't mind a couple of mornin's a week until Gabe gets the plantin' business sorted.'

'You're taking the business on full time?'

'Uh-huh. We've done up the old Parlour. It's why we got a phone, though why beats me. Ain't nobody in a gosh-almighty rush to lay folks away, not the folks we shift fur. Most are so broke they'd be happier burnin' the dear departed on the stove, savin' heatin' as well as the cost of interment.'

~

'Mummy, do you believe in angels?' Sophie sat on the step watching the road.

'Yes I do. Why do you ask?'

'Uncle Gabriel is an angel. Nana May said so.'

'Did she?'

'Yes, I heard her. She said he can't go being a guardian angel all his life. He has to let go of all that nonsense and find himself a wife.'

'And what nonsense was he to let go of?'

'You!'

'What!?'

'Oh look!' Sophie jumped up. 'He's here.'

The pick-up rolled into the yard. Gabriel got down, a denim shirt and pants replacing the uniform. The casual style suits him, although sad to say these days he is anything but casual.

Stiff and formal he stands at the door. 'I'm here about the tower floor.'

'Come in, won't you?'

'No need. I know what's wanted. Just lettin' you know.'

He's gone. As May grows closer to the Challoners so her son retreats.

Adelia can't afford to care. Four months of living in Fredericksburg have put steel into her spine. The dreaming girl en route to a new life is gone. In her stead is a determined character, a woman with no passion other than to hold onto sanity while keeping her daughter safe.

That is the plan. But the stresses of life are taking their toll. Twice last week she was close to fainting, though fainting is not the right word, it's more about swimming through glue.

Mid-afternoon it happened again.

She was on the step-ladder reaching out to trim the wisteria when her mischief-maker mind chose to recall the first sight of Bobby in the tower, music playing and a puppet dancing. *'Ain't misbehaving, saving my love for you…!'*

Bang! All went black.

Eyelids flickering, she swayed.

The step ladder tilted.

'Careful!' A hand in the small of her back guided her to safety.

It was over in a moment, a short yet telling reminder of who's the boss.

Adept at covering her tracks she made light of it. 'Hunger pangs,' she said climbing down. 'I didn't bother with breakfast and now I'm paying for it.'

Gabriel passed his straw hat. 'Put this on.'

'It's too big.'

'Never mind, put it on. And there's this. ' He pushed a five-pound note into her pocket. 'Ma shouldn't have taken it. It ain't you owes for maple.'

'Oh, but I…!'

His jaw tightened.

'Very well.' She led the way to the kitchen. 'Thank you for giving us your time. I know you're busy at the funeral parlour.'

He shrugged. 'Folks keep on dyin'.'

'You're a very serious and sober man, Gabriel Templar,' she said, trying to steer attention away from the fact she was trembling. 'Don't you ever smile?'

'Pa was a drinkin' man. When he was alive he gave me and Ma hell. When he died he give us more. After that there was six years in the State pen, boot camp and Parris Island. Now there's coffins to be made and folks to bury. Not many reasons to smile in any of that.'

'I'm sorry,' she said. 'I didn't mean to offend you.'

'It don't matter. It's water under the bridge. You got that doll handy? Ma wants it for makin' somethin' for Sophie.'

'Hang on a moment.' She returned with the doll. 'This is so beautifully made. If you're not happy at the parlour couldn't you make more? I'm sure you'd find an instant market.'

'Make more?' He ran his thumb over the delicately carved wooden face. 'Why would I want to make more when this one is trouble enough?'

'Well really!' It was her turn to be offended. 'If it was so much trouble I wonder you bothered. No one asked you to.'

'Bobby Rourke axed me. He gave me your picture to work from.'

'Yes, your mother did mention that.' She looked again at the doll. 'You did this from a photograph?'

'I didn't need no photo. I know your face better than I know my own.'

'I don't see how.'

'Uh-huh.' He walked away. 'That's your trouble. You don't see what's goin' on right under your nose.'

~

'Ain't she sweet! Don't you think she's kinda neat!'

Bobby is teaching Sophie to jitterbug. They boogie up and down the billiard room, Sophie giggling fit to burst. It's been a pleasant evening.

No complaints, no tantrums, and no obvious desire to escape.

Bobby is in a good mood which prompted Adelia to offer a haircut.

'Do I need one?'

'It wouldn't go amiss.'

'Okay, then. Let it not be said Captain RE Rourke shirked his duty.'

'If you'd take Sophie to bed I can finish up here.'

'Right-oh! Let's go, kiddo! Last one up the stairs is a rotten egg!'

Squealing, Sophie rushed away, Bobby in pursuit. It's all right, Adelia reassured herself. It's all a bit forced and frantic yet hopefully settling.

Sophie in bed he knelt by the bath, his wounded cheek padded with a towel.

Adelia is careful not to hurt him. And, since they have not as yet exchanged so much as a kiss she is prudent with her body, leaning away, keeping space between them fearful of starting a battle she cannot win.

The trim went well, Bobby breaking open a celebratory bottle of champagne.

She wanted to ask if he need drink but refusing to spoil the moment talked of showers. 'We need a shower attachment for the new bathroom.'

'Don't worry about that. When work on the tower's finished we'll have showers enough for the whole Eighth Army.'

Mellowed by champagne, he talked of the accident. 'The motor bike belonged to a pal of mine. Bloody thing did for me! I turned a corner a bit sharp and ended in a bomb crater, barbed wire popping my eyeball like ripe tomato.'

A couple of glasses later he is not so mellow. 'Sent Stateside I trawled around for a while tryin' civil airlines. I figured if I could drive a Lancaster I could steer their flimsy kites. No good. Not enough for the two-eyed variety let alone a one-eyed dick. Anyway, my Pa left a heap of cash. I started buyin' USAAF surplus. Nothin' ambitious, a mail run or two, interstate taxi-service kind of jaunt.'

'So you don't actually fly anymore?'

'Are you kiddin'? I have to fly. It's mother's milk to me. Jesus, the day I can't flap my wings is the day I check out!'

'And the club?'

'There ain't no club! It's just a bunch of wounded eagles lookin' for a nest. Guys do their bit for King and Country. They bust their asses provin' their worth. They win medals but the minute they leave off dog tags they're nobodies. Forget the gongs, the DFCs, it's the bum's rush! You're out on your ass with no place to go.'

Hand shaking, he lit a cheroot. 'I started the Club because I was sick of bein' shoved around. What I got when I left the air-force was a line of jumped-up fuckers tellin' me what I could and couldn't do. I can't live accordin' to another man's rules. I have to live as I wanna live and die as I wanna die and not shoved from pillar to post by guys who didn't so much as fart in defence of their country.'

Adelia tried to calm him but he didn't want to know.

'It's same with all GIs. They need something to do and a place to do it where they can get shit-faced and nobody bawl them out. Wives and girlfriends verboten! No one to give them the third degree. No one to remind them of yesterday's glory. No one sayin' ain't it a shame, Baby! You were such a great lookin' guy, Baby! And will you for God's sake get surgery, Baby, 'cos your face is enough to make a person vomit!'

Adelia held his hand. 'I am so very sorry.'

It took a while for him to speak. 'It ain't your fault.'

'You've had a rough time.'

'No more than anyone else.'

'I can understand why you need the club.'

'I don't need nothin'. I told you it ain't a club! It's a shit hole for drunks.'

'But it helps the men who go there.'

He shrugged. 'Maybe.'

She poured a glass of wine and held out her hand. 'That'll be two-bob, sir.'

'Two bob?'

'For the haircut.'

'Jees, that's a bit pricey. Will you settle for a beer?'

'I'll settle for a band-aid. I cut my finger a while back on a photograph of one of your buddies and the wound keeps opening up.'

'What photo's that?'

'I found it in the cottage the first night we were here, photographs and other bits. It fell on the mat, a Colonel Bogey type, stiff upper lip and heart of steel.'

For a while he stared seeming to struggle between laughter and tears. He chose laughter. 'Jeez, that is funny!' he snorted. 'Colonel Bogy? That's the guy I was tellin' you about, Ash Hunter, who left me the motorbike.'

'Oh I see.'

'Good old Ash. We were real close, have been since we were kids.'

'Then why did you burn the photograph?'

'I didn't! It was another guy. I brought chaps back from the Mess. We were swappin' stories. I told 'em about Ash, said who he was, and showed them newspaper clips of him getting the Medal.'

'Medal?'

'The Congressional Medal, the big one. I took an album out and some klutz spilt booze all over it, then made it worse tryin' to clean it with lighter fuel. It's okay. I've got more pics.' Bobby smiled. 'Alexander William Stonewall Hunter, a guy so fine you could cut your soul on him never mind your finger.'

'Stonewall!' Adelia couldn't help smiling.

'I know! Poor guy's an army brat following in daddy's boot-steps. It's some time since I saw him. Don't know that he made it back. Oh, but those guys!' He curled his fist. 'You invite them home and they take liberties. It's the last time. They won't be settin' foot on my land again, not now my lady's here.'

He took her hand. 'Does the cut still hurt?'

'It smarts a little.'

'I've got a cure for that.' He slid her finger into his mouth.

She looked away and he grinned, enjoying her discomfiture.

'It's not funny,' she said, smiling.

'It is from where I'm sitting. You should see your face! Talk about shocked.'

'I'm not shocked,' she said, her toes curling at the lathering tongue. 'I'm an old hand at the finger-sucking routine. Sophie does it all the time.'

'I'm not a kid. I'm a man.' He was pulling her closer when the door opened, jangling bracelets preceding the intruder. 'Tally ho!' he released Adelia. 'Bandits at two o clock! I thought there was a whiff of brimstone in the air.'

'I hope I ain't intrudin'.'

'Not at all!' Adelia offered an easy chair. 'Do sit down.'

Mrs Rourke chose another. 'Thank you, I'm not stopping.'

Bobby thumbed the top off a beer. 'What's your poison these days, Ma?'

'I don't drink. Haven't touched a drop since your father, God rest his soul, went to meet his maker.'

'Jeez, let's not spoil the day talkin' about him,' said Bobby. 'Did you come to see Sophie? She's asleep, but Dee won't mind wakin' her.'

'Actually, I'd rather not. It's late and she's been busy with the piglets.'

'That's fine by me.' Mrs Rourke sniffed. 'I'm just recovering from a dose of flu Sue Ryland's brat give me. I wouldn't want another.'

'Here you are, Ma.' Bobby offered a glass of champagne. 'Try that for size.'

'Celebratin' are yer?'

'You might say so.'

'Got somethin' to celebrate?'

'Yes,' said Adelia, 'the trimming of Bobby's hair.'

He gave a twirl. 'And she made a good job of it too.'

'Fancy yourself a hairdresser?'

'More an enthusiastic amateur.'

The atmosphere having taken a sharp nose-dive Adelia retreated to the sofa and taking out a swatch of curtain materials began flicking through.

'What's that you're lookin' at, furnishin' stuff?'

'I'm thinking of new curtains for the long sitting room.'

'I chose the drapes for that room. It was a job lot at the store a couple of years back. I was thinkin' to save money, Baby puttin' every cent in this place.'

'Every cent?' Bobby sneered. 'I got this place for a song and you know it.'

' It's okay havin' luxury tastes,' said Mrs Rourke, 'but if all you got is a suitcase of clothes and money that ain't worth the paper it's printed on, it's best you keep your tastes to yourself. Seems to me a deal of money is bein' spent.'

'There is.' Adelia remained bent over the swatch. 'A great deal.'

Bobby's lips twitched. 'Much more of it and Dee'll have to get a job.'

' I wouldn't mind a job,' she said. 'I mean, when we're done decorating and Sophie's found a school.'

'Back to nursing?' Bobby frowned.

'Perhaps not quite that but similar.'

'Forget it. There's plenty to do here. Ma will give you a hand. She's nifty with a needle. Sewed many a crooked seam, ain't you, Ruby?'

'That's it.' Mrs Rourke sniffed. 'Make fun of your mother.'

'Just joshin'.'

'I know your joshin'. It's like to end up nasty.' She tugged at Bobby's hair. 'She's cut it too short. You need a longer bit over here.' He slapped her hand and she sat down. 'Did you do like I said and ring that doctor?'

'What doctor?'

'The one Mrs Lyons told me about. Her boy Joe as was in the navy got burnt. Now he's got hisself a new nose. And d'you know how he got it? They took skin off his what-you-ma- call-it and grew him a new one.'

'Joe got him a new what-you-ma-call-it?'

'A nose! He got a new nose!'

'A new nose! So what happens when he blows it? Does he get a stiffy?'

'Hey!' Mrs Rourke was affronted. 'I didn't come to listen to dirty talk. And by the by,' she turned on Adelia. 'I hear the kiddie's still seein' May Templar. You got no sense lettin' her visit there, him murderin' his own flesh and blood.'

'Murdering?'

'Yeah murder. He killed his pa, struck him down without mercy.'

'Oh, poor May.' Adelia sighed. 'And Gabriel such a good man.'

'You listenin' to this?' Mrs Rourke jerked her thumb. 'Two minutes and she knows every man-Jack better than folks who've lived here all their lives.'

'Leave it, Ma.'

'I ain't leavin' it. Fifteen years hard labour he was meant to do. They say the Marines got him off but I know it was them lawyers givin' an easy ride. It's all wrong! It should be as the good book says, '*eye for an eye, a tooth for a tooth*.''

'What about turning the other cheek?' said Adelia.

'The Good Book weren't talkin' about murderers. And don't you quote scripture at me, girl. I was studyin' bible when you was havin' your ass wiped.'

'Ass wiped?' Adelia raised her eyebrows. 'I'd be careful with the champagne if I were you, Mrs Rourke. That sounded awfully like dirty talk to me.'

Bobby sniggered and Adelia was ashamed. 'Sorry. I shouldn't have said that.'

'No, you shouldn't, puttin' in your two cents when it ain't wanted. The Templars are hogs grubbin' in dirt. You being British you might not mind who you keep company with but me and my boy got to think of our good names.'

'What good names are those?' said Bobby.

'We've always had a good name, never been sullied, least not til now.'

'Leave it, Ma.'

'I won't leave it! Are you gonna let her talk to me like that, Baby Rourke? It's disgraceful. Comin' and upsettin' things, treatin' me with contempt and mixin' with riff-raff! Worst day's work getting hooked up with her.'

Bobby stood up. 'I said leave it.'

A gag was applied but not enough to stop bile seeping through.

'I'm only sayin' what everybody else is sayin'. You gotta put your foot down, and while you're at it ask why she wears that ring? What is it a wedding ring? Because if it is I call it closing the door after the horse as bolted!'

Adelia stood up. 'I'm going to bed.'

Bobby nodded. 'Go. The evening's spoiled anyway.'

~

She was sitting brushing her hair when he came to her room.

'Sorry about Ma. She can be a real pain in the ass.'

'I didn't help.'

'Wouldn't have mattered what you said.'

She carried on brushing.

He sat beside her. 'What's with the bible quotin'?'

'You're not alone in suffering from God-botherers. I spent a good deal of my youth with Aunt Maud and her passion for the local vicar. What she didn't know of the New Testament wasn't worth knowing.'

'So you're no God botherer yourself?'

'With the blots on my copy book? I hardly think so.'

'Thank Christ for that. I couldn't have borne another.'

Adelia regarded him from the mirror. 'Why does she call you Baby?'

He took the hair brush and began brushing. 'To her I'm still in knee britches.'

'But you're not a baby. You're a man who's seen active service.'

'I know who I am. The thing is how do you see me?'

'What d'you want me to say? I am sorry about what happened to you. How could I not be? And I understand you're a man with manly feelings.'

'Sure I'm a man,' he laid the brush aside, giving her a shoulder rub her muscles rigid under his hands. 'Relax. You're tight as a drum.'

'Am I?' she said bending her head. 'I wonder why?'

Ignoring sarcasm he carried on kneading. 'I bumped into an old friend today,' he said, tricky words out his mouth before he knew it. 'Not a friend so much as the mother of a friend, my buddy's ma. She says he's comin' home.'

'Really,' she said, her voice muffled though her hair. 'That'll be nice for you.'

'Nice for you too. You'll get to meet him.'

'Lucky me! What a bore.'

'Bore?' he said, strangely thrilled by her disinclination.

'Yes, all the Boy's Own hero stuff.'

'He ain't like that. Sure, he's tough but underneath he's marshmallow. Least he was last time I saw him.'

'And when was that?'

'England, '42.'

'England?' She flicked her hair back from her face, pleased of a chance to speak of home. 'Was he stationed near you?'

'Scotland. When I saw him he was on a forty-eight doin' the town.'

'Colonel Bogey doing the town!? He does normal things like normal people?'

'It has been known.'

'I can't imagine it. In the photograph he looks as if he never laughed in his life.'

'Maybe he's got nothing to laugh about,' Bobby muttered. Uncomfortable with the conversation he draped her hair across her shoulder and kissed her neck. 'I don't know what you got against the guy. He ain't done nothin' to you.'

Words hanging heavy in the air he got scared and started pasting little kisses down her neck. She shuddered and he stopped. 'It's all right,' she said, relaxing her shoulder allowing the nightgown strap to slide down her arm. 'Carry on.'

'Is this going where I think it is?'

'Where do you want it to go?'

'As far as it can! Hold on a minute!' He dropped the brush and ran. 'I got more of that Krug in the cellar. It'll help loosen us up.'

He took the cellar stairs two at a time. By the time he hit bottom he was pissing himself laughing. Ma's face! If this is going to happen every time Ruby comes to call, the battle in Dee's green eyes, then the old bag will get a season ticket.

Sprinting through the house he couldn't help but marvel at changes. What a difference she's made. Four months and she's shifted furniture, hung wallpaper, sewed curtains, planted beans and pulled weeds. Shazam! He's got a home.

A case of booze stacked behind a box, he cracked a bottle and drank, champagne running down his chin.

Every nerve in his body shot to pieces he fought to be calm. 'Come on, Captain America, straighten up and fly right!'

Another glug and he's in the hall surveying an erstwhile prison.

Not so very long ago he sat on the sofa with his pistol oiled and ready.

No longer needed on voyage the pistol is locked away.

Bowing his head, he prayed, 'thank you, Jesus.'

Then he did a smart u-turn heading back to the dining room and the spanking new baby-grand. He dug a silver-framed photograph out of a drawer and propped it on the piano. Then stepping back, he saluted smartly.

'And thank you, Colonel Bogey.'

Chapter Eight
A Handsome Man

Friday morning brought liberation, a bicycle on the back
porch, a basket up front and a child's seat on the back. Of
the good fairy there was no sign, however, the meticulous
way in which the bike had been overhauled, and the
diffident manner of giving pointed to one man.

Eager to try it out Adelia loaded Sophie on the back.
They took off, pausing at May's on the way. It's easy to see
why the Templar home fascinated. A two-storey building,
pink tiled roof and walls squashy with age, it flourishes
amid the trees as part of the vegetation. Animals run loose
or are tethered on loose lines. Birds with pinioned wings
squawk and preen in aviaries. Horses peer over fences,
dogs wag tails and cats yawn, everywhere you look
creatures crawl, fly or hop. Only May sits motionless on
the stoop, a tabby on her lap.

Adelia applied the brakes. 'Hello, May.'

'If you've come lookin' for Gabe he ain't here. Sue
came by with her kiddie, Becky, and they've gone lookin'
at a buzzard.'

'It's all right. I just wanted to thank Mister Templar for
the bicycle. It was him, wasn't it?'

'Couldn't be nobody else. He's the only fool willin' to take on another useless piece of junk.'

'What's the matter? Is the funeral parlour not doing well?'

'It's goin' lickety-split. I don't see much of Gabe nor for that matter you. All the sewin' and gardenin', you're a crazy woman. And what now, are you gonna sit or are you off with a hornet's nest in your drawers?'

'I'd love to chat,' Adelia mounted the bicycle, 'but we're going to the tailors later today and so I'm in rather a hurry.'

'It's okay,' said May, tipping the cat off her lap. 'I don't wanna hold anybody up. I got chores of my own. I'm away again. Sister Belle's sickly.'

'I'm sorry to hear that. Is there anything I can do?'

'If there's anythin' to be done you is the one can do it,' said May, then catching a puzzled look waved her hand. 'Forget it. I'm cranky today. Now this Mister stuff? Why can't you call my boy by his first name?'

'I feel awkward. And anyway, you don't call Bobby by his first name.'

'That's because I don't like him. I got time for you and Sophie else why would I work at the Mill but it don't change the way I feel.'

'Does Mister…does Gabriel feel the same?'

'He's a closed man. I never know what he's thinkin'. Pa's drinkin made him like that. It brought us shame, lost us the yard and broke my boy's heart.'

Adelia pedalled to town pondering a broken-hearted murderer.

They stopped at the drugstore where a sloe-eyed brunette called Sue took their order. 'Hi, little gal,' she smiled at Sophie. 'Some bicycle you're riding?'

'Did you see me and mummy on it?'

'I sure did. Hello there.'

'Hello. Could we have a milky coffee and a strawberry milkshake?'

'Sure thing! You want somethin' with that coffee, waffle or piece of pie?'

'Nothing, thank you. I need to keep an eye on my figure.'

Sue grinned. 'You don't need to worry. There ain't a handful of you as it is.'

Hips purring like Rolls Royce engines, she sauntered away back of the store where she met with another girl. There followed a great deal of peering back to their table and whispering. Eventually coffee arrived. Sue perched on a bench alongside. 'You're the gal come from England?'

'Adelia Challoner. How do you do?'

They shook hands. 'I'm Sue Ryland as was. I've seen you out and about and wanted to say Hi but you're always on the move. D'you like it here?'

'It's a beautiful part of the world.'

'And you have a beautiful little girl. My friend and I were saying we never saw such eyes. And dark curly hair! I guess this little honey takes after her Pa.'

'I guess she does.'

An impressive bosom straining buttons on her blouse, Sue relaxed along the back of the bench. 'Set the date then, you and Baby Rourke getting wed?'

'No not yet,' said Adelia, aware that was the case. They'd talked of marrying but that was all, the subject quietly placed on the back burner.

'He talked all the time of you comin'.'

'Did he?'

'Uh-huh, all the time, and here you are!'

'Yes, here we are.'

'That'll be a dollar with the cookies.'

Under scrutiny, Adelia fumbled with her bag, the contents scattering. Both women grubbed about the floor. Sue retrieved the photograph and handed it back. 'Now that's what I call a handsome man. Who is he an old flame?'

'He's a friend of Bobby's.'

'Is he?' Sue stared. 'You know you're some mystery. Years Baby was saying you were comin'. The way he talked you was one of them British princesses on the newsreels that speak through their noses. My gal this and that, we thought he was making you up. But here you are, large as life.'

'Well, not so large according to you.'

'You and him together and him bein' the way he is?' Sue raised her delicately pencilled eyebrows. 'It kinda makes me wonder how you'll manage.'

'Oh we'll manage fine, thank you!' Adelia set down the cup. 'It's what British Princesses do. Finish your shake, Sophie. I'll be outside getting a breath of air.'

Cheeks brilliant, out she went onto the sidewalk. My God, she thought! If this is how it feels under scrutiny no wonder Bobby hates it.

She leant against a rail. Two old men leant with her.

Wheels crunching and shoes shuffling, a funeral procession breasted the hill, a pair of coal black horses rising out of the heat-haze.

Up and up they came pulling a sparkling hearse, ebony spindled wheels floating on a cloud of dust and a pale coffin reposing on a purple mantle.

A tiny Negro boy perched on the wagon, an oversized top hat balanced on his ears. Bless him! He seemed overwhelmed by the occasion, eyes rolling back and forth between the onlookers and the man directing the funeral.

Gabriel Templar walked before the hearse. Dressed in black frockcoat and pants, high-top boots, a white ruffled shirt and silver embroidered waistcoat, he was the hired gun in a Western movie.

The cortege drew level. A sigh passed through the onlookers. And then amid a jingle of harness and creaking of wheels it moved on.

'Oh, that was wonderful,' whispered Adelia.

'Yes, ma'am.' Black-eyed Sue stood alongside. 'Thrifty but never cheap Gabriel sends them off right.' Her breath warm, she leaned close. 'I did hear it was him brought you and Sophie from the bus depot.'

'He did.'

'That's some messenger boy, wouldn't you say?'

'My daughter certainly thinks so.'

'Your daughter's got good taste. See the folk on the sidewalk?' Sue pointed to the crowd. 'Some of them are here out of respect for the departed. All of 'em are here to see Gabe Templar, gentleman and killer.'

'So, it's true then.'

'Killed his Pa? Yes he did! Whump, one stop and that Hodge was gone.'

'Gabriel went to prison?'

'Sure, though he oughtn't. Nobody should go to jail for killing a man like Hodge Templar. Six years he was in that place. Went in a boy and came out a man. It was the Marines got him out and God bless them for it. The Corps saved more than his life. Got folks to see what kind of man they were missin'. Now he's giving up on that. He's done stepped back in time doing what he did before, digging graves for poor folk. There's a lot of folks wonderin' why.'

'I'm sure Mister Templar knows what he's doing.'

'You think so? You wouldn't question why a man so dedicated to the Corps would quit like that? Wouldn't think it odd?'

'I am not in his confidence.'

'You ain't?'

'No.'

'Well, he don't wear no uniform now but still makes womenfolk sigh.'

'You're fond of him?'

'Fond?' Sue laughed. 'I'm more than fond. I'm crazy for the man. I'd like to wrap him in warm molasses and suck him til his bones were dry.'

'My goodness!'

'Goodness ain't what I've got in mind. There are all manner of things I could do for Gabe Templar but will never get the chance. He's set his sights on some other gal, sighing over her for years, though Lord knows why.'

Sophie came out of the store candy in her mouth. Adelia settled her in the seat and was about to pedal away when

Sue called out. 'They say he has a mean streak but I ain't seen it. He's been good to me and my daughter. I guess it's how you treat him. Like them stallions of his, you got to keep a soothing hand on their neck or they're apt to send you flyin'.'

~

That afternoon they drove to Richmond, Bobby's tailor situated above the main avenue. Bolts of cloth were brought for his attention, shirts, socks, ties, were chosen or discarded, a pile of packages growing.

Adelia wore the grey linen suit and sat reading a magazine while from behind a curtain Bobby trashed her taste in clothes.

'Why you wearing that thing again? You look like Orphan Annie. Was there nothing in the closet? I mean, come on! Thousands of dollars of clothes stashed in there, didn't one item take your fancy?'

She turned a page. Yes, she thought, they're lovely but I can't clean lavatories in chiffon any more than I can sit here in a cocktail dress.

She sat up. What was that he said about wearing that thing again?

A chill rippled down her spine. He was in the Mill that day and heard them walking about and phoned from the tower pretending to be elsewhere. And the nonsense about being delayed was all it ever was.

Did she suspect it? Probably, but busy absorbing other horrors had swept that little item under the carpet.

Sad, she gazed out the window at people hurrying by. Who are they and what are they looking for? Is it love they want or compromise? There's plenty of compromise in her life. Last week after the hair trim she thought there might be sex, but what started as an intimate tete-a-tete, a glass of wine to bolster the nerves, fell away, Bobby's passion flatter than the champagne.

During the war his antics were the talk of the nurse's rest room. 'Watch out for the Yank in the Broom Cupboard!' they'd say. 'He has the face of an angel but the cheek of the devil. While you're busy taking his temperature he's busy with his hand up your skirt.' Imposed abstinence must be difficult for him. It would seem the war stripped him of more than his sight.

~

They left the tailors for the zoo. It was hot, Sophie fractious and Bobby the centre of attention. Most chose not to stare showing respect for the man and uniform. Some couldn't look away. He took all with dignity, Adelia's respect rising accordingly. Then he'd be unnecessarily sharp with Sophie and respect would plummet. So went the day, up and down like a faulty barometer.

Toward evening there was as an incident that would haunt her forever. They were walking through a park when a man shouted, 'Hey Bobby!'

Sweat breaking out, he skidded to a halt and then visibly relaxing clipped his forehead in salute. 'Hiya, buddy! How you doin?'

Adelia was introduced as his fiancé. The men talked a while. The man bowed and moved on, whereupon Bobby slumped down on a bench.

'What's wrong?' she said. 'You look like you've seen a ghost.'

'I sure thought I heard one.'

Moistening her handkerchief at a water-fountain, she patted his forehead.

'Don't!' He pushed her away. 'I'm okay. Don't fuss!'

They sat for a while, Sophie playing in a sandpit. Adelia peeled off her hat and shaking out her hair turned her face to the sun.

'You ever hear from that guy who ran out on you?' asked Bobby.

'What?'

'Sophie's father? Did you ever hear from him?'

'No.'

'You still don't remember him?'

'No.'

'What nothin', not so much as a clue in all these years?'

'Not a peep and I wouldn't want to. When are we going to eat?' she said, wanting to change the subject.

'In a minute when I get my breath back.'

Bobby was having a job holding it together. The trip was turning out to be a nightmare. When they were in the tailor's outfitters he nearly let the cat out of the bag. The fitting room with heavy velvet curtains reminded him of a confessional box and the tailor with the tape-measure, Bobby wanted to kneel beside him and confess his sins, how minute-by-minute, twenty-four hours a day he is flying by the seat of his pants.

'Perhaps we should go home now.' Adelia shifted beside him. 'Time's getting on and we don't want Sophie late in bed.'

'No, we can't have that!' he snapped. 'Can't have the little princess upset!'

Bobby closed his eyes. Why do I do that, why do I push them away?

Out the corner of his eye he saw her pulling at her collar. The continual criticism of her clothes was getting to her. Okay, the suit was a Salvation Army reject but let's face it she would look good in a paper bag.

The day she came to Virginia he was in his usual perch. Bruised sexy mouth, cheekbones you could rest your chin on, and golden hair twisted up, she stepped down from that truck like a Goddess.

When they met in Blighty he was not the best-behaved patient. 'Matron!' he was always yelling. 'What does a man have to do to take a piss in this place?'

She would poke her head round the door: 'Is that you shouting?'

'No,' he would snarl, too needy to care about a pale-faced ingénue. 'It's the Japanese fuckin' Sandman!'

She'd whisk away, reappearing with a bottle. 'Here,' she'd say, her eyes like emerald frost. 'Keep your voice down. You're frightening the cockroaches.'

Knocked sideways, he kept an eye out for her. Days went on and he heard she lived alone. No steady guy and no stage door Johnnies queuing for a taste of her lips, she was the Original Snow Queen. At first she didn't think much of him. Why would she when he's chasing tail at all and sundry? But with her in mind he watched and waited. Then the worst happened, a fresh breeze blew into town and overnight the picture changed.

Talking of Ash Hunter, a rumour's going round that he's alive, and you know rumours, they have a nasty habit of coming true.

'Dee?' he took her hand. 'How d'you feel about moving to California?'

'I've hardly got used to Virginia.'

'I know, but I'm seriously thinking of moving on.'

'But this is where you were born. Your mother is here and your friends?'

'Precisely.'

~

That evening he spent the time playing blues on the gramophone and guzzling beer. Come midnight he was out of his scull but still could not slake his thirst. There was only one thing that would settle him and that was sex.

BTBW, before-the-brick-wall, he needed sex like roses need sunlight. Fucking and flying were life's blood. Darting about a tennis court with a leggy sophomore or cruising bars looking for a piece of tail sex was a reason for living. He still frequents bars but more a kidder reacting to a knee-jerk habit.

And why go out when your home is comfortable? Why look for love when love is in the drapes at the window and the gleam of polished floors? For the first time in his life he has a home. If it wasn't for the lies he'd be in seventh heaven, cosy in the conservatory, watching things grow, daisies that stretch out to the sun, and roses, that like Dee are tough and ravishingly beautiful.

Sophie wants a dog? No way! No dogs. No cats. Dogs shit on the grass and cats kill birds. We got moles making a mess of the lawn. Last week he set traps but after he'd done it the thought of the poor blind little buggers trapped was too much. He crept out at night and dug 'em up.

The greenhouse is his heaven - silence, the smell of Kerosene, rain gushing in the barrel and honeybees drunk with pollen, who could want for more?

Is that hilarious or what! A few years back if anyone had said Baby Rourke would spend his thirties fucking about with plants, and that plants were all he could fuck, he'd put a pistol to his head. Peace and solitude is what he needs, messing about with seeds, his tweezer-like fingers extensions of a suffering soul. Butterflies and spindle-shank spiders will never fail in his greenhouse. He sets them free. He knows how it is to be despised.

BTBW, every girl knew what he wanted. He'd wine and dine and then undo his flies. 'Okay, sugar pie, what you got in them lacy drawers.'

Some anteed up. Others moaned, 'why can't you be like your friend?' He'd laugh. 'What, a rifle in one hand and a flower-press in the other?'

It was Alex Hunter they talked about, a guy so bashful he couldn't catch a girl if she were hog-tied. In those days they had nothing in common; Bobby was of the air, Ash was of the earth, West Point was all he cared about. A smart cookie, the guy has total recall. All he has to do is look and it's in his brain forever. A loner, when not at the Academy he'd be on the Heightes, a dog by his side and clapped out BSA motorbike beneath him. A soldier -a West-Point man- he would sell his soul for a rifle and yet loved animals, tickling small-life from burrows the way Templar tickles a trout.

Now there's a resemblance! Both men have the same comic-strip build. The difference is in their beginnings. Raised in a home where good manners prevail Ash could dine with princes, class and cash, his Pappy Frobisher was rich as Rockefeller. Gabe couldn't eat without having a fork explained.

Gabriel Templar! If Bobby could have one wish granted, one black soul sinning, it would be to see that bum laid so low he'd never get up, his handsome face shoved in the dirt.

A shadow slunk by the window, the vixen after the ducklings. She won't get them, not after yesterday him and Dee creating an island middle of the pond.

Deprived of dinner the vixen howls. Howling was his need for sex. Still smarting from Sunday night when he thought he'd got it made he cracked another bottle. Unsteady, he spilt beer on Ash's photograph. 'And you can shut the fuck up,' he said, turning it face down. 'It's nothing to do with you!'

Up the stairs he trolled, singing as he went, *'ain't she sweet, don't you think she'd kinda neat, now I ask you every confidentially, ain't she sweet.'*

One step over the threshold and he is stone cold sober.

Dee slept on her back, her hand entwined in her hair. Breast rising and falling deeply and evenly she sleeps, a murmur from Sophie's room, and eyes closed she rises up on her elbow. All quiet, she sinks down, able to sleep through hell and high water yet a squeak from Sophie and she's awake.

Folding his arms along the edge of the bed he knelt down. Look at her! Eyeballs moving, she is dreaming. Does she dream of her lover?

Maybe Gabe is her fancy or the blue-eyed man with a truer claim.

She opened her eyes. 'What's wrong? Is Sophie all right?'

'She's fine.'

'Are you ill?'

'Nope, just lonely.'

Panic receding, Adelia breathed out. Lord, he stinks of booze. Sadness in his eyes she stroked his hair. 'Poor fellow! I'm such a burden to you.'

'You're no burden.' He drew her hand to his lips. 'You're gorgeous, and I'm a grade-A asshole.' He leaned over. 'Tell me about your day. Here am I home from the office, Mister Nice Guy, umbrella in the stand. You're in the kitchen and I call out, 'hi, honey, I'm home! Have you had a nice day?''

Adelia humored him. 'We had a lovely day, me and Sophie on our bike.'

'What bike?'

'Gabriel Templar left us an old bicycle.'

Bobby flushed. 'Why in Hell do you want that?'

'Because it's useful! It has a seat on the back and is easy to get about. Oh, don't be unhappy about it, Bobby! Please don't spoil it!'

'I'm not spoilin' it. I just wish you'd asked me for a bike.'

'I didn't ask. He gave.'

'Yeah, and for what services rendered?'

'Services rendered?'

'Forget it!' he snapped. 'Finish your nice day.'

Humor gone, Adelia sighed. 'We had a nice chat with May, and went to the nice drugstore where we were served by a nice waitress called Sue.'

'Yeah, good old Sue, she of the open heart and ever-open legs.'

'I like her. She had a firm handshake.'

'I'll bet she did. Her old man, Herb Willet, came back from the Pacific minus an arm. Sue lent him hers. Then when he put an end to himself she went out night looking to raise other things.'

'Her husband killed himself?'

'Yup, a .45 in his mouth took the top off his head.'

'That's terrible.'

'Is it so terrible? I guess he couldn't face life without all his moveable parts and chose his own way out. You have to respect him for that.'

'Surely there's more to life than the loss of a limb.'

He scowled. 'Easy to say when you've both arms and legs. Maybe if you'd lost a limb you wouldn't be so quick to judge.'

'I wasn't making a judgment. I was trying to put myself in Sue's place.'

'Never mind her! She was prowlin' the streets when he did it looking for a guy with bad taste. Gabe, most likely! She always had the hots for him.'

'She's in love with him. This morning she couldn't take her eyes off him.'

The moment it was said Adelia knew she'd made a mistake.

A bull to a red rag, he leapt to his feet. 'I thought I told you to stay away from him. Just because I agreed to May workin' here doesn't mean you're to make bosom buddies of the entire tribe.'

'I wasn't with him. I was watching a funeral.'

'Was Sophie with you?'

'Of course she was! Where else would she be?'

Not wanting raised voices Adelia closed the door. 'What have you got against Mister Templar? Tell me what it is and I might understand.'

'I've got nothin' against him. The guy doesn't figure in my thoughts. What's with the Mister? He's nobody! I don't want you consortin' with his kind.'

'I don't consort. Who do I know to consort with? You don't introduce me to your friends and your mother never comes except to criticize.'

'Why wouldn't she? You haven't gone out of your way to encourage her.'

'I would've loved a relationship with her but she didn't want it. She made that clear when she sent me the equivalent of a poison pen letter.'

'What you talkin' about?'

'This is what I'm talking about.' Adelia took the card from the dressing table drawer. 'See what it says, ''Go home English whore.'

Bobby ripped the card in two, tossing the pieces on the floor. 'Ma didn't put that in your coat pocket. That's not her writing.'

'Then who did?'

'I don't know and I don't care! Don't try changin' the subject. You and Juicy Sue have a likin' for a particular type of man. Bees to honey you stand around watchin' them parade their muscle.'

'Don't be ridiculous! The only reason I was there was…!' Adelia snatched up the torn pieces of card. 'How did you know this was in my coat pocket?'

'You said it was.'

'I said nothing about a coat and nothing about a pocket! Did you do this?'

'Why would I do such a thing?'

'I don't know. Perhaps hoping I would read it and not bother to come.'

'That's crazy.'

'Yes isn't it, but you said yourself you didn't want us.'

'Sure I was scared of you comin' but I wouldn't stick a card in your pocket and call you whore. Only a madman would do that. And another thing!' Face scarlet, he was shouting. 'When are you gonna quit wearing that ring? It's insultin' as Ma says. You're here to marry me not hang onto some old flame.'

'I can't marry you.'

'Why because of a stupid card?'

'No, not that especially, I just can't marry you.'

'But you have to! Everyone in Virginia knows you've come specially to marry me. If you don't I'm gonna look a real fool.'

'Why worry about how things look? Wouldn't you prefer me to be happy?'

'The hell I would! Not after everythin' you've put me through. The money I've laid out, the heartache all these years waitin' for you to make up your mind. I would've thought the least you can do is marry me.'

'And what about my heartache?' she said, picking pieces of card from the floor. 'The lies you've told?'

'Well, that's the way it goes, honey. You want money and expensive doodads you got to take the rough with the smooth.'

'Damn you for sending this, Bobby Rourke!' Furious, she threw the pieces of card at him. 'And damn you again for sending it too late!'

He slapped her, his ring thudding into her knocking her back on the bed.

There was a hush, the slap echoing. 'Jesus, honey, I'm sorry!' He was on his knees by the bed. 'I never meant to do that!'

Adelia wanted to tell him it didn't matter but words wouldn't come, the only sound heard as consciousness slipped away was the running of feet.

Gabriel burst through the door. The situation didn't take much figuring out; she is on the bed and Baby Rourke a fungus crawling all over her.

'Get off her!' He snatched his collar but Bobby didn't seem to care and tore at her gown, his fingers biting her breasts like they were fabulous fruit.

'Get away!' Gabriel threw him to the floor. Breath hissing through his teeth and grey eyes splintered he circled. 'Come on, get up!'

Sophie was in the doorway. He carried her back to her bed tucking her under the blanket. 'It's okay, sweetheart. Mommy's restin'. Now you do the same.'

Bobby pushed by and ran down stairs fiddling away like a bug. Seconds later the car backfired, red taillights disappearing down the lane.

A blue tinge to her lips, Adelia lay silent and still. Her gown torn like that she needed covering. Gabriel looked about for something to cover her. The room was soft. Pale drapes with floppy bows, a cream cover and shaded lamps, it showed a woman's delicate touch. Perfume hung in the air from a box of powder on the table. Unable to bear the sight he took off his shirt and spread it over her. Such visions would tempt a saint and he is only a man.

She opened her eyes.

'You okay?' He was already halfway out the door.

When she didn't answer he came back. 'I'll go and leave you in peace.'

'Stay,' she said.

'Stay?' His heart lurched. Not wanting to get it wrong he said, 'Sure, I'll sit in the chair while you sleep if that's what you mean.'

Making space she moved back in the bed. 'Please stay.'

A moment of panic, rights and wrongs crashing through his mind, and then afraid she'd change her mind he stripped off his jeans and lay down.

'You sure about this?' he said. 'This is me, Gabe, you're talking to.'

As though to quiet his fears she captured his hand and brought it to her breast. Invited by the gesture he spread his hand. 'Lovely woman,' he whispered hoarsely. 'How much of your sweetness is mine tonight?'

In reply she pulled the torn nightgown from her body, tossing it into the darkness. 'How much of me do you see?'

~

Four in the morning he left, the dogs waiting under the willows. The sun was splitting the horizon, every blade of grass and leaf glittering. Toads sang in the river-mud. Crickets scraped their legs. Whip-poor-wills called.

Blistering images filled his head. It was like being at a drive-in watching an X-rated movie. She let him bury deep between her legs and lick and suck her breasts. Whatever he asked she didn't refuse and knowing he'd never get another chance he asked plenty. Now he has to get over it and not kid himself that time spent with her was anything but a one-of.

It wasn't easy shutting it out. The smell of her on his skin made him tremble and he'd see her bent over the bed, his hands about her narrow waist plunging inside her. Or the time she was against the wall and he was on his knees his tongue inside her. Lord almighty! What she thought of him was anybody's guess. A girl like that was made for tender wooing. Last night he was a broncobuster breaking a thoroughbred and yet one more chance to hold her, to kiss the hollow of her throat, and he'd be tender.

One more chance?

'Get hold of it, Gabe!' He laughed, scornfully. 'This is real life not a dream.'

The phone was ringing in the house, Ma tuning into his soul.

'You there, son?'

'How's Aunt Belle?'

'Better then yesterday! You got old Mable Chance to plant today. Make sure that son of hers pays up front. You know what a no-good he is.'

'Quit worryin'. It's in hand.'

'I'll be home Thursday. You eat right and pay no mind to whatever's goin' on at the Mill.'

Pay no mind is Ma's saying. In the past when Pa was drinking hisself silly she'd to screw her lip. 'Pay no mind. One of these days you'll best them all.'

She had her comfortless saying, Gabriel had his. As a boy he'd stare in the mirror, shoulders busting out of a patched shirt. 'What's all this muscle and bone for?' When he was young and they had the wood-yard muscle was good enough to climb a tree or impress a girl. But the yard got into debt. Pa borrowed money. Muscle and bone didn't help anyone then.

There was badness in Hodge Templar that drink let loose. Ma called it 'the brute'. Pa called it discipline and his cure-all a belt behind the privy door.

'Discipline' was all Gabe knew. They moved to Grandma's place where Gabe was apprentice to a coffin maker. He couldn't make coffins and go to school. Truancy folk would call. Pa would get mad and take down the belt.

'Stupid great lump!' he'd holler. 'How come I got a dummy for a son?'

'I ain't a dummy,' he would whisper to the goats in the yard. As long as the manger was filled they didn't care. Their eyes seemed to say, 'pay no mind.' But he did mind and big and dumb and shy was left in the wake of other kids.

Girls were forever tying an honest boy in knots. A mute dressed in black, hair tied in ribbon he'd walk beside a coffin. Freckle-faced girls with pouting lips and pointed breasts would call, 'hi handsome!' They'd huddle up. Hot little hands would rub the front of his pants, and like a flock of birds they'd shriek away. 'We touched Gabe Templar's brains!'

In time he learned to avoid points and pouts. Sue Ryland was the biggest tease. Eyes like damsons and hair like river-water she'd cup his crotch. 'Give me your brains, sweetness. I'll find a use for 'em.'

Desperate to get away he applied to the army and stood naked in line, blushing, when a medic fondled his private parts. 'Okay, Mr Universe,' says the medic. 'We've seen how bouncy your balls are but can you answer a question, how many feet to a yard?'

'Best you ask the bank.' Gabriel replied bitterly. 'It's them got our yard.'

The medic wasn't amused. 'Go home! We've no use for morons.'

Rejected by the army a new humiliation waited, Baby Rourke in uniform lounging against a Cadillac. 'Hey big man, where's your draft card?' he'd yell. 'Is it down your pants along with the rest of the useless tackle?'

Worse was to come. Pa got sick, liver burned out. The need to thrash his wife and boy was stronger than ever. One day in '34 Hodge Templar hit Ma once too often. They took Gabriel away, metal cutting into his flesh. For a time then it didn't matter that he killed in defence of Ma. He went to jail, fifteen years hard labour. Were it not for a world war he'd still be there.

Ma reckons angels come in all shapes and sizes. Charlie Whitefeather saved Gabe's skin. Charlie was his cellmate, wherever Gabe went so did Charlie. Twenty stone of pockmarked muscle he stood between a teenager and hell. Screws looking to kick a kid it was the Navaho Holy man they had to get by.

Ma reckons angels come in all kinds of weather. She says you can't always tell if they come with a ploughshare or a sword. Charlie came with a knife down the side of his boonies. Gabe could whittle. At night the Navajo would read the latest letter from Ma while he whittled dolls for trade.

Charlie loved to read kiddie's books. It was in one of those books Gabriel found another angel. *Sleeping Beauty* it was called, a beautiful girl lying asleep on a bed. He cut the picture out and stuck it on the wall next to Charlie's poster of Rudy Valentino. Every night he'd dream of Beauty except she wasn't sleeping like Beauty, she was up and doing, a nurse's veil on her head.

Spring of 1940 a war in Europe threatened American interests. The Corps got him out of jail, a campaign the War Department was running, 'Serve your Country and Serve your time.' Joining the Marine Corps meant Parris Island and that was worse than any jail. Drill sergeants hated the idea of a con working his time via the Corps. To them he was an overgrown bullyboy in need of correction. They handed out the correction. When he kept getting up, not cursing or whining, the beatings stopped. He went from Private to Corporal, and one day defending a salt-water ditch on Tarawa Island, a BAR in one hand and a gaping hole in his shoulder, he earned another stripe and a reputation.

'You should've got the Medal,' said a Gunnery Sergeant. 'But you're ex-con and so you got nothing. But don't let that stop you, son. You got guts and you got initiative. Be an officer. They are thieves and murderers a plenty.'

Ma thought he resigned the Corps for Adelia. He did, but other pressures helped make up his mind. You need guts and initiative to be an officer. You need to be able to read and write. He can't do either.

Spring of '45 he's in the pick-up pulling in for gas when the bartender from the Hawaiian Bar comes running; Baby Rourke needs taking home, the guy sobbing over a photograph of a girl. It was Gabriel's dream girl, except she's no dream; she is Baby Rourke's nightmare.

All his life Gabe's had a special sense seeming to know things beforehand. He knew when Ma was going to be sick and when the river's about to overflow. There were days when he woke knowing what was going to happen like yesterday and the call saying Mrs Chance passed away. He wanted to say, I know, Mrs Chance already tole me. He kept quiet. It's enough they know him as the town murderer. He don't want them thinking him some crazy prophet.

Week after week he would bury strange feelings pushing them down and down but no matter how deep he buried them like plants or clouds they couldn't help but rise. When an animal was sick he sees the sickness as a mist over the diseased part. If he can fetch that mist out then the part will mend. Trying to survive, to be normal, he would carry pushing feelings down. Weeks would go by until

Hello, energy would rise, pushing and shoving, wanting to expand, until boom! It would blast out his fingers!

That's how the stuff in the stable came about, the carvings being magic caught in wood and stone.

Hodge took a hammer to them. Gabriel came home to find him trembling. 'That stuff's not natural. So I busted it.' It was drink talking. His stuff was as he left it. 'What you talkin' about?' he said. 'You busted nothin'.' But Pa shook his head. 'I busted it but it healed itself right up again.'

Sixth sense, Ma calls it. Gabriel doesn't know what it is only that where Adelia is concerned it works overtime and always has. Like a doe when her young is in trouble or an eagle when the nest is threatened he knows when she's in trouble. Has always known! As a kid he knew that somewhere in the world was his other self. She'd come in dreams, bright and shining. They'd play, diving and swimming in sunlight like otters in a pool.

It was no otter that day in the Harbour.

Quarter after eight that night Bobby came looking, telling his woes, could Gabe collect them from New York 'cos he was too sick to go. Gabe was already dressed, uniform pressed and hair shorn within an inch of his life.

He knew the invitation was coming and is marching up the ramp approaching the desk and she is there, dazed beauty offering her hand. 'I know we haven't met,' she says, a voice like rough velvet. 'But thank you for coming.'

'Haven't met,' he'd thought, his hungry eyes counting the silken down on her cheek. 'We have met. You do know me. You're just forgettin'.'

It was Bobby who tried to run her down at the Diner. Son-of-a-bitch! Gabe recognised the car and told him if he so much as breathed on her bad he would lay his miserable soul to rest for once and always.

Last night because Bobby breathed on her wrong and a dream became flesh. Now Gabriel has an ache in his gut and certainty of trouble ahead. He knows he should stay away but if the Lord God Himself were to lean down and say, 'Stay away from that gal or you'll burn in hell,' Gabe would have to burn.

Chapter Nine
Latest Morgan

Adelia parked the bike outside the children's home, and rang the bell at the reception desk. 'My name's Adelia Challoner. I called earlier?'

'Ah, yes, Mizz Challoner. Take a seat.'

Nervous, she perched on the chair. Five minutes later the receptionist put her head round the door. 'Is it about the part time job at the commissary?'

'Yes, two mornings a week.'

'Would you mind filling in a questionnaire?'

She began filling in the form. Then a smiling redhead offered her hand. 'Hello Adelia. I'm Sarah Parker. How are you getting on with the form?'

'I'm having a problem with the medical section,' said Adelia thinking here we go, trotting out the same old garbage. 'I was involved in an accident in '42, the usual stuff, a bomb fell on a building and I...'

'Mizz Parker!' The receptionist held out a phone. 'The call you've been waiting for, person-to-person, London, England?'

Mizz Parker leapt to her feet. 'Excuse me, I must take this.'

Adelia returned to the form and 'precise medical history.' How precise is precise? Should she mention the amnesia? Living with it doesn't mean she's come to terms with it. So many limitations, she can't catch a bus without a note in her purse, ' *My name is Adelia Challoner. I live at the Mill, Fredericksburg. In the event of illness contact Captain R Rourke.*'

Pathetic, a child with a note from its mummy!

Attention divided between a blackbird pulling on a worm, Mizz Parker chattering on the phone, and last week's mistake, she gazed out the window.

I need to work, she told herself, maybe then I'll stop doing silly things.

Last week she did a very silly thing. She had sex with Gabriel Templar.

Events leading to the silly deed are fuzzy. Bobby was being difficult. They argued. He slapped her. He says not. When she showed him the bruise he denied it. 'You fell and hit your head. You know what you're like.'

Slap or not she'd suffered a major attack, a 'fugue.'

Fugue? Surely only medicine would give a musical connotation to a cruel mental condition. During the last four years doctors have used all kinds of words to describe her condition. She looked up the word fugue: '*a principal theme, holding the interest of composers, performer, and listeners of Western music in the same way that a sonnet engages poets.*'

Adelia sees her illness more a cuckoo that sleeps in every bed, eats the food, drinks the cellar dry, runs up a gas and phone bill, and when bored vacates leaving the nest in chaos. In the throes of this illness the cuckoo does what it wants including seducing a good neighbour. Gabriel

Templar is a wonderful man, but with Sophie across the hall and Bobby close by? She is utterly ashamed.

'Hi there, Adelia.' Mizz Parker is back. 'I know I've kept you waiting but I truly can't be sorry. Nothing is going to bring me down today. I've had the very best news. My brother, a serving soldier, who we thought was lost, is coming home.'

'That's wonderful!'

'Isn't it? We've had a time worrying about him.' Mizz Parker bent closer. 'He's Special Ops, very hush-hush, and so we never know what he's up to.'

'You should go home and celebrate,' said Adelia. 'This is too happy a day to be bothered about hiring dinner-ladies.'

'Hold on! I do want to talk about you. Let's go into my office.'

It was cosy in her office, a thick carpet on the floor and an imposing desk.

'So you want to work in the commissary?'

'Put it this way I need to work and children need feeding. If I am honest the nursery facilities are the main attraction. We've only been here a while. I'd like Sophie to mix with other children.'

'How old is she?'

'Three and a bit. It would be all right to leave her in the crèche?'

'Sure. I brought Petey and Dave when they were younger. They're too grown now to be seen with mom. I see you are a nurse. Where did you train?'

'St Bartholomew's, London.'

'Good heavens! Wouldn't you prefer to nurse here? A St Barts nurse would command a decent salary, far more than you'll get slinging hash.'

'Slinging hash would suit me fine.'

'And Bobby, will working behind a counter suit him?

'You know Bobby?'

'I should come clean. I had an ulterior motive for wanting to speak with you. I'm fund-raiser for the hospital. I'm not involved with hiring of staff but I caught the tail end of a phone conversation and was curious.'

Adelia's spirits sank. Oh no, not another one!

'We're a close community and though I don't live in the 'Burg these days I can't help tuning in to local gossip. My mother said Bobby was getting married and that his fiancé was here. When you rang I thought to say hello. Is he okay? I've seen him in Richmond flying about in that scarlet hot-rod.'

'Yes, he loves the car. I don't drive myself but want to learn.'

'I couldn't be without my car. Having to rely on another to run me about would drive me nuts. But about Bobby, my brother asked after him. They were buddies when they were younger.'

'I see. Did you tell him of Bobby's accident?'

'I hadn't the heart. It didn't seem right to fill in the sad details over the phone.'

'And when is your brother coming home?'

'We don't know for certain, probably a week or two.'

'It must've been a worry for your family.'

'It wasn't good. Dee, it's been swell meeting you. I probably haven't been as diplomatic as I ought but I couldn't let the opportunity go by without conveying my regrets to Bobby and to say Alex will be in touch.'

~

Gainfully employed, Adelia took the long route home. Sophie and Bobby are in Richmond getting a puppy so she can take her time. As she rode along the lanes she indulged an innocent pastime, a trick she learned in the war called 'finding a face to cover pain.' At Bart's nurses took care of their own, it wasn't so in St Faiths. After the accident she woke to find she'd been sidelined to a ratty annexe. Out of sight and mind she asked of her job with children and was told she didn't have one. Matron said she could work nights at the Annexe but that was all. She said Adelia had behaved like a tart and had nothing further to say.'

Nothing to say! What a lie! From Matron to the lowly ward maid Adelia was topic of the day. Demoted to the Annexe geriatric ward, or the Bin, as it was called, she worked through even though pregnant.

Bobby got her out. Memories of that day are few. He came with roses. 'Come on! You're out of here. It's time to lose this job and seek your fortune elsewhere.'

'I can't,' she'd said, heaving a trolley into the sluice, emptying slops down the drain, the bump straining her uniform. 'I need the money.'

'Forget the money and forget this job. You're not a nurse you're a skivvy.'

He took her hand and ripping the apron from her waist marched her from the hospital giving the finger to the night sister. 'See this girl!' he'd hollered. 'If she was a skinny bitch with face like stewed prunes would you treat her the same?'

The night sister had bridled. 'Here in Faiths we treat everyone the same.'

'Do you?' he'd yelled back. 'Then God help the patients is all I can say.'

Lost and lonely, it was around that time she found relief in make-believe, creating blue-eyed lovers. These days her fancy is for Bobby's friend, Alex Hunter. It is the steady look in the eyes that does it - that and Bobby's sales-pitch.

'What d'you mean sales pitch?' he'd said when challenged.

'You're always singing his praises,' says Adelia. 'Talking of his courage and yet what a shy sort of man. You sound like you're advertising the latest Morgan.'

'Hah!' Bobby had grinned. 'Come to think of it he is very like a Morgan, plenty of power on top but underneath a real pussycat.'

Riding her bike in the sunshine Adelia thought it a shame the pussycat wasn't here enjoying the day. But then Colonel Bogey would never ride a bike; possibly a tank or jeep but never an old-fashioned Raleigh, however worthily maintained.

'Damn!' Her thoughts were veering to Gabriel Templar.

How perverse is her illness. During an attack her life is viewed through layers of gauze and the people behind the gauze puppets. When Gabriel touched her it was heaven. He spoke, he moved, and joy shrieked through her soul. So many layers of gauze that night had it not been for a faded shirt she might've dreamed him.

'Hello there, Mizz Dee!' A voice rang out. Horses grazed across the river, Sue Ryland with Gabriel, hair flowing about her shoulders and cream riding britches sparkling against faded denim.

'Hello Sue! Hello Mister Templar! Thanks for the bike!' she called, a blush staining her cheeks. 'It will be very useful.'

He nodded.

'Say, Dee,' called Sue. 'My Becky was asking if Sophie would come over.'

'Lovely! I'll mention it to her when I get home. Bye!'

Head down, she pedalled away. She pedalled and pedalled until she could peddle no more. Oh, his face! He hates me. And who can blame him.

At the bridge she leant against a parapet staring at her reflection in the water. She is so lonely. 'Where are you, Colonel Bogey when I need you?'

In her mind's eye he was beside her, a khaki sleeve brushing her arm. He had a deep Southern drawl and was asking if she recalled a church in Suffolk and a mouse sitting on the altar.

'Why would I remember that?' she said. 'I don't know you.'

He laughed. 'Yes, you do. I am…!'

A fish broke the surface of the water.

Ripples spread over her reflection and another face appeared beside her.

Gabriel. 'You wanna lift?'

Puzzled, she looked up. 'Didn't I just see you with Sue?'

'Yeah, a couple of hours ago.'

'A couple of hours ago? What time is it?'

'Coming up for six.'

'Six! I thought it was about three!' She'd been standing on the bridge for an hour or more, arms chilled and grit from the parapet embedded in her skin.

'You want that lift?' Adelia opened her mouth to decline but he was propping the bike in the back of a vast motorized hearse. 'Is that something new?' she said.

'I picked it up in a sale.'

'Do I have to ride in it?'

'There ain't nothin' else, unless you wanna risk the footpath and the river.'

'Right,' said she miffed by his tone. 'Where do you want me, in the front with you or palely loitering in the back, a rose on my breast?'

'Hah! Now there's a question.'

It was late. Dark clouds were rolling over the river. She must have cycled further than she realised. Sophie will be wondering where she was.

'Sophie's okay. She's with Becky. I dropped her on my way to pick this up.'

'What?' Adelia was sure she hadn't spoken.

'Becky's a good kid. Ain't no harm gonna come to her there.'

'I was only saying to Mrs Parker Sophie needs kiddies of her own age.'

'Mrs Parker?'

'Sarah Parker, at the children's home? I went for a job today.'

'Did you get it?'

'I start next Tuesday. Now look!' She turned to him. 'I need to talk about what happened the other night. I've been putting it off, but you giving me a lift like this, and well...*carpe diem*...it seems the right moment.'

He shook his head. 'I don't want no explanations.' They journeyed on in silence until he turned. 'And what's this carper whosis? You tryin' to be funny?'

'What!'

'You and your words and your cut-glass voice! You mockin' me no knowin' I don't read so well? Is that what the big words are about?'

'Of course not! I wouldn't dream of...! It would never occur to me to....! And if you think that...then you must think me an awful person!'

He growled under his breath. Adelia closed her ears. They pulled into the drive.

She slammed the door. He lifted down the bicycle and was gone.

'Oops!' said Bobby. 'I think you and the undertaker have come unstuck.'

She opened the door and a pup flew at her.

'Sophie calls him Biffer. He's cute but leaky, pissed over the kitchen floor three times already. I fixed him a box in the boiler room. It's warm in there.'

'You little dear!' Almost in tears she buried her face in warm fur.

Bobby watched her fuss over the pup. 'You and Gabe had a falling out?'

'He's a horrible man with horrible opinions.'

'That's an improvement on last week. Was it specific or a general set-to?'

'I'd sooner not talk about it.'

'Suits me! I wouldn't care if we never mentioned his name again.'

'And Sophie, you were happy to let her go with Sue?'

He shrugged. 'I thought it might broaden her education.'

'You don't look well.'

'I'm not feeling well. I was waiting for you to come then I could go to bed.'

'Go! I'll bring you a hot drink.'

Adelia put milk on to warm. Then she phoned Sue. By the time she got back the room was in darkness, drapes pulled and Bobby a hump in the bed.

'Here you are. I put a couple of spoons of honey in it to help you sleep.'

'I thought you'd gone,' he said, voice muffled.

'Sorry about that. I lost track of the time.'

'I mean, I thought you'd gone for good! Not that I'd blame you if you did.'

Downstairs the pup was howling. 'I'd better sort Biffer out.'

'No, stay a minute!' He grabbed her wrist. 'There's something I need to tell you. Somethin' bad. It's been playing on my mind.'

'Let me sort the pup then I'm all yours.'

'Okay.' He slumped back in the bed.

She brought Biffer upstairs and setting the box in the corner pressed her finger to her lips. The pup sighed and settled. She took off her sandals. 'What did you want to tell me? It sounded important.'

'It ain't, least not in the scheme of things.'

'Have it your own way.' She stepped out of her shorts. She was struggling with the clasp on her brassiere when he reared up.

'What you doing?'

'I'm getting into bed. If we're to make a go of this we can't sleep in different houses. It's the two of us, our backs to the world.'

He stared. 'It ain't no use you getting in with me.'

'Why isn't it?' she said, pulling back the cover.

'I'm impotent.'

She slid between the covers, pounding the pillow, punching anger away. Then she reached out, drawing him close. 'We'll see about that.'

~

They had breakfast in the kitchen. 'More scrambled eggs? Are you sure?'

Bobby pounded the table. 'More eggs, woman! I need sustenance.'

Adelia smiled. 'For a man claiming impotence I thought you remarkably tangible.'

'Impotence my ass! You've been conned by the best chat-up line ever,' said Bobby, grinning, and wolfing eggs.

'That's far too complicated for me. Shall I tell you about my nice day?'

He took her hand, kissing her fingertips, his lips greasy. 'You can tell me anything as long as it's not that you're leaving me.'

'I'm not going to leave.'

'And you'll be with me when I die.'

'Don't be morbid.'

'No, you've got to promise you'll be with me when I die.'

'I'm not sure I can make such a promise.'

He dragged her hand over his heart. 'Do it! Swear you'll be with me when I die.'

'I swear I will be with you when you die.'

'There,' he said. 'Now you're committed.'

'Do you want to hear about my job?' she said to break the tension. 'I'm a part-time dinner-lady slinging hash.'

He pursed his lips. 'D'you get paid?'

'A pittance, pocket money for Sophie.'

'You don't need to sling hash for that. I got all the pocket money you need.'

'I know, but it will make me feel better plus the fact there's a crèche.'

'I might've known it was something to do with the kid. But sure why not! Today I'm the Easter Bunny. Knock yourself out!'

Adelia was at the sink. He came behind her, and pulling her dressing gown over her shoulders slid his hands about her breasts. 'That was some loving you gave me last night, Mrs Rourke. Who taught you to do that?'

'No one taught me.' She blocked a picture of Gabriel Templar, of his body thrusting into hers. 'It seemed natural to do it.'

'Natural is good,' whispered Bobby, lifting her gown, cupping her bottom, his fingers working inside her. 'I'm all for natural.'

Working like the devil to block mental images she closed her eyes but it wasn't Bobby brought her to orgasm, neither was it Gabriel. It was another who caressed her, blue eyes heavy with desire and his mouth languid.

Later, at the meal table she talked of the children's hospital. 'I met a friend of yours today by the name of Sarah Parker.'

He spilled his drink. 'Sarah Parker?'

'Yes, hospital admin.'

'And what did she have to say?'

'She was quite chatty, actually. It seems her brother, who everyone thought missing, is alive and well.'

Bobby went to the veranda pushing the doors open. 'Alive and well, you say?'

'She said you'd be pleased.'

He tossed the cheroot out into the darkness. 'I am. I'm very pleased.'

Out in the hall the telephone rang. When he didn't move Adelia took the call.

It was a woman for Bobby. Fingertips icy, he took the phone. 'Mrs Hunter! How are you?' he said, face expressionless. 'Yeah, I just heard.' They talked and then he replaced the phone. 'Ash's Ma. He's okay but won't be home til Christmas.'

'At least they've heard from him.'

'Uh-huh, at least.'

~

Around five am the outer door slammed and the Morgan was out of the drive. Adelia switched on the light. There's no understanding the man. One minute he's a cat with the cream now he's sulking.

Unable to go back to sleep she took the pup for a walk.

It was raining, a fine drizzle whizzing her hair into a million curls.

Biffer ran ahead floundering through bracken. He was heading for the Eyrie.

A settler's remembrance of home, the house rose up through the mist, a leftover from another age. Though in ruinous state, tiles missing on the roof and rainwater spouting from broken guttering, Adelia liked it so much more than the Mill.

The pup wriggled through a gap in the hedge, ran across the overgrown lawn and in through a broken side door.

She followed. It was gloomy inside, rain dripping through broken shutters. The pup ran up a wide staircase and began scratching at a door whining to be let in.

The door opened. Gabriel Templar stared down.

She stopped dead. 'I'm sorry. I didn't know you came here.'

'It's okay.' He bent to scratch the pup's ears. 'It ain't my house.'

'No but it's finders-keepers.'

'Finders keepers. What does that mean?'

Thinking he was being difficult again, she shrugged. 'I suppose it means if you find something that was lost it becomes yours.'

Long frame unwinding, he straightened. 'Are you lost?'

She hesitated.

He said it again. 'Are you lost?'

A wall to her innermost heart began to crumble.

Voice cracking, he said it a third time. 'Are you lost?'

'Yes.' She scrubbed her cheeks and nose with her sleeve denying tears.

'And have I found you?'

'Yes.'

'And can I keep you?'

She ran up the stairs and leapt into his arms.

Chapter Ten
Sporadic Signals
Spring of '48.

'So do it, and do it right this time for Chrissakes!'

Bobby leaned out of the window, keeping an eye on workmen clearing the last of the scaffolding while threatening a salesman on the other end of the phone that if the new carpet wasn't fitted today it would be cancelled.

Two years it's taken to get the tower right. To be fair it isn't Templar dragging his feet. It's plumbers, electricians, and every other charlatan this side the Mason-Dixon Line. A coat of paint on the boards, new shutters, a copper roof and roses around the door, Paradise, you might say, except for the owner bent on making life hell.

Sophie was at the table fiddling with bits of cloth Dee had given her. 'Daddy,' she said, holding up a stuffed rabbit. 'Who does my Easter Bunny look like?'

'A patch over one eye? Now who could it be? Give me a clue.'

'It's somebody very special. Somebody you know.'

'What with a green nose? I don't know any rabbits lookin' like that.'

'Don't be silly, Daddy,' she giggled. 'You know very well who it is.'

She sounded so like her mother his heart gave a wrench. Eyebrows shoved together, he leant over the table. 'Silly? Now what kind of a thing is that to say to your Pa?' he said. 'I've a mind to tan your backside.'

Fright sucked the shine from her eyes. She ran from the room.

'Sophie! Honey, don't run!' he shouted. 'I was only teasing!'

A draft whipped through the window flipping the curtain over a framed photograph. Bobby flipped the curtain back. 'Sorry, buddy,' he muttered, knowing his temper caused Sophie to run. 'My mouth will get me killed one of these days.'

Needing to pee again he went to the bathroom and then to wash a couple of painkillers down with beer from his secret stash. These days he's always in pain. Dee tries new diets but nothing works, when he isn't peeing he's on the john, shit running from him. It's why his shorts are on the line, the ones with built-in diapers. Adelia made them so he wouldn't be ashamed.

Two years not married, and never likely to be, Dee sleeps in the cottage and him in the house. They tried sharing a bed as they tried sex. He never gave it a chance, no more able to rely on his pecker than he could his leaky ass.

Drawn to the photograph he sighed. This is one he cut out from Stars and Stripes' magazine; Ash getting the Medal. Six foot three in his socks, miserable son-of-a-bitch, he salutes General Ike without a glimmer of a smile. Ash was the best friend a man could ever have. The day is coming when Bobby will have to meet him face-to-face.

Alone with uncomfortable thoughts he fiddled with the frame, moving it around searching for the best light.

'Not another photograph!' Dee came in behind him. 'We've enough of those downstairs without them cluttering the bedroom.'

'It's just the one.'

'One is enough, thank you.' She pushed open the closet door. 'What tie shall you wear for the RAF reunion?'

'I don't care.'

'What's the matter? You sound peeved.'

Bobby stared in the mirror. A well-groomed man stared back, hair and nails neatly trimmed, a neat shirt under a neat sweater to go with neat pants and a neat eye-patch covering a not-so-neat hole in his face.

'I ain't peeved.' He did a little soft-shoe shuffle. 'I got a chipper house that nobody wants to share, a chipper daughter who runs every time I open my mouth, chipper friends who fly my planes, drink my beer, but don't care if I live or die. A chipper mother who runs me ragged, and an Oh-so-chipper woman who says she cares but who is screwin' the hired help. What's to be peeved about?'

Stillness came over Adelia. 'Must you drink so early? You know what it does.'

'What does it do?'

'It turns you into a man I don't know, last night a prime example.'

'What was wrong with last night?' he said, recollecting a boozy rendezvous with guys from the club, raucous singing and plenty of falling about down stairs.

'And now all this shouting! If it's the reunion bothering you, don't go.'

'I have to. I'm guest of honor. You're going too, don't forget that.'

'Am I? Then I'd better get a good night's sleep. Make sure I do you justice.'

Do him justice? She stands by the window light accentuating every flaw in her face. Not that there are natural imperfections! Virginian sun lending a creamy tone to her skin, darkening her eyes by contrast, she is divine but tough and getting tougher, a battle going on inside and the coils over-heating.

There are days when she's unable to sustain the fight. Then another Dee appears, a stand-in so to speak, prowling the house and garden in satin skirts and high-heeled pumps. A fabulous woman who will dance and sing, and talk to hogs and chickens and folks only she can see. A woman who wanders a twilight zone so damned loving you could drown in her.

'What will you wear tonight, the scarlet chiffon?'

She grimaced. 'I suppose.'

A closet full of gorgeous clothes and she's in dungarees! The only time she wears anything else is when madness brings out a personality more potent than the land-army girl. Frustration zipped through him. 'Of course, if my stuff don't appeal you can always wear them bastard dungarees!'

'True!' Her eyes flashed. 'I could always wear the bastard dungarees.'

An uptight British accent making a simple cuss downright filthy, Bobby exploded with laughter. 'Say, do you remember the first time we went to Washington? You wore that crummy suit and me with my pants tied up. What a pair!'

'You were incredibly brave.'

'There's nothing brave about buying suits. If you want to talk brave,' he gestured to the photograph, 'then this is your guy.'

She rolled her eyes. 'So you keep saying.'

Adelia carried the laundry down. Ash Hunter! If she had to listen to that guff one more time...! When Bobby first spoke of him she thought hero worship never hurt anyone but there's hero worship and there's obsession. Photographs everywhere, even in the outside loo! She left it there but with the face turned to the wall.

Last night he had friends over. This morning the pigsty was cleaner than the sitting room. Dirty, dishevelled and loud, they gathered in the yard. She appeared with sandwiches. There was shuffling and wiping of hands down trouser legs. She left and off they went off again, hollering like shipwrecked mariners.

Why does he let them do it? Does he not value his home? She would've been happy to entertain them in a decent manner but they don't want that and neither does he. Lost souls, they prefer perdition to paradise.

If all of his friends are like that what price the hero? She's sick to death of Ash Hunter and she's not alone. Mention him and Gabriel's jaw would snap.

'You don't like him?' she says.

'It's not him. It's the way he's touted.'

Adelia knows what he means, that whenever he's mentioned a silver salver slides on a table, Alexander Hunter naked complete with apple in jaw.

~

Come midday Bobby was freaking out. What with the carpet-fitter banging and the pain in his head he's at the end of his tether. Now Sophie's plunking out the same five-finger exercise. 'Can't she find anything else to play?'

'You know your daughter,' Adelia walked by towing the vacuum, Biffer, the Airedale, biting the machine. 'She won't give up until she's mastered it.'

'She's not my daughter. If she were she'd be flying a plane not a piano.'

'Time to pack up, Sophie! Daddy's got a headache.'

'And don't use all the hot water!' Bobby is obsessed with bathing. Convinced he stinks he showers five times a day. The specialist said it is a '*psychosomatic problem augmented by damaged olfactory nerves.*' Medical science and its practitioners! What are they but quacks offering bottled piss to punters!

In '44 medics said not to expect miracles, they could save his right eye but only a new Michelangelo could refashion his face. That said the rest of his anatomy was beyond repair. Nurses would wash him. Young girls fresh from the convent - innocence on their cheek and plastic gloves on their hands -would move him around. He'd give them the old razzmatazz but it was a waste of time. Those ghostly virgins could've raised the dead quicker than his dick.

Occasionally, he'd glance down and his poll was crowing like daybreak. Sporadic signals, said the medics. Sporadic signals? What the fuck did that mean? Did it mean he still had change in his trouser pocket? No, sir, a spout to piss out!

Adelia can work miracles but lately her hands are losing their touch. He is falling apart, so scared he can't speak. So he shouts instead.

'Are you going to bathe, Sophie, or what!'

'It's not fair. Uncle Gabriel's fixing the lights and I wanted to see them.'

'It is fair and he is not your uncle!'

As well as preparing Easter dinner Dee has organized a Hunt-the-Egg for kids at the hospital. And where is Gabe but up a ladder hanging fairy lights! Dee likes lame ducks. Not only do kids come for tea their mothers come. Bobby didn't mind the mothers but takes exception to Uncle's weekly reading lessons.

Moron, he thought, hating the square shoulders and clear expression! What kind of man sits next to the woman he wants to fuck to hear her teach ABC?

At first Bobby enjoyed the humiliation. He couldn't believe a guy would put himself in that position? They keep the fucking under wraps. Once or twice a month he'll wake in the night to the outer door closing. He stays mute. If getting humped once a month keeps her at the Mill so be it.

'Gabe?' Bobby looked over the newspaper, he loves winding him up. 'You ever come across a guy called Alex Hunter in your travels?'

'General Hunter's son?'

'That's him.'

'I don't know him.'

Bobby snickered. 'Unlikely, I suppose, you two movin' in different circles.'

Sensing trouble Adelia arrives still towing the goddamn vacuum.

'You are very pale.'

'So would you be if you had my head.'

She sighed. 'What's the matter with everybody? May's not herself today.'

'Her chest is playin' up,' said Gabriel.

'If she's unwell she should stay home.'

'What d'you mean stay home?' Bobby interjects. 'She's helping out tonight.'

'There's no need. I can manage. It's only your mother.'

'Don't matter who it is. The point of a maid is to lighten the load.'

'May isn't a maid. She's a friend.'

'That's your trouble. You can't have hired help for friends. It doesn't work. And are you ever going to finish with that vacuum!'

Off went the machine. A minute later it was on again.

'Hey!' His head was killing him as is the RAF reunion on his mind and her piddling job at the hospital. Why did she need to do it? He saw little of her as it was. 'Fuckin' thing!' He yanked the plug from the socket. 'I want that off!'

Forgetting the cable was on a retracting reel he flung the plug across the room.

Like a lariat it whipped back, catching Adelia in the chest.

Hand to her breast, she ran. He would have followed but Templar was down the ladder, a look in his eyes as lethal as the screwdriver in his hand.

'I didn't mean it. It was an accident.'

The bloke never said a word, just picked up his tools and went on through to the cottage.

~

They sat in the kitchen looking over exercise books. Adelia leant on the table. 'It's really coming along, don't you think?'

Gabriel frowned at the neat lettering. 'I still get my ds and bs back to front.'

'Don't worry about that. The main thing is to enjoy what you do.'

Does he enjoy it? He stared at the book. Two years ago he accused her of mocking him because he had trouble reading. Next day she offered help. 'There's no shame in not being able to read. The shame would be in not trying.'

It was the toughest thing he ever did sit beside her copying letters, muck from the graveyard under his fingernails and Baby Rourke looking on, but he hung on ignoring wisecracks and Ma's forebodings. He got a reward. For the first time in his life he can sign his name without thinking the world's trying to shake him down, as he can read a newspaper and pay bills.

It doesn't end there. With a sudden love of good music he's gone and bought a phonograph.

Ma reckons he's got above himself. It ain't that. Where before he was closed, thinking it not for him, now it offers comfort to his soul. Best of all is this, sitting in the kitchen, music on the radio, his thigh alongside Adelia's and threads of her hair clinging to his sleeve. They laugh and share a joke and sometimes when she is needy and doesn't feel too guilty they share more than that.

'I do,' he said.

'Do what?'

'I do enjoy it, Mizz Adelia, ma'am.'

She giggled. 'I've such a cheek. You must want to slap me at times.'

'Sure, and kiss the bits I slap.'

Blushing, she bypassed the comment and offered a parcel. 'I'm thrilled with what we've accomplished and in celebration of your passing-out parade, Sergeant Templar, here's a little something for your birthday.'

'How did you know it's my birthday?'

'Your mother told me.'

Gabriel opened the parcel. Books, one about a sculptor called Cellini.

She saw him questioning. 'I saw the carving you did for Miss Matty when Boo died. You have a wonderful talent. Wouldn't you like to do something with it?'

'Like what?'

'I don't know maybe carve beautiful things for beautiful places like the man in this book. Be the artist that you are.'

He took the book but said nothing about his stuff in the barn.

Then she gave him a bible. 'I wanted you to have something of mine.'

Leather-bound, the pages edged with gold leaf, it was *'awarded to Adelia Emma Challoner for punctual attendance in Bible studies.'* There was personal stuff inside, a baby-ribbon, a pressed flower and a newspaper cutting;' *August 29th, 1934, Elizabeth and John Challoner, united in love.'*

Overcome, he could only mumble his thanks.

'Read from it?' she says. 'Just open and read wherever your eye rests.'

Bibles are filled with long names that nobody could read, not even the preacher at the Mission. Gabriel scanned the page searching for a word he knew. He started to read: 'My beloved spake and said unto me, rise up, my love, my fair one, and come away. For, lo, the winter is past...!'

At first he didn't know what he was saying. When he did get it the words blew him apart. It was a love-letter, a man telling his adoration.

He set it down. 'I can't do it.'

She began to read and suddenly she was the sculptor, words falling from her lips as white chips of stone. He watched and wondered what she was thinking.

Adelia was thinking of Alex Hunter. She couldn't get him out of her mind.

The other day she asked, 'why the hero-worship?'

Bobby had shrugged. 'Probably because he's the only hero I know.'

Last night she dreamt the man stood at the bottom of the bed dressed in camouflage gear, stripes like tiger's claws on his cheeks and a belt full of weaponry. In the dream she shouted. 'Get out of my bedroom!'

He smiled and said. 'Go to sleep. You've children from the hospital coming.'

Throat sore when she woke, she shouted again. 'Spying on a person when they're trying to sleep? What kind of a dream are you?' He said he was a lonesome dream. She then said he should visit the Mill. 'Then your friend can tell *you* how wonderful you are rather than me.' The vision faded until only the dagger on his beret. 'Maybe I will,' he said. 'I could use the rest.'

~

It was evening, the remains of Gabriel's birthday meal on the table. Ruby is chiding Sophie. 'Quit kicking, child. I've headache enough without that jarring me.'

'Get down, darling.' Adelia tried appeasing another. 'The pancakes are delicious.'

May sniffed. 'They'd be a lot better if I'd had the kitchen to myself.'

Bobby sat watching. Dee looks exhausted. It's her fault! Five am she's up making candles from remnants of tallow. Penny-pinching! He hates it as he hates the dungarees. He knows why she scrimps and scrapes, she hates being beholden.

Tonight she's a knockout, hair in combs and breasts gleaming above a strip of black velvet. Needless to say Ma isn't happy. It's hard imagining Ruby as pretty. She must have been once since she stole Bucky Rourke from under May Templar's nose. That's how the feud began.

'Shall you light the brandy?' says Adelia.

'Gabe!' The devil tempting, Bobby got to his feet. Knowing who's out back washing dishes, he calls out, 'Come and set fire to the pud, will ya?'

In he comes, Mister Humility in white T-shirt and denims. Dee asks him to stay and share a drink. He refuses and goes back to the kitchen. Pink circles in the middle of her cheeks Dee doles out the crepes. Her high color doesn't escape Ma.

'You should cover up! Easter is for celebratin' Our Lord's sacrifice, not an excuse for showin' all you got. And him with his tongue hangin' out! He ought not to be encouraged. Give him an inch and he'll take a yard.'

'No!' Adelia throws the spoon down. 'You can't insult people and eat the food they serve. I'll not have it! Mister Templar is a good man. He doesn't deserve this.'

'How would you know?' Bobby refilled his glass.

'What?'

'I said, how do you know he's good? You got a twenty-four hour memory block. You can hardly make judgments about the men in your life.'

'There hasn't been that many to make judgments.'

'There's been one and unless the rules have changed one is all it takes.'

Hurt, she looked at him. Into the silence the phone rang.

A familiar voice sounded in his ear. 'Happy Easter, Bobby.'

The phone fell from his fingers. By the time he'd picked it up he'd managed to regain a measure of composure. 'Ash, old pal! How you doin'?'

'I'm okay. I understand you've had a pretty rough time.'

'No worse than anyone else. Where you callin' from?'

'London Airport. I'm about to board the plane. I wanted to call and wish you the best for Easter.'

'Same to you, Buddy.'

When he returned to the table Ma was still holding forth. Looking at all the troubled faces Bobby thought to chuck in a new stick of dynamite. 'Forget it Ma. This time next year we'll be in California and new friends to insult.'

~

It was late. They stood at the bottom of Sophie's bed, Bobby drunk and giggling and Dee trying to shut him up. A fur-covered purse shaped like a cat, he set Sophie's present at the end of the bed. 'D'you think she'll like it?'

'She'll love it.'

Sophie's face was a pale blur through her curls. Bobby thought of the first time he saw her sleeping. Up she got, bolt upright; finger to his lips he'd dived in his pocket pulling out a biscuit. 'Mummy says I'm not to take sweets from strangers,' she says. 'I ain't a stranger, sweetheart,' he replies. 'I'm just a sad old bogeyman.'

That night she took the biscuit and went back to sleep. Next couple of days she wandered the house whispering, 'Mister Bogeyman? Are you coming out to play?'

She never calls him bogeyman now. He is daddy.

'Christ!' he wiped his eyes. 'I wish to God I could call back time.'

'Don't we all,' says Dee.

It's late. Ruby is snoring in a chair. Gabe's taking down the lights. Dee is clearing the table. Bobby is finishing the last of the Beaujolais.

'I thought you'd given up on the idea of California,' she said.

'I thought so myself.'

'What about me?' Ma opens her eyes long enough to interfere. 'What will happen to me when my only flesh and blood is miles away?'

'What happened when I was doing my bit for the old country? '

'I suffered.'

'Now you won't have to. I'll be safe in the bosom of my family. You could always come with us,' he said, knowing she was too selfish to move.

'Leave the Mission and my duty to the congregation? The pastor wouldn't like it.'

Hate in her eyes she turned on Dee. 'This'll be on account of you and your heathen ways. He's takin' you away before you disgrace him.'

Dee swept out and the lights fused. That was Easter.

Ruby took a cab home. Come midnight Gabe was leaving.

Drunk, Bobby flung his arm about him, muscles and tendon stiffening under his touch. 'Not going yet are you, old sport? Stay and have a drink.'

'I don't drink.'

'Aw, come on! Dee? Fetch out another bottle of champers?'

'It's late.'

'Late nothing, it's Easter Sunday! Our last in Virginia!' He popped the cork. 'Let's drink to us three? You, me, and the old sport.' They took a glass each and solemnly came together, a tickle in Bobby's head making him dangerous. 'What's the toast?'

'Peace on earth,' says Dee tightly. 'And goodwill to all men.'

'It's Easter, honey, not Christmas.'

'The toast stands.'

Their glasses came together in a chink, Templar sipping like it was nitroglycerin.

'What's your toast, old sport?'

'Don't know that I have one. '

'I've got one! How about absent friends?'

'Yes,' she says. 'Absent friends.'

Bobby frowned. 'You thinkin' about the missin' link again, Sophie's father?'

'I was thinking of my father and mother.'

Arms across his chest protecting his heart Gabe is saying nothing, those arms cause the tickle in Bobby's head to become a shriek. Then to top it all Gabe gives Dee a wooden rattle. 'You mind the time you mowed the grass and cut the leg off that frog? How you ran about next time tryin' to scare 'em away.'

'Do I?' She shuddered.

'Now all you gotta do is rattle and them frogs will skedaddle.'

'Thank you.'

'That all?' says Bobby. 'Don't he get a proper thank you? I mean, a twenty-four carat present like a frog clacker deserves more than thank you.'

'I've already given him my bible.'

'Well now, a bible!' Jealousy whipped through him. 'I didn't know you were a religious man, Gabe. Where d'you get the callin' Death Row?'

Gabe made for the door. Bobby should've let him go but a piece of last year's mistletoe hung over the door as simple and innocent as a time bomb.

'A kiss under the mistletoe!' He saw it. 'That's the way to say happy birthday!'

'No,' said Adelia, fists clenched. 'It's a very silly way.'

'What's silly about giving a pretty woman a peck on the cheek?'

'Bobby,' she said, 'I don't want to do this.'

'Yes, you do. You've been hangin' on for years. So go on, get it over with.'

Sounds in the house dropped away.

'Go on!' He demanded his voice ugly. 'Kiss her, dummy!'

Gabriel gazed at Adelia. They'd never kissed before. Until this moment there had been an unspoken acceptance of the sacred and of crossing a line.

'We shouldn't do this,' she whispered.

'I know,' said Gabriel, 'but it is my birthday.' Then he was leaning down, the warmth of his body preceding the kiss. Briefly, sweetly, his lips touched hers.

'Happy Easter, Adelia.'

'Happy birthday, Gabriel.'

Book Two
The Hero

Chapter Eleven
Memory Lane

The cabby slued round in the seat. 'The what?'

'The Black Swan.'

'There ain't no Black Swan, Captain. A bomb got it summer of '42, blew it, and a field of cows halfway to the moon.'

'Sure.' Alex nodded. 'Forget it. I was thinking out loud.'

'The Mucky Duck,' the cabby grinned. 'A good old place, a bit scruffy round the edges but you always got what you wanted, a decent meal, clean sheets and if you were lucky a dirty little girl.' He opened his mouth to make the wartime crack about Yanks being overfed and over-here but aware of cold blue eyes and a combat crew-cut brushing the roof of his cab thought better of it.

The Yank whistled him up outside the station. 'Drive until I tell you to stop, ' was the instruction, which is okay, the meter ticking nicely. But they've been driving an hour and still the bloke stares out the window like he could swallow Needham whole. 'Were you here when the old place burned down?'

'I was.'

'So this is a trip down memory lane.'

'You might say so.'

'And then you're on your way home?'

Alex shrugged. Beyond a 48 hour touch-down a couple of years back it's so long since he was home he's not sure he has one. This beaten up old country with the stink of cordite in the air is as much home as any place. That's why he is here, as the cabby said, a trip down memory lane.

'Where to now, Captain?'

'Colonel, if you please.'

The cabby saluted. 'Yes sir, Colonel! Fancy a peep at the new Black Swan?'

The cab putted down the narrow streets. As they crossed the square the town clock struck the hour. The first time Alex heard those chimes he was with Adelia doing the tourist thing, admiring the sights knowing that what they admired today might tomorrow be a handful of dust. Six years on the town and the clock remains upright. It is flesh and blood that has fallen.

The cabby grinned. 'Don't seem a minute since I was running your lot around. I'd pick up one of your lads. We'd circle the square, him giving her what-for on the back seat, and then go back for another. Happy days, ay, Colonel?'

Alex Hunter's happy day began August 1st 1942 and ended August 2nd. Major Hunter, 1st Battalion, US Rangers, as he was then, was due to leave for Italy. He had planned to spend a day in London but a letter from home told of a friend in hospital and so instead of the Houses of Parliament and Big Ben he took the motorbike to Needham and to St Faith's. It was a joke. The old friend wasn't thrilled to see him. Even with a leg in plaster Bobby Rourke was up to his old tricks, a woman waiting in the wings he couldn't wait to be rid of Alex.

Got up like a matinee idol, silk scarf and dressing-gown, he'd hobbled up and down the tiny room glancing at his watch and dropping hints. Then with a knock on the door he threw Alex out. 'Don't let me keep you, sport!' he says. 'Last day in Blighty you have a thousand things to do and a thousand whores to fuck.'

Alex was on his way out when he collided with a nurse. 'Sorry,' he'd said. 'Perfectly all right,' she'd replied. 'No harm done.'

There was harm done, everlasting harm. That face, the veil scooping back her hair gave her the look of a postulant nun. Unable to leave he hung about the grounds sharing a porter's lodge. 0700 hours next morning she came through the gate and what did he do but offer to buy her a coffee.

A well-brought up girl, she walked by yet something must've appealed because after a little pleading she gave way and smiled. That smile was a dagger to his heart. Twenty-four years old, six-three in his socks, two hundred pounds of muscle, he'd found the girl of his dreams and wasn't about to let her go.

If it hadn't been for the motor bike she might have got away.

'Can't stay for coffee,' she said. 'I have to feed the animals.'

The animals were pets holed-up in a wreck of a house on the edge of town.

'You live here?' he'd thought the place unfit for a rat let alone a postulant nun.

'It's my Aunt's place,' she'd rushed from pen to pen. 'I know it's pretty grim but it's all I have.' He told of Ranger Camp in Scotland and how he had to be in Southampton the following day. Caught up in the urgency of the moment he made a drama of it, rambling on until an invitation to spend time together became the Last Stand at the Alamo. Catching the look in her eyes he'd laughed. She laughed with him. On the way to her Aunt's place she rode holding onto his belt. On the ride back her arms were tight about his chest.

'You're going to love Virginia and Virginia's going to love you!' he shouted. The wind took his words and scattered them as time has scattered his dreams.

'Here we are, Colonel,' the cab pulled alongside a building. 'The Oast House it calls itself now but underneath it's the same old knocking shop.'

August 1st, 1942, the Black Swan was packed to the gills. The carpet was rolled back, a phonograph played and black market booze flowed.

Couples danced cheek-to-cheek. Until the war he didn't know how to dance. His father, General William Hunter US Army retired, is a dignified man, the son and heir must be the same.

That night they danced. She was weary as was he but afraid of losing a second they circled the room. Then one, or both, wanted a room.

'The old Mucky Duck,' the cabby sighed. 'A girl, a bed, and a bottle of beer, you were in heaven. In those days you never knew if the girl you were with was the last. So you gave her a good poke in case she was.'

Alex stared at the windows. As he watched the Black Swan rose out of the ground like a vast mildewed calliope, the walls encrusted with pigeon shit and the glass doors imprinted with the heat of a thousand male hands.

It was on the top floor in room 11 he gave a good poke. Clumsy, he didn't know how to kiss much less make it easy for a virgin. Being in love kicked the hick out of that country-boy. Overnight he graduated from a fumbling jerk to the hottest GI in town. Crazy in love, he did things only whispered about by Baby Rourke and other sexual athletes back home.

'The Germans got it. Three in the morning an incendiary bomb on the brewery next door,' said the cabby. 'Whoosh, up it went, bed bugs and all! Cor, mate, can you picture it?

Six years and he hasn't stopped picturing it. Picturing things is what he does best. Lieutenant Colonel Ash Hunter, aka the Camera, has the eidetic memory that allows him to relive everything seen or done. The Camera is an apt name for his particular function. Click, a shutter will fire and whatever is seen or heard is retained forever. Click, documents rewritten at will, maps and drawings reproduced. Click, conversations recalled. Click, a church with a hole in the roof.

'Cabby, is St Giles' Church still standing?'

'Depends what you mean by standing.'

St Giles was already a ruin in '42, weeds in the font and rooks in the rafters.

Adelia thought it peaceful. 'Ruin or not God can still hear our dreams.'

Alex had asked her dream. 'That you'll come back to me.'

Sunlight shining through the rafters and a field mouse on the altar Alex made a promise. 'No matter what happens I will come back.'

That day he made a vow, but God having other things on His mind took His Eye off the ball and a few hours later she was dead.

~

It was too much. Enough of a bleeding heart, he got the cabby to take him to the airport. Now he is sitting on board a plane watching the English coastline fold away under the wing. The last two years of his life have been on hold. Attached by a circuitous route to an intelligence unit in Berlin he is required to go anywhere in Europe at a minute's notice. The bulk of his time is spent in covert activity, tapping radio broadcasts, reading documentation and deciphering codes. Between times he makes trips to the Soviet sector of Berlin and is returning Stateside fully expecting to go further afield to Singapore and the Philippines.

Lately Korea is port of call, trouble on the 38th parallel. If there's not a war soon between South and North Korea his name is not Alexander Stonewall Hunter.

His job is difficult to define. The official title is Communications Expert, the department adding a touch of authenticity having him lecture on navigation and reconnaissance.

Sarah, his sister, calls what he does special ops. Flair for romance has Sarah. There's nothing special about long spells of mind-numbing boredom interspersed by sudden spates of activity. He bides in unattractive rooms, sleeps on thin mattresses and eats dull food. No social life and no friends, doing what he does, moving from place to place listening and watching brother officers are wary. It doesn't matter that he's earned his battle scars or that he didn't set out to be a code-breaker. To the average Joe he is a spook prying into private lives, a non-combatant who wears the uniform but lives outside the code.

Code-breaking skills belong to the Camera. First and last he is an academy man yet somewhere between Scotland and the Ardennes he gained a reputation for the keenest eyes and sharpest ears. Hence he was co-opted into military intelligence. But that was then. He determined to come up for air and so when a position at the War College came up he pressed for it.

Sure, there is covert activity involved. While the Camera is operational the army will make use of him. But he's going to try to settle, maybe get married and have kids. There have been women but nothing lasts. One of his sister's friends might change that. Whoever she is she'll have to be tough and extra patient. It's not easy playing second fiddle to a ghost.

Ghosts? The word has meaning. There were times when born of despair, buddies dying all about him, he felt her presence, smelt her perfume and knew her breath on his brow.

It happened in the Ardennes while he lay in a ditch, his knee shot away.

Her spirit, soul, call it what you like, came to him - no gaseous cloud or wailing banshee, simply a warm heart beating against his own.

He told no one about that, not even his Godfather, Joe Petowski, killed at Anzio. What could he say? That the spirit of a beautiful blonde girl was his guardian angel? Hoo-yah! In your wet dreams!

Back in '42 when the bomb dropped he was blown out the window and down to the ground and out cold for twenty minutes. What happened to his beloved in those twenty minutes? He doesn't know! The number of times he tried to get back inside! Once he got as far as the bar, vaulting a blazing counter, his hands on fire, but then firemen dragged him away.

MPs arrived. In the melee he was knocked out. Mercifully, then there was nothing. Next he's on a train bound for Scotland and the Ranger camp.

Hope was harder to kill than Adelia. Confined to quarters, his hands in need of dressing, he spent hours calling Suffolk hospitals. Always the same reply: 'No one of that name and description here.' Beyond the faceless no-goes he was forever on the phone to one who witnessed the fire.

Bobby Rourke was in the square that day and saw Alex dragged away, and like the good friend he is promised that if there was news Alex would get it.

Bobby even checked the aunt's house, boarded up, he said, pets all gone.

A funeral might have helped, given an ending, at least, but bodies brought from the fire were said to be beyond identification. All Alex has of time spent with her is a snapshot taken in Suffolk- Adelia in nurse's uniform holding a monkey some photographer guy was hawking about the square.

The photo, a ring on his finger, and endless memories, that's it.

In the plane he tries to sleep but can't get away from the past. Anzio, it's always Anzio, Joe Petowski in a ditch, his upturned helmet acting as a bucket for dirty Italian rain and honest Polish blood.

Click, the Camera whirs and a prisoner, Alex, is paraded alongside other Rangers through the streets of Rome. Click, he escapes, and remembers the flight over the Italian border hidden in a cart under a pile of manure. From Anzio it was the Ardennes where, though badly wounded, he held a gun placement for twenty-four hours.

For that act of foolishness he was awarded the Medal. Big deal! Hand on heart he'd trade every citation ever won for a kiss from her living lips.

Click! The Camera rewound back to '42, stopping just before the bomb fell.

It happened so fast there was no time to really say goodbye. They were woken by sirens and the sound of heavy ack-ack.

Incendiary falling, every detonation closer than the last, he was helping her to dress when an explosion, and shock waves, threw them apart.

Boom! Alex was slammed against the barricaded window. The room is frosted with ice! The blast is shredding her clothes, petals of silk shriveling, first her skirt and then her underwear.

For one horrible moment she is framed in the doorway, some unseen force lifting her until a scarlet glad angel she is poised in the air, her lion's mane of statically charged hair flying in the up draught.

Boom! A second blast takes out the window before sucking him down to the street. Heaven help him, it's all there in his head, endless footage, flames from the hotel roof piercing the sky and a fireman rolling a hose.

Blood in his eyes from a cut forehead, he is running from one group of bedraggled men and women to another. So scared he can't think he is shouting, 'Come here, Adelia! It's me Alex! Sweetheart, where are you?'

A terrible memory, a clash of sight and sound, ambulance bells jangling, men and women in nightclothes their faces blackened.

He remembers one woman turning to another. 'Ere, Dot,' she says. 'D'you hear the big bloke shoutin'? Geezer thinks he's calling his bloody dog.' And why wouldn't she say that, it's how he was, a rabid animal.

One face stands out in the crowd. There he is, Baby Rourke leaning on a crutch, his brows singed and madness in his eyes.

'Say, Bobby!' Alex shouts. 'Did you see her?'

'Who?' Bobby stares, an expression on his face that even now Alex can't fathom. 'Who we talking about?'

'Your nurse, Adelia! She was with me in the pub! Have you seen her?'

'No, sport. I haven't.'

Alex never did know why he was in the square that day, but guesses he was being Bobby and a girl in one of the rooms. Scuttlebutt says he's suffering now, drunk most nights, blind in one eye and on his way out.

Poor guy! As soon as he gets back Bobby will be the first port of call.

The plane is touching down at Charlottesville.

Exhausted, he sleeps and dreams of a garden with green lawns and roses. Set back of the gardens is a lath and plaster house, a beautiful place, one of the old 'black and white' Tudor houses seen in England.

A girl in jeans and a straw hat is trimming the roses.

The heels of his boots crunching the shale he walks toward her.

'Hi,' he says. 'It's me Alex.'

She turns. It is Adelia. 'I know who you are,' she says, returning to the roses. 'You're Colonel Bogey, the Yank that loved and left me.'

Chapter Twelve
Vernas

Hearing of the RAF Reunion dinner and Bobby up for a medal Alex dropped by the hall to support him. The guest of honor didn't show. No word of explanation just an empty seat on the rostrum. Alex left and was walking through the parking lot when a sporty-job came out of the shadows almost gunning him down.

What the hell! He leapt aside.

'Ash buddy!' The car squealed to a halt. 'I'm so sorry. I didn't see you!'

Bobby Rourke, you mad bastard! Alex was ready to give him a piece of his mind but seeing him anger died. My God! If he hadn't heard the voice and recognized the RAF blues and customary silk scarf he never would have known him.

They shook hands. 'Were you trying to kill me?'

'Sorry Ash. It's my eyes or lack of 'em. But don't worry. I'll get you next time.'

'Where did you spring from?' said Alex wrestling with the shock.

'Same place as you. I went in to offer apologies. I didn't mean to let anyone down but the missus was sick so I couldn't get away.'

'Sorry to hear that. Is she okay now?'

'She's fine, one of those women things.'

Bobby took a flask from his pocket and tipping it back took a long pull.

'Man!' Alex whistled. 'You're gonna have a head tomorrow.'

'Forget my head! What use is it except for a gargoyle? Got a gasper?'

Alex offered his case, the photograph of Adelia clipped inside. Shocked by the state of his old friend he took a time lighting a cigarette. Jesu, now he knows what Sarah meant by the walking dead.

'I guess I'm not the pretty boy I was.'

Bobby smiled…at least Alex thought he did. With that scar who could tell?

'I'm sorry.'

'You'll be more so when you know the cause. Your old motor-bike did for me. It tossed me off its back like a mule with a bug up its ass.'

'I'm sorry,' he said again.

'Me too, but what can you do. It's as my missus says, water under the bridge.'

'You're married now.'

'And with a kid! See this?' Bobby took a snapshot from his wallet. 'The creature with the brawny arms you'll recognize as my Ma. The little gal with the big eyes is Sophie Emma Rourke. Look at the expression on her face. She can't stand Ruby and ain't got the sophistication to hide it.'

Alex took the photograph and Bobby lunged at him.

'You son-of-a-gun!' he said excitedly. 'You've been holding out on me.'

'Holding out?

He pointed to the ring. 'You've been and got yourself hitched!'

'I'm not married.'

'But you're wearin' a ring and a wedding ring at that!'

'It's something I wear.'

'Oh you are kiddin' me.' Bobby's face fell. 'Don't tell me you're still carryin' the same bloody cross?'

'What cross is that?'

'You know what I'm talkin' about. All that stuff in Blighty! Fucks sake!' Bobby tossed the cheroot into the dark. 'Why couldn't you have found a woman? It would have made all the difference.'

'It's not that simple.'

'It is that simple! The past is the past.'

'Yes and what's dead remains dead!'

There was a pause, Bobby's mouth opening and closing. Then he shrugged. 'We do what we must,' he said. 'The trick is learnin' to live with it.'

'Never mind the past,' Alex stuck his hands in his pockets. 'How are things in your neck of the woods?'

'SSDD. Same shit, different day.'

'Does your wife like Virginia?'

'She would if it wasn't for people tryin' to shove her around.'

'What people?'

'Ma for one.'

'Uh-huh.' Recalling Mrs Rourke, a mean-fisted woman with a habit of quoting scripture, Alex's sympathy was with the wife. 'You-all live together?'

'Hell no! You couldn't put them in the same pen. There'd be murders! What you going to do now you're home, live with your Ma and the General?'

'My plans are loose. Until I know what's what I have to be near the Pentagon.'

'You still in the cloak and dagger business?'

'What business is that?'

'Yeah, right! Any truth in the Korea poop you read in the papers, North and South on the brink of war?'

It was dark in the car-lot, hardly the place to chat, yet Bobby seemed reluctant to leave. He talked of the past, laughed and joked, but there was only one real topic of conversation, sooner or later everything coming back to the missus.

'I guess you were too choosy to find yourself a nice little Fraulein. You always were a picky kind of guy.'

'I don't know that I was.'

'Well, you never put yourself out, did you, 'cept maybe this one time.'

Alex let it go. What could he say?

Bobby slipped dark glasses over his nose. 'You talk about me lookin' bad but you look a little frayed round the edges.'

'I guess so.'

'You know what you need? You need a fortnight's R and R at our place, a week sleeping and another week eating Dee's apple-pie.'

'And the domestic strife? '

'Ah, that's nothin'. You'd be okay. Ma never comes round these days, thanks be to God. Go on! Come! You'd be doing all of us a favor.'

He was gone. The last remark sounding like a challenge he jumped into the car and sped-off, red taillights disappearing through the darkness.

~

He wasn't gone for long. In fact, for the next month Bobby Rourke was all and everywhere, a blonde on one arm and a redhead on the other.

The first time it happened Alex was in the Baker's Dozen, an army haunt in Washington, sipping a beer killing time before an interview. Who should wander through the door but Bobby with his arm about a busty redhead?

Thinking he was about to meet the wife Alex got to his feet.

No sir! The idiot was hustling the woman out and winking over his shoulder. 'If anyone asks you didn't see me. I was with Verna.'

The following Saturday, Alex, brother-in-law Maurice and his two boys, were at a ball game. There's Bobby waving from the stands with a different redhead. The third encounter was a lollapalooza. Alex had dropped his mother at the beauty parlor and was heading back when the sports car overtook him.

'Say, Ash?' He shouted, this time with his arm about a blonde. 'Me and Verna are off for a furtive fumble over Chesapeake Bay. Fancy a ride?'

The guy was ever two men, Robert E Rourke, Ace pilot, and Baby Rourke, womanizing drunk. Alex never calls him Baby, he won't subscribe to a soft-peddle image that encourages the guy to be less than he is. They've been friends for a long time. The family doesn't understand the friendship. There have been times past when Alex didn't understand.

Discipline and duty are key words in the Hunter household. Regulated by his father's strict code of conduct - and his own struggle to come to terms with an eidetic memory- Alex lived an orderly life. According to his sister, Sarah, he's a stuffed shirt. It's true when he was young he spent a lot of time alone, not so much from choice, more the reverberations of a heavy father plus his own reticent nature. When not at the Academy his youth was spent drilling on the Green, or bird watching, field glasses about his neck and his dog by his side.

Bobby was a mixed bag. Slim and adventurous, and with a great line in wooing, he swooped about town in the latest car, the Chevy's tail fins rivaling the quiff in his hair. When the General complained Alex defended the guy. What do you expect? He's only trying to rise above his mother's shabby way of living.

Before she took to bible punching his mother was a hustler and his father a plumber with a Midas touch. Bucky Rourke made a mint of money in copper mines, enough to purchase a house next door to the Hunters; when he died life then for Bobby was all about flying. He attended the Academy for a time but was never a serious campaigner. Planes! While other kids collected baseball cards he flew daredevil stunts in an air-circus. In '39 he went over the border to the Royal Canadian Air-Force and from there to England, Needham, Suffolk, and the war. Living so close they drove the General crazy, spilling their trashy way of life about the quiet suburb. Sarah kept her distance but for other reasons, namely her and Bobby once having a thing going.

A complex character, yet damn good fun to be with, Bobby could have you pissing your pants in no time, whereas Alex is a sober kind of guy. Strong on loyalty, he likes sport, the theatre and music. He hates confined spaces, wool next to his skin, and falseness of any kind, and admits to being something of a prude. It is said he is a good friend when in trouble but a rigid disciplinarian, in other words a stuffed shirt. One thing is certain, his stuffed heart is broken.

~

Coming home was a mistake. The minute he got out of the cab, the family gathered on the step, he knew he should've stayed away. Everything and nothing had changed. His parents were collapsing inward, Ellen, his mother, so fragile he feared to hug her, father as bull-headed as ever yet faded like a sepia portrait.

Sarah, the socialite, wears her hair and her nails a bright shade of red, her opinions - and her laughter- as brittle as her nails. Maurice Parker, Sarah's husband, a surgeon at the Veteran's Hospital, has the same earnest intellect yet is sadder, balder! Their boys, Dave and Pete, are wild savages with a mouthful of iron. As for the larger-world, former colleagues are on their second divorce and tethered to a telephone discussing alimony and the Dow Jones.

Virginian women are fabulous but intimidating. Crossing the room at one of his sister's soirees is like crossing a minefield. Alex comes out the other side with raspberry pockmarks on his face and handprints on his butt. Sarah works overtime arranging dinners for two. Trying to fit in he locked his ring away and did his best to be charming but found he was mentally rearranging his date, nose for a nose, eye for eye, and laugh for a laugh. By the time the meet was over he was gazing at a hybrid, his date's identity muddled by that of a phantom.

It's got so he's considering putting the ring back on his finger. He misses it, misses the weight and is forever staring at the pale circle on his finger.

On his birthday wearing the ring came under question.

They were dining at Sarah's. All was going well until Mother talked of GI Brides: 'I met Isla Blair in town with her new daughter-in-law. Such a nice little thing! And a cute granddaughter, a real picture in a blue straw bonnet.'

'Now don't get broody,' said Sarah, 'I've done my bit. It's for Alex to oblige.'

Mrs Hunter sniffed. 'If it's down to him I'll never get a granddaughter.'

'I don't know. He might surprise you yet. Sure, he has a couple of grey hairs and a stiff leg but there's life in the old dog yet.'

'Thank you, Sis.'

'You're welcome. Seriously though, I did think you'd find a wife. You'd be quite the fashion. Washington's littered with female émigrés. They are reversing the oversexed and over-here jibe; nowadays it is British girls who are over here.'

The General threw down his napkin.' I don't hold with the GI program. Women and their undernourished brats bringing disease into the country! We got enough of our own without taking on other country's misfits.'

'Are they misfits?' said Mother. 'Isla's daughter-in-law seemed a nice girl.'

'Of course they're misfits! You only got to read the papers to know what kind of women they are. '

'I for one feel sorry for them,' said Sarah. 'Think how you'd feel if you came all this way and found Ruby Cropper your mother-in-law?'

'Don't talk about that woman at the dinner table!' said the General.

'I thought you liked Bobby's fiancée.'

'I do. I thought it was Ruby Cropper you were on about. Sure, I like Miss Dee. At least she has hogs and stuff, doesn't batten on the country looking for a handout.'

Alex added his two cents. 'If a woman marries a US serviceman surely she's entitled to a handout.'

'Not on my pension she ain't! I didn't work all my life to support a bunch of layabouts. I dare say back from Berlin and Gay Paree you were okay with the deal. I'm not. You want to bring a foreign woman home to the US go ahead and do it but don't look to me and your mother for support.'

Alex set down his glass. 'Bringing a wife home isn't next on my agenda but if the situation changes I'll let you know. I saw no layabouts in Berlin. There were those looking for a good time, aren't there always. The majority were trying to stay alive. As for anyone throwing herself at me I don't recall any of that.'

It was the worst thing he could have said.

'Aw, dearie me!' drawled Sarah. 'Did you miss out, baby brother? Did no-one make a pass at you? No cute girl gazing into your big blue eyes?'

'Now quit with that, daughter,' said the General. 'No need to be personal.'

'There's every need,' said Sarah. 'We can't have the dear boy lost and alone. You must take him up to the hospital, Maurice. See what you can do to spice up his life. Maybe introduce him to one of your more sexy nurses.'

'I don't want any of that.' Riled by the conversation, the words were out before they could be gainsaid. 'I had my own nurse and she's dead, killed in an air-raid.'

There was silence. Then his mother nodded at his father. 'I told you something was amiss. You and your fixations! Why can't you leave the boy alone?'

'How was I to know?' protested William Hunter. 'He never tells me anything.'

Alex pushed away from the table and went out on the veranda.

It wasn't long before Sarah appeared. 'Sorry.' She slipped her hand into his. 'I didn't know.'

He shrugged.

'Was she lovely?'

'Very.'

'Did you love her?'

'Yes.'

'I'm sorry. What was her name?'

'What does it matter? She's dead. Her name died with her.'

Sarah went back into the house. He stayed in the garden. Click, suddenly Adelia was beside him, naked save for her panties and his socks. They were in the hotel room. She was demonstrating the finer points of a tango. 'Not like that, darling,' she was saying.' You're supposed to be indicating passion not calling a cab.'

She flung herself about a while and then grimaced, the dog tags cold about her neck. 'How d'you bear these things? They're cold against the skin.'

He'd stalked her. 'Come here, baby. Daddy will warm you up.'

Giggling and breathless, she'd backed away.' Don't you dare come near! I don't think I can stand another lesson in love.'

~

Sarah threw a party, Alex under siege with kisses and handshakes. He couldn't breathe, especially when she started in again with questions.

'Did your girl come from a good family?'

'Her folks were dead.'

'How old was she?'

'We didn't discuss age.'

'Did you meet while in Scotland? Was she like the Blair girl?'

'We didn't meet in Scotland. And no, she wasn't like the Blair girl.'

'Was it sudden? Did you look across a room and suddenly there she was, the girl of your dreams? I can't imagine it. You're not a sudden sort of fellow.'

'You don't know what sort of a fellow I am.'

'Yes I do! You're my brother.'

So it went on. Torquemada and the Inquisition had nothing on Sarah.

Ten-fifteen the doorbell rang, a flash of RAF blue lounging in the porch.

'Evening, squire.' Bobby stood swaying on the threshold.

'Come on in, you sonofagun!' Alex hauled him in. 'A party wouldn't be a party without the Baby.'

'Hush up, old buddy!' He laid a finger across his lips. 'You mustn't call me Baby. The missus doesn't like it.'

Alex walked out into the drive. 'You've brought Mrs Rourke? '

'Mrs Rourke!' Bobby followed him out. 'Don't tell me Ma's here. The General won't like that.'

'Not your mother, you fool, your wife!'

'She can't make it. Sophie's got hives, been in the raspberry canes with the dog. Hi Sarah.' He bowed, silk scarf brushing the ground. 'How you doin'? '

'Hello,' said Sarah, coolly. 'Excuse me. I see Ma calling.

'Ouch, frostbite!' Bobby waggled his fingers. 'Sarah and me used to be real close but not anymore. Too many Vernas I fear.'

Alex steered him to a seat. 'A drink or have you had enough?'

'I'll have a double Tequila Slammer with a cherry on top.'

On the way to the bar Sarah collared Alex. 'What's he doing here? '

'Why?'

'He's drunk.' She chewed her lip.' I can't stand seeing him that way.'

Anger flared. 'What's your problem with the guy? Cut him some slack will you? He's enough to contend with without you giving him a hard time. '

She rolled her eyes.' For a grown man you are incredibly naive.'

'What do you mean?'

'You're naïve about Bobby and always have been.'

'Why, because I don't care that his Pa was a tinker and mother a whore? '

'No, because you don't see what kind of a person he is.'

Click! For some reason Alex associated the comment with Needham Square and the photograph in his cigarette case, Adelia holding a monkey. 'Bobby's okay.' The words felt like echoes. 'He's a clown. It's his job to make people laugh.'

'Let's hope he keeps you laughing. He's giving others cause to weep.' She barred the way. 'Has it occurred to you to wonder why with all his money he chooses to live in a rundown pile in the middle of nowhere?'

'Maybe he feels awkward about his looks.'

'Then why troll round Richmond with blondes and redheads? Awkward, no! He doesn't care who sees him. It's others he keeps hidden, the woman and her daughter. A couple of years in Virginia and apart from a trip downtown they go nowhere. I've met them, Sophie at kindergarten and Dee slinging hash at the hospital. So lovely, they might've stepped out of a renaissance painting. Does he appreciate them, does he hell! Apart from a woman who cooks and a guy helping out...handy man, for want of a better word, they're alone in that place.'

'You seem to know a lot about them.'

'Word gets around.' She sighed. 'I wonder if Pa minds him being here.'

'It'll be the glitter of the DFC if he doesn't.'

'Don't be sour, Alex. I know you're having a hard time being home but you'll be better once you've got your own place. Found anywhere yet?'

'I've a couple of places in mind.'

'You don't sound too enthusiastic.'

'What's to be enthusiastic about? It's a place to live in.'

'I don't think your nurse would agree with you on that.'

Alex stiffened. Sarah was her father's daughter. Once she has the bit between her teeth she won't let go. When he stayed silent she lost her temper.

'You've a lot to answer for, Alex Hunter. You hurt Ma not coming home sooner. You hurt the General too, not that he'd dream of showing it. A couple of hit-and-run visits wasn't right. They love you and were afraid for you. Now that you are home I hope you're not going to shut them out.'

Alex tuned Sarah out. He watched Pete, his nephew, playing ball with a dog and thought back on the afternoon in '42, Adelia and a dog playing fetch.

She would throw the ball and the dog would catch.

Click! As clearly as he could see Pete he saw Adelia and that dog. Up went the ball into sunlit Suffolk skies. Alex leaned back to watch it rise. The ball hovered, started to fall, and out went his hand to catch it!

'What are you doing?' said Sarah.

He shoved his hands in his pockets. 'Nothing.'

'I know why you don't like any of my friends. It's that memory of yours. Why bother with flesh and blood when a dream is alive and kicking?'

'Leave it, Sarah! I've survived all these years without your help.'

'But that's it! You're surviving but you're not living and it's not good for you. You're a good-looking man. You have poise and charm. The girls are mad about you. They say you are sexy but bruised.'

'I'm not interested in what the *girls* say. I'm interested in being left alone.'

'Don't worry, you'll be alone.' She strode away. 'Acceptable bachelors are thin on the ground but not so thin a girl wants to compete with the dead.'

Alex slid into the conservatory. Another asylum-seeker was already there, the General with a bottle of rye and a couple of glasses.

'Listen to 'em,' he said, gloomily. 'Goddamn typewriters, what do they find to talk about?' Lingering with pride on the Medal ribbon his glance passed over his son's jacket. 'I hear you're in deep with them intelligence boys. Be careful. Get in with them OSS types and you may as well kiss the full bird goodbye.'

From the open window there came a chorus of female laughter, Bobby Rourke's soft drawl mingling with the hissing of sprinklers.

'Now there's a man wears his scars with pride. I didn't think much of him when he was younger but he came through. Did you know he was here yesterday? Your mother found him and Miss Dee wandering the grounds.'

'What is all this about his wife, the whispering and secrecy?'

The General was affronted.' There's no secrecy in my dealings. I take as I find and I find her a lady. Miss Dee is a nice girl with real nice ways. And there's her kiddy, cute little moppet. If you get in with a decent crowd, you never know, I might yet have me a granddaughter like Sophie.'

Enough is enough! Alex packed a bag and was on his way out when he saw Maurice. 'Hi brother-in-law, how's the world of plastic thermocouples?'

'As well as can be expected, thanks. What about you? '

'Nothing wrong a Huey out of here won't cure.'

They leant on the banister gazing down on the mass of people about the buffet table, the women in cocktail gowns, teetering heels and dipping cleavage.

'Look at all that red meat! How's a guy to be a vegetarian when that's on offer?'

Alex grinned. 'How are the boys?'

'Pete's into girls and Davy green slime from Mars.'

'Are they planning to follow in the way of their father's surgical boots?'

'According to them a surgeon's a glorified butcher. It doesn't stop them taking the butcher's hard-earned cash.' Maurice gestured to the bag. 'I had hoped you were staying. It's a long time since I talked with someone sinister.'

'I have to get out.'

'It's okay. I understand. You're grieving.'

There was a burst of laughter, Bobby working the room.

Maurice sighed. 'Poor guy, the war really did for him. It can't be easy being him. Can't be easy living with him either! He has a treacherous temper, naught to sixty in no time. All praise to his lady for hanging in.'

'I keep hearing about the mysterious Miss Dee. Is she all I've heard?'

'Depends what you've heard.'

'I heard she's good to look at.'

'About that you heard right. I'm not normally bowled over by the Nordic blonde thing but I make an exception for her.'

'The General seems taken with her.'

'Your father is a closet gentleman. A damsel in distress is sure to find favor with the General.'

'Is she in distress?'

'I would say so.'

'Why, from the Vernas?'

'Hardly. She really is quite lovely. Not a woman to be left alone for long.'

'Judging by the gossip Bobby and his wife are the only cud worth chewing.'

'You two should get together. You share the same interests.'

'Excuse me!'

Maurice laughed. 'When he's not talking about his wife he's talking about you. The guy's got a crush on you. Always had! We laugh about it.'

'It's not funny. I can't move for him on my tail.'

'Really?' Maurice stared across the room. 'Did you actually invite him?'

'I forgot.'

'Then why come? He doesn't want to be here. You can see he's uncomfortable. It's my guess the man's here with a purpose and I'll guess again saying you are that purpose.'

'Why? What does he want? '

'Go ask.'

Chapter Thirteen
Reunion

Asking questions of a desperate drunk hardly seemed the right thing to do, nevertheless, Alex found himself doing exactly that.

'You okay?'

'I'm chipper, thank you for askin'. How's yourself?'

'Better than you'll be in the morning.'

'You're right. It's time I was home. My missus will be worryin'. Whoops!' Bobby lurched against the wall. 'I fear I have imbibed too much of your excellent liquor.'

'You figuring on driving home?'

'I wasn't figurin' on swimmin'.'

'Give me the keys.' Minutes later they were on the Richmond Road, Alex feeling oddly stage-managed but unable to decide who managed whom.

Bobby sat with eyes shut, the purpose of his visit, if there was a purpose, under wraps. Considering the amount of booze he'd put away it was a wonder he could breathe never mind sleep yet drunk or sober he was back to being smart.

Always a fancy dresser, even after a morning at the airfield he'd emerge with manicured nails. The girls adored him. He traded on that adoration, strutting his balls like a cockerel spoiling many a decent girl. He wasn't entirely to blame. His mother taught him to despise women and he learned well. Nowadays, if those girls had a mind they could pay him back by offering a mirror.

'You okay? '

'Chipper.'

'Things all right at home?'

'Wizard. Say, are you ever gonna come and meet Dee? '

'Sure, time and the army permitting.'

'What's wrong with now? You could sleep over. I'll drive you back in the morning. It's not like there's anyone at your place, the General and your Ma staying at Sarah's. I heard 'em say so. Of course if we're not good enough…?'

The Cedars, the Hunter's house on the Green, cannons on the lawn and antique rifles mounted on the bedroom wall, is more a museum than a home.

'I guess I could stay a night.'

'Don't do me any favors.'

The miles passing Bobby slept again and then woke yawning. 'So, what d'you expect to find at our place then, old sport, moonlight and roses? '

'Is there moonlight and roses?'

'You'd better believe it, the brightest moonlight and richest roses. '

'Is your wife a rose-grower?'

'Nah! She likes 'em but hasn't time or patience. Struggling to make ends meet in the old Country made her practical. If she don't grow it we don't eat it.'

'War makes for self-sufficiency.'

'Yeah, but you can take it too far! We got chickens and we got hogs. The idea was to turn 'em into meat and sell 'em. Trouble is she can't bring herself to kill anythin'. So now we got a run full of stringy chickens and pen full of fat hogs.'

Alex laughed but Bobby didn't. 'Crazy, she is. You wait til you see her. You'll think I keep her short of dough. When they first came I kitted them out with the best. She keeps Sophie a princess but dungarees is what she's all about.'

'So who grows roses? '

'Me, they are my passion. '

'How did that come about?' said Alex, smothering a thought, vis-à-vis passion, and assorted Vernas.

'Boredom is how it came about, boredom and gardenin' magazines brought into the hospital! Roses and hospitals? Yes, I'm expert in both.'

'Was it a good hospital?'

'As hospitals go I suppose so but I got no faith in modern medicine. Most medics don't know what they're doin'. As for nurses they're nothing short of gorillas.'

'I thought British nurses were okay.'

'Of course you did! Maybe if you'd been through what I've been through you'd see it different. It's about recognisin' the enemy. When you're in a plane you know him. You can identify the craft and the ensign. Hospital nurses are associated with angels, all the white gear and veils. By the time those angels had finished with me I could've turned a flame-thrower on the lot.'

'It's not been easy for you.'

'Damn right! You know the medics told me I'd less than a year to live?'

'They were wrong.'

'Bet your ass they were wrong!' Words raw as the scars on his face, Bobby sat twisting his wedding ring, as many twists and turns to the ring as to his tale. 'The way those angels maul a man is unbelievable! They walk in and without a by-your-leave do all manner of unmentionable things to your body and soul. When I was first knocked out it took two of them to wipe my ass. I wouldn't want a woman of mine wipin' my ass. I'd sooner put a bullet in my head.'

'What about you?' He turned. 'You still thinkin' on that girl?'

'I'd sooner not talk about it.'

'I understand. I get like that about Dee. She was hurt in an explosion. Somethin' called recurrin' amnesia. Nothin' serious, you know, but faintin' fits and trouble rememberin'.'

'How did you two meet?'

'How did we meet?' There was a pause and almost audible click of a needle falling into a groove. 'She was a nurse at the eye hospital.'

Alex suppressed a sigh. Before the war you could tell when Bobby was lying, his face was a giveaway. Now with the purity of the right, the angelic side, and a sudden switch to the left, the suffering face of Christ, you can only guess.

'Hold on!' He tugged Alex's sleeve. 'That's the road.'

They swung off the highway, the car bouncing down narrow lanes, the smell of the river in the air, darkness closing in and eyes of night creatures shining.

They rounded a corner, pulled in through open gates, and came to a halt.

All was darkness but for a lamp on the porch, the flame a pulsing beacon.

'I love this place.' Bobby wound down a window. 'But I did wrong bringin' her. Back home she knew where she was. Now she's nowhere.'

'Is she homesick?'

'She's crazy.'

'What?'

'The medics reckon she's crazy 'cos she walks and talks in her sleep.'

'Most folks talk in their sleep.'

'Yeah, but do they make conversation with walls? No, she's not crazy, she's as you say homesick. She needs the right kind of home and the right kind of man to be there when things get rough.' Bobby's eyes slued sideways. 'You know, a mean sonofabitch who won't let her get pushed around. Someone like you, Ash.'

Alex recoiled. What the hell? Is this the purpose Maurice talked about? Has he been lured here as a possible minder for a crazy woman?

His reaction must have shown on his face because Bobby grinned. 'Stand easy, soldier,' he said, voice not matching the grin. 'I was only kiddin'.'

It was cramped in the Morgan and heavy with the smell of booze and stale urine.

He got out. 'I'll take a rain check on the visit, if you don't mind, and walk to the Green. It can't be far and I need the air.'

'But why when there's a clean billet here.'

'You don't need me here. You've problems enough. '

'Problems? What do you mean problems?'

'It's not that so much. I don't feel happy about staying.'

'Then go!' Bobby lost his temper. 'Fuck off! Who needs you?' He held out the keys. 'Here, drive yourself home! No need to walk. Me and Dee sweat blood to get this place right. We don't want no Big-shot Colonel favourin' us with his presence.'

His hand shook so the keys rattled. Alex was ashamed. What is he doing? He should be supporting the guy not joining in the general condemnation.

'It's okay, Bobby. Lead on.'

They went in though a side door, bumping into furniture and falling about, Bobby refusing to switch on a light. They ended up bottom of a metal staircase.

'We had the tower made into a suite,' he said. 'Sitting room and shower lower floor and bedroom upstairs. Go get some rest.'

They were about to part when he pressed Alex's hand. 'This time tomorrow you and me will be goin' our separate ways. I just want you to know I did it for the best.'

Too weary to care about the ramblings of a drunk, Alex climbed the stairs, stripped to his shorts, hung his uniform in the closet, set his watch and tumbled into bed.

~

That guy really messed with his head. No sooner did he lie down than he was dreaming of a former haunt, Eastern Berlin, six foot drifts of snow outside the cathedral and inside a choir singing a Bach cantata: '*Komm, Jesu, Komm*!'

More a nightmare than dream, a straggling line of skeleton-thin men and women shuffled down the central nave. Gaunt with threadbare clothes they sang for bread, a carved wooden statue of the Madonna singing with them, a spine-chilling sound issuing from a painted mouth.

Soprano, alto, and base, the melody rose and fell through the frost-chilled air, weaving in and around the columns of what was once a great cathedral.

In the everyday world of wartime Berlin Alex was a US soldier. He was well fed and warmly clad in a wool-lined battledress and heavy army boots. In the dream he was like the rest wearing rags and nothing on his feet but matted socks.

One of a ragtaggle queue he stumbled forward. So hungry he couldn't think he stood head bowed before the statue. The Madonna ladled rice into his bowl but good God, the hand giving out the food was flesh and blood and the voice issuing from the mouth was Adelia's!

He woke with a shout to a child weeping and footsteps passing by his head. A dog scampered by, claws scraping, the circular tower acting as an amplifier.

Then a woman did sing a lullaby - Miss Dee comforting her daughter.

Resigned to a wakeful night he lay listening. It was worth coming if only for the view. Through panes of glass oceans of star-studded skies stretched out forever, and the cream-colored drapes held back by twisted silk were as restrained clouds.

A door led to a metal walkway and fire-escape. A stained glass window, a Tall Ship gliding across an ocean, was set into the door. Moonlight cast shapes on the ceiling. Watching these patterns shift and change Alex felt as if he were aboard the ship drifting on an endless night with stars and with that voice keeping him company.

He envied Bobby. It shamed him to think so. But yes, envied the house, the shining windows and rose-perfumed garden and the daughter and the dog with the scratching claws. Most of all he envied Bobby's passion for his wife.

That voice! It raised every hair on his body, scratching his nerves until he could bear it no more.

'For Chrissakes shut up!' He rose up on his elbow. 'You're killing me!'

The singing stopped.

Amazed that he should behave that way he got out of bed. What is wrong with him that he should yell at the woman for singing in her house!?

It was a clear night with a view of the garden. He leant against the cool glass. How long he stood there he doesn't know, maybe an hour or maybe only a moment.

A flicker of movement caught his eye. A door slammed and a woman came away from the house to stand among the willows, moonlight shining on her face.

Adelia was in the garden.

What?

'Adelia is in the garden.'

Don't be absurd! Logic suppressed the thought.

'I'm telling you Adelia is there in the garden. Look you fool!'

Breath misting the window, he stared. Then he scrubbed at the glass.

No question about it! She was there in the garden!

'It is her! It is! I'd know that face anywhere!'

Boom! He kicked the door open, vaulted the rail and ran down the fire-escape and into the garden.

All was quiet. For an age, heart pounding, he stood on the wet grass listening.

There was nothing.

Of course there was no one! This is the Camera and the voice and the night.

He went back and dressed. A tidy mind observing tidy habits, he stripped the bed and left via the fire-escape instinctively taking the path of the lone phantom.

Moonlight for a guide he trod a well-worn track, the path edged with stones and the shrubs clipped. It was straightforward yet such was his mood he lost his bearings fighting ghosts of yesteryear and the living tangle-wood of today.

He climbed a bank and pushing his way through a wall of thorns stood before a house and tall chimneys with a snake of white smoke.

The moment he saw the house he knew it. Lath and plaster walls, blackened timbers and battered mullions at the windows, he knew it all, even to a rug of clematis and blue wisteria that raced hand-over-scented-hand up the veranda.

Sensing well-known ground the Camera ran amok. With sickening speed a series of pictures flashed through his mind: he was inside the house running from room to room, searching for someone, running, running, and all the while gaining speed until with a cannon boom he slammed to a halt outside an attic door.

'Whoah!'

Shaken by the experience he grabbed at a hedge. Thorns jabbed his skin, a token of the fact he was not dreaming.

He pushed through the hedge and scrambled in via a side door. Moonbeams playing on mouse droppings and the skeleton of a bird, he climbed the main staircase. Up he went, the treads damaged and banister broken into a library where the wall behind the shelves was marked with echoes of a thousand books.

It was dark at the top of the stairs but at the end of a passage a strip of light under a door lured him on.

The door was off the latch. Someone was inside. He felt the silence, heard the bated breath and knew eyes to be watching and waiting.

Gently, he nudged the door. It swung open.

A lamp stood on the windowsill and a fire burned in the grate.

Adelia lay asleep on the floor wrapped in a rug and a pair of strong arms.

Was he surprised to find her there? Surprise was not the first emotion. First there was intense joy. Heart swelling joy, lungs filling and breath catching in his throat!

Thank God she is alive, was the thought.

There followed hurt and a thousand bitter thoughts and feelings.

Unable to speak, a tangle of sound in his head, he stood hearing the echo of a flesh and blood Madonna who sang of a teddy bears' picnic.

This was the face that had haunted him for so long.

Slowly, he became aware of eyes watching and of muscular knees that formed a cradle for a baby to lie in, a blonde baby with an immaculate face.

Adelia had survived the fire. She was here in Virginia not a phantom in a garden or a handful of ash in a Suffolk cemetery. She is a living human being, the General's damsel in distress, Sarah's Miss Dee, and Maurice's Nordic Ice Queen.

This is the dream of many a year.

The nightmare.

The lie!

He turned and walked away.

Chapter Fourteen
Walking Through Walls

Bobby has been invited to a party. 'A drinkin' party,' he said revving the car. 'Guys swapping dirty stories, you wouldn't like it at all.' He came home last night bringing a friend with him, both drunk and falling about downstairs. Biffer barking woke Sophie, and then would you believe the friend told Adelia to shut-up!

Furious, she was tempted to kick the door down but thought of the nonsense that would inevitably follow and went to see Gabriel instead.

They made love. She slept in his arms and dreamt she was in the Mill, drifting through the tower walls as they were butter. Walls and floor shining with brilliant light, the turret room never looked like this when she's awake. She seemed to be part of the light and yet at the same time mortal, able to breathe, to hear the tick of a watch, and see Bobby's friend asleep in the bed.

Whoever he is he had a gun under the pillow, the butt glittering in the moonlight. He talked in his sleep. 'Help me, Joe. I can't breathe.' She came closer and he said her name. Startled, she woke and rushed back home to take Biffer for a walk, returning head clear and armed for the day.

Bobby had already left. There was a note on the kitchen table. *'Had a call from the club, trouble with fuel lines. Give my regrets to the Colonel.'*

Fuel-line my eye! He's done what he always does when needing to escape, invoked the flying club. Now she must suffer Alex Hunter alone.

She sped about scrambling eggs and brewing coffee. Then, hallelujah, May appeared. 'Thank goodness you're here. We've visitors.'

May grunted. 'So I heard.'

Sophie ran into the kitchen. 'Mummy, there's a man in the tower with ribbons on his jacket.'

'Is there indeed.'

She ran back up the stairs. 'I'll ask for a piece of the blue ribbon for Coco.' 'Sophie!' Adelia called. 'Don't bother our guest!' Then she thought, damn it, let her go, see how Colonel Bogey feels when his peace is disturbed.

Bright sunlight woke Alex. A little girl in striped pjs stood by the bed a toy monkey under her arm. A chocolate-box beauty with cupid's-bow mouth and pale translucent skin she pointed to his jacket. 'Has your mummy any more of that?' she said of the Medal ribbon. 'Coco's awfully fond of blue ribbon with stars.'

'Sorry, honey,' he said dully, 'that's all there is.'

Head in his hands he sat at the side of the bed. God, what a night, his world juddering to a halt! Such a shock, yet he managed to get outside the house before vomiting his disappointed dreams into nearby bushes.

He tried walking away. Pride said forget it! You don't belong here. Get the next plane out! But a greater part of Alex, a backbone that would not bend, wasn't going anywhere. Back he went to the Mill and like goddamn Rapunzel climbed the tower to sleep and wake to a child with eyes as blue as the ribbon.

'Ugh!' He stumbled to the bathroom throwing up again.

Sophie followed. 'Shall I go get Mummy? She looks after me when I'm ill.'

'No.'

'Daddy's gone away. He said to say sorry.'

'I bet he did.'

'Were you drunk last night?'

'I can't speak for your daddy but I was stone cold sober.' At the bathroom door he barred her way. 'I'm going to shower. Better cut along to your mammy.'

Icy water drummed on his thick scull. What in God's name is this about? Years he's carried that torch and all the while she's right here under the family nose.

Man, is he a fool! Here was he thinking her spirit protected him through the war, bringing him through the flames and gunfire of Anzio, sharing a makeshift pillow with rats and lice, and all the while....!?

Years he carried this cross believing he was responsible for her death and what has he to show for it, a sham wedding ring and Judas for a friend.

'Hello Mister Soldier!'

The shower curtain was twitched aside. Sophie shimmied out her pjs and got under the shower with him squealing as the cold water hit her tiny frame.

'I don't think so.' He put her outside the shower.

'But I always get in the bath with Mummy.'

'I'm not your mammy.'

Teeth chattering, she stood waiting. Yielding to a determined child he wrapped her in a towel and sat her on a linen basket while he dressed.

Off she went, prattling. 'I know who you are,' she said. 'I saw you at the drive-in movies. You wore a hat and rode a white horse and Mummy said look! There's Roy Rodgers alias Alex Hunter.'

'Is that right?'

'Uh-huh. And the other day in the library choosing a book she said how about Tom Thumb? It will make a change from Alexander the Great.'

'Chrissakes, Adelia!' he muttered. 'Why didn't you just take my pistol and shoot me when you had the chance?'

Sophie was off the linen basket drying his feet. 'You've got thick feet.'

'I know,' he said, 'they go with my thick brain.'

'Gabriel's got thick feet.'

'And who exactly is Gabriel?'

'He's my friend. He plants people in boxes, covers them with flowers, sings a song and off they go to Jesus.'

That took some working out. Hah! He thought, sourly. Adelia's having an affair with an undertaker. How Gothic is that!

The kiddy began running in a tight circle, puffing and panting, her face red and cheeks blown out. 'I want big legs,' she said, 'then I can run and run.'

'Hey now!' He picked her up. 'Take it easy.'

She sagged, heart pattering, against his chest. 'I know why you're here.'

'You do?'

'Uh-huh. You've come to take me and Mummy away. '

'What!'

'Mummy told Daddy you'd take us away one day and then he'd be happy.'

Alex set her down on the floor. He didn't know what she was talking about and wasn't going to try. It's some new hell of Baby Rourke's making.

And you know kids, they get stuff muddled.

'It's none of my goddamn business anyway.'

'Ooh! 'She slapped her hands over her mouth. 'You mustn't swear! Mummy will smack you. It doesn't hurt! It only hurts when Nana Ruby does it.'

'Your grandmother beats you?'

'Uh-huh, "spare the rod, and spoil the child."'

Alex was disgusted, a bible-thumping bully for grandma, a drunk for a father and mother having sex with the local he-man? What kind of life is that for a child?

A sharp rap on the door sent them springing apart.

'You in there, Sophie Challoner?' a homespun voice enquired. 'Because if you are, and you ain't out in two shakes, I'm comin' in to get you.'

Sophie fled.

He took a clean shirt from the bag, the khaki not unlike the man, stiff with starch, a smooth line and no unsightly bulges. Shirt pockets pressed flat, house and lockers keys about his neck with dog tags, cigarette case and lighter in the right breast pocket of his jacket and wallet and pen in the left. The jacket snug and the pants a second skin a belt was superfluous. As sister Sarah likes to point out, his pants are too damn scared to fall down.

He looked in the mirror trying to see what she'd see. He has changed, the war took care of that, yet likes to think he is a cultured man, good to his family and kind to waifs and strays. As for looks, six three, two hundred and ten pounds, plus a few scars and a twisted knee, he is still pretty much the man she swore to love.

He took a card from his wallet, wrote a couple of lines propping it and a twenty dollar bill behind the mirror. The twenty is for a cracked pane in the door, the business card a bitter hope she might feel the need to get in touch.

An inch long rip in the sleeve from last night, he zipped his jacket into the bag. A last glance in the mirror then he ran downstairs following the smell of coffee.

A deep breath at the kitchen door and he is inside.

~

Sunlight flooded the kitchen spotlighting a yellow tablecloth and vase of Morning Glories. No sign of Adelia. The homespun voice belonged to a middle-aged woman at the stove. 'The Missis sends her apology, a hog due to drop her litter. You're to get started on your breakfast. Eat hearty. There's plenty.'

A loaded plate was slapped on the table. He pushed food about the plate.

'You from these parts, Mrs...?'

'The name's May Templar. I help out here a couple of mornin's a week. My boy has business in town that takes his time, but when he ain't there, he's here.'

'What business is that?'

'Valley Rest Funeral Parlour.'

Sensing a loose lip, he probed. 'Worked here long?'

'Long enough. Me and Delia have our differences but I like her, which is as well 'cos she don't get help from no place else. Know Ruby Cropper, do you?'

'Not socially.'

The help was unhappy, spitting out words like they burned her mouth.

'She's Delia's ma-in-law, not that she's any kind of mother to anyone. Ruby's the one caught Bucky Rourke. Him and me were real cozy until she comes swingin' her hips. He never wed her, gave his money but not his name. She's hopin' her son will die and she'll get her hands on the cash. Comin' home rat-assed every night we'd all do better if he did.'

May Templar spat on an iron. 'Don't know why she puts up with it. Ain't many women willin' to look after a grown baby. He's handy with his fists. Never lays a hand on Sophie. She'd skin him alive if he so much as breathed on her.'

Alex pushed back the chair. 'The sty, you say?'

It was a cloudless day vapor trails crisscrossing in the sky. Maybe yesterday's friend rides those trails, the guy with a pig's bladder for a face and dark glasses protecting his lying eyes.

Alex is working himself into a rage. Years of loving the woman and feeling responsible for her death mingled with bitter loathing for Bobby.

He marched down the path. Rounding the corner of a shed a dog came at him, paws covered with grime. 'Stay back, ' he said, trying to dodge it.

'Gabriel?' A voice called from inside the shed, a voice heard last night the same tight English vowels. 'Gabriel, is that you?'

'Negative.' His voice stuck in his throat. 'Alexander Hunter.'

'Oh!' There was a profound silence. When she spoke again there was an edge to her voice. 'I'm sorry you were disturbed last night. Sophie had a nightmare and you know how it is with children they see bogeymen everywhere. I'd love to chat but am tied up at the moment. Shame! I was looking forward to hearing of your exploits. Never mind! Another time perhaps? Safe journey!'

A dismissal? Getting his marching orders? No Goddamn way!

A couple of minutes later she called out. 'I can hear you, Biffer. If you're doing something you shouldn't you're in trouble.'

Still Alex held tight, every muscle locked in defiance.

'Damn that dog, and damn Colonel Bogey!' Shapely backside first, she backed out of the shed. 'Him and his negative! Why can't he say no like everyone else?'

Color flooded her cheeks. 'Oh, you're still here. Sorry about that. I thought you were Gabriel. I sent my daughter to find him but no joy.'

Alex lost patience with the dog. 'Get down I say!' he bawled, the shout echoing about the garden. Down went the dog like a stone.

'That's pretty impressive,' she said, untying a scarf that bound her hair. 'I imagine you get a similar reaction on the parade ground.'

Dumb as the dog at his feet he stared. Such a face you'd never forget, high cheekbones, eyebrows like dark arrows winging upward, her nose straight and elegant, a Botticelli angel couldn't be lovelier. The climate suited her, giving her skin a creamy tan and her eyes bitter-mint green in contrast. Her hair was darker than before, the Virginia sun streaking it with silver. Instead of the shoulder-length bob she once favored it now runs a natural course tumbling about her face in unrestrained glory. There was the same delicate bone-structure, same fragile wrists, tapering fingers and narrow waist, yet her body had ripened, the dungarees and sleeveless vest accentuating long legs and high full breasts.

Inner strength in every line, her feet in battered work boots and resolve in every muscle and fiber, she stood her ground.

A blackbird darted between them. Blossom fell on his head. He waited for her to fling her arms about him and apologize. He got nothing. No shame. No guilt.

'Well, Colonel?' she said dryly. 'Are things as expected?'

'Excuse me?' he said, cut to the quick by the scorn in her voice.

'You were staring.'

This composure was too much. He leaned over her. 'Bobby not around?' he said bitingly. 'Cut and run has he like the scheming liar he is?'

Eyes suddenly wary, she asked, 'what has he done?'

'What has he done? You ask me what he's done!'

She shrugged. 'I can see you're angry but I don't know why.'

Incensed, he spun in a circle. 'All this time and she doesn't know why!'

Pale now, she held up a hand. 'Sorry but you must take this up with Bobby. I haven't time to worry about it.' She was away crawling back into the shed. 'I've a sow dying in here. If I don't do something I'll lose the piglets.'

Alex had choices. He could walk away and never see her again or stay and learn why. Hand-made boots in the mire, he stepped over the fence and through the opening. When he appeared on the other side she rolled her eyes.

'What are you doing?'

'I thought I might be of use.'

'But you're covered in muck! Look at your trousers!'

'Pants can be cleaned.' He peered into the gloom, piglets on a bed of straw, the sow in extremis blood issuing from her hindquarters. 'What's the problem?'

'One is stuck in the birth canal.'

'What can I do?'

'Well…' She hesitated. 'There's a hot-water bottle under the straw. You could empty it into a bowl and bathe those that are weak.'

Five of the piglets were strong rooting for a teat. The rest struggled.

He immersed them in the water. She talked to the sow, 'Come on, Hilda, old girl. Let me take your little baby away then you can have a bowl of porridge.'

Aware of her so close, Alex became two men, Colonel Bogey, as she called him, rigid with offence, and the other man – the soft underbelly - the guy who'd called her sweetheart hurt so much he wanted to weep.

There was movement outside, the dog barking. The undertaker had arrived.

Gabriel Templar crawled through the opening. 'What's happenin'?'

'She's gone and the piglet too,' said Adelia.

'Move over. Let me try.'

'I've got it.' She drew back, her lap drenched in blood and a tattered mass in her hand. 'Do what you can for Hilda.'

She left, scrambling from the sty.

He watched her go. 'Is she okay?'

No reply.

Alex took in the shoulders and rippling muscle where vest and pants parted company. Templar wore his hair long yet jeans washed to a velvet pile, and with good boots under a rim of dirt had the hallmarks of a soldier.

'You were in the Marine Corps.'

Templar swung round.' What's it to you?'

Whoah! Startled by the loathing in his eyes, Alex asked, 'do I know you?'

'No, nor likely to. '

'You're uncivil.'

'And you're not wanted! Sooner you clear out the better.'

The message was double-barreled, straight from the hip. Adelia's belligerence was born of guilt; this man's resentment was up close and personal.

'What is your problem?'

'You're my problem, army, mine and everyone else's!'

'How so? Until today I didn't know you-all existed. '

'Maybe not but we sure knew you did.'

Eyes red and face scrubbed, Adelia returned. 'Will you take her?' she said to Templar. 'Give the hams to Mrs Sparrow. I couldn't eat them.'

Wiping her nose on the back of her hand, a gesture so like her daughter, she turned to Alex. 'I've asked May to run you a bath. You and Gabriel are about the same size. I'm sure he has things that would fit until you can make other arrangements.'

'Don't trouble. I've spare in my bag.'

'You'll stay for lunch.'

'No thanks.' He was about to walk when the Camera fired, recollection of last night and Bobby talking of a crazy woman.

He skidded to a halt. She was talking, apologizing for sins Bobby might have committed. Alex tuned her out and last night in: '...*hurt in an explosion. Some condition called recurrin' amnesia. Nothin' serious, faintin' fits and trouble rememberin'.*'

Fainting fits and trouble remembering? Jesu, he thought, she doesn't know me!

'Do stay.' Her voice faded in again. 'If only to make Sophie feel better.'

The sun warm on his head, the day was suddenly glorious. Doffing his hat he offered his hand. 'Colonel Alexander Hunter, US Army, at your service.'

Bemused, she stared, and then took his hand, sunlight glinting on the ring he gave. His fingers closed about hers. Warm flesh and blood is under his hand.

She is alive! And so he can live.

Chapter Fifteen
Scarlet Chiffon

Lunch was an awkward affair.

Sophie was upset and leaned on his knee. 'Why did Hilda have to die?'

'She was old, I guess.'

'Coco is old, ' she said, hugging the toy monkey. 'I don't want him to die.

'Coco can't die.' Fresh pair of dungarees crackling, Adelia came into the room. 'He's a toy monkey and therefore immortal.'

'Is Daddy immortal?' said Sophie stroking the monkey's face.

'No, darling. He only thinks he is. Cream, Colonel?'

'Thank you.' He accepted the cup, his ring chinking against her ring.

Alex was seeing all with fresh eyes, how dependent they were on one another, how the child nestled into mother and mother to the child.

'Bobby said you'd been ill. He mentioned an explosion in '42?'

'I was caught in an air-raid.'

'He said there were complications.'

She smiled a tight smile. 'You must have had quite a chat.'

'You preferred me not to know?'

'You and Bobby are friends. I thought he might've told you.'

Her glance flickered over him. 'Sophie? Get mummy's sewing box. And while you're there sort out a pretty shade of wool for Daddy's cardigan.'

She waited until the child had left. 'What is it you want to know?'

'What happened that night?'

'I couldn't tell you.'

'You don't know.'

'I don't remember.'

'You don't know how you got out?'

'I was unconscious. I woke in St Faiths with a lump back of my scull. I believe a fireman pulled me out but the fire and preceding day are a mystery.'

'That must be difficult to live with.'

'It has its moments.'

'Do you remember anything at all of that night?'

'I get the odd flashback. '

'Of people you were with?'

'There was someone but I know as little of him as I do this tiresome illness.'

It was hard keeping quiet but with so little information at hand Alex could only keep to safe ground. 'What do medics say?'

'The standard reply to any question is, given time the situation should resolve itself. I hate it when they say that, sounds like I'm holding onto the thing.'

'And are you?'

Her eyes flashed. 'You've obviously never seen anyone in the throes of this. If you had, you wouldn't ask such a question.'

Sophie returned with the workbox and then returned to lean on Alex's knee.

'Sophie likes you.'

'The feeling's mutual.'

'Pass your jacket. I'll mend the sleeve.'

Tormented, he laid his cheek on the kiddy's curls. Help me, little Sophie, he prayed, tell me what to do. Seeking inspiration he gazed about the room, his glance alighting on yet another photograph of him. 'What's with the photographs?'

'That's Bobby's none-too-subtle form of brainwashing. You're his hero and he wants you to be mine.'

'You're kidding!'

She bit the cotton on the reel. 'I am not.'

'No wonder you're abrasive.'

'Am I abrasive? I'm sorry. You deserve better whatever Bobby's intention.'

The telephone rang, his sister on the other end. A short chat and then Adelia returned to her seat. 'We had a luncheon date at your house today.'

'Did you know I was Sarah's brother?'

'I had worked that out.'

'Bobby didn't tell you?' The deception burned.

'He thought you were dead.'

'I thought so myself. You had a dinner date with my mother?'

'And the General but with all the pig business I forgot.'

- 221 -

The General passed over for a pig! Alex couldn't help smiling.

'You find that amusing?'

'Well, you know, the General and all.'

'It's not at all amusing. Unless you've lived with it you can have no idea.'

'Then tell me!'

'I couldn't possibly. I don't know you.' She passed the jacket. 'It's not the best, but it'll hold. Perhaps you'd like me to phone for a taxi?'

The chat over, he is being shown the door.

Sophie was asleep on his lap. Adelia took her from him. 'You have remarkable eyes, Colonel, so like Sophie's. It's all right,' she said smiling. 'I lay no charge at your door. You can't help it if you share the same color eyes as her father.'

'Excuse me?'

'Bobby didn't tell you?'

'Tell me what?'

'He isn't Sophie's daddy.' She took the child for a nap leaving him stunned.

~

Twenty minutes later she was back. 'Bobby tells everyone we're married and that Sophie is his even when they know it's not so. Strange, I thought he'd told you.'

'There's a lot he hasn't told me.'

She blushed. 'And with good reason if your reaction is anything to go by!'

'No,' he said, feelingly. 'It's not that you and Baby aren't married, it's…!'

'Don't call him that!' She cut him short. 'He's a man not a child.'

There was a rap at the door, Gabriel Templar with a basket of logs.

Alex was on fire, every nerve twitching. He wanted to grab her and ask about Sophie's father. Sunlight flashed on a photograph frame and he knew.

'Jesu!' Delight and anguish combined, a roar broke from his lips.

When she stared he grabbed her hand. 'You're right! I am every bit Colonel Bogey! I have to be not to make the connection. But it was his lies that threw me!'

'Lies?' She snatched away. 'If by that you mean his little fabrications I'll tell you what I tell his mother, Bobby's untruths hurt no-one but Bobby.'

'A lie told to cheat and steal is a hell of a lot more than a fabrication!'

'Would that we all had such a clear set of rules.'

'Rules help keep a man alive!'

Adelia clenched her fists. This man and his infernal questioning, why is he here? And where is Bobby when she needs him? Come to that, where is Gabriel?

Gabriel sits in the window mending a rein. Sophie has switched camps and is for the Colonel. It can't be helped. A handsome, educated man in a uniform that hints of danger he is everything a child would admire. In contrast, Gabriel is a proud and prickly individual. Local people said he quit the Corps because he's a coward. He's no coward. He knows how to save life and when to end it.

'Last spring I found a hare in a trap,' she said. 'It was crying. Gabriel stopped it. He is the bravest man I know.'

There was silence. Looking up she encountered the Colonel's gaze. She dropped a spoon and picking it up bumped heads with him and was stopped by his eyes.

'Your eyes,' she whispered. 'They're so like…'

She swayed. 'No,' she whispered.

'What it is?' said Alex. 'What's happening?'

She was falling. He bent to catch her but Templar beat him to it.

Gabriel carried her to the window seat and leaning back began to sing. It happened so fast and was dealt with so calmly you wouldn't think a woman fainted only that she took a nap. Sunlight shone through the windows creating a halo about Templar's head, the two taking on the perfection of a Rodin pieta.

Minutes ticked away until Alex could bear no more. It was the look in Templar's eyes, so proprietary. He leapt to his feet burning to silence the singing.

'Try it,' Templar drawled. 'It won't be easy. I'm no half blind cripple.'

'Keep talking like that and you will be.'

'Okay, we can take this further but you'd do better waitin' until she's back and with her daughter…or should I say your daughter.'

Alex didn't ask how he'd figured it out. 'You may think you know something,' he whispered, 'but you know nothing.'

'I know all I need to know. You're the sonofabitch left her to die.'

'Keep your voice down! I don't want her finding out this way.'

'You don't want her findin' out period!'

'She needs to know but at the right time and in the right place.

'I wouldn't be talkin' if she could hear. The only way she'll find out is if you tell her. Are you gonna?'

'I don't know. You must do what I've had to do all these years, wait and see.'

'Wait and see what, an army jackass playin' with a man's feelin's?'

'Depends on the man and his feelings.'

'There can't be stronger than mine. My heart aches for her. It ain't the only part.'

'Don't speak that way!' Alex was incensed. 'Don't even breathe in an offensive manner while she's unable to defend herself!'

'You got some nerve talkin' about offensive after what you did.'

'I did nothing I could help! When the hotel went up I was blown down to the pavement. By the time I came round the girl I loved was burnt to a crisp.'

'She weren't burned.'

'I know that now. I was told she was dead,' said Alex bitterly. 'A friend told me.'

Templar got it. 'He told you she was dead? How could he do that?'

'You tell me.'

Templar sat chewing over the new information. Then he stared away out of the window. 'This sickness is dangerous. She needs help.'

'And she'll get help.'

'Look out! She's wakin'.'

Adelia's lashes were fluttering. Within seconds she was shaking violently, and then with a hoarse cry was on her feet and running.

'Sit tight,' said Templar. 'She'll bathe, change her clothes, maybe put on a fancy dress. It's a sufferin' thing. The first thing you gotta do is learn to suffer quietly.'

Upstairs the tortuous sounds of retching continued. Alex went to the stairs. 'One day I'll maybe see you in a different light but now I can only feel contempt for what's gone on in this house. Bobby Rourke will answer to me. You can bow out.'

'And if I don't?'

'You will. It's as you said. She needs help and I'm the man to give it.'

~

Adelia hung over the lavatory pan, and then, damn it all if *he* was beside her scooping her hair away from her face holding her taut against him.

Slowly nausea passed. She sat on the side of the bath, Alex Hunter wiping her face with a towel. 'I'm afraid you find me unwell,' she croaked.

'How often do you feel this way?'

'I've lost count.' She waved him away. 'Please go. I'm finding this very difficult.'

Left alone she showered and cleaned her teeth and then sat at the dressing table. The sun was shining but she was chilled to the bone. With each wave of ice-cold nausea there was a sense of the walls exhaling and the décor changing with every breath. Conscious of Sophie next door she began to dress.

She opened the closet trailing her hand over the hangers.

Such clothes! It was a pity she never wears them.

A red chiffon gown hangs at the back of the closet. A fanciful thing, sequined bodice and Ostrich feathers, it is more a Burlesque show than a barbeque on the lawn. To wear it well a woman needs to believe in herself. Adelia believes in nothing yet will wear it. A woman needs armor when going into battle.

She made for the stairs.

'What the hell...?' Alex stared. A fabulous woman strolled down the stairs, a showgirl, scarlet high-heeled slippers on her feet and diamonds in her ears.

'Oh hello,' she says, extending her hand. 'You must be Alexander Hunter. Bobby said you might be dropping by. Welcome to the Mill.'

A bolt shot through his heart. What is happening?

Fingertips trembling like the fronds of a sea anemone she gave him her hand.

It was icy cold.

'Have you eaten?' she said.

'I had dinner.'

'Good. That means more time for talking.' She drew him down on the sofa beside her. 'Did you have a good journey? Sophie and I came via the Edmund B, seven days of pitching and tossing. I would imagine it is much smoother by plane.'

In all his time in Special Ops Alex had never come across a situation like this. He didn't know how to handle it. No use looking to the coiled spring in the window seat, one eye on Adelia and the other on the stairs, but then he doesn't want help. Only by being in the thick of it can he know what he's up against.

'You're perhaps referring to the plane ride back from Berlin?'

'Was it Berlin? I thought you were in London, well, Suffolk, actually.'

The hair on his head sprang to attention. 'You thought I was in Suffolk?'

'Yes, though I don't know why. Bobby said you phoned from London.'

She was searching through a fog looking for data. He could help by simplifying.

'I did phone. I called to wish you-all a happy Easter.'

'Ah yes, that's it. So you've been home some time?'

'Couple of months.' She went to withdraw her hand but he held on. 'I do know Suffolk. I spent a day there once. It is a pretty county.'

'Isn't it?' Her face lit up. 'My aunt had a cottage there. You could sit by the window and watch the seasons pass.' She grimaced. 'That's if you could scrape ice off the glass in winter and paw prints in summer! Maud lived for animals.' Freeing her hand, she ran her fingers through her hair, silken fronds flickering. Then she smiled. 'It's good to see you, Colonel. You don't know how I've longed to meet you.'

Well, he thought, smiling back, if this is lunacy I'll have it on ice.

She leaned forward. 'It is you, isn't it?' she whispered. 'You are the one I see in my dreams, the blue-eyed soldier with a friend called Joe?'

'Joe?'

'Joe Petowski. He died in a ditch.'

'Indeed he did.' Electrified, he waited.

'I tried to help but it was too late.' Like a child, lashes like feathers on her cheek, she crept closer. 'Have you come to take us away?' she asked still whispering.

Whispering in response, he gripped her hand tighter. 'If that's what it takes.'

'I knew it,' she said eyes glowing. 'I said to Bobby, keep on like this, keep trying for top dollar and one of these days he'll come and I'll say okay!'

Confused and hurt, he retreated along the sofa. 'You're unwell. You need to rest.'

Beauty fled from her face. 'I've embarrassed you. I'm so sorry.'

'Gabriel!' She was on her feet, color draining from her face. 'Help me!'

Long fingers dug in his shoulder. 'Leave her be, Colonel.'

A soldier yielding to experience, he released her.

'Step away, honey,' Gabriel said. A marionette jerked by a string she stepped back from the sofa. Alex had time to wonder at the brightness of her eyes before she crumpled and was caught. 'Has she fainted again?' he said.

'What d'you mean again?' Gabriel bore her away. 'She ain't woke from the last one.'

~

Adelia was happy. Diamonds in her ears and hair secured by sparkling combs she sat at a dressing table applying a rich, red lipstick to her lips. 'Voila!' She smiled and a stranger smiled back, a woman with lips like cherries and skin like satin.

Sophie sat on the bed watching.

'How do I look?' said Adelia, twitching the bodice a shade lower.

'Like a movie-star.'

'Excellent!' She dabbed the perfume stopper between her breasts and behind Sophie's ears. They tangoed about the room: "*Pardon me boys! Is this the Chattanooga choo-choo, track twenty-nine…*'

Sophie giggled. 'It is you, isn't it, Mummy?'

'Of course! Who else would I be?'

Minutes later, or so it seemed to Adelia, she heard her daughter say her prayers, switched off the light, and gathering her skirts floated downstairs.

Colonel Bogey was leaning against the fireplace, a strained look on his handsome face. For a second she was tempted to jump into bed with Sophie but good manners will out. 'Colonel Hunter,' she put on her best smile. 'Welcome to the Mill.'

There was an awkward pause while he tugged on his tie and then her hand was taken and gently pressed. 'I'm glad to be here.'

The lamps were lit. The table had been cleared. Sophie's jigsaw was out.

Gabriel sat in the window-seat mending a leather rein.

'Gabriel!' Relief more powerful than any drug spread through her bones. She ran to him. 'Thank God you're here. I thought I'd have to suffer that awful bore on my own.'

He frowned, his eyes sending out a warning.

'What?' Her hands were rigid. 'Did I say something I shouldn't?'

Gabriel was pale, his lips chapped from working outdoors. She took a pot of cream and smoothed it on his lips. 'Have I ever said you've the most kissable lips?'

'Uh-huh,' he carried on mending. 'Lots o' times.'

'And how right am I.'

Colonel Bogey was still by the fireplace. 'Are your lips chapped, Colonel.'

'I don't know.'

'Lean down.' He leaned. She smoothed cream into his lips. 'Better?' His breast rose and fell in a great sigh. 'You poor thing! You look worn out. Have you been fed?'

'I ate earlier.'

'I see you're wearing a ring. Are you married?'

'There was someone.' He lifted his hands. '...but the war.'

'I know,' she sighed. 'It does that, breaks people apart before they've started.'

The record on the gramophone was running down. She sifted through the rest.

'Here's a lovely one.' She put it on the turntable. Music filled the room, Adelia singing along: *"I'll be loving you always, with a love that's true, always, when the things we plan need a helping hand..."* Do you know this song, Colonel?'

'I heard it once in Suffolk in a hotel called The Black Swan.'

'The Black Swan? I know it well.' She spun away. 'Care to dance, Gabriel?'

'Not right now.'

'Gabriel's a wonderful dancer. I caught him one night boogying away on his own thinking no one could see him. Isn't that right, Sergeant Templar?'

'Uh-huh.'

'Would you care to dance, Colonel?'

They circled the floor, Alex giving her bare feet a wide berth. Poor fellow can't dance. I'm pushing a barrow with square wheels. And so sad! Pain oozing from every pore! 'Your family must be pleased to have you home. Are you here to stay?'

'My plans are dependent on another.'

'Have you a place of your own in Virginia?'

'No, but I'm on the lookout. I've seen a place back of the woods, run-down but with distinct possibilities.'

'You don't mean the Eyrie? That's a wonderful house. It's completely out of the way and perfect for a hush-hush job like yours.'

'Hush-hush?'

'Bobby says you're a spy.'

'Bobby exaggerates.'

'But you do carry a gun and you don't need a gun to be a twitcher.'

'Twitcher! How do you know I like to watch birds?'

'Didn't you tell me?'

'Not in the last twenty-four hours I didn't.'

Adelia thought she'd been dancing with the Colonel for a minute or two. It's longer than that. When they first circled the room the clock showed five-thirty. It was now ten past eleven. She is stuck in a repetitive nightmare, a fugue, *'characterized by the systematic initiation of a principal theme.'* A somnambulist, she wanders downstairs, dances and sings and then passes out only to wake again.

So it went on, a needle in a groove. Gabriel Templar had seen it all before. For Alex it was like losing her again. 'Wouldn't you like to rest?'

'I'd love to,' she panted. 'But don't know how.'

Overcome, he pressed her hand to his lips.

'Oh!' she exclaimed at the scars on his palm. 'What happened to your hand?'

'I tried leaping a burning staircase.'

'Why ever did you do that?'

'Someone I loved was trapped in a fire.'

Eyes solemn, she nodded. 'You would do that, a man like you. Was she saved?'

'Yes, thank God.'

'It's a nasty scar. I have a scar at the back of my head.'

'Kiddies, let's not compare scars.' Bobby was at the door. 'I'm bound to win.'

Bang! The fragile peace exploded.

'He…hello Bobby,' Adelia stuttered. 'We were just talking about you.'

'Who's we, you and the dancin' fool or Gabe left out in the cold?'

'Okay.' Gabriel was on his feet. 'We all know what's goin' on here so let's take it nice and easy. It's delicate china we're handling' not toughened steel.'

'Holy Christ!' Bobby shook his head. 'I wish I'd had you for nurse when I was missin' my eye. Talk about dedicated, you'd have fixed me up in no time.'

'All I'm sayin' is there's no need for hollering' and fightin'.'

'It's okay, pal,' Bobby patted his arm. 'I know exactly what you're sayin'! 'Greater love hath no man than he lay down the love of his life for an enemy."

'What's the matter?' said Adelia.

'Nothin'. Everything's chipper, ain't it, Colonel?'

'Adelia?' Alex cut him dead. 'May I give this number to my service?'

'Of course.'

He strode out and she left gazing after him.

Bobby went to the bottom of the stairs. 'Scramble, princess!' he shouted.

There was the patter of feet on the landing. Sophie hurtled down the stairs and into his arms. They lay on the sofa, the child clasped to his chest as treasure trove.

He gazed at Adelia. 'Look at you done up like a dog's dinner! Who's it for this time, General Patton out there or a dozen other guys I've yet to hear about?'

So much anger and so much noise, she couldn't answer. There was something she needed to tell Bobby. It was about the Colonel. But the words wouldn't form in her mouth, so instead she told of Hilda.

'We lost Hilda today.'

He shoved Sophie aside. 'What d'you mean *lost*? Hilda was a hog. You don't *lose* a hog. You *lose* your maiden aunt.
'

'Sophie and I were fond of her.'

'I dare say but it's a crazy way to talk. Next you'll be saying we've lost a chicken, or a couple of ducks off the pond, or....'

'Coco?' offered Sophie, trying to be helpful.

'That's right, honey! Coco the Clown!' He grabbed the toy monkey pantomiming a funeral slow-march. 'Roll out the hearse, Gabe! We'll go into mourning, black armbands and veil. Maybe have a fly-past, me and the boys from the club in arrow formation. We could get General Patton out there providin' an escort. Eight of the nation's finest accompanyin' the coffin. Just think of it, a solitary bugler up on the hill playing taps...'

Sophie burst into tears.' I don't want Coco to die.'

Adelia's vision cleared. Time and space fused. Suffolk and heroes dying in ditches vanished, only her child's tears and crazy Dee Challoner dressed as a tart remained.

~

She sat on the stairs. Gabriel sat with her. 'Sophie's sleeping.'

'She's okay. No need to worry.'

Ashamed of the gown and cleavage like the Cheddar Gorge she hugged the toy monkey to her chest. 'Was I very bad?'

'You were fine.'

'Look at my feet? And my nails! And there's mud on my dress.'

'You were lookin' out for the piglets.'

Gabriel was mending horse tackle, plaiting leather reins, his long fingers flicking back and forth. Watching those hands Adelia felt a love so deep and wide it couldn't be silenced. 'Gabriel, I want to tell you something very important and I want to tell you now while I've the nerve.'

'No.'

'I must! Please let me, because if I don't tell you now I may never.'

'I don't wanna hear.'

'But Gabriel!'

'No!'

Choking back a sob she ran out through the French windows. Gabriel watched her go. Then there was Bobby beside him breathing whisky in his face.

'Fool! Why didn't you let her say what was on her mind?'

'She didn't know what she was sayin'.'

'The hell she didn't!'

'She don't need to say what's on her mind.'

'No, but you do!'

'I got nothin' to say.'

'Liar! You got everythin' to say! Moon and June and the whole sweet sufferin' mess! And what's more you gotta say it now before the big guns move in.'

'What are you doin'?'

'I'm tryin' to give you advice. I know that man out there on the phone. He's a bulldog. Once he gets his teeth into somethin' he'll die sooner than let go.'

'Why are you tellin' me this? When you went out the door this mornin' you hated my guts. What's brought a change?'

'I haven't changed. I still hate your guts. I hate his more.'

'You are one sick critter.'

'Maybe I am,' Bobby snarled. 'But I ain't the one wastin' time while the woman I adores is out there howlin' at the moon.'

Gabriel picked up the twine. 'There's a time to fight and a time to let go.'

'Maybe, but now ain't it, not while army britches has the bit between his teeth!'

'I got no rights over her.'

'Only the right of the man who loves and is loved back! He left her to die!'

'Maybe he did. Maybe he didn't.'

'I'm tellin' you he left her! I know. I was there! Go seek and destroy!'

'I can't. I might destroy her.'

Bobby turned away. 'You're gonna regret this, Gabe. They say pride comes before a fall. Well, by God, your pride is gonna make you fall!'

~

She was sitting on an upturned bucket when he found her.

Alex took off his jacket and hung it about her shoulders.

She gazed at the sty. 'Where do you think we go when we die?'

'It's not anything I think about.'

'I suppose you being a soldier you can't afford to.'

He upturned another bucket. 'Maybe not, but it doesn't stop me believing in a power greater than ourselves.'

'There has to be something, because if this is all there is then it's nonsense. And all those wonderful things, pigs and people, are so much smoke in the air.'

'It wouldn't make sense.'

'I'm sorry about earlier,' she said. 'Sorry you had to see me make a fool of myself and the people I love. I don't do it on purpose.'

'I never thought you did. But you can't leave it. You must take advice, even if it's only a word with my brother-in-law, Maurice Parker.'

'I mended this,' she said, drawing his jacket about her shoulders. 'Arguments with your best friend and running repairs from a crazy woman, what a home-coming!'

'You're not crazy.'

'And Bobby? Is he still your best friend?'

'No ma'am, and before you ask I can't tell you why.'

'How correct you are, Colonel, and how certain! I wish I had your certainty.'

'Appearances can be deceptive. Right now the only thing I'm certain of is that you and Sophie are in need of protection and that I am committed to that protection.'

She turned to look at him. 'Why are you?'

There was nothing he could say. The situation is complex. Now is not the time for another bomb to be dropped on the Challoner household.

Adelia sighed. 'It's all right. You don't have to explain. I'm sure you have honorable reasons for wanting to help...and we do need somebody.'

He took her hand. 'Then let me be that somebody!' Her hand lay limp within his grasp. She doesn't like me, he thought, sadly. She thinks I'm a boring old fart.

'No,' she said, divining his thought. 'I think you're wonderful.' So saying she gently kissed the scarred palm. She then placed the jacket on his lap and went inside.

He sat for an age reliving the touch of her lips. Maybe there is a chance, he thought. Maybe I can go in and say, 'I am Sophie's father. The man who loves you.'

All was quiet in the house. He climbed the stairs. He would speak to Adelia in the morning but first he wanted to take another look at his own flesh and blood.

Sophie! His child! How her Nana and Gramps are going to love her!

Sophie's bedroom was along the corridor, the door slightly ajar. He pushed and the door swung open. She was asleep and so was Adelia, her arms about her daughter.

They were not alone. Bobby was with them.

Showered and changed into sweater and pants, hair wet and face pale, he lay with his arms about them both.

The right side of his face so young and vulnerable, it was a shock seeing him like that.

Alex closed his eyes. What did he know of their life? He's only scratched the surface. Looking at them now he sees that despite problems they had love for one another. They are a family. The fact that he is Sophie's natural father carries no real weight. He is an outsider.

Opening his eyes he found Bobby watching. Silently and purposefully Bobby held his gaze. Then he closed his eyes shutting Alex, and the world, out.

Chapter Sixteen
Big Guns

Adelia was packing bottled pears into her basket. 'Can you collect Sophie from ballet class this evening?'

Bobby frowned. 'I thought May was doin' it?'

'She can't make it. Oh, and while you're at it better pencil in the next concert date. They're doing 'Midsummer Night's Dream' and Sophie's a fairy.'

'Not that tin hut again! Those kiddy seats gave me hell last Christmas.'

'You didn't go last Christmas.'

'You're right. I did the Easter thing.' Bobby grinned. 'Say, do you remember that fat ginger-haired kid gettin' fouled up in the curtains? '

'Do I? I was mortified you laughing at the poor child.'

'Poor child nothin'! Sophie can't abide her. She says she's a drogue.'

'Well, she shouldn't. And what is that word drogue?'

'It's a dummy used for target practice, a worthless piece of trash anyone can take potshots at. It goes by the name of Baby Rourke.'

Adelia carried on filling the basket. He might be bent on a fight but it's Mission day today, no time for petulance.

'Did you hear what I said?'

'I heard.' A feeling of suffocation came over her. 'Why d'you do this? Why tear us to pieces? We had an agreement. We were to care for each other, share what we had but as free people not prisoners!'

'You're not a free woman. You're the local axe-man's moll.'

'Axe-man? Any more labels you'd like to pin on your best friend?'

'Who you talkin' about? Not Hunter, I hope! Some friend he turned out to be, throwin' his weight around tellin' me and Gabe what to do.'

'It was Gabriel I meant.'

'Him my best friend?' Bobby snorted. 'The guy pokin' my wife!'

'Will you stop that? I am not your wife and never will be! For heaven's sake, Bobby...!' She ground to a halt. He looked terrible. 'What's the matter?'

'Me and Dutton from Aviation had a set-to. The jumped-up little creep had the nerve to say I was a danger to myself and whoever I carry.'

'And are you?'

'I'm a better pilot with one eye than most other Johnnies flittin' about this 'burg!'

'If you say you're safe to fly then you are. I have every confidence in you.'

'You do?' He rested his forehead on hers. 'Why can't you be like other women and marry me for my money? You could do whatever you wanted. It's not like you're goin' to be saddled with me for long. We both know there's a time-limit on my ass.'

The door was open. Biffer played with a grape, tossing it in the air and catching it without making a dent in the skin. It was a lovely day, too lovely for sorrow.

She took his hand. 'Come to bed.'

It's not difficult making love to Bobby. All you have to do was look beyond the outer covering. Hands oiled, she sat astride him working down the long planes of his back trying to put life into his body. So thin, buttocks wasted, bones sticking through. 'Don't go out tonight. Stay home and I'll make us a slap-up meal.'

'Fine.' He rolled over. 'Meantime make a meal of this.' There was nothing to make a meal of, only loose skin and white knuckles clutching the blanket.

She put every ounce of feeling into it. It was no use. The more she tried the more he clutched the blanket. Then, oh God, a tear slipped from under his eyelid.

'Don't cry.' She hugged him tight. 'It's not the end of the world.'

'It is if the hospital is right. They reckon this time next year I'll be blind.'

'I thought you crying over sex!'

'What sex?' He laughed through his tears. 'I gave up on that months ago.'

'Then why the fuss about me and Gabriel?'

'Because you're not about sex, you're about love.'

'I love you.'

'You don't. You *care* for me but you love Gabe and fancy Ash Hunter.'

'I don't understand you!' She pulled on a sweater. 'One day I've spent in Alex Hunter's company. You can't fall in love in a day!'

Bobby sat up. 'I never said you were in love with him. I said you were in love with Gabe. But wait a minute! Maybe I got it wrong. Maybe it is him.'

'Oh, don't do this! Don't make a thing of him.'

He pushed off the bed. 'I'm makin' a thing of nothin'. I've just realized where me and Gabe Templar have stood all these years, bottom of the pile.'

~

When the hearse pulled into the yard Adelia ignored it. Yesterday May said she wouldn't be returning to the Mill nor would she be taking Sophie to kindergarten. No explanation, never mind how Sophie felt, she took off her apron and left. And she isn't the only difficult one. Gabriel hasn't been near the house in days.

People can be so rude, Alex Hunter a case in point, sneaking off last week without a word and leaving a twenty-dollar tip! It was a pity because until then he had surpassed Bobby's endorsement. Tall, dark, and severely handsome, even when caught up in messy domestic affairs he remained courteous. Shame, and shame again!

'Mornin'. Gabriel rapped on the door. 'Any chance of a cup of coffee?'

'Depends if you're in a better mood. That other miserable character, your friend, Bobby, went out earlier with a face like thunder.'

'He ain't my friend.'

'You seemed pretty friendly last week.'

'That's him throwin' a smoke-screen.'

'Smoke screen! If you want coffee you'll have to help yourself. It's Mission day.'

'Wanna lift?'

They drove in silence, Gabriel watching the roadside for injured animals.

'Where've you been this last week?'

He shrugged. 'No place particular.'

'Just staying away?'

A sure sign he is irritated, he clicked his tongue yet still said nothing.

Adelia closed her eyes. Last night she had a dream. A regular item from Cloud-Cuckoo-land she was dressed in black underwear, a hat on her head and pearls about her neck. In the dream she was about to step into a frock when a door slammed. She woke knowing she was dressing for a funeral.

She yawned and Gabriel, ever prescient, said, 'nightmares again?'

'Yes, the Merry Widow.'

'Maybe it's tellin' you somethin'. '

Adelia doesn't know what it was telling only that it comes when she is afraid. Last night she woke to find Bobby crouched over the bed, the clock's luminous dial reflected in his eyes. She feigned sleep until he slipped away into the darkness. She lay listening, and then slept and dreamt of funerals.

~

The Mission was a shack on the outskirts of town where local women gathered to sell homegrown produce. Adelia took bottled pears, two-dozen eggs, and a dozen posies of flowers. Bobby is scathing about her efforts. 'You can't make more than ten dollars.' He doesn't understand ten dollars earned is better than twenty given.

She set her basket by Emilee and Matilda March, elderly spinsters who live in Taft House and bake delicious cakes. Business was brisk, ladies leaving early to hear a new preacher.

Adelia doesn't attend church; many of the sermons seemed to be aimed directly at her. Most of the town's people are amiable but the Mill is a cause of gossip. The one with the most to say is Ruby. She comes on Mission days, her last port of call jelly donuts from the Miss Marches. Today she is waiting to pounce on Adelia.

'Did you know Baby's seein' his lawyer? I said he should be thinkin' on meeting his Maker and not talkin' to lawyers.'

'I'm sure that gave him comfort.'

'Don't get smart with me, sister,' she hissed, 'you're runnin' out of allies. May Templar's given notice and from what I hear her son's not far behind. Not that he'll stay away, a dog stays close to its vomit.'

'You are disgusting.'

'It ain't me that's disgustin'. Had your fill of a murderer you move on to richer pickin's in that army feller. And him Bobby's best friend! Ain't you got no pride? Are your appetites so vile you need another dancin' on your coat-tails?'

Adelia shoved the basket on the bike. Ruby followed. 'That's it run away! Sooner or later the General's son is gonna know you for the two-bit tramp you are.'

Furious, Adelia pedaled down the road. 'What did Bobby do to deserve a mother like you?' She paused at the drug store to get her breath back. A soldier the size of a barrage balloon sailed out the real-estate office to a sedan parked on the other side of the square. The soldier opened the door, Alex Hunter emerged.

Buttons sparkling, he crossed the road and doffed his cap. 'I left a card at your place thanking you for your hospitality. Forgive the delay. I was out of the country.'

'That's perfectly all right. Do call again. We...Sophie...will be pleased to see you.'

He nodded, replaced his cap, and left. Adelia gazed after him. That's all very well, Colonel, but what was the twenty dollars for, a seat at the Burlesque Show?

~

The latest lipsticks are in the store. Adelia was trying a sample when a sultry voice breathed in her ear. 'That soldier-boy you were talkin' to earlier? Is he the one bought the Eyrie?'

Bought the Eyrie! Adelia made her way to the house. Gabriel's worked all his life with that in mind. He will be so disappointed. She got there in time to see a real-estate board hammered into the ground and padlocks applied to doors.

Gabriel stood by the gate.

'I am so sorry,' she said.

'Don't matter.'

'You wanted it.'

'There are a lot of things I want. Don't mean I'm gonna get them.'

Locked out again she could only stand by. The man is as much a mystery now as when she arrived in Virginia. Though May has talked of her violent husband Gabriel never mentions that time. Adelia never asks. Murderer or not he is kind, people bringing sick animals to him to be made well.

He's not the easiest person. Prickly as a porcupine he lives behind a wall of silence.

Not so long ago he broke through the wall and was happy.

Now the wall is higher and deeper than ever.

'I would imagine the new owner will treat the house well,' said Adelia.

'You think so.'

'He seems a decent sort of person, don't you think.'

'He's sure got you foxed!'

'Why are you so angry?'

'Why are you so blind?'

~

Gabriel watched her walk away that day with a sick feeling in his gut. It's all over between them, couldn't be otherwise with Hunter about. Handmade boots and meticulous cuffs, he's met his type before. Career soldiers married to the military they are regular ball-busters who'd sooner break than bend.

That morning in the pig sty, if Gabe had had his way he'd have plucked the knife from his boot and stuck it in his neck. Why did it happen? Things were good until he arrived. Now events are moving fast, work at the Eyrie, new floors and windows. A pool being dug and a sister of Hunter's seen about town spending money.

Money means nothing to the Eyrie. If the house doesn't like you, it won't let you in. Records lost in the Civil War nobody knows when it was built. Amy Parfitt, the oldest resident of Fredericksburg, says it's a copy of a house in England, timber hauled across the Atlantic years ago. She reckons the Mill was built the same time, timber coming thousands of miles and bringing bad luck with it.

Gabriel knows nothing about bad luck. The house was his sanctuary for years. There are watchers in the Eyrie, glistening things that come out at night, faded shreds of another time with memories of their own. One thing is certain, if those watchers don't take to you, Colonel or gravedigger, you are not welcome.

He's got a planting today. The Valley Rest emporium was left to Gabe when he was in the State Pen, a gift from old man Smith.

It was Hodge Templar got him working there many years ago. Spooked as any highly-strung stallion, eight-years old and rubbing down coffins, he feared what he would find. He found nothing but empty bodies. There's no more need to be afraid of an empty body than there is of a spider shriveled under glass.

Simeon Salmanovitz taught him the business, showed the difference in wood, silky blonde Beech, slippery Elm and durable Oak. He taught the tools of the trade, the chisels and planes and the powders and paint. At ten Gabe knew how to embalm a body and paint a face giving a glow to cheeks sallow in life.

On planting days he rode on the box behind the horses or played mute, pacing alongside the wagon, his tow-colored hair in a black velvet bow.

Years have rolled by but he's still the mute and the things he's learned, Pa, Charlie Whitefeather, the Corps, silver creeping things in the Eyrie, Bobby and Adelia, they all come down to one certainty, there's more to life than living.

'Giddup!' With a lurch the hearse started out, plumes on the horse's heads nodding. Gabe is pernickety about the rig, don't matter that only the empty pockets use Valley Rest, there's style in the rig, a swish of wheels and hooves clip-clopping along the road. As the wagon rolls out so mourners fall in behind, men and women in dusty clothes all knowing they will take the same journey one day. Today it has Lemuel on the box, tiny for his age, and Hiram, his father, an Eastern prince. By the time they reach town they've attracted a following.

Approaching the cemetery a jeep whizzed from out a side-road, Sophie sitting beside an old army type on her way home from school. The old guy popped a respectful salute, his grizzled face suddenly young and handsome.

Gabriel recognized him as General Hunter. It's as Bobby said, big guns are being hauled onto the field; divide and conquer, for where the child goes the mother will follow.

~

'Don't worry,' said Sarah, picking mud off her heels. 'The General may be clumsy with people but he's wonderful with children and horses.'

Adelia filled the kettle. 'Whatever he's got it works for Sophie.'

'I used to be like her. I couldn't wait to get a hug from those arms but the medals always got in the way.' She stared round the kitchen. 'This is real homely. Do you-all congregate here or is this your private bolt-hole?'

'We start out in other rooms but tend to gravitate here.'

'They say the kitchen is the heart of the house.'

'So I believe. Will you excuse me a minute? I need to change into shoes.'

Trying not to rush Adelia went through to the garden room to pull off her muddy boots. Why is Sarah Parker here? What does she want?

Two-thirty and a toot of a horn, Sarah in a bright blue coupe and her father in a jeep. 'Hello there!' she called. 'We were passing and thought to drop by.'

Mizz Parker is always immaculately turned out. Sophie is an ardent admirer of her and her boys and stands before the mirror combing her fringe a la Sarah and cooing over Davy's eyes, as for the General he's the teddy bear she always wanted to hug.

While not exactly friends they have formed a tentative acquaintance. Adelia likes Sarah. She is a kind woman with a strong sense of justice. Patron of the hospital with her father she's the engine behind the drive for modernization.

She's more than once offered Adelia a job. 'Stuck out there with only pigs to talk to it's not civilised! Get Bobby to buy you a car. Mobility is freedom!'

'Good of the General to collect Sophie.'

'Pa's a real softie. He's desperate for someone to spoil, and though he loves the boys they were never at the spoiling age.'

'I appreciate his kindness.'

'How is Bobby?'

It wasn't the first time Sarah had asked after him. Adelia suspects she once cared for him and for that matter still does. 'He thinks he's going to die.'

'Is there nothing to be done?'

'There is something,' said Adelia. 'The Aviation authorities can let him keep the airfield. Bobby was born to fly. Grounded, he'll die.'

~

Bobby does think of dying but right now is in no particular hurry and spends the afternoon lying on a strange bed while a strange woman blows his dick.

He was looking at the ceiling watching a spider spin a web. The window is open. A breeze blows and rattles the web. The spider drops. Up it goes, whoops, down again. Up and down, it is a real trooper, much like the whore blowing his dick.

'Any luck, girl?' He patted her head. 'Anythin' stirrin' in the undergrowth?'

She shrugged and carried on blowing. He was reminded of Adelia. Not that she blows him! He wouldn't let her. Down there with that stink, I don't think so!

The sight of Dee in bed will get him all fired-up, the spirit willing but flesh not so. Any attempt usually ends with his tongue locked into her pussy. She has trouble with the big O but again, like the spider and the whore, she tries. Sometimes it happens, toes dug in the sheets, but silent, every feeling drilled through those toes.

That's okay. He is happy for her and soothed by her good intentions, but Jesus God, he'd be a darn sight happier if he could push his hands under her butt and poke her with something a whole lot stiffer than good intentions.

Bobby is scared, and not just for himself. Two years in Virginia and Dee's no better. If you could chart the ups and downs you'd see she was worse. The fainting fits and sleepwalking, her talking into thin air and laughing with ghosts, a shrink seeing that and she'd be in a straitjacket on route to the Eastern State.

Adelia Challoner is walking-on-the-wild-side crazy! It's a nice kind of crazy, gentle and sweet, the kind that does no one harm. That's how Bobby sees it and he should know with a ringside seat for every show. She wouldn't hurt that spider let alone her daughter but the people that run this shitty world don't recognize harmless.

If they knew her, if they lived within her warmth they'd scramble to be close. She's a budding angel, kindness personified. Witness the pigs she can't sell and chickens she can't kill, then there's taters and beans and all else that springs from under her hand. The Mill that shines and glitters because she makes it so! As for Gabe, thanks to her the not-so-dumb Dummy can read and write.

And what of Bobby Rourke? But for her he'd have long since bought the farm. The way he mistreats his body, the booze and the whores, by rights he should've rode in Gabe's crystal wagon months ago. The Big question is this, who's gonna take care of the carer when he finally climbs the Stairway to Heaven?

That spider up on the ceiling is waiting for his supper. So is Hunter.

The day Bobby went to Sarah's party he was scared. Consultations with surgeons had long since marked his card, the renal unit saying that with a liver the size and texture of Stilton cheese he had the life expectancy of a squid.

That day he began to weave a web of his own luring Hunter to the Mill. He didn't expect it to work. It was a whim, a hope that if he brought them together then the tragedy of '42 could be undone.

The plan worked but not for Bobby. Go figure! Earlier today Dee accused him of not recognizing a friend. He laughed when she said it but it got him thinking. Some folks believe what goes around, comes around. God knows what he did to deserve Ruby for mother. In '45 he was a mess, hand-to-mouth and drunk every night. You'd think she woulda pitched in. Nah! It was Gabe. Not only did he fetch Bobby from the Hawaiian Bar he cleaned up his shit. It was he who slaved to get the cottage right and it's him always at the Mill. He is the guardian angel they all run to.

Well, it's payback time. Yesterday Bobby went to see his lawyer and there arranged to throw a Grade a Platinum-coated spanner into the works. Like the spider he wove an intricate web of his own and if it goes as it should then life in Fredericksburg is never going to be the same.

'So, you see, little spider,' he gazed up at the ceiling. 'It ain't only the Lord as moves in mysterious ways. It's Baby Rourke.'

The whore lifted her head. 'You say somethin'?'

'No, my dear. I was talkin' to the spider.'

The whore returned to her ministrations.

Hello! His eyes flashed open. Something is stirring in the undergrowth! The whore, bless her britches, has worked a miracle! Turned on by the idea of throwing a spanner into the military works, his cock is crowing for all its worth.

Cock-a-Doodle Do!

~

Gabriel came to the Eyrie. The attic is as he and Adelia left it, the remains of a fire in the grate and an oil-lamp on the ledge. He lit the lamp, a signal to say he is waiting. Pushing wide the window he leaned out. A million stars swung in the sky, the whole of heaven spread out in a sequined blanket. Crickets leapt in the wet grass, flowers exhaled and the Eyrie called his name, 'Gabriel! Gabriel!' Something big and soft and silver flitted across the sky, an owl lofting up into the Cypress Tree.

It was on a night like this Pa died. Gabe came home to find Ma hurt. His fist wound back and flew. He went to jail. Were it not for a war he'd still be there.

Were it not for Adelia he'd still be in the Corps.

The other day he was thinking about that. Nobody liked anybody on Pariss Island. When you're told you're a useless, dumb cunt of a kid twenty-four hours a day what is there to like. One day the kicking stopped.

The Gunnery Sergeant kept a Pinto, half pony, half donkey, back of the mess. It hung its head over the wire hollering. Gunny was about to put a gun to it. It was scared, eyes rolling. But Gabe put his fist into its mouth and pulled the stump. It quit crying. Baby Rourke is like that Pinto 'cept there's not a fist big enough to twist the rotten stump out of his head. God could do it but He needs to move fast because the guy is losing it and Adelia asking for a bolt on the cottage door.

This was yesterday. 'You want a bolt on the door?'

She carried on dragging the kiddy's bed into her room. 'Sophie was cold in the night so I thought I'd move her in with me.'

Gabriel fixed her with a clear eye.

'Don't look at me like that,' she said. 'I know what I'm doing.'

Afraid of what Bobby might do Gabe stayed away from the Eyrie. He didn't want to add fire to fire, but tonight driven by need set the lamp in the window.

It doesn't pay to look back on their loving. If getting his ashes hauled is all it was he could've stayed in the Corps. Girls will do anything for a Marine, undo your flies with their tongues, lift your peter out, stick a finger up your ass and sing a chorus of My Old Kentucky Home without removing their bubble-gum.

Sex with Adelia was straightforward and fast, her guilty feelings in the driving seat.

Was it love? He knows what he feels but couldn't answer for her. What was said in the heat of passion is lost in the day.

He stood still. She was behind him, breathless, her eyes as big as owl's.

'You've been runnin'.'

'Yes.' She laughed a stumbling kind of laugh.' Not running so much as talking.'

'Talkin' to who?'

'General Hunter and his daughter.'

'Was he there?' he said, both of them knowing who he meant.

Arms hugging her breast, she stood by the fire. 'He's away on Army business. Not that I asked. His father volunteered the information.

'Ask what you like. I don't care!'

'Why are you like this? If this is about Bobby's flattering nonsense you can forget that. He hasn't a good word for his former friend. He says he always suspected him of being an arrogant s.o.b. and now he's certain.'

'He is arrogant.'

'I didn't get that impression.'

'You've changed your tune. Not so long ago you were sick of the sound of his name. Seems to me you're no better than Bobby. You're both fickle as flies.'

They stood looking at one another, her bosom rising and falling. Gabriel reached out. Flattening his palm about the back of her neck he pulled her toward him.

'Don't yell at me,' he said softly.

'I'm not yelling.'

He silenced her with his mouth. 'You've been paintin',' he said against her lips, taking hold of the collar of her coat pulling it down her shoulders.

'How do you know?' she whispered.

'You got white spirit in your hair.'

He stripped, kicking his denims across the room. Her coat slithered to the floor, her nightgown following. She was in his arms.

'Is this the end of you and me?' he demanded. 'Is he gonna come between us?'

Honest to a goddamn fault she said. 'I don't know.'

Chapter Seventeen
Cuckoo

Alex was caving in the Allegheny Mountains. It was a deep system, unstable, a difficult climb at any time but for a man who loathed confined spaces doubly so. Even now the thought of being stuck in a lift brought him to the edge of panic. Which is why, abhorring personal weakness, he put himself through this.

They have been out most of the day and were on the return journey, his partner belayed at the lip of a shaft and Alex ascending a ladder. It was late. There had been frequent rock-falls. As a result the air was foul and getting more so, Jamie Macintyre singing filthy rugby football songs while breaking malodorous wind.

'Chrissakes, Jamie! What have you been eating?'

Macintyre laughed, light from his helmet bobbing.' That'll be last night's curry sauce. It was so hot I could've dried my socks on it.'

Captain James Macintyre, DSC and bar, crazy Aussie, coal black eyes and stomach like a washboard, was interned during the war. Digging tunnels by night and playing football over the tunnels by day he was a maverick none could tame. A genius with wires and a fuse he blew himself out of the camp into Special Ops.

'Hey, Camera! What's with you and the blonde Sheila?'

'Blonde Sheila?'

'I saw you talking to her last week.'

'There is no blonde Sheila.'

'Sure there is. I saw your face, you were a goner, and I heard you ordering flowers. Hope you're doing more than buying flower because you're not getting any younger. You don't want to...Whoah! Look out below!'

A great flake of rock broke away from the lip. It slid down the port side knocking Alex off the ladder. He fell, the lifeline screaming through the karabiner coming to a violent stop to hang upside down entangled in the ladder.

'You all right?' yelled Macintyre.

He was far from all right. A hot pain in his chest and difficulty breathing suggested broken ribs. It wasn't a long climb back. Had Alex been less tired he'd have made short work of it but by the time he was over the lip he was exhausted.

That night in the emergency room he could barely keep his eyes open. Three months have come and gone since he bought the Eyrie. While the asking price was covered by Pappy Frobisher's legacy the bills keep coming and so not wanting to hire men for every job he moved in. Stripped to his skivvies in the summer heat, a blowtorch in one hand and hammer in the other, he cleared lofts, lagged pipes and plastered ceilings.

A grueling schedule, he would leave the Academy at 1800 hours, arrive at the Eyrie around 1900, work, sleep, and be back on the road by 0700.

It is taking its toll. In class yesterday, twenty pairs of eyes following a pointer, he stopped mid-sentence, a fog where his brain used to be. Saturday perched on a ladder cleaning a hand-painted ceiling he slept where he sat, waking to the smell of burning and a cigarette scorching the new wood-block floor.

The house is jinxed. Everything that can go wrong goes wrong. Moronic workmen did more damage in one day than centuries of wind and rain. One fell through the roof bringing the chimney down in the process while another left a tap running. Damage to the yard is sacrilege, a spruce hacked down and a greater part of the wisteria ripped from the wall.

It wouldn't be so bad if someone appreciated his efforts. There's only a cat brought out of the rain. The Eyrie his ass! He's a military Cuckoo putting time and effort into a nest that doesn't want him while dreaming of a mate that doesn't like him. Talks between the Mill and the Eyrie are at a standstill. Conscious of doing damage he stays away. The General is not the most diplomatic of men. If he thought Sophie his granddaughter there'd be no holding him. Anyway, Alex doesn't need his father lousing things up. He is doing okay on his own.

Last week he wired his boss for need-to-know on Templar. What came back sent him racing to the Mill. Adelia answered the door. He didn't beat about the bush. 'Did you know Templar spent time in the penitentiary for murder?'

'Yes.'

'And it didn't worry you?'

'His father was a drunk. He beat his wife and his son.'

'That's no excuse for murder.'

'I doubt Gabriel was looking for an excuse.'

Alex knew he was being an ass but couldn't stop; he said Sophie shouldn't mix with the likes of Templar. Eyes blazing, she went for him. 'Bobby knows who he is. It was he suggested Gabriel collect her from kindergarten. If Sophie mixing with Gabriel doesn't worry the man that gives us shelter why should it worry you?'

Not satisfied, Alex called on his driver, Frank Bates, an old and valued friend, to lend a hand. As of today the friend will be picking up the slack.

~

Gabriel is running late. The furnace that fires the ovens was choked with silt. He stayed to clear it. As a result he is late collecting Sophie from school.

He loves the kid. She is so bright. Gabriel likes jigsaw puzzles. She likes them too, the more complicated the better. A favorite is the 'Battleship Potemkin.'

You'd think a Marine might have an advantage but no, she knows every piece. Same with playing cards, she'll be shouting snap before you've turned the card. Adelia let him in on the secret. 'It's her memory. She's memorized the wrinkles and blots back of the cards.'

Bright and loving is Sophie, but not as loving as she used to be. She has new friends, the General, his wife and his daughter chief among them.

Traffic heavy, he arrives at the school to see a sedan pulling away with Sophie in the back. Tyres shrieking, he spun the wheel, broad-siding the sedan.

'Where you goin' with that kiddy?'

The sedan was flying an army pennant. The driver in service greens wound down the window. 'I'm taking Miss Sophie home.'

Gabriel pulled on the door but it was locked. 'Get out, Sophie!'

The driver reached back a hand the size of an anvil. 'Stay put young lady. My orders are to see you safely home. Hanging about a laundry chute ain't safe.'

'I was late,' said Gabriel. 'I got stuck in traffic.'

The driver wound up the window, adjusted his shades, and drove away. 'That's your problem, son. Not mine.'

~

The last of the furniture was delivered to the Eyrie, Sarah, Maurice and the boys helping out. 'The chandeliers look great,' said Sarah. 'Which reminds me, how about the following Saturday for housewarming? Check the diary, Maurice!'

Maurice was admiring the view. 'This is bliss.'

'Expensive bliss,' said Alex.

'Even so, I'd swap Georgetown for it.'

'And live in the middle of nowhere!' said Sarah. 'You'd be bored silly.'

'No,' said Maurice, 'you'd be bored silly.'

'Cooee!' Alex's mother came through the Orangery, and the General, trim in fatigues and forage cap behind her. 'My goodness! You have been busy.'

'Some view!' said the General. 'I shouldn't wonder if this isn't premium land.'

'Say!' He unhooked the field glasses and stood scanning the terrain. 'There's Miss Dee and Sophie yonder picking apples!' He took off. 'Give me a shout if I'm needed. I'm going to say howdy to your neighbors.'

It was late afternoon when he returned. He wasn't alone.

They were coming by the pond, ducks taking off in a flurry of wings, Sophie running ahead, sneakers twinkling, and the General escorting Adelia.

Sarah coughed. 'Don't look now but we've company.'

'My, isn't she something!' murmured Ellen Hunter. 'Look at the Pre-Raphaelite hair! And the carriage! You'd think she had a poker down her back. You can see why Bobby wants the world to think they are married.'

'Well they're not. She doesn't go into details but doesn't lie about it either,'

'So what is their relationship about?'

Sarah shrugged. 'I don't know, sufferance maybe, sufferance and obligation.'

'Sounds to me like the average marriage.'

'Hush! Here's Sophie.'

Sophie ran into Mrs Hunter's arms.' Are you coming to see my ballet?'

'And what ballet is that, sweetie-pie? '

'It's at the school. I'm to be Mustard Seed. Mummy's made me a bumblebee costume with wings and antennae. Will you come?'

'We'll see what Mummy says. 'Adelia? What about this ballet?'

'It's not so much a ballet as amateur dramatics.' Adelia hadn't wanted to come but the General would insist. 'Sophie is a fairy.'

'What about us old folks?' The General swept Sophie into his arms. 'Do we get to watch this little fairy do her stuff?'

'It's very small beans, General, just a piano and babies in tights.'

'Sounds cute to me. Don't you think it sounds cute, Sarah?'

'It is cute. I've seen rehearsals.' Sarah took Adelia's arm. 'Someone here I'm not sure you've met? Alex, the grim looking male in the rainbow colored war-paint, is my brother.'

Adelia didn't want to see him. Coming round to the house digging ancient dirt, how dare he? But then he pulled out of the water, naked but for a pair of shorts, drops of sunlit water highlighting the bruises on his upper torso.

'He's been hurt.'

'Yes, the idiot fell down a hole.'

'Excuse me.'

Vaguely aware of Sarah's surprise she set out across the grass.

The moment was picked out in colors, everything known, water splashing in a pool and the hum of a generator, the sun on her face and the need to beside him. All so very familiar. 'What have you done?'

'I took a fall.'

'Those bruises look painful.' She reached out and was surprised by the warmth of his skin when she is so very cold. When he flinched she said sorry. Then he grabbed her hand crushing her fingers. She could only stare. 'Bobby thinks you're a fraud. That you're not who you say you are.'

'Come.' Bypassing curious stares he steered her round the pool.

'What about Sophie?'

'Sophie's with her adoring public. It's you we should be thinking about.'

He ushered her into the Orangery and closed the door.

Aware of shining wood-block floors and fresh paint and simple lines, 'you've made it all so beautiful,' she said. 'The Eyrie must be delighted.'

He laughed a bark of wry amusement. 'You'd think so. Do take a seat. I'll throw on some clothes and arrange for my mother to look after Sophie.'

Adelia sat on the sofa. The Mill is a dangerous place. It's a relief to get away, Bobby gone missing for days on end returning gaunt and forlorn.

The warmth of the Eyrie reached out to enclose her. She kicked off her sandals and curled up on the sofa. She heard Alex come in, heard the chink of cup on a saucer and a cat purring.

She gazed at a fat tabby. 'You have a cat?'

'This is Willow. I found him in the garbage pail. Are you feeling better?'

'What did you say to Sophie?'

'I didn't get a chance to say anything. Sarah's taken them to the movies.'

He leaned against the door. Adelia regarded him under her lashes. The last time they met he was angry, face a tight mask. Now, on his own territory in jeans and bare feet he is younger and infinitely more dangerous.

'I need to speak to you about Sophie,' he said.

'Why do you?'

'I told you I was committed to your protection. Do your recall that?'

She nodded.

'My work requires me to be readily available. I can't be as close as I would like and so I've enlisted help. Frank Bates is a friend. He'll keep an eye on Sophie.'

'No need. I take Sophie to school in the morning Gabriel brings her back.'

'Frank will take up the slack.'

'There is no slack,' she said hackles rising. 'I admit it's tricky and conflicts with work but I've no reason, or desire, to change the arrangement.'

'His prison record should give a reason.'

'Gabriel is a good man. I trust him with my life.' She fumbled with the clasps on her sandals. 'I must go. Bobby will be home and I need to be there.'

'Let me help.' He knelt fastening the buckles, holding onto her ankle the warmth of his hands passing through her body. Adelia tried not to look, the resentment she felt that settled resin-like about her heart when he criticized Gabriel melting.

Desperate, she said, 'your girl would love what you've done to the house.'

'I did it for her but then everything I do is for her. '

'You must have loved her very much. '

'I was mad about her! I still am.'

Mad about her! The impassioned words rang about the Orangery. He moved closer. 'Adelia?' He took her hand. 'Do you recall that evening in the garden?'

Speechless, she nodded.

'I feel that kiss. It burns me. There isn't a place on my body where that kiss is not. It's here!' Using her hand he touched her throat. 'And here.' He flattened her hand over her breast. 'And here!' He laid her hand on her lap, heat scorching back. Then he carried her hand to her mouth. 'It's here,' he whispered, prizing her lips apart, moving closer until his mouth was only a breath away.

'Don't!' she pulled back.

They were thus, a frozen tableau, when a rap on the window sent her reeling.

'You gonna leave me on the doorstep all night?' Bobby was at the window. Palms either side his face and wounded cheek a flattened mass, he stared through the glass. 'What's this tea-and-sympathy with the neighbors? You tellin' folks what an unhappy gal you are and what a sonofabitch old Bobby is?'

'Alex was helping me with my sandals.'

'Oh, it's Alex now is it?' he sneered. 'What happened to Colonel Bogey? Same as happened to Mister Templar I suppose, gone with a change of wind?'

Alex leapt forward. 'Get out of my house!'

'I ain't in your house, old sport. I'm in the garden.'

'Get out! I can't have you within fifty feet of me and mine!'

Adelia headed toward the door. 'Let's go, Bobby.'

Arms folded, he leant against the glass. 'I'm stopping where I am. Orderin' me about like a servant! Who does he think he is?'

She pulled him away.

'Okay, I am going, but I'll be back,' he yelled. 'You think you hold the aces but you don't. Possession is nine tenths of the law, buddy, and don't you forget it!'

~

Back at the house he turned on her. 'Were you discussing me back there?'

'Of course not!'

'Of course not!' he mimicked. 'Why discuss me when you've better things to say, like how much is the price of beans and how it feels to be fucked by a prick!'

'We were talking about May leaving and me getting to work.'

'May left because she couldn't stand to see what you were doin' to her boy.'

'Oh hush! Sophie will be home soon. We don't want her walking in on a row.'

'She won't care. I'm nothin' to her. She calls me daddy but it's words.'

'Sophie loves you and would love you even if she knew the true situation.'

'And what is the true situation with you and Hunter?'

'There is no me and Hunter. He offered the use of a car and a driver.'

'Like hell that's gonna happen! Bad enough when the blond idiot chauffeured you around! Be dammed if I'll let the next in line make a fool of me.'

He picked up the phone and dialed. 'Superintendent, please.'

'What are you doing?''

'I'm phonin' the children's home. Hello Superintendent? This is Captain Rourke callin' to say my wife won't be comin' any more. She's been overdoin' it and with her psychiatric problems it's not the best idea. You didn't know? Oh, yeah, nothing too dreadful, a bang on the head during the war but we can't take chances. Yes, I'll give her your best. Good day to you!' He slammed the phone down. 'Now you don't have to worry about work, because you don't have any.'

Adelia was distraught. 'How could you!'

'I'm not finished.' He got into the car, started the engine and drove back and forth over the bicycle. 'There you go! No work. No bike.'

She flew at him. He slapped her and Biffer growled.

'Hey!' Bobby cuffed the dog. 'Snarl at me and I'll have your hide for garters!'

'Leave him be!' She tried pushing Bobby away.

He slammed her against the wall. 'Don't you push me! I've had it with people trying to shove me around.' He slapped her again and Biffer launched into the air, hitting Bobby on the chest bearing him back into the water barrel.

'Mummy!' Sophie was at the gate.

'Back off!' The General hauled Biffer away. 'We don't want no rabid dog doing harm.'

'He's not rabid!' said Adelia. 'He was trying to help me.'

'Okay!' Bobby set the barrel upright. 'Drama over! Everybody settle down.'

The General stared. 'What were you doing that the dog turned on you?'

'He didn't turn on me. We were foolin' around, weren't we, Biff?'

The dog hunkered down.

'Come here, boy! It's okay.'

The dog crept forward to lick Bobby's hand.

'See!' said Bobby. 'No problem.

'Keep an eye on it. We don't want it turning on Sophie.' The General turned his back on Bobby. 'Miss Dee, you and Sophie should spend time with us. I was only saying to my wife, it's time we got to know you better. Maybe introduce you to our friends, show you the other side of Virginia.'

Bobby took offence. 'What d'you mean other side, blue collar versus white?'

'Take it how you like.'

'Let's go.' Sarah took the General's arm. 'We came to ask if Sophie might stay overnight. It's vacation and the boys would love to have her.'

'What about ballet class?' Adelia asked.

'We'll take her. I'm sure you could use the break.'

Bobby pushed forward. 'Don't I get a say in this?'

The General stared. 'You got objections to Sophie staying with my daughter?'

'I've no objections to Sophie stayin' anywhere. I want to be asked.'

'You've been asked. '

Sophie started to sob.' What's going to happen to Biffer?'

'Nothin's goin' to happen,' said Bobby.

Sophie ran to hug him and he turned away. Weeping, she dropped on her knees by the dog hugging him. 'Bye-bye, Biffer,' she said.

Chapter Eighteen
Opera and the Ballet

'Run me to Richmond, old sport! I need you to sign a couple of papers.'

Gabriel swung the Morgan out of the drive, autumn's dead and dying leaves cannoning over the red bonnet. 'What kind of papers?'

Bobby adjusted his dark glasses. 'Nothin' heavy! Witness a couple of trust deeds, that kind of thing. How's your Ma? We don't see her much these days.'

'She's fixin' to stay in Baltimore.'

'Does that mean you'll be movin' out with her?'

'If I can sell the Parlour.'

'Take her some roses from the yard.' Bobby started coughing, veins on his forehead standing out. 'I was plannin' to plant more next year but that won't happen. It's all up with me, my dear, as they say in the theatre.'

They drove onto the highway the Morgan sharp under Gabriel's hands and Bobby hunched in the seat, scarf blowing in the breeze and shades over his eyes.

'Ever been to the theatre, Gabe?'

He shook his head.

'Me neither. Lately I've been watching Sophie practicin' ballet. Do you like ballet?'

'I know nothin' about it.' Gabriel is finding the new Bobby hard to handle. This U-turn, the enquiries and invitations to dinner make no sense.

They drove awhile and he started up again. 'You could learn about ballet.'

'Yeah, sure.'

'Why not? You're as good as the other dancin' fools. But you'd have to become part of the classy scene. Gabriel Templar, esquire, a wad in his pocket and a beautiful woman on his arm! That'd make 'em sit up, by Christ!'

The last was said with such venom Gabriel swung him a look. Other than grinning Bobby wasn't telling. 'Okay! First we cut along to my lawyers, throwing some serious spanners in the works then to my tailor. I need a jacket and so do you.'

'No thanks.'

'Come on! New clothes, new haircut and a new life? We should all have a chance at a new life. It should be written in the contract: '*Every soul having fucked up his first attempt shall be given another.*' Believe me if I had my life over you wouldn't see my ass for dust. London, Rome, the Far East, I'd be Lawrence of Arabia reborn.'

Caught up in the dream Gabriel nodded. 'The Himalayas.'

'Yes, sir! Hitching a ride to the top of the world!'

'That's some dream.'

'It doesn't have to stay a dream. A shit-load of money and you can go anywhere. But you gotta get an education! Maybe go to Paris and grab some knowledge.'

'If you say so.'

Bobby glanced sideways. 'So there's nothin' I can tempt you with? What about treasure money can't buy? Say, a delicate piece of bone china about to go on sale to the highest bidder? Can I tempt you to that?'

Gabriel wouldn't lie. 'That above all.'

'Semper fuckin' Fi Sergeant!

'Yes, sir, Captain, sir, Semper fuckin' Fi!'

~

The Hunter family lunched on the Eyrie terrace. 'Looks like rain.'

'Don't say that, Pa. I've worries enough as it is.'

'You've done great, Sis,' said Alex, indicating balloons and colored lights among the willows. 'It's all very Fourth of July.'

'I had to do something or people will think it a wake rather than a house warming. I've invited a couple of the girls to make the numbers so don't be standoffish.'

'I'm never standoffish.'

'You are! Megan Richardson reckons you could freeze the pants of a whore.'

'Megan says the nicest things.'

'Yes, well, if we don't watch out you'll be on the sidelines auditioning for a wallflower. That is unless the lovely Miss Dee puts in an appearance.'

It's a week since the incident by the pool. Nothing is said yet plenty hinted. Sarah is fishing. Alex declines the bait. The General swallows it whole.

'I hope she does come and gets to be amongst civilized people.'

'You know he got her fired?' said Sarah. 'Some garbage about mental problems! Mental problems, my eye! Any problem she has is on account of him!'

The General nodded. 'The man's a loose cannon. I never did get what you saw in him, son, but seeing he's your friend you should go straighten him out.'

'No!' said Ellen Hunter. 'This is Bobby Rourke's affair. You must stay out of it. The girl's made her choice and must do what we all do and see it through.'

'Why must she?'

'Because, Alex, that's what marriage is about.'

'They're not married.'

'Makes no difference! Married or not the same rules apply. She made her bed and uncomfortable though it is she must learn to lie on it.'

'Does that go for your granddaughter?'

'Excuse me?'

'Does that apply to Sophie?'

'What are you saying?'

'I'm saying Sophie is mine. I'm asking if Adelia has to lie on an uncomfortable bed do you want your granddaughter to do the same.'

There was a stunned silence then Sarah shrieked. 'I knew it! I saw the look in your eyes by the pool and knew you had major history. That's why I'm going to the house. I've been trying to find out what's going on but she wouldn't come clean.'

'It's not that she wouldn't come clean. It's that she couldn't.'

Explanations developed into a council of war. Sarah was jubilant, Ellen Hunter less so. The General was bellicose.

'Let's hitch our asses over to the Mill. You grab the missus. I'll take care of Sophie. Ain't nobody stealing my granddaughter.'

'You can't grab anyone.' Maurice grasped the gravity of the situation. 'A set-up like this needs tact and diplomacy not a Sherman tank.'

'To hell with diplomacy! That house is a powder keg.'

'If Adelia were stronger it would be easier,' said Maurice.

'She is strong!' said Sarah. 'Any woman who puts up with Bobby *and* his mother while running a home and coping with a foul illness has to be monumentally strong! I couldn't do it. I'd have thrown in the towel the moment I saw his face.'

'That's because you've an axe to grind,' said the General tactlessly. 'Loose cannon or not he earned his scars fighting for his country.'

'He did not,' said Alex, bitterly. 'He got them riding a motorbike into a wall.'

He left them to it and working out frustration took an axe to the blackthorns. His house will not to be hidden behind bushes. Life has been like that covert -from now on everything is to be out in the open. That's why he sent an invitation to the house-warming. Bobby will see it for the challenge it is.

Alex set about the bushes. There was a rustle behind him, Gabriel Templar. Their glances met. A realtor's board was on the path, 'Sold' scrawled across it.

Though not a man for gestures Alex couldn't let the moment pass. He took the billboard and snapped it in half tossing the shards at Templar's feet.

~

Adelia was going through the closet trying to find a dress for the house-warming. She rattled through the hangars and there sandwiched between monstrosities was the black velvet sheath. Cut low over the breasts and skimming the hips, she looked like a Victorian Saloon dancer. Then she turned, the mirror revealing a swooping plunge of velvet that met a mile on the wrong side of her tailbone.

Back it went into the closet. 'I'm not going!'

'You are!' said Bobby coming in the room. 'I told that interferin' sonofabitch chauffeur of yours to pick us up at nine.'

'If there is interference you've only yourself to blame. Since you put paid to my bike I'm reliant on the kindness of others.'

'You don't need to be. I can take you anywhere you want to go'

'Not with a quart of whisky inside you.'

'I can hold my liquor.'

'So why is Gabriel driving us around?'

'Gabe's a pal not your lover's bodyguard.'

'Why would Alex Hunter need a bodyguard?'

'Because he's the army's secret weapon! Get Hunter on your team and you don't need stuff you see in the movies, cameras disguised as pens microdot film and the like. He is the camera and the film and can recall entire conversations in any language you choose. Russian, French, German, it makes no difference to him.'

'You're fond of him. You can't hide it.'

'I was once. Not anymore.'

'Then you oughtn't to go to his house-warming.'

'Baby Rourke ain't about to walk away from a challenge. Where you off to?'

Adelia put on her coat. 'Biffer's gone missing.'

'Since when?'

'Since this morning. Did you take him with you?'

'Nope.'

'Then where is he? He's not eaten his food. He must be hungry by now.'

'Don't worry about it. You know Biff. He'll turn up when he's ready.'

~

She walked out into the rain. House warming? As if she'd set foot in the Eyrie after what happened! But what did happen? Only that Alex pressed her hand about her body and those parts of her body ache so much she can't think.

'Biffer! Where are you, boy?' Rain seeping through her coat she walked on, her feet following a familiar track. Gabriel was in the barn chipping at wood.

She tapped on the door and he threw a tarpaulin over his work.

'You never show me your work.'

'Nothin' to see.'

'Have you seen Biffer on your travels?'

'If I do I'll send him home.' He picked up a plane and began smoothing a plank of wood. Slauugh! The plane spun along the surface curls of wood flying away.

She watched. 'Is it true you're selling up?'

'It's on the market.'

'Why didn't you tell me?'

'I wasn't sure what I was doin'.' Slauugh! More curls of wood, Gabriel bending over the plane his shirt coming adrift from his pants.

She tucked his shirt into his pants. 'You need bigger shirts.'

Spurning her touch he leapt away.

'Gabriel! Why are you being this way?'

Tears in her eyes, she turned. He was after her snatching her in his arms. He carried her to the shed and began stripping her clothes. He carried on until her pants were round her knees. Then he laid her over the plank of wood, curls of wood entangled in her hair. 'Is this what you want?' he said, ripping open his flies and pushing inside her. 'You want a feel of Gabe Templar's brains?'

Denying an answer his mouth fastened over hers. Adelia tried to respond but couldn't. It was too ugly. 'Don't.' He didn't seem to care and reaching above grasped a metal strut pulling against it, his body slamming against her.

'Oh, don't!'

'Why not?' he grated. 'I'm bein' what you want me to be, a dumb piece of ass to use as and when you like!'

Adelia began to weep and he pulled away. She slid to the floor. He bent trying to lift her. She pushed him away. 'Why did you do that?'

Face a mask of pain, he shrugged.

'I loved you,' she said and turning ran.

~

Alex gazed across the wood. 'She's not coming.'

'I never thought she would,' said Sarah. 'She knew how dangerous it could be.'

'I guess not.'

'Why don't you tell me about her? Has she changed much in the years?'

'Have I?'

'The years away have made you a stranger.'

'I couldn't come home. I needed forgiveness. Berlin was a world I helped spoil. I was scared to come home in case I spoiled this world.'

'And Bobby? How do you feel about him?'

'I don't know. Until Adelia and Sophie are safe I shan't know.'

'She may not want you.'

'I'm aware the odds are stacked against me.'

Ten o clock the doorbell rang, Bobby in RAF uniform, a silk scarf about his throat, a bottle of Krug under one arm and Sophie on the other.

'Evening folks!' He doffed his cap. 'Sorry to be late but there was a hold-up, fashion-wise. My daughter didn't know what to wear.'

Alex heard his father draw in his breath. 'Steady, General.'

'And you did invite him,' murmured Ellen Hunter. 'Good evening, Captain Rourke, Adelia not with you?'

'Unavoidably detained.'

'Sophie, how pretty you look! Did mummy make that dress?'

'Yes and my Juliet cap.'

'Lovely.' Ellen held out her arms. 'Come and give Nana a kiss.' Sophie flew to her and was carried away, Ellen, Maurice, and the boys an envelope about her.

'Why do I get the feelin' of wagons circlin'?' said Bobby.

'Because blood will out,' said Sarah. 'You've only to see the child to know she's a Hunter.'

'Yes and a Challoner! Don't forget that essential piece of magic. It makes the difference, vintage champagne or vinegar.'

'Why you…!' the General raised his fist.

'Dad!' Alex propelled him away. ' Show Sophie where she'll be sleeping. You?' he beckoned, 'the study.' He closed the door. 'Give me a reason why I shouldn't put a pistol to your head and put you outta your misery.'

'Do it! Put me out my misery!'

'Shooting is too good for you.'

Bobby perched on the desk. 'Come now, Ash, don't go fallin' into clichés.'

'You are a cliché. Where's Adelia?'

'Detained. Got a gasper?' Out of habit Alex pushed his cigarette case across the desk. Bobby peeled back the eye-patch. 'Well, what do you know?' He stared at the photograph. 'It's my little nurse! You've had this a while.'

'Like the woman it never left my side.'

'Confident, aren't you?'

'Not confident determined. Why are you here?''

'Because you invited me! Why, do you think there's an ulterior motive? Friends don't have ulterior motives. They're straight with one another, straight and true as old

Gabe's dick and that is muscular, if you know what I'm sayin'.'

He started coughing. He coughed so long Alex poured him a glass of water.

When he started again it was still on the subject of Templar's dick.

'Stow that shit!' Alex hissed. 'What is it you want?'

'I want you to stop takin' them away from me,' said Bobby fingering the cigarette case. 'I know how it looks. You're seein' what most see, a wreck tryin' to hold onto a girl who doesn't love him but that's only part of the equation.'

'And Templar? Where does he fit into the equation?'

Bobby grinned wolfishly.' You don't like that, do you, the thought of that good old boy doing his bit for Uncle Sam.'

'You sick sonofabitch. I don't know why I'm listening to you.'

'You've no choice. You're in over your head like the rest of us. Go careful, old sport, or you'll end up using whores and giving Gabriel license to fuck your girl.'

'If I ever get that desperate I'll give you the pistol and you can shoot me!'

'Nah, that's not goin' to happen. It wouldn't cross your mind to use a whore when needy. You're a pain now and you were a pain before the war.'

'I had no idea I was such an inconvenience.'

'You weren't an inconvenience. You were my friend.'

'What kind of friend destroys a man's dreams?'

'I'm still pretty much your friend.'

'How d'you work that out.'

Bobby shrugged. 'Maybe I had an ulterior motive comin' here. Maybe I came to tell of my plan to shake the bats out of Dee's belfry and make her remember you.'

'Are you saying that's what you did?'

'I'm sayin' maybe I ain't such a bad friend after all.'

'You are a piece of shit and the sooner you're out of our lives the better.'

'Saddle up, Guvnor!. There was a knock on the door. 'Templar's here.'

'See this man out, will you, Frank? His business is done.'

'I've plenty more to say but I can wait,' said Bobby, straightening his tie. 'I'll go and collect Sophie. Her Ma will be missin' her.'

'Mizz Sophie is with Mr and Mrs Parker. They left ten minutes ago.'

'Interferin' bastards!' Bobby leapt away. 'Why did you have to come back, Ash Hunter? Why couldn't you have died like everyone else?'

'Shall I follow him, guvnor?'

'Might be a good idea. Show Templar in.'

'Go steady! He's still riled about me taking over the kindergarten run.'

Templar walked in, a mirror image of a man spoiling for a fight.

'What did Bobby want?'

'Something and nothing.'

Templar paced the room. 'Five hours I was trapped with him the other day! Five hours listenin' to rubbish about ballet. Now he's out chasin' whores and when he ain't he's threatenin' to hurt Adelia. Why haven't you come clean?'

'If I thought it would help I'd stand on top of the Empire State Building and scream the truth. I'm doing what I can within the bounds of honesty.'

'A rabid dog doesn't recognize honesty.'

'Possibly not but I do.'

Templar snorted. 'You Academy candy-asses are all the same. Don't you know while you're busy polishin' your buttons a woman is gettin' hurt? '

'Is that all you came for?'

'There's more.' Gabriel swung his fist. 'Sonofabitch, you couldn't leave me anythin'! You had to send your tame bloodhound to get Sophie from school.'

It was all he managed to say before Bates dropped on him stomping his face.

'Have you done?' Alex was spiting blood. 'I don't mind trading insults but not at the cost of my carpet.'

Templar left, blood streaming from his nose and mouth. 'I'm done for now but I'm warnin' you, hurt her again and I will kill you.'

~

Adelia dreamt she wore the scarlet chiffon and a scarlet wide-brimmed hat. Then the scarlet chiffon dissolved until she was in her underwear, *black* underwear and a black straw hat. In the dream she took the compact from her bag and began to powder her nose and then to wretch the scent overpowering.

She woke to a powder puff rammed over her nose.

Terrified, she pushed Bobby away. He grabbed her by the throat. They struggled in silence until he ran and the Morgan screeching out of the drive.

She wanted to call Gabriel but couldn't not after what he did.

There is a card hidden under her pillow. She dialed.

'Colonel Hunter's service! Can I help you?'

She slammed down the phone. Three minutes later it rang.

'You called my service.'

'Is Sophie with you?'

'She's with my sister and the boys. Are you all right?'

'Yes. No! Just a minute!' There was a noise outside. She threw the window open. 'Biffer is that you!' A shape pressed round the water barrel. It was the vixen at the bins again. She picked up the phone. 'It was the fox.'

'I'm on my way!'

'No! Don't come!'

'What's wrong?'

'Biffer's gone.'

'Let me come over. I can help you look for him.'

'Please don't! Tell me about the party instead! Was Sophie happy?'

'Sophie's fine. The party would've been better if you'd been here.' There was a pause and then a sharp intake of breath. 'You know that I am in love with you.'

'Oh!' Her heart turned over.

'Have you anything to say to me?'

She shook her head. 'I must go. I'm glad the party went well.'

'It went as expected. We had a situation. A thief stole from my house.'

'I hope it wasn't anything of value.'

'It was a cigarette case. It has little value yet it held another thing that is very dear to me. Do you want to know what that is?'

A dog howled. She dropped the phone and huddling into her old red raincoat took the hurricane lamp through the orchard.

It was thundering. Rain driving into her face she walked on.

'*You know that I am in love with you.*'

Until now she hadn't known what that meant. They were magical words.

'*You know that I am in love with you!*'

Lifting her face to the sky she turned in wide slow circles, dancing in the rain, the lamp aloft and her hand to her heart holding onto a gift.

Chapter Nineteen
Babies in Tights

Seven in the morning the phone rang, Gabriel, sharp and to the point. 'I can't make it tonight. Tell Bobby he'll have to get some other sucker to drive.'

Five minutes later Bobby is downstairs and dressed and ready to go out and looking as though he'd slept in his uniform.

'Would you like me to press that before you go out?'

'Nah, this'll do.' He grabbed her round the waist and whizzed about the kitchen manic in his mood. 'How you doin' today, Nurse Challoner?'

'I'd be a lot better without midnight visitors trying to choke me.'

'Midnight visitors?'

'You frightened me.'

'I was only foolin' around.'

She pulled her collar aside, revealing a dark bruise. 'Some fooling.'

'Did I do that? I guess I was a little heavy handed.'

'I guess you were.'

He stroked her hand. 'You know I'd never really hurt you.'

'I know no such thing,' she said, tearing pieces from an exercise book and scribbling 'LOST DOG' notices. 'I'll never forget the look on your face "Bobby Rourke rehearsing for his big scene, 'the night I murdered my English trollop!'

'English trollop? Yum, I like the sound of that.'

'You were trying to kill me.'

'I was not. You'll know when I'm killing you. I'll give you plenty notice.' He clasped his hands about her caressing her breasts. 'You're in a foul mood this morning. What's up, withdrawal symptoms now Gabriel's flown the coop?'

Sick of every Tom, Dick, and Harry doing what he liked she slapped his hands away. 'You can stop that!'

'Whoo, tiger, you are in a mood! What time's Gabe picking us up?'

'He's not. He phoned to say he can't make it.'

'That's okay I'll drive. Whoops, I can't! I'm minus a car.'

'Minus a car?'

'I left it someplace and can't remember where. Why is Sophie not home?'

'They were bringing her but I said stay. I don't want her fretting about Biffer.'

'He'll turn up. You know Biffer.'

'I thought I knew you and look how wrong I was about that!'

The doorbell rang, Sergeant Bates. 'The Colonel's compliments, could you use a driver tonight?'

'Way to go Alex!' yelled Bobby. 'Make the most of it! Your days are numbered!'

'Please thank the Colonel for me. He's a lifesaver.'

'Lifesaver?' Bobby squawked. 'You don't know the half of it!'

Adelia ignored him. If she can get Sophie through the concert tonight then tomorrow is another day.

Suspecting Bobby involved in the dog's disappearance she distributed 'LOST' notices about the town, and then a quick call on *Belle Couture* and back to scrub the Mill from one end to the other. Their passports and the thirty pounds she hid in their old suitcase, it isn't enough to buy passage home but it's a start. Breaking a promise to stay has to be better than Bobby breaking her neck.

She will miss America. She had grown to admire the people. Life in England will be hard. They will have to rent rooms and find work. Ballet classes will have to go. They will have a bed, food on the table and freedom, but that's all.

'It is enough.'

~

Bobby is locked in the garage with the car engine running. He's made up his mind. If it's a case of kill or be a killer he's not ready to sell his soul to the devil.

Lord! He sank down on his knees. All he wanted was to wander about her room, maybe pick up her stuff to sniff and touch. It's not the first time he's watched her sleep but she whispered that name. It was the straw that broke his back.

Being up close and personal to murder is new. Death is immediate in Bomber Command, faulty equipment, Bf109s about your head, ack-ack, take your pick.

With a Lancaster it's a disembodied voice in your ear: 'Steady! Steady!' Then it's bombs away -business over. There is nothing distant about throttling a woman. It's as up close and personal as you can get.

A man does all manner of things for all kinds of reasons. Like the day he elected to join Bomber Command. Why do that? Why steer those big buggers about the sky when you were born to ride a winged Pegasus?

Last night in her room when he held the powder puff under her nose he had a choice. The moment his hands were about her throat the choice was gone, a darker Bobby taking over, one who got a buzz from the helpless look in her eyes. It had the same effect as sporadic signals, a hard-on fit to fuck a donkey.

Last night she called for help and someone came. A shadow fell over the bed, a breeze ruffled a candle flame, and a voice said, 'no, Bobby.' It scared the bejasus out of him! He was out and on the road before she'd chance to draw breath.

All night sitting chucking booze down his throat he thought about it. Something came to her aid. So he decided if someone has to go it had better be him.

Everything's prepared, a hose in the exhaust and flying jacket padding the doors.

Showered and shaved in best blues, DFC pinned to his chest, he is ready. Dee is out, Sophie is cushioned in the Hunter bosom, Ruby is Ruby, he is good to go.

He won't leave a note. The cigarette case clasped in his hand and the photograph inside tell the tale. Let Colonel Alexander Stonewall Hunter explain that!

'Okay! Here we go!' He turned the ignition.

It fired and then stalled.

He turned it again. Stut-stut-stut!

'Fuck's sake!' He climbed out of the car, lifted the hood, fiddled with the plugs, and got back in again. 'St..tt...tt..tt.tt..tt!'

It's okay! No problem. He has a back-up plan, a .38 from his pocket. Brains splattered over the windscreen, not the neatest job but what d'you do?

He cocked the pistol. It tasted of machine oil and phosphates from the greenhouse. Words tripped through his head, a quote out of Tale of Two Cities where Sydney Carton says, 'it's a far better thing.'

He quit that. It's not a better thing. It was a cowardly shitty end for a hero.

He pulled the trigger. Click!

The sun shifted, clouds scudded across the sky and a voice whispered in his ear.

Sighing, he put the gun in his pocket, unplugged the hose and opened the garage door. Then pausing, he leant through the car window and keyed the ignition.

Broom! The engine sprang to life.

~

The sedan drew up outside the Mission, Adelia and Bobby in the back and Sophie up front. 'Marjorie Collins has a cold, Sergeant Bates.'

'And that means...?'

'I'm to dance Puck.'

'Do you know her part?'

'I know everybody's part.'

'You memorized them?'

'Uh-huh. Can you do that?'

The Sergeant grinned. 'No, but I know a guy who can.'

They got to the hall. Yellow and brown striped wings streaming out Sophie skipped ahead. 'Bye everybody!'

'Bye, princess!' shouted Bobby. 'Break a leg or whatever the hell you say!'

He's in a strange mood, high and then belligerent. Right now he is staring at Adelia's suit. Dark navy New Length skirt and fitted jacket with a Mandarin collar, a black straw boater, high-heeled pumps and elbow length white gloves, she is as calm and contained as an elderly matron.

'What's this, a new outfit?'

'I bought it earlier.'

'Where d'you get the money?'

'It's the last of my wages from the children's home.'

'You sure you haven't been filchin' the odd buck from my pocket? You wouldn't be the first. A whore took every cent last night.'

'No doubt she earned it.'

'Ooh, sharp!' He pressed his lips against her ear. 'Careful,' he whispered. 'The last thing you want tonight is sharp.'

'Why is that?'

'You'll find out.'

The Hall was packed, the Hunter clan seated halfway down. Alex turned to watch them enter and Adelia gasped, his face cut and bruised.

Bobby whistled. 'Looks like somebody took a baseball bat to your hero.'

'Was it you?'

'You kiddin'? This is Genghis Khan we're talkin' about not Winnie-the-Pooh. He's a Colonel in the army. He tells his men to take a shit and they say what color.'

'For God's sake!'

He shrugged. 'Well, it's true.'

'Do we have to sit with them?'

'What and miss the fun? I should say we do!' He stomped down the hall, towing her behind him. 'Come on! Toot sweet as they say in Gay Paree!'

At the row he saluted. 'Evening all. Welcome to the best show in town, but be careful where you put your blue-blood asses, the seats ain't to be lived with.'

The row swiveling in a single sliding motion they shuffled along.

Adelia took her seat and sat gripping her gloves.

Alex was on her right. 'How are you?'

'Better than you by the look of things! What have you been doing war-games?'

'War-games?' A flicker of a smile touched his bruised lips. 'I would say that's about right. Any news of the dog?'

'No and there won't be.'

The lights dimmed. There was a rattling of curtains. Sophie ran onto the stage, antenna quivering dramatically. 'How now, spirit! Wither wander thou? '

'Yup,' the General nodded.' That's my girl.'

~

It was as she said, babies in tights. She tried to relax but was conscious of Bobby chewing his finger-ends one side and Alex Hunter absorbed and silent on the other.

The seats were hard and her head ached. 'Have you an aspirin, Bobby?'

'You want I should get you some?'

'Perhaps at intermission?'

'Forget intermission. I'll go now.' With that he limped out.

Alex leaned toward her. 'Sophie's enjoying herself.'

'She is a born actress.'

'Which is more than can be said for her mother!'

'I'm no good at hiding. That's more her father's line.'

Alex sat in silence a reined-in expression on his face. Then he said, 'there isn't a man in this room who wouldn't be proud to have Sophie for a daughter.'

'Thank you. And thank you for what you said on the phone last night.'

He slapped his chest. 'I meant every word!'

Intermission and curtains rattled. People were standing, stretching their legs.

Sophie ran toward them. 'You came!' The General snatched her up. 'You bet we did. How could we stay away when our own little star is up there shining?'

'Mommy, did you see me?'

'I saw you, darling.'

'Did Daddy?'

'Yes he did. He's popped out for a moment.'

'Can I take Nana and Gramps to meet my friends? They've never met a real-live General.' Off they went, a flotilla, the tiny pilot leading the General by the hand.

Alex Hunter turned. 'I need to speak with you. May I call after the show?'

'What about Bobby?'

'What I have to say he needs to hear.'

'As you wish. Excuse me.'

Desperate for air she went into the garden. Gabriel sat on a bench in his funeral suit, silver waistcoat shining. He was as bruised as Alex Hunter.

I'll be damned, thought Adelia bitterly. They've been fighting.

She approached. 'Please don't say you were playing war-games.'

He got to his feet. 'Marines don't play games.'

'Why are you out here? Why not inside with your sparring partner?'

'I figured best to steer clear. Didn't want folks laughin'.'

'Hah!' Adelia snorted. 'Me and mine have provided this town with non-stop amusement for years. Why stop now?'

They walked in and a ripple went round the hall. Head high, she marched to her seat. Alex was on his feet. Disdaining explanation she sat down. Seconds later the General and Mrs Hunter resumed their places, Sarah's eyebrows shooting skyward.

The ballet resumed. Then Bobby reappeared drunk and spoiling for trouble. Down the aisle he came leaning on a walking stick. At their row he did a double take. 'Well, if it ain't my pal Gabe wearin' the same badge of courage.'

'Oh my God!' Adelia moaned.

Alex's hand closed over hers.' Ride it out. It'll get worse before it gets better.'

'Don't touch me!' she flung away. 'But for you none of this would be happening! '

Color coming and going Bobby shuffled along the row. 'Howdy champ!' he thumped Gabriel's shoulder. 'What did he do, put you through a meat-grinder? '

'Belay the chatter!' snapped the General.' You're spoiling the entertainment.'

'Spoil nothin'.' Bobby dropped into a seat. 'We are the entertainment.'

~

The ballet dragged on, the audience shifting and sighing. Last year Adelia came with Gabriel and May. They grumbled about the seats, waved at Sophie, laughed when scenery fell over and ate hot-dogs in the interval. It was fun. This is hell.

Bobby leaned toward Gabriel.' So you gave him a thumping'. I'm glad. It's time somebody put him in his place. I don't know why he's here. A thing like this, my daughter's ballet class, it's for friends and family not ex-buddies.'

People were staring, a woman in front giving them a hard look.

'What's your problem, lady?' Bobby shouted. 'Ain't you seen the Three Stooges before? ' He took a cigarette-case from his pocket. 'Smoke, Gabe?'

'I don't smoke as well you know.'

He leaned across Adelia proffering the cigarette case.' Gasper, old sport?'

'No, old sport!' he spat. 'But go for it! Maybe then we'll get some peace!'

It was said with such emphasis Adelia glanced down. A photograph was tucked among the cigarettes. She bent to look and Bobby snapped the case shut.

It was Sophie's solo, a spotlight illuminating her face. Bobby chose the moment to fondle Adelia's thigh. 'What say when this is over we have a show of our own?'

Knowing he was trying to provoke a quarrel she suffered his hand.

Alex Hunter found it impossible to do so.

'Why don't you stop making a Jackass of yourself?'

'Why don't you!' It was the opening Bobby was waiting for. 'Comin' here when nobody invited you, tryin' to steal my wife and daughter from under my nose.'

Up on the stage Sophie faltered.

'Stow it the pair of you,' said the General. 'You're upsetting Sophie, '

Bobby laughed. 'And we can't have the precious kid upset!'

'Pull yourself together, man. You're making a spectacle of yourself.'

'Don't tell me to pull myself together, not and what I've had to put up with.'

'Pipe down, Mac!' someone shouted.

'No you pipe down!' Bobby bounced to his feet. 'It's okay for you with your comfortable lives and honest wives. You don't know what I've to contend with.'

'Bobby, please!' Adelia took his arm but he pushed her away causing the other three men to surge to their feet.

'See this?' He waved his arms. 'See the dogs in heat fightin' over the same tasty bitch! See the army man, the ribbons and medals? He's a liar and a cheat. Top brass spit and polish yet underneath no different to you and me.'

'Don't involve me in your dirty business!' the General bellowed. 'This is between you three and shouldn't be hauled out before the entire world.'

The ballet ground to a halt, parents taking the children away.

Sophie stood alone in an empty stage.

'Out of my way!' Adelia shoved Bobby aside.

He grabbed her arm. 'You're not going anywhere til you know what's goin' on.'

'Bear with it, ' said Alex. 'He has a purpose.'

'Purpose!' she stormed. 'What are you talking about?'

Bobby sprung the cigarette case. 'See this photograph? It's been hidden in this case for years. And do you know who it belongs to? Why him, Colonel Bogey.'

'Oh, get out of my way!' She didn't care about a silly photograph. She only cared about Sophie and ran lifting her down and leading her from the hall.

It was raining, big silver dollars falling from the sky. Bobby was on her heels.

'You don't get it, do you? Don't get who Hunter is.'

'I don't care who he is.'

'You would if you knew.'

'So who is he?'

'I'm Sophie's father!' A voice rang out.

Her feet ground to a halt. The words made no sense.

Alex said it again. 'I'm Sophie's father.'

She can't have heard right. 'Sophie's father?'

'Yes.'

It came to her then - whir, whir, cogs and gears locking into place - the General and Mrs Hunter's interest in Sophie and Sarah's visits to the Mill, the questions.

'And the General and Mrs Hunter are her grandparents?'

'Yes.'

The photograph? She's in nurse's togs, cloak about her shoulders...her hair is shorter...she is smiling into the camera, a monkey perched on her arm.

She looked at Gabriel. 'Did you know about this?'

'I figured it out.'

'And you didn't tell me!'

'How could I?'

'Mommy!' Sophie tugged her arm. 'What about my real daddy?'

Alex knelt in front of her. 'I'm your real daddy.'

'No.' She turned to Bobby. 'This is my daddy.'

'See?' he said triumphant. 'My little girl knows who I am and she knows who you are, a lyin' coward.' He turned to Adelia. 'See this guy all tricked up like a chocolate soldier? This is the guy who left you to die.'

'Don't start that again,' spat Alex. 'You know the liar here just as you know I didn't jump from any window. You saw what happened. You were there.'

'I was not.'

'You were! I saw you in the square.'

'I was in the hotel saving Adelia.' Bobby stuck his face up close. 'How d'you think she got out, old sport? You think firemen did it? Poor bastards were too busy mannin' the pumps to worry about an idiot girl.'

He turned to face Adelia. 'I saved you. Me, what's his name the flier. And him, Colonel Alex Hunter, Medal of Honor, blah-di-blah, is a goddamn liar!'

'Bobby,' she whispered.

'I was in the hotel when it hit. I carried you down the back stairs. I knew about those stairs 'cos that's who I am, Baby Rourke, womanizer and drunk.'

'I didn't know.'

'I wasn't gonna tell you.'

The General pitched in. 'I don't care what you did. You're not getting Sophie.'

'Leave it, Dad,' said Alex. 'We can't do this. It isn't right.'

'Right? Bobby leapt at him. 'You talk about right, you sanctimonious shit!'

The first punch was wild skating off Alex's shoulder. The next was on target his head recoiling and the medal about his neck flipping from under his collar.

The next punch caught him. And the next! How could it miss when the target stood with arms at his sides, disabled by some inner code of honor?

'Don't!' Adelia cried. But Bobby had a taste for it and kicked Alex's legs from under him. Gabriel grabbed Bobby's wrist. 'That's enough! You made your point.'

They struggled until Bobby ran away into the darkness.

Eyes like pack ice Ellen Hunter snatched Sophie. 'We'll take Sophie. She's better away from this. You and my son have a lot to talk about. '

'You dropped your coat.' Gabriel draped it about her shoulders whereupon it slid down settling on the ground like a wet cat. He bent to pick it up but she shook her head. 'No. Leave it.'

Shoes absorbing water and suit soaked she walked away. In the distance someone was calling her name but she didn't stop. Bobby saved her! Alex Hunter was Sophie's father. Bobby saved her! Colonel Bogey left her to die!

A car pulled by the kerb water baling over the sidewalk. 'Ma'am!'

Water running off his bald head Sergeant Bates unfurled the umbrella. He shepherding her into the car and closed the door. 'Where to Missy?'

Where to, she thought, desolately, where is there to go?

Slowly the car moved off. How could he do it? And how could Bobby lie? And Gabriel knew! And Sarah and the General! It's all been a lie!

They drove through lanes and by-roads. She didn't know where they went. It might have been Mars. And why after this isn't memory rushing back? If it was as doctors said she needed a key to unlock the past what is this but a key!

The car swung through a gate. 'Here you are, missy, home at last.'

She sat staring straight ahead.

'Come on. You've had a shock. You need to be indoors. '

The door was open, yellow light streaming out over the wet shale.

'No,' said she, digging her heels in. 'I'm not going in there.'

There he was, Colonel Bogey, big and menacing, his hair wet with rain.

'Thank God you're here,' he said.

'No!' she said, hoarsely. 'You can go to hell!'

'Baby, don't.'

'Don't you baby me!' she shouted. 'Don't you dare!'

A towel in his hand he came toward her a Matador and she the maddened bull. 'No!' She slapped him.

'I love you.'

'Liar! 'She slapped him again hitting his shoulder, co-ordination shot, unable to bridge the gap between her hand and his bruised face.

He draped the towel about her shoulders. Then his arms were around her and he was picking her up and her head was breaking apart and she was falling.

Chapter Twenty
Howling

Adelia opened her eyes to a long rectangle of a room with a whitewashed ceiling crossed by oak beams. All was in shadow, heavy drapes at the leaded windows and a single lamp by the bed. The air was scented with a familiar mix of faded wisteria and apples. She was in the Eyrie, in Alex Hunter's bed, and he was standing by the window. Events of the evening crowded in, the last melodramatic act of a third-rate farce.

'Sophie?' she muttered, her voice a hoarse whisper.

'She's with Sarah and Maurice.'

'What time is it?'

'A little after twelve. Is there anything I can get you?'

Icy cold, she drew the sheet about her. Why was she here and in her underwear? She should be home taking the emergency suitcase from the closet.

'You could lend me money to get back to England.'

'If that's what you want.'

'It's what I want.'

She slept. When she woke she was lying on a couch, a man's shirt over her.

He sat opposite, a wary look in his eyes.

'What time is it?'

'Twenty after three.'

'Why am I here and not at the Mill?'

'Given the circumstances the family figured this the best place.'

'And stripped me of my clothes?'

'Sarah put you to bed. Your clothes were wet.'

'Put me to bed. What am I a baby to be packed off to sleep?'

'You were ill. You needed to be safe.'

'And this place, alone with a liar and cheat, is safe?'

'It's the safest place I know.'

She shook with rage. 'How dare you make decisions for me? You and your beastly secrets! What have I done that you should treat me with contempt?'

'Contempt is the last thing I feel. I can only apologize for what happened. You should have been the first to know.'

'Perhaps you prefer me to go on thinking of you as a friend.'

'I am and always will be your friend. Believe me, from the moment I knew you were alive I've wanted to tell you but events got in the way.'

'Whose shirt is this?'

'Mine.'

'Why is it covering me?'

'You asked for a shirt to cover you.'

She shrank away. She doesn't recall asking for a shirt any more than being here on the couch. It is that out-of-step feeling. Experience has taught her to try remaining calm when on the edge of an attack but the thought of being alone with this man was worse than the threat of illness. 'I need my clothes.'

'They're in the laundry room.' Wincing, hand to his ribs he got to his feet.

Ugly memories slammed forward. 'Why didn't you defend yourself?'

'I was obliged to stand and take it.'

'Why were you?'

'He saved your life.'

'So it's true. You did leave me to die?'

'I didn't leave you! I wouldn't leave anyone like that! It's against my instincts as a man and a soldier. If only you'll listen I can tell you what happened.'

'Tell me then.'

'We were dressing, nearly out and safe, but then the brewery next door was hit. The blast took out the door. You were thrown across the room. I was sucked out of the window and down a couple of floors. I landed amongst bushes out cold. By the time I came-to the building was on fire.'

'Why didn't you come looking for me?'

'I did.'

'And?'

'And information received was that you hadn't made it.'

'You mean you were told I was dead?'

'That's about the size of it.'

'But surely you didn't leave it like that?'

He leaned against the window, the first pale light of dawn reflecting in his face. 'The source was reliable. At the time I had no reason to doubt it. '

'Source? Information? What are you, a machine? You're talking about my life!'

His shoulders twitched. 'I'm sorry.'

'And so you should be! It's not for me to judge what you did that night. I can't remember what you did. But you should have told me the moment you set foot in the Mill.' She leaned forward, her head in her hands. 'Perhaps it wasn't important. Perhaps I was only ever a convenient ship in the night.'

He continued to stare out the window. When he spoke it was with the same detached tone, a stranger recalling the past. 'You have been many things to me but never convenient. To be frank, there have been times when feelings for you have been downright inconvenient. And while I can't defend myself against all of your complaints I can at least defend myself against doubt of my love.'

He turned to face her. 'I have loved you for six long years. I've carried you every second of those years and I can say, hand on heart, I don't regret a moment. Perhaps if we'd waited in '42 what followed could've been avoided, but when the heart's involved waiting is intolerable.'

'That doesn't explain subterfuge here in Virginia.' She put out her hand, spreading her fingers looking at the ring. 'I take it we're not married.'

'Negative.'

'And Bobby? He said he'd followed us to the Black Swan; does that mean he knew you and I were, for want of a better word, lovers?'

'He knew.'

'But if he knew I was alive why didn't he tell you?'

'Presumably to punish me.'

'For what?'

'Leaving you.'

'Did he tell anyone here in Virginia about it?'

'It seems not. I believe he has since tried to point me in the right direction.'

'Why didn't you tell me who you were?'

'I didn't know how the truth might affect you and Sophie.'

'Oh do tell the truth,' she said wearily. 'I am sick of the other stuff.'

Still he gazed out of the window and still a cloud hovered over her heart. Go on, Adelia, said her courage. Ask the question that you, and he, are waiting to hear.

'This reliable source, the one who told you I was dead, was it Bobby?'

He nodded and the last piece of the puzzle fell into place. It was about punishment but not the punishing of Alex Hunter. This is Bobby punishing Adelia.

A skinny woman in nude-colored underwear and laddered stockings, she pushed past and ran for the bathroom vomiting pain down the lavatory.

Splashing water on her face she squeezed toothpaste on her finger jabbing it about her gums. Dark-circled eyes gazed back, her face as white as the paste round her mouth.

He tapped on the door. 'Let me help you.'

'It's Bobby who needs help,' she muttered. 'Not me.'

Exhausted, she crouched in the corner of the cavernous bathroom. She didn't weep when she arrived at the Mill and found feces on the floor. She didn't weep when Bobby turned out to be a drunk. She wept when she thought Sophie's father a ghostly presence and wept again when

Gabriel broke her heart. But now, even knowing she is the cause of so much unhappiness she can't weep. But she can howl, and does so, the bathroom reverberating.

Alex opened the door. He picked her up, carried her to the bed, stripped off his clothes and pulling back the covers pulled her in with him. She fought him but not for long. 'Sleep,' he said, his breath ruffling her hair. 'Or we'll both be howling.'

~

The telephone woke him. Bright sunlight was streaming through the window and Adelia asleep in his arms. He snatched the phone. It was the General.

'You okay, son? Your mother couldn't rest until I called.'

'I'm okay. How's Sophie?'

'She wept as in only natural. Then Sarah turned that mutt of theirs loose and she wept more thinking on her own dog. What about you, any repercussions?'

'Not yet but there will be. Got to go, Dad. Don't want to wake Adelia.'

'She's in your bed? '

'Uh-huh.'

'Is that wise?'

'Probably not.'

What a night! Keeping her in one place was impossible. No sooner was she in bed or a chair she's pacing from room to room worrying about Sophie and Bobby. Bad enough when she wandered the Mill in a bright red dress and bare feet but at least then she was happy in her madness. Last night she engaged in conversations he couldn't share, looking to an invisible counselor, someone she called Joe, Alex's buddy killed in Anzio.

Since learning of her condition he's talked with medics. Maurice referred him to Jacob Feldstein, consultant psychiatrist at the Veteran's Hospital, who specializes in war related psychoses. He offered opinions but wouldn't speculate. 'It's one thing to hypothesize an illness quite another to live it.'

Ain't that a fact! When the woman you love is locked in a world you can't see getting answers from people you can't hear hypotheses are just so much bullshit.

The phone rang again. Sarah. 'How is she, bro?'

'Worn out, like me.'

'Do you want Maurice to come over?'

'Thanks but after last night I think a priest a better idea.'

Eyes closed, Adelia reared up. 'Don't let me forget to feed the pigs,' she muttered. Then she lay down again still asleep.

He lay on his side looking at her marble face wondering if the attack was over.

Click! Gabriel Templar is sitting in the window seat at the Mill, talking of her illness: *'It's a sufferin' thing and the first thing you gotta learn is to suffer quietly.'*

It came to Alex then the supreme quality of Templar's love. Was he, Alexander Stonewall Hunter, equal to it? 'I don't know,' he whispered, wiping dried toothpaste from her lips. 'But I'm going to give it a damn good try.'

~

Alex showered, and dressed. Frank Bates was in the kitchen finishing a cup of coffee, a pack on his back. 'Going someplace, Frank?'

'I figured you didn't need me around.'

'You have a home here for as long as you want it.'

'Thanks, Guvnor, but I'll stay awhile with my sister in New Jersey. Give you space. How's the lady?'

'Sleeping.' Alex made calls, putting his boss, in the picture. He then called Daniel Culpepper, legal provision to be made. Until the illness is understood Adelia is a danger to herself and Sophie. Then he left to see what's happening at the Mill.

Trying to diminish a hard-on the size and weight of a heat-seeking missile he ran all the way. Four hours they shared a bed. While he wasn't about to take advantage it was enough to drive any man wild.

All was quiet, no sign of Bobby and every pen empty, not a chicken or hog in sight. Then Templar shinned over the fence.

'I took 'em all. I'm just returning the eggs.'

'I'll tell her. She'll be relieved.'

'She okay?'

'Coming through.'

~

Frank was gone when he got back. The boiler was churning, Adelia taking a bath. He gathered her clothes and hung about in the passage. The bathroom door was closed. Twenty minutes and no sound he rapped on the door.

'You in there?'

When there was no answer he opened the door. She was in the tub, her arms over her breasts, and soapy hair piled upon her head.

He set her stuff on the chair and turned to leave.

'Thank you,' she said.

'For what?'

'For Sophie.'

Drawn like a magnet, he knelt by the tub.

She touched his bruises. 'Your mother will never forgive me for hurting you.'

'The only way you can hurt me is to hate me.'

'I don't hate you.'

'Won't you kiss me?'

She hesitated, and then leaned forward touching her lips to his forehead.

'I've missed you so much,' he said, 'every day aching for you.'

Things went a little haywire. She's coming at him like an express train.

He didn't like it. 'Take it easy.'

'Isn't this what you want?'

'No.'

She leaned over her knees. 'Then I don't know what you want.'

He unhooked the shower working water through her hair. 'I'll tell you what I want. I want you to trust me. I want you to be proud of me and feel I'm the only man in the world for you and that nobody can take my place, no matter how good or fine. I want you to eat, sleep, and breathe, Alex Hunter.'

'You don't want much.'

'I want it all.' He wrapped a towel round her, lifted her out of the bath and through to the bedroom. 'I'll leave you to get dressed.'

'Don't go.'

'I don't want to go but neither do I want you thinking I'm some hit-and-run bullyboy looking for a quick lay.'

'I don't think that.'

'Good, because you were never a wartime pit stop. You are everything to me. And now that I've found you it isn't about salving my conscience. It's about my soul. I was born loving you. I shall die loving you.'

'Oh,' she whispered. 'You make me shake inside.'

Match to a flame, he grabbed her wrists. 'I want to make you shake inside. I want to push so much of me inside there's no room for anyone else. I want you to scream with joy not howl with pain. I want you to give me a son for my daughter. I want you to hunger for me as I do for you. But if that's not what you want then tell me, because if we step over the line there'll be no turning back.'

'And the consequences?'

'To hell with them.'

~

Adelia woke and he was drawing the sheet away, cool air caressing her breasts. There were none of the heated words that accompanied the first frantic couplings. Lord, what a fire there was, his body straddling hers, his hands about her waist and his thick penis ramming into her, hot delight streaming from every nerve of her body while he muttered, 'you will love me! You will!'

She'd wanted to say, 'I expect I will but there's no need to kill us both in the process.' The less she said the more he demanded, reflections in the looking-glass taking on the erotic contortions of a carved frieze in a Hindu Temple or a page from a porn magazine hidden among Bobby's 'Rose Grower's Weekly'.

All day long he pursued her, pausing to feed her delicious scrambled eggs and sweet wine, the wine of his kisses more intoxicating. Now he was hungry again, and quietly, coaxingly, drew her close. 'Kiss me, baby,' he said. She offered her mouth and he sank over her, his whole body given to the kiss. Lowering his head he sucked her nipples. When he moved downward she shuddered in anticipation. He laughed softly. 'No howling or the neighbors will be sending for the cops.'

With hands like sandpaper he is parting her thighs, now his tongue is teasing her, tasting her soft lassitude creeping through her bones. He doesn't mince words. 'Is that good?' he said, working his fingers inside her. 'You want this?'

Silently, thrillingly, she began to spasm. He rolled her over onto her belly, and drawing her to the edge of the bed pulled her onto his penis, thrusting long and deep. He's pulling her head back and she's arching and gasping.

'Yes, come on,' he's muttering. 'Tell me about it!'

Still he's beating into her until she's crying out. Lamplight falls on his face, such need and such determination in his face she's overcome. 'You didn't leave me.'

'I didn't leave you.'

'And you really do love me?'

'You bet I do! What's more you love me. That much you haven't forgotten.'

The clock woke her. Alex lay stretched out on his stomach, feet over the edge and face squashed in the pillow. When he said he wanted everything it was not statement so much as a declaration of war. Three days locked in a velvet battle, there wasn't a part of her he hadn't invaded.

'What?' he says when she's quiet. 'What's going on in that head of yours?'

Bobby is in her head. Three days ago Alex went to feed the animals.

When she asked how it went he said the animals were at Gabriel's.

'How do you know?'

'He told me.'

'No word from Bobby?'

'I don't know and I don't care!'

He did care; it showed in his face as it did in hers. Alex tried to push the care away, a kiss for every part of her body. 'Once more round the block?' he said.

'Lovely,' she'd whispered. It was lovely but sad too their bodies joined in silence, a shadow gathering and Bobby's blind amber eyes dead center.

Chapter Twenty-One
Frog-Clacker

Bobby returned from a heavy all-night session at the Hawaiian Bar. '*Open up the doghouse*,' he boogied along to the kitchen, '*two cats are comin' in.*'

Shaky on his feet he fell against the door. 'Hush, Baby, old pal,' he giggled finger to his lips. 'You'll wake the righteous from their sleep.'

He stood listening. Dee would be dead to the world but Sophie, his lovely little princess, has ears like Dumbo and will run to meet him.

Smiling and giggling he waited. Then he remembered. He is alone.

The fun went from the day. Beer from the icebox, he sat brooding.

The night of the raid he was at the Black Swan. He'd seen Ash waiting for Dee, spied on them, saw them meeting in the hospital grounds and one look at the big stiff's face knew he'd caught the Big One.

So what did Bobby do but borrow a jeep and hunt them down. First they went to Auntie's in the boondocks and then they trailed about all day without so much as holding hands. When they finally pulled into the Black Swan car-lot Bobby tootled in after them pitching his tent by the

Jukebox. Did his devoted nurse see her patient sitting in the corner? Did she hell! Too busy gazing into Hunter's eyes. A bit of shuffling on the dance floor and then they went upstairs.

Was he sick! Tick-tock, he stayed behind with the regulars, watching the clock and sipping warm beer while listening to the same tune on the jukebox.

Whump! A bomb dropped from the sky and all hell let loose!

At first he's fleeing for his life. Then seeing the damage to upper floors, girls and guys jumping from windows, he prized the lock off the cellar chute and fought his way back up. The door to Room 11 was off the hinges, she was on the floor but no sign of Ash, a window frame swaying in the breeze and Armageddon at the gate.

Flames searing his eyebrows, he snatched her up and ran down the stairs popping up from the cellar like a soot-streaked rat.

But for her pants she was naked. He wrapped her in a blanket and flagged an ambulance. No sooner did it leave than Alex stumbled across the square.

Eyes popping, he grabbed Bobby. 'Did you see her?'

The devil got Bobby's tongue. He outdid St Peter denying Adelia four times.

Weary now, he leans against the door. Fondness touched his heart, and though he tries to fight he remembers Ash visiting St Faiths. A mere Major he was in those days and what do you know he'd given up his last 48 to visit a buddy.

Was his buddy glad to see him? Noh, he fucking wasn't! He couldn't wait to get rid of him and Ash too well-mannered to complain took it on the chin. 'So long, Bobby,' he said. Then he opened the door and there she was.

The rest, as they say, is ancient history.

'Except it ain't ancient,' Bobby muttered. 'It's alive and kickin'.'

Ash may be telling the truth about being sucked through the window. He never was a liar but unable to live with that Bobby pushes the thought away.

That day in Needham Square a scuffle broke out Ash going crazy; it took three guys to hold him down. A fat Polack by name of Joe took over. Whump, a whack to the chin and he's in a van on his way to Southampton, leaving the real hero to hightail it back into St Faith's.

It didn't end there, Ash forever on the blower. Bobby talked him out of visiting. '*Bodies brought from the hotel were burned beyond identifying.*' Which was true! Just not true of Dee. She was caged in an annex with geriatrics and cockroaches. Back in his role as Yank in the Broom Cupboard, he was first by her bed. When she woke he waited for her to speak of Alex. She said nothing.

A bomb fell, the world shivered and shook. Nobody's world shook more than hers.

What a come down! In a day she went from Miss Icicle to a lying bitch. At first Bobby was inclined to agree. Then he witnessed a couple of the blackout fits and became her protector. Adelia and 'the bump' became his family.

Strange, he looks back on that time with tenderness. He was at the clinic when Sophie was born, roses in one hand and a beer in the other. Maybe that was how a true obsession with Dee began. Now they're gone and he is alone.

'*Open up the doghouse…*' As usual he's up in her room stroking and sniffing. The fancy stuff hangs in the closet along with the sable coat Gabe brought back.

Bobby's sick of going to bars. He is sick of his bowels and scars that fester, sick of hobbling along with a stick and people staring. Most of all he is sick of Bobby.

He tried putting an end to it but lost his nerve thinking God was watching.

Well God isn't watching!

God, like Bobby, is blind!

'I should've killed her when I had the chance!'

Picking up a box of face powder he hurled it across the room. Opening the closet he wrenched stuff from the hangers, tearing at it, silk and chiffon rupturing under his hands. Then he did the same with her pathetic suitcase, the passports and thirty Judas quid she hung onto always planning to leave.

He trashed the lot. She can go to Hell but is taking nothing with her.

~

Alex was still sleeping. She slid out of bed, dressed quickly, and left closing the door behind her. It was a heavy morning, oppressive. She took the short cut over the fence into the orchard. The Morgan is under the willows, the front fender staved in and the bonnet warm from the sun.

Upstairs she found chaos. Sophie's things hadn't been touched but her room was trashed, her clothes piled on the bed with perfume emptied over all, and their old suitcase emptied, passports torn up. Perched on top of this funeral pile was a costly Guy Fawkes, the sable, scarlet nail polish dribbled over the fur.

Screaming frustration, she scooped up the clothes and opening the fire-escape door tipped the lot over the rail, rainbow-colored silks and satin billowing out, diamante jacket catching on a sail the sequins falling as metallic blossom.

By the time she was done she was covered in nail polish. She took a shower and was reaching for the shampoo when it came to her.

She gritted her teeth. 'You've had a ripping time while I was away.'

'I did.'

'Feel better now?'

'Much.'

She stepped out of the shower and he passed her the towel. He looked awful, a transparent look that made her heart ache. 'You look tired.'

'I ain't tired.' He lunged at the doorframe doing chin-ups. Up and down he went, braces creaking and tobacco stained fingers like grappling hooks.

Suddenly he fell, collapsing to the floor arms and legs sticking out.

Gingerly, she leaned forward. 'Bobby?'

'Hoopla!' He sprang to his feet in a horrid kind of somersault.

She screamed with fright.

'Jumpy ain't you, honey-chile?' he said, shadow boxing steam, his fist gliding past her nose. 'You should exercise and maybe lift weights. If you're going to be out three nights on a trot you need to be fit.'

Skin damp, she struggled into her pants and dungarees. Then she went to Bobby's room collecting Sophie's toy monkey from the bed.

'What you doing?'

'Getting Coco.'

'You're not takin' anythin' out of here.'

'There's nothing to take.'

'And that's only right. I paid for it. I keep it.'

She set the monkey back. 'Just as you like.'

'Nothin' is as I like. Where you and your playmates are concerned it's me forever makin' compromises. In '42 it was Hunter. Last week it was the town loon. This week it's Hunter again. Who'll it be in '52?'

'I don't know, but one thing is sure it won't be you!'

Careful, Adelia, she bit her lip, every nerve screaming. She knew she was in danger but couldn't keep quiet. Damn it all, he's so self-righteous!

'You never cared about me,' he said.

'And what have the last years been about then if not caring?'

'I don't mean that kind of carin'. I mean what you had with Gabe.'

'Don't bring Gabriel into it. This is nothing to do with him.'

'It's everythin' to do with him. If he had more of the necessary you wouldn't be botherin' with Hunter.'

'Money has nothing to do with it. And don't set Alex against Gabriel! They're from different worlds.'

'I know, one has hot and cold running water the other an outside crapper!'

'Why must you reduce everything to cash and sex? Ten cents or ten million he will always be Gabriel to me.'

'Listen,' he reached out, tracing the bib on her dungarees. 'You and Gabe? If you wanted to do your thing it's okay with me.'

'Bobby!'

'No, I'm sayin', it ain't an issue just so long as you stay with me. I mean, I didn't really stop you before, now did I?''

'Bobby, please!'

'Haven't you got a conscience?' he said puzzled. 'Doesn't it worry you what you've put me through?'

'Yes, it worries me.' She turned to leave.

He grabbed her wrist. 'You must think I'm crazy lettin' you can come and go as you please.' His grip tightened. 'You think you can stay out all night and come home and shower? What kind of a husband would let you do that?'

'You're not my husband.'

'That's a technicality and you know it. And what about Sophie? You think you're gonna set up home across the way and me let it happen?'

'He is her father.'

'I'm her father. If I was a good enough father last week I'm good enough for the rest of her life!' He twisted Adelia's arm. 'Because of you I've put up with all kinds of hell, people laughing, thinking I'm a clown without the wherewithal to keep a woman happy. You can go but she stays even if I have to go to court.'

'No court in the land will allow you to keep a child when her true father lays claim. The only way you'll see Sophie is if I say so.'

He slapped her then, drawing blood from her mouth.

'Don't you hit me!' She caught up the nearest thing to hand, the frog-rattle, and hit him with it. 'I'm sick to death of people treating me as they like!'

Clack! Clack! The noise echoed about the room.

Bobby started to laugh.

She ran out onto the fire escape.

'No you don't!' He barred the way. 'You're not leavin'. You're getting' on that phone and bringin' my daughter back where she belongs.'

'You must be joking! No way I'm bringing her back to you and this lunatic asylum! How could you tell Alex I was dead?'

'Is that what he told you? The man's a liar.'

'You're the liar. I have a problem remembering but some things are burned in my brain forever. Like the photograph of you by the B17 plane, Baby Rourke prior to his accident. And those burnt in the grate the day I came. You did that so I wouldn't see Alex and remember him. And the card in my pocket calling me a whore? You've been lying since we met. But that lie, that I was dead, beats them all. How could you do that to your best friend?'

'And how could you leave your best friend for him?'

'I haven't. I'm still here, more fool that I am.'

'I'm not talkin' about now! I'm talkin' about Suffolk. I was good to you. I looked out for you when everyone else called you crazy. Who was it took care of you? Who bunged the baker a wad so you had a place to live? Who

bought food, payin' black market prices so you wouldn't go
hungry? Who was it? Tell me!'

'You.'

'Yeah, good old Bobby! You broke my heart. You chose
my best friend over me but I still loved you enough to offer
you a home.'

'Yes and I'm grateful.'

'I don't want your gratitude! I never wanted it! It's like
the clothes in the closet. You thought them beneath you as
you thought that of me. I bought the clothes. I disposed of
them. I bought you and can dispose of you.'

Cracks in the glass fanning out like a spider's web he
flung her against the fire-escape door. 'I hate these things,'
he looped a dungaree strap about her neck. 'No dresses to
give the poor Bobby a hard-on, just plain wear. Ain't that
right?'

'Yes that's right,' she kicked out. 'But it didn't stop you
trying!

'Well, how about this? A couple of days with Hunter
and she's feisty! Good was it? Have lots of lovely wet sex
did you? Fuck all night and all day?' He twisted the straps
tighter. 'Come on, Miss Dee, tell me all about it!'

'I'll telling you nothing!'

'That's it…struggle! It won't get you anywhere. Earlier
this week I pledged my soul offerin' my miserable life in
exchange for yours. God said don't bother. Not so long ago
I begged Hunter to put me out of my misery. He wouldn't
do it either. But you know what it's not me needs puttin'
out of misery, it's you.'

Adelia was choking. Her eyes burned. Her lungs burned. The sky behind Bobby's head burned. High in the air she heard the cuckoo call. 'Cuckoo!'

Then there was nothing.

No cuckoo.

No sky.

And at long last, no Bobby.

She slid down onto the fire-escape. Bobby staggered back, his hands still at her throat. There was the rushing sound of a high-velocity aircraft. A man's legs cut through the dusty air kicking him down. As he fell an arm came about his neck cutting off his air supply. Murderous gray eyes stared down at him.

'I didn't mean to do it,' Bobby gasped. 'I didn't mean to kill her.'

Gabriel didn't care what he meant to do. He kept on squeezing until that miserable life began to fade and there was bubbling in Bobby's lungs and regret that he never saw Paris or went to the opera or ballet.

Abruptly, pain and sound rushed back.

'Don't!' Alex punched Gabriel clear. 'He's not worth it!'

'But he killed her!' said Templar scrambling toward Adelia.

'No he hasn't. Not if I can help it!'

Alex dragged her across his knees. Tipping her head back he pinched her nostrils and breathed into her mouth. He struck her breastbone and massaged her heart. Once and counting: one thousand one, one thousand two, one thousand three, breathe.

Her breast rose and fell.

'Come on!' he yelled. 'Don't lie there! You got Sophie to think on!'

She coughed.

'Come on! Come on!'

Coughing and choking, she lurched upward her eyes staring and frightened.

On his feet and pulling her with him Alex took her head between his hands and blew into her face. She recoiled, gulping air, her lashes quivering.

He blew again. She took another gulp of air and then sagged against him, holding on to his waist a red weal appearing about her throat.

Alex's knees went. Suddenly he was shaking so he didn't know who was supporting whom. 'Thanks,' he said to Templar.

'I did nothin'.'

'You did. He was coming again. She wouldn't have survived a second shot.'

Bobby was on his feet and scrambling down the fire escape.

Neither man watched him go.

'What brought you?' said Alex.

'The frog-clacker. And you?'

Alex was silent. God knows what brought him, maybe a ghost. He was asleep and dreaming of Joe Petowski who was calling, 'wake up, Camera!' he was shouting. 'Adelia's in trouble!'

He woke and the bed was empty. Through an avenue of apple-trees he'd run and so afraid his spirit ran before him lofting over the orchard. That's when he saw the fight on the fire escape and Gabriel seemingly walking on air.

Down in the yard a car started up, the engine revving.

'I should've killed him,' said Templar.

'You didn't need to. He's dead already. He just doesn't know it. But he's done damage. God knows how much of her is buried under the pain.'

Gabriel turned away. 'But for you she'd be buried under somethin' more final.'

Chapter Twenty-Two
Teddy Bear's Picnic

'Look at those tiny polar bears, Adelia!' Sarah pointed to the window display. 'Don't you think they'd look cute on the tree?'

'Yes, very.'

'Suzy Hawkins, a friend of mine, is a whiz at tree decorations. Suzy and her crowd are coming over Thursday finalising the details for this year's Gala Ball. Why don't you get Alex's Man Friday to buzz you over? '

'That's kind of you but Miss Mattie and Miss Emilie are coming to tea.'

'Not to worry, perhaps another day. Come to lunch and do wear that hat! You look like a Russian Countess travelling incognito. I believe I shall co-opt you onto the fund-raising committee. Maurice keeps telling me we need more glamour. By the way, Alex, I've tickets for you for the Gala.'

'I don't know about that, Sarah, our plans are still loose.'

'Tighten them! It's the New Year's Eve Ball. Everybody will be there.'

Alex felt Adelia shudder. 'It's time we were moving. We've a meeting at Sophie's school at 1500 hours. I'll call you later about the Gala.'

'Yes do but only to say you're coming. I've told everyone about my brother's beautiful wife-to-be so I want you there.'

Alex kissed his sister's cheek. 'Thanks.' She returned his kiss, whispering in his ear. 'No thanks necessary but next time bring the real Adelia.'

In the car he glanced at Adelia. 'You okay?'

'I'm fine.'

Fine? If gazing out of the window is fine then she's fine. If fine is leaping to her feet whenever he enters the room or looking to do chores every minute of the day - helping Bates take out the trash or in the kitchen with cook peeling potatoes- then she's fine. And if fine is returning his kisses with her lips but not her heart, withdrawing inch-by-inch, then she's fantastic!

The noose about her neck did more than bruise her throat. A spark has been quenched, Adelia Challoner's flash and kindle doused. By day she sits by the window and at night is locked into nightmares. She freezes whenever he's near. Most days he keeps his hands in his pockets afraid to touch her.

Living close to the Mill doesn't help, not a speck of light seen, the tower an accusing finger pointing to the air. God knows why he thought it would.

Sophie copes with the change better than her mother. Confused by the state of affairs, not understanding why Daddy Bobby, as she now refers to him, cannot be with them, she settled with a minimum of fuss. She rarely asks questions seeming to know the subject taboo. The family are a mixed blessing. Crazy about their granddaughter they try to juggle it all, but while the General has a soft spot for Miss Dee Alex's mother is hostile.

Gossip filters back via the children's hospital, how Bobby was ill-used by his woman and best friend and decent charity thrown back in his face, and is always seen in his red car, a bruised turtle in a hand-painted carapace.

Frank Bates is now Sophie's permanent minder. They get on well, the big man and the child, yet it's hardly a satisfactory situation. Gabriel Templar is the one person nobody wants to discuss, and this, more than any other reason, caused Alex to put the Eyrie on the market.

It is snowing. 'Are you warm enough?'

'How could I be cold in this?' she said adjusting the collar of her coat.

Dark grey wool with black sable collar, double-breasted with twisted silk frogging down the front, it is an elegant garment designed along the idea of a military greatcoat. She wears a hat of the same fur. Hair pulled back from her face, spikes of dark fur on her white forehead, she is breathtaking.

'Sarah's right. You do look like a Russian Countess.'

'Is that good or bad?'

'From where I'm sitting it's impressive.'

'The question is will Sophie's new school be impressed?

'They'll be so impressed they'll up the fees accordingly.'

When she came to the Eyrie she came with a pair of coveralls and a faded shirt. Coveralls and shirt were consigned to the bin. The shirt was retrieved and now laundered and pressed is in the bottom drawer of her dresser.

Alex doesn't care that she came empty-handed. He gets a kick from hustling in and out of female shops, Sophie clinging to his hand and sales-girls twittering. Adelia loath to accept gifts he doesn't want her feeling obligated. He wants her to be happy and in love. At the moment he has neither.

~

The car pulled away from the school gates. 'So, what do you think?'

'I think she'll love it.'

Bright classrooms hung with Christmas decorations and an impressive list of academic achievement on the walls it seems a decent school.

'Are you happy for her to go there?'

'Perfectly.'

It is quiet in the car, wiper blades sweeping snow from the window. Adelia wants to tell Alex how much she loves him and how her heart is filled with gratitude for Sophie but she can't. Words pile up in her head yet it's Bobby's face she sees first thing in the morning and last at night. Who will take care of him if she's not there? Who will feed him and keep him clean?

If only she had something to do to! The Eyrie runs itself. Alex is an army-man and self-sufficient. Sergeant Bates is Factotum. A woman comes and cleans three times a week, a cook organises the meals. There's a gardener so that's out. Other than care for Sophie she has nothing to do.

In Washington today she tried explaining to Sarah.

Sarah shrugs. 'He tried to kill you.'

'He didn't mean to. He wasn't himself when he did that.'

'It doesn't excuse what he did.'

'I owe it to him to help him.'

'You owe him nothing. Not even regret.'

Beside her Alex sighed. 'I take it you don't care to go to Sarah's Thursday.'

'Perhaps when I know her and her friends better.'

He was silent a while. 'Would you sooner go home to England?'

'I hadn't thought about that.'

'Neither have I but I should. I was so locked into having you with me I never thought to ask if you wanted the same. I mean, why should you? All I am is the guy with the good fortune to be in the right place at the right time.'

Adelia opened her mouth but he held up his hand.

'Let me finish! We can move house and move State but would it be the answer? You should have the opportunity to lead your own life. Choose what you want for yourself and Sophie. You were brought to Virginia on a lie. I couldn't stand to think you were with me on another.'

'I'm not with you on a lie.'

Snapping the lighter shut he pulled on a cigarette. 'I can't believe I've railroaded you into a situation without thinking it through. You must be allowed to be your own person. My Pappy left me well provided. I can set up a trust and you wouldn't be taking anything I'm not willing to give.'

'Alex...'

'Don't get me wrong! It's not what I want. But we shouldn't think about what I want only what's best in the long run.'

Adelia began to cry, huge gulping sobs.

'God, don't cry!' he said, pulling her into his arms.

'I'm sorry. I can't get his face out my mind. He was so unhappy. And he didn't mean to do it! But I don't want to leave you. I love you!'

'You do?'

'Of course I do!' She realised it was true. 'Why would we want to go to England? You are my home. Sophie and I would be lost without you.'

She flung herself at him, kissing his eyes and mouth and any other bit of him she could reach. He laughed then, a great joyous bark. 'Hey now, take it easy!' he said, nestling her into his side. 'We don't want to alarm the driver. I got plans for when we get home. I don't want you stealing a march on me.'

The ride home was good, Alex healed by her words, but then they pulled through the gates, Frank ran toward them and he knew there was trouble.

'He's got Sophie!'

Adelia's face was ashen. 'What do you mean got her?'

'I was out back with my head under the hood. I thought she was okay. A minute ago I heard the phone. I went to check and she was gone.'

Adelia started running toward the woods. Alex grabbed her. 'Don't rush in until we know what's what.' He turned to Frank. 'Have you rung the police?'

'I was about to when I heard you coming.'

Alex turned to Adelia. 'Stay here. We'll get her.'

'I'm coming with you.'

'Negative! We don't want to spook him.'

'It's me he wants to speak to. If he sees you it will only antagonise him.'

'I can't let you go there alone.'

'You can. Bobby won't hurt Sophie. I know he won't.'

~

Bobby didn't think Sophie would come. He sat gazing out of the window, watching snow fall. There was a knock on the door. She looked real pretty, a blue velvet coat with round collar, black patent boots on her feet, a ribbon in her hair, and the bag shaped like a cat swinging from her arm.

'What you got in the bag, hon?'

'Secret things,' she said setting it down.

'Oh secrets!' He went to the window. There was no sign of anybody yet. But they will come. Dee won't leave her daughter alone with him.

He put the kettle on and then checked himself in the mirror. Not too bad. Maybe he could've had a closer shave but he couldn't see to do it.

'How have you been, princess? Still doing your ballet?'

'I go to Madame Julie's now.'

'Madame Julie, ay?' He can hear a car!

'My new ballet teacher.'

Seconds later they pulled into the drive. They'd come in the Packard not through the copse but right to the front door! This is Alex setting the tone, once a soldier always a soldier.

They arranged it last week, him and Sophie. Sunday evening she called the club to see how he was, and then innocently spilling the beans about her Mom and Alex were going to check out her school. That was when Bobby invited her to tea and asked her to keep it secret.

Monday he waited at the window until the Army car swung by on route to the Eyrie. Then he called Sophie and like a good daughter she came.

There's a sound outside, snow crunching underfoot. A tap on the door!

A quick glance about the sitting room! He'd tried to do it as she used to do it, best Worcester tea-service and cake-stand, pastries on top, fancies in the middle and cucumber sandwiches on the bottom - the bread sliced so thin it took the top off his thumb.

There was raspberry Jell-O in the blue dish, Greek ladies in togas smiling through the Jell-O. There was cream, silver forks for the pastries. Napkins. Smiles! It was everything for a civilised afternoon tea.

A sniff of the armpits making sure everything is okay, (he'd padded the diapers and put rubber knickers over his shorts so he should smell as sweet as the new mown.) A quick glance in the mirror - eye patch in place - a polish of shoes on the back of his best RAF blues.

He opened the door.

'Hello, Bobby.'

'I see you got a military escort,' he said, Hunter, Bates, and an army driver by the car machine-guns for eyes.

'Can I come in?'

He stood aside, resisting the need to bow and say, after you Duchess. Today wasn't about clowning. Today is about…about…truth is he doesn't know what it's about other than to apologise for what he did.

Then again it's nothing to do with being sorry and more about giving him out there the finger! Indeed there's satisfaction to be had in shutting the door in Ash's face. Squirm, you bastard! See how it feels to be afraid.

He turned and Adelia is kneeling by the chair arms about her daughter.

'May I take your coat?' he says, all politeness. Trembling, she passed her coat and is revealed in a knitted dress, soft wool clinging to every curve.

'And yours, Miss Sophie?' he said, watching as she shed her coat, a pretty tartan taffeta dress underneath with a lace collar.

'Great dress! You goin' some place after?'

She nodded gravely. 'Petey and David are coming to Nana's for tea. We're having a fancy-dress party, masks and things.'

'Sounds like fun,' he said reaching out to rumple her curls.

'Come here, Sophie!' Dee called.

The fear in her voice stung him. 'I'm only lookin' at her.'

She gazed at him. Shamed by the look in her eyes he went into the kitchen and fiddled with the teapot. The heavies stand by the car, Bates like a bronze Buddha and Hunter in an overcoat, snow making a cape of his shoulders.

When he returned with a tray Dee was perched on a chair and Sophie clamped to her side. 'So what is it these days, princess, one lump or two?'

'Negative,' she said, Hunter in her voice, a clean crisp note overriding the drawl. 'My daddy says sugar's not good for my teeth.'

My daddy! His hand shook spilling milk the full weight of what he'd lost thundering home. Until today the house was a nightmare from which he had hoped to wake but now, Sophie in her tartan frock and Dee a new coat, this is reality. They'll never come home again.

'So what's in the bag?' was all he managed to say.

'Christmas presents.'

She gave him a parcel. He opened it, squinting at a multi-coloured blur, a blanket made of bits of cloth.

'It's a blanket I made to keep your legs warm when you're flying.'

'Gee!' he said, recalling the two of them in the den some weeks back, Sophie labouring over the stitches and Dee helping. 'You made it yourself?'

Cheeks pink, she nodded. 'Mummy cut out shapes and I sewed them together. See this?' She pointed to a patch. 'That's Mummy's skirt. And that is Mrs May's blue dressing gown. That's Gabriel's shirt. And that is your...'

Overcome, a mongrel pissing on the floor and God rubbing his nose in it, he bundled the rug aside and took up the second parcel. 'And this?'

'It's a sweater Mummy knitted.'

He dragged the one he wore over his head and scrambled into the new the smell of her in every stitch. Shaking, eyes filling up, he fished behind the sofa, passing a box with the name of a New York furrier on the lid.

'Pass this to your ma, will you?'

'I don't think so, Bobby,' said Adelia.

'If you don't want it burn it! It's only a coat.'

He had another parcel for Sophie. She opened it. It was Coco all gussied up in a new uniform and with a bright red eye-patch at his left eye.

'Oh my monkey!' she cried, cradling it in her arm.

He passed the jeweller's box. 'This is to go round your wrist.' Eyes like saucers, she opened the box. It was a gold bangle. He slipped it on her tiny wrist. 'It's got a message inside, to my princess from Daddy Bobby.'

'Oh, daddy!' She threw herself at him sobbing. 'I miss you. I want you to come live with me and Mummy and Daddy.'

Dee was crying too, tears running and not attempting to wipe them.

That finished him. His heart was breaking, tearing in two. Suffocating, he pushed Sophie away. 'Sit with your mother! You're wetting my sweater.'

Stricken with grief he slumped in the chair. Where did it all go wrong? This time last year the house was soaked in Christmas. There were coloured lights and tinsel, the smell of cooking, turkey and mince pies. There was Sophie and kids from the ballet school singing carols, Ma on the sofa, Gabriel hanging mistletoe over the door and good old Biffer following him around.

Now the dog is dumped on the airfield, its leash a coiled snake under the rocking chair. The house is a morgue. He's moved into Dee's bed but all he gets is night sweats. He's dying. And he's blind. He can't see the dials on the instrument panel. Washing is piled in the baskets and pots in the sink. The garden's run to seed and the roses are covered with mildew. The hogs and the chickens are gone. There's nobody! And he's so lonely he could die!

'Is there anything I can do for you?' Dee whispered.

'No, nothing,' he said. 'I done it all myself.'

The clock struck six, still they sat, cakes and sandwiches untouched and the tea cold in the pot. Nobody rammed down the door, no gunfight at OK Corral. There was silence and love and pity coming at him in waves.

The clock struck the half.

'We have to go soon,' said Dee. 'Sophie has her party tonight.'

'Oh yeah that's right, a fancy dress,' he hissed. 'You goin' as Delilah and Ash Hunter as a fuckin' snake in the grass.'

Sophie dropped her bag on the floor.

Dee picked up the bag and with an almost audible click rose to her feet.

His words, his stupid, stupid, profanity, had set her free.

She helped Sophie into her coat. 'Thank you for the tea. It was good of you to go to so much trouble. Next time perhaps you'll have tea with us.'

'Okay,' he said, still sitting. 'Don't forget your presents.'

'We won't.'

Sophie kissed him and then tucked the toy monkey under his arm. 'Coco says he wants to stay with you.'

'Sure, sweet-pea,' he said, too exhausted to return her kiss. 'And thanks for the blanket and the sweater.'

Dee unlocked the door. 'Goodbye, Bobby. Thank you for everything.'

Long after they were gone he stared at the door. 'Don't mention it.'

Chapter Twenty-Three
Auld Lang Syne

'Mummy!' Sophie looked round the door. 'Rosie's wetting the floor again.'

'For heaven's sake!' Rosie is a Christmas present to Sophie, a retriever pup, with brown eyes, golden fur, a huge appetite, and a weak bladder.

Adelia flew down stairs, snatched the puppy, shoving newspaper between it and the floor while trying to keep the hem of her robe clear of advancing puddles.

Frank Bates passed, a wilted Christmas tree under his arm. 'She don't seem to have got the trick yet, ma'am.'

These days Frank is a permanent fixture in an apartment above the garage. If she was doubtful of sharing their home a glimpse of the holster strapped to his chest -and memories of the Mad Hatter's Tea-Party as Alex refers to it - plus the nature of the military trips they make together - cause her to think again. Special Ops, Sarah calls it. Adelia doesn't know what it is but as time moves on and tension rises — uniformed men in confab in the sitting room - she is glad of Frank.

Rosie under one arm and Willow under the other she returned to the bedroom. Sophie is in her father's dressing-room fastening his cufflinks, his bass voice rumbling below her high flute; she and the boys stay with their grandparents tonight, Adelia and Alex accompanying Maurice and Sarah to a Gala Ball.

It's fancy dress, Sarah persuading a theatrical friend to let her borrow from the wardrobe department, hence she's to be Peter Pan, Maurice Captain Hook, a stuffed parrot on his shoulder, and Adelia Tinker-bell with silver bustier and tinsel wings.

There should have been a pirate outfit for Alex but it was too small. Recalling him in the bedroom last night, moonlight throwing Bacchanalian shadows on the wall, she stifled a giggle. Is there a man like him? Fierce and tender, he makes love to a military campaign, her satisfaction the ultimate victory. 'I say in there! Why am I always the one clearing up?' she said, applying a fresh coat of nail polish. 'Rosie's everybody's dog, not just mine.'

'Ah, but you have flare,' said Alex coming into the bedroom, Sophie hanging on his shirttails. 'We couldn't do it half so well, could we, sweetheart?'

Sophie grinned. 'No Daddy.'

'Traitor.'

'Who me or your daughter?'

'Both. Sophie, make sure Rosie has her supper. It's Mrs B's evening off. And don't leave it for Sergeant Bates! It's his New Year too.'

'Okay!' She dashed off down the stairs.

'And don't say okay!'

'You're fighting a losing battle there, Mammy.' He moved behind her tying his tie in the mirror. 'She's in love with Petey and his every other word is okay.'

'It could be worse. It could be affirmative.'

'Was that insubordination I heard, Tinkerbell?'

'No, sir, Colonel, sir!'

'You sure?' He swept her hair aside his lips to her neck. 'Only if I were to put you on a charge and confine you to quarters we'd never get to the Ball.'

'Oh, let's not go,' she swiveled to face him. 'Let's stay here.'

'Nothing I'd like better but we promised Sarah, and I mustn't be greedy and keep you to myself,' he said stooping to press his lips to her breast.

'You're mean,' she said. 'I've polish on my nails and you're taking advantage.'

'Mean am I?' He locked the door. He stripped off his shirt. Never one to do anything by halves he kept on until there was a man so secure in himself he could crouch, entirely nude, knees braced and erect penis exposed.

'You are wonderful,' she said softly.

'Ah, shucks, lady,' he blushed. 'No more of that you'll have me swollen headed. But what the heck, my head's no different than other bits of me.'

Tongue gently probing, he kissed her, and then turned her round to undo the clasp on her brassiere. 'Is this one of them complicated fastenings I hear about?'

'Hear about?'

'I've been around. I'm no green horn when it comes to beautiful women.'

Drawing her close, he rubbed his chest over her breasts. 'I've ached to do this. Night after night I've thought of nothing else, you and me in the warm darkness.'

He pulled her to him. 'Hold me,' he said harshly. His lips sought her breast, his mouth warm enclosing her nipple. 'Hold me as you held Sophie. Show me how it was when you fed our baby, and then I can see and remember.'

She bound him close. 'I do love you.'

'Thank God for that. There's something I need ask. Don't worry!' he said. 'I'll not enquire into the past. Your life and mind are your own. I'm just grateful you're here.' He took a ring box from the drawer. 'I bought this in Suffolk when I went to look at the old place. I saw the color and thought of a window in Suffolk.'

~

'We're poor little lambs that have lost our way, baa, baa, baa..!'

It was late by the time Bobby got to the Eyrie. Swigging from a bottle and singing he slewed into the drive. It was cold, icicles hanging from the willows and he'd swallowed so much bourbon he might've been in the Tropics.

Bottle under his arm he slammed the knocker, the noise a rifle shot. 'Yeah, baby! That's the noise we wanna hear, disturbin' the neighbours at their evenin' prayers.'

The door opened, Frank Bates in cardigan and slippers.

Bobby saluted. 'Evening, Squire. I've come to see the mistress of the house and to convey heartfelt good wishes for the comin' New Year.'

'The mistress and the master left ten minutes ago.'

'Don't tell me I've missed the late/late show! I wanted to catch that show. Best lookin' hoofer in town! Never seen titties like 'em! Make your eyes stand out.'

'Go home, Captain, and sleep it off.' The door closed.

Whistling, he made an unsteady way back of the house to the orangery where an oil lamp burned. The night of the house-warming Adelia took a lamp like this and went walking through the woods looking for Biffer. Then all alone in the middle of nowhere she started to dance her hair flying like ribbons on a Maypole.

He was watching from the bushes. Seeing her dance like that he was sure Gabe Templar was nearby. But it wasn't him she danced for. It was Ash Hunter. Something had been said, a word or gesture that had brought her alive.

Flicking open a pack of cheroots he hung over the lamp, taking a light from the hissing flame. The smell of oil stung his nostrils and smoke filled his eyes.

'Your stagelightin' stinks, Dee!' he bawled. 'You should get one of your studs to carry torches like they did in the old days. Whooee! I'd give my left nut to see the mighty Hunter tipsy-tosying about in his army socks. That'd pack 'em in the aisles!'

Sniggering, he took a strong pull of whisky, and then carefully wrapping the bottle in a paper bag lifted his arms and began twirling like a ballerina.

"Missed the Saturday dance...heard they crowded the floor...couldn't bear it without you...don't get around much anymore..."

Several crablike turns about the porch and then he lost interest. He would've been here earlier but went to a movie and got sidetracked by Sue Ryland. Phew! That was one hot tomato. Strong hands, she don't mind groping in the dark with a friend. Cupping his hands, he yelled, 'keep your lumberjack paws to yourself, pussy! Times may be hard, but they're the only thing that is.'

If Ruby had been a better mother he might've been a better man. When he came home from Blighty minus an eye she let him lie in shit. Then when Dee came to help Ma gave *her* hell. 'But it wasn't all bad, was it, sweetheart,' he whispered.

Despite their troubles there were days when he was happy; summer days pottering about in the greenhouse tending roses, sunlight on his face and Biff at his feet.

She was always there, a straw hat on her head and a smile on her lips. They'd share their brand of compensatory sex and try to get along but driven by demons he'd take to the wharf picking up whores. He'd get drunk hoping the whore would go away but most fiddled with his useless tackle and stole his bankroll.

It is snowing, the willows trailing branches like ghostly fingers.

Adelia reckons the world is full of ghosts and the Eyrie and places like it halfway houses for the lost. She says it's why she lights a lamp at evening guiding them home. Bobby doesn't believe it but figures to take out insurance.

A moth flew out the willows. Peony wings heavy with snow it bumbled into the flame. Hating to see it burn he squashed it underfoot.

'Okay, little soul,' he said sadly. 'You're home now.' He took the hurricane lamp. No-one yelled stop thief, Bates and the sympathetic un-dead know that like the moth his wings are tattered and that he needs to rest and not burn.

~

It was nearly midnight when Adelia began to feel uneasy, until then all was well.

Earlier this evening a madly, sexy man strolled out the bathroom. Dazzling in white tie and tails, whiskers stuck to his cheeks, Alex shot his cuffs. 'What d'you reckon?'

She had laughed. 'What are you supposed to be?' Holding up his coattails he swiveled, a cotton-tail stuck to the seat of his pants. 'A wolf in sheep's clothing!'

It is all very nice. The Gala Ball is going well. Sophie is with her grandparents. They've seen a house in Richmond they like. She hasn't had an attack in weeks and is to be married on Thursday. She should be happy but...?

'What's wrong, honey?' Alex smiled. 'Some oversize baboon hustling my baby?'

'It wasn't a baboon. It was a wolf.'

He nipped her nose with his teeth. 'Yes, and if you look at me like that I shall eat you. Then you can do that delicious thing with your mouth and drive me nuts.'

'You're not supposed to remind a lady of her indiscretions.'

'Why not when her indiscretions feel so good?'

He turned to talk to Maurice and suddenly Adelia couldn't breathe.

'Excuse me, I must powder my nose.'

Head aching, she leant against a sink.

'Everything all right, Miss?' the attendant asked.

'I'm rather warm.'

Then Bobby called her name. '*Adelia!*'

'Bobby?'

Bang! A mirror on the wall shattered, glass flying everywhere. She ducked yet when she looked again the mirror was unmarked.

Shaken, she returned to the ballroom.

Jacob Feldstein barred her way. 'Can a gorilla beg a waltz with Tinkerbell?'

Ears ringing with the sound of breaking glass she twirled about the floor, rubbing shoulders with exotic characters like Bo-Peep who danced with Little Boy Blue and Red Riding Hood waltzing with a lion, his tail draped across his arm.

'How are you these days?' said Jacob.

'Not too bad, thank you.'

'You know, there have been major developments in the field of war related amnesia. I was wondering if we could meet and discuss your case.'

Adelia knew he was talking but only heard Bobby. She searched the room for Alex and saw him on the phone in the lobby, hand about his ear shutting out noise. Maurice and Sarah were with him. Then all three turned and looked at her.

Heart pounding, she ran. 'What is it?'

'There's been in an accident.'

'*Ten! Nine! Eight!*' Revelers about them began counting the chimes to midnight.

Sarah dashed away, 'I'll go get your coats.'

'*Five! Four! Three!*'

'Where is he, Maurice?' asked Jacob Feldstein.

'Richmond.'

'*Happy New Year!*'

'Better be prepared.' Alex pushed through the throng. 'He's in a bad way.'

'Shall we come with you?' said Sarah, handing their coats.

'Negative. Keep the General informed, as for the rest it's need-to-know.'

They left the ballroom to people singing, words floating out in the air:

'*Should old acquaintance be forgot and never brought to mind.*
Should old acquaintance be forgot for the sake of old lang
syne.'

~

It shouldn't have happened. One minute he's taxiing down and then Biffer's on the runway wagging his tail pleased to see the bastard who abandoned him.

Bobby hit the brakes, slid on the ice, correcting, correcting! What did Biff do but follow the skid. There were two choices, save himself or the dog.

He chose Biffer and swung hard starboard. A grinding noise, the wingtip hit the ground sparks flying. The tail did a neat flip. The Mustang hit the concrete bunker. Boom! Bobby's face is slammed into the instrument panel and feet up his armpits.

He passed out, regaining consciousness inside pitch black nothing.

Sounds echoed, his labored breathing, glass tinkling and metal complaining, and what sounded like rotgut whisky dripping close to his elbow. He could hear but couldn't see. Could think, but couldn't feel. Could breathe but couldn't move.

'Oh,' he thought. 'So this is what it's like to die.'

Not impressed! Other than the suicide pantomime with hosepipe and pistol he'd always thought he'd go out in a blaze of glory, spinning earthbound, wings on fire, Johnny-in-the Stars. This isn't anything, not even an anti-climax.

Then pain kicked in and he changed his mind. 'Jesus!'

There wasn't a part of him that didn't scream in agony.

'Jesus Christ!' It was so bad he passed out again. When he came-to pain was removed, as though his mind said, 'fuck it! I can't take any more of that.'

On a normal day rescuers would be raking him from the wreckage but this is the club airstrip middle of nowhere. Furthermore, it's New Year's Eve, the guy manning the control tower pissed out of his brains by now.

Why is it so dark? Okay it's late but he ought to see some form of light.

Cold fear emptied out his belly. It was dark because he couldn't see.

Pain overwhelmed him. He passed out again and woke to light being carried toward him as though by a train coming through a very long tunnel.

Portside there were two silver buttons about three or four inches apart and a whimpering and scratching and the sensation of warmth close by.

'Biffer, you little sod!'

The dog lay across his chest. So weird, he knows what Biffer looks like, body and curly fur, yet here in the darkness there's only eyes shining like tiny beacons.

What kind of person am I, he asked? That dog loved me and I treated it like shit.

'Sorry, Biff,' he choked up. 'If it's any consolation life isn't the same without you.'

The silver buttons winked and shone love pouring out, like the hurricane lamp Bobby will see them through the darkness and come home.

'Oh!' The pain was so bad it is no longer a pain, it was his soul screaming.

All about him voices whisper and laugh and sing, unearthly voices, and then clear as a bell he heard Adelia.

'Hang on, Bobby,' she whispered. 'I'm coming.'

'It's okay,' he said. 'Don't rush. I ain't goin' anywhere.'

The bottle of bourbon was dripping. There was a stink of gasoline and electrical discharge. Hell! That's not bourbon leaking. That's a severed fuel pipe!

'Get out, Biffer!' he yelled. He didn't mind being fried but the dog needs to live.

'Get the fuck out!' he shouted again but Biffer hunkered down.

There was rippling in the air like gates being opened.

The light coming down the tunnel was close.

Then an enormous voice boomed out. 'You in there, Bobby?'

'Yes sir, I'm in here,' he replied, scared and excited, his soul desperate to fly away.

'You hang on. I'm comin' to get you.'

'Don't be long,' says Bobby. 'Biffer's here and the plane is about to blow.'

Then someone, something, was beside him and the plane, what was left of it, filled with a light so pure and bright it scorched what was left of his earthly eyes.

Hands came down and pulled him out. There wasn't any pain.

'Get Biffer!' he says. 'Don't worry 'bout me.'

'Okay, Bobby, whatever you say.' Strong arms bore him from the wreckage, though they didn't feel like arms, more a soft blanket, or feathers, or wings.

~

The Richmond Road was pretty clear. A watery speck would rise out of the night, a car streaking toward them filling their car with light and then fading into darkness.

The windscreen wipers flicked back and forth keeping time with her words.

'Do you remember when the fox tried to get the ducklings? We built that island in the pond. You said you hated the fox but that night you put out scraps. Then there was the time the rook fell down the chimney. You spent ages levering the board off the grate. Later that same bird ate your chrysanthemum buds, ungrateful wretch.'

Alex knew she wasn't talking to him. She was trapped in the same desperate illness and doing what we all do in the face of death - recalling better times.

He never really hated Bobby, not even when he'd tried to kill Adelia. But the way the guy seems to know when folks are happy and snatches that happiness away is enough to make anyone hate.

A Masarati overtook them on the outskirts of Richmond, Feldstein giving the A-Okay as he passed. Alex's not sure about him. Ambitious, good-looking and with the physique of a linebacker, darkness lurks beneath the slick surface.

'Feldstein is taken with you,' he said, trying to lighten the journey. 'I guess I've got my work cut out keeping your admirers in line.'

She sat with her hands in the pockets of the latest sable.

Alex doesn't care for the coat. He wanted her to return it. She refused. 'It's not a coat,' she said. 'It's a hair shirt.'

~

They turned into the hospital complex and she clutched his hand. 'It's okay,' he said. 'I'm right there with you.' He wound down the window looking for a porter. But it was New Year's Day and nobody around.

'Shall I wait in reception?' she said.

'Okay.' Alex lives by the rules, ambulance lanes must be kept free and so he parked accordingly, maybe if he'd been less tidy he'd have got there in time.

Car parked, he set off at a jogtrot. In the reception area there were deflating balloons and a balding Christmas tree but no Adelia. A ladies toilet was across the way. Thinking she was inside he waited. Minutes ticked by. A door opened, a tired-looking orderly in a blood-spattered coverall wheeling a drip-stand in.

'Excuse me, ma'am?' he said. 'Did a blonde fairy go by you?'

'A blonde fairy?' The orderly walked on.

He rapped on the toilet door. There was whispering and shuffling. A nurse with tinsel on her hat looked out. 'Can I help you, Brer Fox?' she said, grinning.

Catching sight of his face in a mirror he ripped the whiskers off. 'Have you seen a woman in costume go by, tights and wings?'

'Yeah, emergency. You go through the double doors and turn left passed hematology and then onto pharmacy and then turn....!'

It was eerie walking along the corridor, doors and glimpses through small square windows of night-lights pooling on ashen faces.

Cursing, he slammed through. Why go off like that? Why couldn't she wait?

Quickening his pace he strode on, imagination working overtime. He could see her running along the corridor, the sable falling from her shoulders, breath catching in her throat she calls out, 'hold on, Bobby! I'm coming!'

Shoes in her hand, Adelia ran through the reception area, bypassing the desk where a nurse with tinsel on her cap was kissing a porter. Then double doors, left, right, and left again, a voice in her head giving directions, flickering neon lights, she was a girl running through black and white cellophane squares.

Double doors ahead, a metal panel at the bottom kicked and dented. Not stopping to breathe she pushed the doors open. Bobby was in there and so was Gabriel.

'Oh, Bobby,' she whispered. 'What have you done?'

Everything was a mangled mess only one pale hand lying top of the sheet.

She held his hand to her breast. Behind her Gabriel shifted his feet.

'Was it you who found him?'

'I heard the plane come down.'

'How did it happen? It was an accident, wasn't it? I mean, he didn't…'

'No! It was an accident! Get rid of that idea!'

'You sure?'

'I'm sure. He swerved to avoid Biffer.'

'Biffer was there?'

'He said so though there weren't no dog in the plane when I got there.'

She bent over him. 'Bobby you were so brave.'

'That you, Dee?' He moved his head.

'Yes, I'm here.'

'It was Biff,' he whispered. 'He was waitin' on the runway like he used to. There was ice. I couldn't hold her.'

'Hush! Rest!'

'No! I can't rest until I've said my piece. You there Gabe?'

'Uh-huh.' Gabriel came closer his work-worn hands twitching.

'Thanks for getting me and Biff out. I did think you were someone else come to get me. You know, your namesake in the sky?'

'That ain't hardly likely.'

'It is!' Bobby's eyes were swaddled by thick binding yet he seemed to see beyond the hospital ward. 'I saw who you are. I used to think you were a dummy. Boy, was I ever wrong. But it's okay! I've fixed it so you will be okay.'

'Rest Bobby.'

'No!' He was fighting for every word. 'I want to explain why I did what I did.'

'You don't need to explain anything.'

'I do! I did it because Ash is a soldier. Sooner or later he'll leave and you'll be alone. I did it because, although I'll be lookin' out for you and Sophie, you need someone on the ground.' He was struggling to breathe, spitting out words with supernatural strength. 'I did it because she's my daughter and I worship the ground she treads. I did it to set Gabe free. But most of all I did it because I love you.'

'It's alright!' She pressed his hand. 'Everything you said is here in my heart.'

Bobby began to cry. 'I'm scared! I figure God is gonna kick me downstairs with other sinners and I'll be one of them lost and lonely souls you told me about.'

'You'll never be lost, Bobby! I won't let you!' She was on her knees by the bed. 'I'm going to light the lamp tonight so that you can find me.'

'What if you forget? You ain't good at rememberin'!'

'Then Gabriel will light it, won't you, Gabriel?'

'Sure.'

'Promise?'

'Promise,' they both said.

Bobby sighed. 'Then I guess I can go. Kiss Sophie for me. See you, Gabe.'

'See you, Bobby.'

He was gone.

They waited a minute then Gabriel touched her shoulder. 'You got folks worryin' about you. Should I send them in?'

She shook her head. 'Not for the minute.'

Gabriel left. Drained and tired, she sat trying to get her breath back. She should pray but what can she say that God doesn't already know.

A trolley stacked with washing utensils stood by the bed. She remembered such trolleys from St Bart's , they are for preparing a body for the morgue.

At Bart's she was taught to respect the dead, to leave the corpse at peace for an hour before going to the morgue. God's Hour, it was called. During the war beds were at a premium, the deceased cheated of his hour.

Adelia thought of the nurse in reception with tinsel on her cap. She thought of Ruby on her way here, and of Bobby who loved to be smart, and looping her hair in a knot took off her coat to tie a towel about her waist.

Peeling back the sheet she saw the full extent of his injuries, the lower torso strapped in a protective cradle, the remains of his legs tied together. There was little to be done about the stench and waste matter yet she could tidy him up.

Filling a bowl she washed his shoulders and armpits. Even in death he was difficult, his body difficult to turn. It was hard work, her spirit quailed yet she persevered.

There was a paper shroud on the trolley a frill round the neck and vent at the back.

She pushed and pulled him into it and then spread a clean sheet over the bed.

'There,' she shed the towel apron and washed her hands. 'It's the best I can do.'

His belongings were piled top of the locker, his wallet et cetera, and a tortoiseshell comb she used to wear in her hair and Coco the toy monkey.

There were bits of metal in his hair. As she was combing them out a single brown curl slid lovingly about her finger. It was too much! Weeping, she fell on her knees.

'I'm sorry, Bobby. I tried my best but it wasn't good enough.'

The door behind her opened. 'Not as sorry as you're going to be.'

Adelia scrambled to her feet. 'Ruby.'

'Yes me, his mother who should've been sent for first.' A handkerchief to her nose Ruby hung over the bed. 'I always said that plane would be the death of him.' She scooped items off the locker into her purse. 'It stinks in here. Somebody ought to open a window,'

'Aren't you going to kiss him?'

'Why would I do that?'

'He died swerving to avoid Biffer.'

'More fool him. You wouldn't catch me swervin' for a dog.'

'Don't you want to hold him and tell him you love him?' Adelia was desperate for Bobby to know his mother loved him.

'I said all I needed when he was alive. I ain't huggin' no corpse. I leave that to the hypocrites as killed him.'

'I didn't kill Bobby. I took care of him.'

'So, you cooked a few meals and mended his clothes? You were paid for it, and paid well by the look of that coat.'

Adelia wouldn't argue not with him lying here. She set Coco on his pillow. 'I'm going now, Bobby, but don't worry, I won't forget the lamp.'

She reached for the sable but Ruby snatched it away.

'I'm takin' that,' she said. 'Thanks to you I got little else comin'.'

'What do you mean?'

'I mean this, when I heard about the plane I went to the house and took a look in the safe, as is my right being next-of-kin. It was cleared out.'

'I didn't do it. I don't have anything of his.'

'I know. I've seen the Will.' She waved Bobby's wedding ring. 'This is all you got, the gold on his finger. You ain't got the house either. He left it to charity.'

'Bobby left his money to charity?'

'He did, "an unnamed charity to be revealed at the reading of the Will."'

'I'm glad. He'll sleep easier because of it.'

'He might but I won't. He's given every cent of my money away. It's your fault and you're gonna pay!' She punched Adelia in the jaw. 'All I wanted was a daughter-in-law to look up to me and a grandbabby to love but all I got was you.'

'Look at your clothes!' She tore at Adelia's costume. 'You're a no-good tramp who wormed her way into my boy's affections. Well, he can't help you now.' She hit out again, Adelia falling and striking her head against the iron bedstead.

Disturbed by the jolt Bobby slipped down in the bed his arm dangling. Reaching down to grab Adelia's hair Ruby encountered his hand.

'Ah!' she shrieked. 'He grabbed me!'

Stumbling, Ruby lost her footing in soapy water and grabbing the handrail tried saving her balance, the bed grating across the floor. Realizing it was she pulling the bed she wrenched sideways. The bed came to sudden stop. Pillows dropped creating a backrest, and strapping on lower limbs forming the angle, Bobby sat up.

Ruby screamed.

Hands over her ears to shut out the din Adelia crawled under the bed.

The door burst open, Alex skidding to a halt. 'What the…?'

The room was in chaos, the floor awash with water, oxygen cylinders hissing, the bed dragged slantwise and a foot in dusty spangled tights peeping from underneath.

Alex crouched down. Blood dripping down her forehead, Adelia was facing the other way. Coat gathering fluff, he crawled to get to her but seeing what she could see was stopped; Bobby hung over the side of the bed, arms stiff in the shroud and tears like the tracks of a snail seeping from under his bandages.

'Chrissakes!' he yelled. 'Somebody do something about Bobby!'

'Hush.' Adelia put a shaky finger to her lips. 'Don't shout or you'll wake him.'

Alex pulled her out.

Teeth chattering, she huddled against him. 'Is it over?'

'Yes it's over,' he said, bitterly.

Templar having told him she wanted to be alone he was pacing the corridor. Then, thinking she could use a hot drink he went to the cafeteria returning to this.

'Were there many hurt?'

'What?'

'The bomb?' Adelia muttered. 'Did it do much damage?'

'The bomb?'

Jacob Feldstein put a finger to his lips. 'Where are you, Adelia?' he said.

'Where am I? In St Faith's, I suppose.'

'And where is that?'

'Needham, the corner of Wellington Street.'

'And who is this?' Feldstein pointed to Alex.

Silence! She closed her eyes, eyelids flickering as though reading from an inner manual. 'Major Alexander Hunter, US Army, in transit. That's right isn't it?'

Jacob Feldstein nodded. 'It's my guess she taken a step back in time.'

'No shit,' said Alex sourly, utterly sick of doctors and their jargon.

'No listen! She focused on *Major* Hunter. Not Colonel. She's regained the past and is back in '42. Don't you see, all else after that day may not exist!'

'All else after that day? But that would mean...!'

'She has forgotten her daughter.'

'Oh Jesu!'

'But don't despair! We can deal with this. Catch it while it's young.'

'Enough!' Alex held up his hand. 'This will do for now.'

'Is it wise to leave it? We don't know what problems may be accruing.'

'I don't know about wise but I don't want to hear any more. We'll deal with it as we can.' Aware of Ruby Rourke sniveling he jerked his thumb. 'Get that woman out of my sight or there will be one hell of a problem.'

He led Adelia out. At the door she paused to look back. The bed was covered now, a white mound and Coco sitting on the pillow.

'Oh, look!' she said sadly, 'someone's left a toy monkey.'

- 363 -

Chapter Twenty-Four
Will and Testament

'Ham and eggs and scrambled eggs for the lady? Anything to drink, sir?'

'What would you like to drink?'

'I'll have a pot of tea. China, if you have it?'

'Don't have tea, ma'am, China or otherwise.'

'Then a hot chocolate.'

'We're fresh out of chocolate.'

'A strawberry milkshake?'

The waitress clattered away, returning to rearrange grease on the table.

'Hardly the wedding breakfast I had in mind,' said Alex, gloomily. 'But then it wasn't the wedding I had in mind, knocking on some old guy's door his wife in curlers standing in for witness.'

'I thought the judge and his wife were very kind.'

'They were, but I wanted white lace and orange blossoms. I wanted my mother and father to be proud, and my army buddies to drool as you walked down the aisle. I wanted Sophie as bridesmaid in a cute Bo-Peep type outfit.'

Adelia smiled. She may not know her daughter as she should yet she does know Sophie Emma Hunter would never wear a Bo-Peep outfit.

What an extraordinary feeling to walk into the house to feet running down stairs and Alex whispering, 'here's your daughter.' There must've been a phone call, instructions on how to greet a forgetful mother. Lip quivering, Sophie took in the state of her mother's face. 'Hello, Mummy.'

People talk about the rush of love that comes when a new baby is placed in the mother's arms. The rush came that evening when she came to say goodnight, Adelia asking of the doll in Sophie's arms.

'I call her Sally but she's really you.' And indeed the doll did bear a resemblance. All that was missing was the bruises and the black eye.

Three weeks ago Major Alex Hunter, 1st Battalion US Rangers told of her life here in Virginia. He is Colonel Hunter now, the same handsome face and powerful physique yet with silver in his hair and scars on his body. And she is no longer a girl. She is a woman who until recently lived with one American serviceman while bringing up the child of another.

Stunned, ashamed, she heard a tale of physical violence and lies, a sanitised tale at that, Alex too much the gentleman to recount the dirty secrets - and there must be dirty secrets, why else would Bobby Rourke's mother shout, 'whore!' while being escorted from the hospital premises.

Alex spoke of duplicity and of a plane crash and death. There were gaps he couldn't, or wouldn't, fill. Sophie was a mine of information. While inheriting her father's eyes and stubborn will she is also possessed of the same phenomenal memory. At first information was confined to 'Daddy, Sergeant Bates, and my Nana and Gramps.' After a while, a delicate inner barometer gauging time, Sophie widened the field.

Her thoughts and language are of a child yet Adelia learned a great deal.

'This is Barney, my lop-eared rabbit,' they walked the Eyrie gardens. 'Before Barney I had a rabbit called Flash, a hamster called Pinkie, two terrapins and a pig called Hilda. Hilda died. Gabriel took her away. I had a dog called Biffer but Daddy Bobby lost him. Gabriel has lots of animals. He made my doll.'

The name Gabriel so often on Sophie's lips Adelia asked about him. Alex said that he and his mother helped out at the Mill. 'If you want to know more about your life in Virginia he's the one.' She declined to ask, her closet revelation enough, clothes she didn't know she owned and a face she barely recognized, the hair long and curling and the eyes decorated with bruises.

Hardest of all is renewing acquaintance. She found warmth in Sarah Parker's embrace and concern in Maurice's smile. The General is a darling but Ellen Hunter is cold. Much water flowed under the bridge and most of it turbulent.

Jacob Feldstein likens this new amnesia to the excision of a tumour, Bobby Rourke being the cancer. Adelia relies on inner conviction, as the day in '42 was returned so one day shall the years spent in the Mill.

Difficult to grasp is affection for Bobby Rourke. Did she really follow him here with thoughts of marriage? That is a mystery as is the idea of entrusting her child to him. Baffled, she stares in the mirror. Who are you? Then to compensate for folly a face looms in the mirror behind her, a wonderful face, wise and devastatingly handsome.

'Hello baby,' the lips will smile. Most beloved and most revered Colonel Alexander Hunter is there and in a blink of an eye she is transported to the country he loved and to a house she might have dreamed.

He is alive. She has borne him a daughter. They are married.

The rest she can bear.

'Finished the milkshake?' said Alex. 'We need to break the news to Sophie.'

'Yes, thank you, and do cheer up.'

It seems her husband is a great romantic. He bemoans the loss of a wedding.

'It's important to start off right. I don't want another six years without you.'

'Why on earth should you have that?'

'Things happen.' Silence, and his general air, causes her to wonder if there's something her soldier husband hasn't said. There have been visitors to the Eyrie, solemn-faced men with braid on caps.

'If it bothers you,' she said. 'We could have a party on our first anniversary.'

'Then again,' his eyes flashed, 'we could have a double celebration, our wedding anniversary and my son's christening.'

'Jumping the gun a bit, aren't you? I've only just inherited a daughter.'

He took her hand. 'I'm crazy about Sophie yet I'm also certifiably nuts about my wife and am paving the way for when she has something to tell me.'

Adelia kissed him. 'Rest assured, Colonel, you'll be the first to know.'

~

Leaving the Diner they encountered a lady a-lighting a Greyhound Bus.

Alex tipped his cap. 'This is the lady I was telling you about, Mrs Templar.'

Adelia extended her hand. 'How do you do?'

The woman briefly pressed her hand. 'Mizz Adelia.'

'Forgive me if I don't respond in the way I should. I've had an accident.'

'Uh-huh, Ruby Cropper beat you. I did hear about it.' Mrs Templar stared at Adelia. 'I've been at my sister's, thought I'd get a bite before the bus moves on.'

'The weather's changeable,' said Alex, turning up his collar. 'Can my wife and I give you a lift?'

'Wife?'

Adelia blushed. 'The Colonel and I were married this morning.'

'You must be real pleased Colonel.'

'Indeed I am. Can we offer you a lift?'

'Thank yer I'll take the bus. My boy will be at the other end. He'll be anxious if I ain't where I should be. ' Hat on one side, she stomped toward the Diner. Then she paused, and looked back. 'I'll be sure to tell him the news.'

~

Adelia received a letter from Bobby's lawyers. 'They want me to attend a meeting the day before the funeral. It is to do with his Will.'

'Do they need you? It's common knowledge he left his money to charity.'

'That's what I said,' Adelia was hanging a picture. 'Is that straight?'

'Nudge it to the right. So why do they want you?'

'For the same reason we're to attend the funeral, the deceased's last wishes.'

'That would be right, a pain in the ass even beyond the grave!'

'If it worries you I won't go.'

'I'm not worried. I don't want the guy interfering in our life.'

'He's dead. How can he interfere?'

Alex took a shovel to the snow clearing the path. He was worried but not about Bobby Rourke. He is more concerned with a suggestion that a certain Camera might be useful behind the 38th parallel. A cable was sent to his boss, a joker with theatrical leanings. '*Dear Aunt Samantha. Scenery's wonderful but could use a decent Camera. A home model would be best. Foreign copies so unreliable. If you do find a suitable brand, make sure it can function in a sticky climate, Love from Sadie and the boys.*'

Idiots! The message implies choice when there is none.

The second hint of trouble came via a call from Jamie Macintyre. 'How's married life? Make the most of it because it's you and me for sunny Seoul.'

Hell, he thought, rolling up his sleeves and shovelling snow. Why now when everything is good? And this, a lawyer informing Adelia of an ex-lover's contempt! If that's not nerve enough I've been asked to act as a pallbearer.

Click! Smarting at every word Alex recalled the letter. '*Hi, buddy,*' the scrawl looped across the page. '*These days I'm short on friends and so I am asking you to do me and my unquiet spirit a favour and carry me to my rest. I always figured when I hit the big one it would be in my bucket and me charred bones. It worked a little different. Even so, for old time's sake, I'm asking you to carry those bones. Yours in hope, and with apologies for being as ass, Bobby.*'

'The hell I will!' Alex muttered.

'Talking to yourself, son?' the General came out to see him.

'Bobby Rourke's lawyers want me as pallbearer.'

'The gall of the man!' The General took a spade. They worked side by side for a time until the General sighed. 'These dying-wish situations work on a man making him feel obligated. Not that Rourke deserves consideration, although he did right by his country and the British did give him the DFC.

'Uh-huh.'

'I dare say they'll be sending a bunch a RAF types to the funeral and that phoney Dutton will be sporting a handlebar moustache. But a pallbearer? Have you asked your lady what she thinks?'

Adelia was upstairs telling Sophie about Bobby's death.

Sophie wept. 'And will Gabriel put him in a box and put him in the ground?'

'Bobby won't be in a box, only his empty body. The real Bobby who loved you and brought you to Virginia is in heaven. Nana Challoner is with him, and my father, your other Gramps, and other good friends.'

'And Coco?'

'Coco?' Adelia remembered the toy on the pillow. 'Oh, yes, he'll be there.'

'Will Daddy Bobby have the blanket I made to put over his legs?'

'I'll find out.'

Later that evening she sat down beside Alex. 'She's terribly upset.'

'What did you say?'

'What we agreed, the funeral on Friday. She wanted to know how he died. I blamed the weather for the accident and the weather again for the delay.'

'You can hardly tell her the truth, that he's in deep freeze while his mother contested the will and the only reason he's being decently buried is because the lawyers have said accept the annuity or get nothing.'

~

That night Adelia had a dream. A 'For Sale' sign hung outside the Eyrie. Flowers in the garden had died and the willows lost its branches. Black underwear, black straw hat and single row of pearls, she was dressing for a funeral. Then in the dream a door slammed, Adelia waking to the echo of running feet.

Horrible dream! Alex lay with his hand across her belly. She tried to sleep but the dream brought fear that the warmth of his hand could not relieve.

A robe about her shoulders she padded along the passage. All was peace in Sophie's room, Rosie on the bed and Willow, the cat, curled up beside.

She made tea and sat gazing out of the window. Such a beautiful night, a scene from a Christmas card! From the window she can see the Mill tower.

A lamp had been lit in the tower window filling the room with golden glow. It triggered a memory, a tall man carrying a lamp, a light about his head as with the Good Shepherd in Holman Hunt's, 'The Light of the World.'

A face rose in her mind. Then Alex was beside her and the memory slipped away. She took his hand. 'Is the house still on the market?'

'Do you want it to be?'

'Don't sell it,' she said trying to dispel the dream. 'Let me keep the Eyrie.'

~

The lawyer, Daniel Culpepper, met her at the Mill. 'Hold onto your coat, Mrs Hunter. It's cold inside.'

'What about my boots? They're heavy with snow?'

'Keep them on. There are no carpets to soil. The place has been stripped.'

'Have the others arrived?'

'There's only one other party involved and he's here. Your daughter is a beneficiary but we'll speak of that later. There was another but the lady in question has on advice declined to be present.'

He led her to a room overlooking the garden. There were three chairs, a bouquet of white roses on the table relieving the sour smelling air.

Curious, she gazed about. So this is where we lived. This room has her handiwork, no question. It's likely she papered the walls, and maybe laughed in here, and cried, and shouted.

'It's cold,' she said.

'If you're cold I can light a fire,' this from the other occupant of the room.

'Mrs Hunter, may I present Gabriel Templar.'

They shook hands, the man in well-washed denim and Adelia in black sable. An arc of electricity zipped from his hand to hers.

'Oh!' she gasped.

He released her hand. 'I'll get wood.'

'I understand you're experiencing memory problems,' said the lawyer. 'Would I be right saying you don't recall the house or the man who lived here?'

'I'm afraid not.'

'So you don't remember this room? Such a pretty room before the vandals got at it, lemon coloured curtains and a cream coloured chaise over there.'

'You've been here before?'

'Yes. Culpepper is my name. I was Bobby's attorney.'

'I'm sorry, Mr Culpepper. I would like to be able to remember you.'

'Oh, not at all! It must be a dreadful experience to lose the people and friends one has made. Quite shocking!'

Gabriel Templar piled wood in the grate, flames sprouting under his hands.

The lawyer propped spectacles on his nose. 'Shall we get on with it? The sooner we get this over the better, don't you agree, Mr Templar?'

'I don't know why I'm here. Can't be nothin' in that paper concernin' me.'

'There's a lot concerning you, sir. You are the chief beneficiary.'

'That can't be right! There's nothin' of mine here save a couple of unpaid bills for wood. Everythin' belongs to Mrs Hunter.'

'Mrs Hunter has two small legacies and the choice of three items to be taken from the Mill. Her daughter inherits a sizeable sum, one hundred thousand dollars, to be exact. Miss Ruby Cropper, the late Captain's mother, will receive a lifetime annuity. The bulk of the estate goes to you, sir.'

'No, sir!' Gabriel leapt to his feet. 'I don't want that!'

'Please sit down, Mr Templar.'

'But I don't want it! I just don't!' Long legs pushed out and hands between his knees, he sat, face white as the snow on the window.

Adelia stared. This is the man Sophie's always talking about. But what was he to Bobby? And what to me that he defends my interests with such passion?

'Mrs Hunter?' Daniel Culpepper coughed. 'My client has asked that you accept these roses, a bouquet to be delivered every week of your life. And this item,' he passed a jeweller's box, 'as proof of his love and devotion.'

It was a wedding ring, inscribed: 'to Dee, with everlasting love.'

'There is a letter to be opened after the interment.'

Adelia accepted the bouquet. The letter and ring went into her bag. She wouldn't wear the ring but neither could she refuse it.

'Then we have the choosing of items from the house. As you can see there's nothing left. I am trying to get property returned but the person who removed them considering them hers I'm encountering difficulties.'

'There is an item I would like,' said Adelia. 'My little girl is very low at the moment. She made a blanket for Captain Rourke. If we could find that and give it to the funeral director I feel sure it would help.'

'It's in the tower,' said Gabriel Templar. 'I'll go get it if you like?'

Aware of the lawyer fidgeting Adelia said, 'why don't we bring this unfortunate business to a close. I am happy Mister Templar will benefit from the will. As for items of furnishings I'd sooner Mrs Rourke kept them.'

'I feel it only right to say this Will is a second draft,' said the lawyer. 'The first left the estate to you, Mrs Hunter. Then in the fall of '48 the Captain changed it, leaving the bulk to Mr Templar.'

'And I'm sure that's perfectly right,' said Adelia.

'It ain't right!' Again the man was on his feet. 'The money is yours. I don't want you thinkin' me a thief.'

'Nobody thinks you're a thief,' said the lawyer. 'I know you to be a right and proper man and that the Captain relied on you a great deal.'

'I was useful to him but the money and us bein' here is his idea of a joke.'

'I hardly call half a million dollars any kind of joke.' The lawyer passed a sealed envelope. 'Read this and you'll see you're missing the point.'

'I'm missin' nothin'!' A caged lion, Gabriel Templar paced the room. 'I got a house of my own. I don't need this and I don't need the money.' Then he turned to Daniel Culpepper. 'And I'll tell you somethin' else I don't need lawyers.'

'There's no need to be offensive. I'm simply trying to do my job. But since you're so clear about what you do and do not want, perhaps you'll instruct me as to what I should do with my client's body.'

'Beg pardon?'

'Captain Rourke wanted his body buried here beneath the blue spruce. Knowing how his mother would react he asked if you, Mr Templar, would be the one to see his remains buried according to the terms of the will.'

'I can do that with or without a will.'

'I'm afraid you can't. The will is specific. The remains can only be brought back to the Mill if you accept the bequest. If you refuse the money and the house and all that goes with it, the planes and air-field et cetera, then all will moulder away, as will my client's body.'

'Oh, but you can't do that!' said Adelia, finding her voice. 'You can't leave him where he doesn't want to be.'

'He wanted the Mill cared for by the people he cared for.'

'It's too sad!' she cried, thinking of Alex and rumours of war as much as Bobby Rourke. 'A man should be brought home to rest. Not left out in the cold. '

'I couldn't agree more.' The lawyer packed up his bag and left. 'This was important to Bobby. Read his letter. I think you'll hear a cry for help.'

Gabriel Templar sighed. 'I shouldn't have gone off like that.'

'It's difficult for you and though I don't remember my time here it's clear Captain Rourke intended you to have the money.'

'Maybe so but it don't make it right,' he said. That man had strong feelins' for you. He didn't mean to leave you with nothin'.

'He didn't leave me with nothing. He gave my daughter a wonderful gift. I shall always be grateful. Mister Templar, I've no right to advise you but I can't help thinking you should accept the Will.'

'It's only money.'

'True, but haven't you a dream to fulfil?' She wanted to lift the unhappiness in his face. 'Something you want more than anything in the world?'

'Sure, but money won't make it happen.'

'How do you know? The future hasn't happened. It's still open. I'm not suggesting money is everything but think what you could do with it?'

'What about you?' he said, turning toward her. 'Ain't you got a wish? '

'I need to be careful about wishing. It seems to me my life has been hazardous enough without tempting fate anew.'

He smiled and the sun came out. 'That maybe true, ma'am,' he said softly, 'but my, weren't you dazzlin'.'

Confused by her feelings, unable to look at him, she pulled on her gloves. 'At least think about taking the Mill. I'm sure you and your mother could make this old house a paradise.'

'Paradise is just a word. What's the good of Paradise if you don't have your own angel inside the door?'

They climbed the tower stairs. The blanket was on a sofa. It smelt of cigar smoke and roses. 'Sophie asked if Bobby had her toy monkey.'

'He's got it. I brought him back from the hospital. I was thinkin' to take care of him but his mother came hollerin' sayin' he was to have the parlour in town. And that was that. But I do know the toy monkey was with him.'

Adelia took a last look about the room. Seeing an oil-lamp on the windowsill she asked if she might take it. 'Do you think anyone would mind?'

He shrugged. 'Who is there to mind?'

Outside in the snow she offered her hand. 'Thank you.'

He took her hand. 'For what? Takin' what's rightfully yours?

'For being a friend to a man who needed a friend.'

Chapter Twenty-Five
Marble Angels

The day of the funeral dawned bright and clear.
Snowploughs cleared the streets, folds of dirty snow both
sides of the road. By 1400 hours the sky was overcast again.
Not a good day for a funeral. Captain Robert E Rourke
DFC was a hero and a local character whose life and death
were equally dramatic; consequently St Jude's is packed, a
threatening storm keeping no one away.

Adelia and Alex sat in the Packard watching mourners
arrive. A chauffeur driven Chevrolet rolled up to the door.
The last passenger had to be helped out, Mrs Rourke,
heavily veiled, a black-bordered handkerchief to her eyes.

'Will you look at that!' said Alex scornfully. 'She looks
like a cross between a bee-keeper and a bomb-disposal
expert.'

'Hush.'

'Well, look at them! They never came near the guy
while he was alive. Now he's dead they're like flies. This
funeral is a sham.'

'All the more reason for us to be here.'

Alex was disgusted at the way Adelia had been treated,
not that she needed the money. It was the principle of the

thing. Years of her life and what did she get but bruises and a rusty oil-lamp! 'And I agreed to act as pallbearer.'

A delicate perfume in his nostrils she kissed him.

'What was that for?'

'For being a big man with a strong sense of honour.'

Greatly mollified, he shrugged. 'It's enough his mother misbehaves without me doing the same.'

Adelia was powdering her nose, powder sprinkling the lush sable.

'Why do you wear that coat? You know how I feel about it.'

'Actually, I don't.'

Of course she doesn't! She doesn't know this is a replacement, the first sable destroyed the day Bobby tried to kill her. Jacob Feldstein phoned. Alex had told Adelia some of what happened while she lived in the Mill but nothing of Bobby trying to kill her. He played it down as he plays down her relationship with Templar. Feldstein doesn't approve; he reckons she's a right to the truth.

Alex demurred. 'She's not to be put through unnecessary stress.'

'And Templar?' said Feldstein. 'Is he under the heading of unnecessary?'

Alex wouldn't budge. 'If she can forget Sophie she can forget anyone. I don't want it being me again.'

Feldstein had laughed. 'She's hardly likely to forget you. The way you've invaded her heart and mind I doubt God could shake you free.'

Invaded her heart and mind? Alex didn't like that. What is he, an army of occupation? No way! The last thing he wants is to be another Bobby.

'Are you all right?'

Clearly nervous she adjusted the veil on her hat. 'This is a bit Garboesque, don't you think but at least it hides the last of my shiners.'

'You know you don't have to go through this pantomime. A month packed in deep freeze? That's not a man they're burying today, it's a compromise.' He shuddered. 'Anybody does that to me I'll come back and haunt them!'

'Nobody would dare. You're much too big and scary.'

'Scary my ass! You and Sophie twist me round your fingers.'

Closing her eyes she pushed her face toward him offering a kiss. Suddenly he was afraid. 'I don't know why you want to do this, not after the way he behaved leaving his money to the hired help.'

'I think Mister Templar was more than that. From what the lawyer said he'd been a constant support to Bobby.'

'And you weren't?'

'I don't know what I was. I only know Bobby Rourke gave Sophie and me a home and that I owe him for that.'

'You owe him nothing, not even goodbye.'

The compact closed with a click, the engraved words 'angel with amnesia,' flashing in the light. 'If I can't at least find it in my heart to say goodbye to him then the years here in Virginia have been wasted.'

With a shock Alex realised they were quarrelling. 'I'm anxious about you.'

'And I'm anxious about you, all the hush-hush telephone calls and news on the radio, Korea and possible troop mobilisation.'

'A soldier has to do what a soldier has to do.'

'I understand that. I'm a soldier's wife and won't make a fuss so long as the soldier in question understands my life is worthless without him and that he has to do what I need him to do, and that is to come back in one piece.'

'I'll try.'

'No darling,' she took his hand to her breast. 'Trying isn't good enough. You have to promise. Swear, hand on heart, you will come back.'

Her breast was under his hand. Click! Time rolled round again. He made the promise, as sacred as the promise once made in a ruined English church.

'I swear by all that's holy I'll come back.'

A car door slammed, making them jump, returning them to the present.

'Come on then let's get it over.' Swinging her knees over the seat she clutched at the sables, her face as innocent and wayward as a girl raiding mother's clothes closet. 'I'll sit at the back. No one will notice me.'

~

No one will notice? She entered and the congregation turned as one, the cause of gossip and speculation scrutinised from her hat to the soles of her high-heeled boots.

An usher hurried forward. 'Follow me, Mrs Hunter, a reserved pew.'

Adelia looked askance. 'Reserved pew?'

'You don't have to do this.'

'Yes, I do,' she said squaring her shoulders. 'I really do.'

He offered his arm and with a rustle of silk and a twitch of his shoulders they started down the aisle. At the transept a woman hissed, one of Ruby Cropper's ragtaggle relatives. Alex faced them down, one by one the ranks of dusty hats turning away cowed by his proud bearing.

A modern day Moses parting a sea of blackened crows, he marched down the aisle, settled his wife in the pew, and then lifting her hand to his lips he bowed before, arms swinging, he marched back down the aisle.

In the porch he removed his greatcoat to reveal immaculate greens and the Medal of Honour about his neck.

Yes, sir, Colonel, sir! If you're going to do a thing do it right!

There were six RAF lads, cadets of slight build and nervous chins. Then the eighth bearer strode into view, Gabriel Templar, it had to be, in black velvet frockcoat and pants, sunlight flashing on his hair.

Alex left the organising to the RAF thus he found he was up front with Templar as partner sliding his gloved hand beneath the pall encountering a rock-hard forearm. Weight unevenly distributed the bearers jiggled about. The church was a hothouse, the scent of roses mingling with the smell of melting tallow. Bobby's favourite colour was predominant, the altar heavy with sumptuous red roses, pillars and pews garlanded with scarlet posies, a froth of satin ribbons more in keeping with a wedding that a funeral.

Chandeliers blazed and down the length of the central nave a white taper stood either side of the pews, lines of flickering flame creating a runway, myriad points of light converging toward the altar and a wooden trestle.

Pure theatre, it had Baby Rourke's tricky hand in every detail.

Alex marched forward his gaze fixed on Adelia's pale profile.

Click! Unexpectedly the Camera rewound on a reel of ancient film. Polished boots paced the flagstones, silver spurs chinked, St Jude stood under a gilded canopy and the Madonna's arms are filled with roses.

Candle wax burned. The organ played the Battle Hymn of the Republic.

'*Mine Eyes have seen the Glory of the Coming of the Lord! He is trampling out the vintage where the grapes of wrath are stored. He has loosed the fateful lightning of His terrible swift sword, His truth is marching on.*'

Alex shuddered. I've done this before! *We've* done this before! I've walked this path carrying another wooden box. The man on my left was the man I marched with and the woman waiting in the pew Adelia.

Click, the film slowed, stopped, and continued forward.

The sense of mystery vanished swept away by the twentieth century and the wreath nestling on the pall, pink rosebuds, 'love from Sophie,' on the card.

'*I am the resurrection and the life, saith the* Lord,' the promise tolled through the church. '*He that believeth in me though he be dead, shall live…*'

The coffin on the trestle, the RAF lads were seated left. Adelia on the right rose to let Alex through. Templar turned as to join the left.

Alex thought to give the crowd fresh meat to chew. He barred Templar's way. 'Since he went to the trouble of putting us together we should stay together. That way the Christians get to score over the mangy lions for once.'

'Yeah.' Templar was quick to grasp the irony. 'If I was to desert the Christians in their hour of need the Lord would never forgive me.'

Alex moved into the pew towing Adelia behind him. Templar sat down and folding his arms stuck his long legs out.

Alex smiled. Pity, he thought, another life we could have been friends.

~

Gabriel's head was in a whirl. Yesterday was bad, but this crammed in a pew next to her and the world watching is purgatory. Desperate for distraction he picked up a bible. Words swam under his gaze: '*My beloved said unto me rise up my love, my fair one, and come away, for lo, the winter is past.*'

It was the poem they read together. Oh, but he misses her! Not a day goes by without him hoping to catch a glimpse always thinking how they used to be together, how she'd tease him, eyes sparkling, and the days they would walk the river bank, sun shining and the promise of tomorrow.

It's all gone, lost forever.

The last meeting, the day she came looking for the dog, left the foulest taste in his mouth. It didn't matter that he did all on purpose to frighten her away or that the Lord God had whispered in his ear, 'Do not fret, my Gabriel. There are many ways to show love.'

He was determined not to come but then he read the note and understood why he is suddenly a rich man. '*As of today, old sport, your situation, cash-wise, is vastly improved. In return I ask three favours. First, carry my coffin. Second, transfer what's left of me to the Mill. Third, take care of our girl. Why didn't I give her the cash? Would you put thousands of dollars in the hands of an amnesiac without taking out insurance? You're the insurance, old pal. Go to it!*

Best of luck, your pal, Bobby.

PS: For Chrissakes get a decent education!

The first two favours he can manage. Offer money and Ruby won't care who carries the coffin or where the body lies. The third favour is pure fancy. A man like Hunter beside her, what insurance can she need? Yet if she was in trouble he'd travel through hell and high water to save that particular Christian.

With that Will Bobby lit a real bonfire. When Gabe got back from meeting the lawyer Ma was waiting. 'I always knew you'd win,' she said. But what has he won? Money can't buy the woman next to him, sitting hand-in-hand with her husband their fingers meshed like the gears in a clock.

Money is money, it ain't a life.

This funeral! So much hot air puffed about the church, people talking of Bobby, saying what a good guy he was and how brave. He wasn't good yet he sure was brave when Gabriel found him in the wreck.

It was screaming that brought Gabriel to the airfield. 'You said you'd be with me! You've got to keep your promise!' Adelia he was calling for. Now she's beside Gabe, coat creeping on his knees and perfume in his nostrils.

In desperation he opened the bible again, the ribbon marking the same place.

Grim and disbelieving, he read of honey-tasting lips and kisses sweeter than wine, the powerful language striking home. Then the page wavered and a gloved hand reached out smoothing it down.

Adelia was reading over his shoulder. 'I love this poem,' she said.

'Yes,' he said. 'So do I.'

Silence grew, a door creaking. He opened his mouth to speak but the RAF Captain was there. 'I say, get a move on, old chap. We're on again.'

The men trooped out, Gabriel Templar and Alex Hunter millionaires rubbing shoulders. It's okay. I'll do what Bobby wants, Gabriel decided. I'll go to Paris and get an education. I'll climb the Himalayas. I'll travel the world and be free but still Adelia's face possessed him and his thoughts were of her.

The cortege was passing the Statue of the Annunciation, the Madonna worn and the Archangel riddled with beetle. Gabriel said a prayer. 'Lady, take this love from me and I'll carve You an angel that will outlive the church.'

~

It was snowing outside, the doors swinging in the wind and snow blowing in.

Disconnected, a stranger at a stranger's funeral, Adelia followed the coffin into the storm feeling as though she hurried toward her own grave.

Yesterday she was at the library at the local paper section researching Captain Robert Rourke. In another paper there was an article about Alex being awarded the Medal of Honour. It seems she loved and has been loved by heroes, so she thought until *Forget-me-not*.

It was the name of the shop. She was ordering flowers for the funeral when the General came by. 'What's my favourite daughter-in-law doing in here?' said he. When she said she'd ordered a bouquet for the funeral he was shocked. 'Flowers for a man who tried to kill you!?'

Tried to kill her! Oh my word! She'd understood things at the Mill to be difficult but never that. The General had registered her shock. 'Forget it,' he'd said pecking her cheek. 'It's yesterday's news.'

It might be yesterday to him but not to her. She's anxious now wondering what else she doesn't know.

'Mrs Hunter?' A man loomed out of the snow.

'General Jentzen! I didn't expect to see you here.'

'I didn't expect to be here.'

'Did you want to speak to Alex?'

'Uh-huh but don't worry. The spat we were anticipating is proving a damp squib. We're likely to call halt to mobilisation. Peace in our time, and all that.'

'Isn't that what Neville Chamberlain said?'

He smiled wryly. 'I believe that was the case.' He glanced at his watch. 'I'd better be moving. Would you ask the Colonel to call me?'

Adelia watched him go. Peace in our time? Why don't I feel reassured?

Snow was falling thick and fast. Threading a way between the tombstones she found a spot beneath the outstretched wings of a marble angel.

It was blowing a gale. She held onto her hat with her right hand and a letter with her left. It was from Bobby dated the day he died.

'Dee, you said you'd never leave me. You swore you'd stay til the day I died. I need you to remember that promise and light the lamp for me.

PS. I was sitting thinking about us and it struck me how dark it is. I miss you and I miss Sophie. I miss sitting on the veranda with Biff of an evening, him scratching his fleas and me sipping a beer. I miss it all, Bobby.'

She gazed at the coffin. Such a small coffin! You'd think a man leaving such a void in her head would need bigger.

~

Alex was right, the funeral is a sham. The majority had already left. A handful remained about the grave stamping feet and checking watches. Even the preacher was in a rush to be gone. The only ones with an interest in the proceedings were the bearer party and they were experiencing problems.

The coffin had to be hefted up a steep incline, the bearers slipping and sliding. They arrived over the grave and shuffled into line. Ropes were extended and threaded through. Suddenly a shout went up. 'Look out!'

One of the RAF bearers lost his footing and then another, his feet sliding from under. The coffin tipped. 'Whoops, butterfingers!' hissed a voice behind her. 'It looks like poor old Baby Rourke's comin' down to earth with a bang.'

Adelia couldn't bear to look yet at the same time couldn't look away.

'Don't let him fall!' she cried. The idea of that poor lump of frozen meat crashing to the ground was too terrible.

Stark images were etched against the skyline, Alex and Gabriel face to face, the coffin between them and their feet planted deep in the snow.

Snow whirled, muscles cracked and ropes strained. Shrieking winds drove coattails high in the air. The two fought to support the coffin, Adelia fought with them, gasping in relief when it was finally lowered into the ground.

'Thank God,' she whispered.

'I shouldn't think God's within a mile of this place,' said the man behind her.

'It is pretty bleak.'

'This'll be his Ma stashin' him here. He didn't want to be in this dump. He wanted to be with his roses. He ain't likely to find peace here.'

'Oh, don't say that!' said Adelia, the wind snatching her hat, racing it away among the graves. 'I couldn't bear to think of him wandering in the dark.'

'Ain't you the woman that used to live with him?' said the man. 'And didn't you forget him? I wouldn't have thought you cared where he wandered.'

'Why, you rude beast! How dare you speak to me like that?'

She whirled to face her accuser but there was no one, only a smiling angel, her hat hooked over a marble finger. The angel smiled. All was still, the storm fluttering within the stillness as snowflakes in a glass paperweight.

A snowflake detached from the rest and fluttered down landing on her lips in the softest kiss. She lifted her hand to wipe it away and Alex pounced, ice melting under his lips. 'Did you think we were going to let poor Bobby hit the deck? We wouldn't do that, would we Templar?

Close to tears she grabbed his jacket. 'Don't you ever do that,' she said, shaking him. 'Don't you ever go away without telling me!'

'I'm not going anywhere, sweetheart. Others may go but I'm staying put.'

Over his shoulder she saw Gabriel Templar leave.

She sighed. 'That's what they all say.'

That evening when Alex was in his study she lit the oil lamp brought from the Mill. The flame fluttered and grew a crocus of light filling the funnel.

She prayed for Bobby Rourke. 'Let him see this light and find his way home.'

No thoughts or feelings, her mind undisturbed snow, she gazed out across the land. All was still, not a breath of wind, every leaf on every tree sheathed in snow, only the stars communicating with earth.

The Mill tower is suffused in white. Trees laden with snow hang across the skyline like intermission curtains across a stage. Beyond the curtains there is a debt being fulfilled - an oil-derrick moving up and down - Gabriel Templar digging frozen earth before opening a coffin to bring his patron home.

Adelia saw a movement in the snow, a dog coming out of the copse, perhaps the fox she feeds every night. But no, it is a dog, a curly-coated Airedale and so terribly thin and wasted struggling through the snow.

It stopped at the veranda.

She crouched down.

Lamplight flickering in amber eyes the dog gazed at her.

'Come on,' she said, softly. 'It's all right.'

Up the steps it came, crawling on its belly, tail wagging feebly.

Adelia picked it up and up wrapped it in her coat.

Paws upended, exhausted and trembling, it lay in her arms.

It smelt of wood shavings and roses. This must be Biffer, the dog Sophie mourns, the fox she's been feeding every night! It's been living in an outhouse, and coming every night to the Eyrie for food.

Adelia kissed the poor half-starved face and carried him into the warmth.

'Welcome home,' she said.

Chapter Twenty-Six
0600 Hours

It is the 2nd of July 1950, a lovely spring day, and Sophie's birthday. They loaded the Packard with rugs and a picnic basket, threw the dog in the back, waved cheerio to Mrs B and headed off to Chesapeake Bay in convoy: Sarah, Maurice and the boys in the second car, the General and Ellen in the third.

They took a trip round the Nature Reserve, goggled at lions and tigers while chattering monkeys stole windscreen wipers. They ate hotdogs and played softball, Adelia in pedal pushers running like a jackrabbit, while Sophie and Becky turned pirouettes on the grass.

Four in the afternoon they found a café that served spicy chowder and hot buttered clams. When the kids started getting fractious the convoy turned for home. They should have left it there but the General wanted to make an evening of it and so they all ended up at the Eyrie. It's not what Alex wanted. Three days from now he's shipping out to Korea.

'Is it warm enough for a Barbeque?' said Adelia.

'With a bit of luck it'll turn cold and they'll all clear off.'

'It has gone on a bit but never mind Sophie's had a lovely day.'

'I wanted this evening to be the three of us.'

'They'll soon be gone and then the three of us, and if you're lucky and promise to be a brave little soldier,' she slid her hand between his legs, gently squeezing, 'eventually there'll just be two of us.'

Hips swaying, she went to the yard. If she'd done that before the call from the DOD his answer would've been to steer her into the laundry room, close the door, bend her over the icebox, and give her the fright of her life, but Korea on his mind his body is willing but the spirit mighty slow to respond.

She noticed and when he was in the bathroom came to enquire.

'What's wrong?' She closed the door. 'You've not been yourself all week.'

'I've a lot on my mind' he said sluicing water over his face.

'Korea business?'

'It's not helping.' He was stripping off his shirt when she took over. Baring his chest she began printing little kisses on his skin causing his muscles to twitch and ripple. 'I don't think we need this.' She unbuckled his belt. 'Nor these.' She shoved his pants down. Then she was on her knees probing his shorts.

'Is the door locked,' he moaned.

'Forget the door, Colonel Hunter,' she whispered, easing his throbbing penis out through his fly. 'Concentrate of what's going on down here.'

Laughing and groaning at the bulging state of himself he did just that. Eyes wide open and Camera clicking he concentrated. Make the most of this, Colonel Bogey, he told himself. It may never come again.

Ten minutes later she'd changed her shirt, plaited her hair, and was talking to his mother. Other than a curve to her lips you'd never know that demure young wife just screwed the brains out of her husband.

~

Alex leant against the door listening to his mother holding forth about schools. Adelia was there but with a poker-straight spine is not happy

'The General and I are thinking ballet-school,' said Ellen. 'So much natural talent, it would be a pity to go to waste. There's a very good Academy in Richmond. The principal and I are old friends. I could arrange a meeting.'

'Don't you think she's a little young to be looking so far ahead?'

'The sooner the better.'

'But are we certain ballet school is what she wants,' said Adelia. 'Sophie talks to me of flying.'

'That's nonsense! Women don't fly planes.'

'I wouldn't say nonsense,' said Alex. 'I heard the air-force is about to launch a campaign with exactly that in mind.'

'But not to fly,' said the General. 'It'll be more about paper-work and such. It'll be some time before we see a gal steering one of them jet-planes.'

'The world is changing,' said Adelia.

'Maybe,' said Ellen tartly. 'But Sophie mustn't be encouraged to fritter her life away. She must use the talents God gave her and not daydream. This flying nonsense is a leftover from Bobby Rourke and shouldn't be given credence.'

Silence fell over the supper table.

Adelia rose to her feet. 'We will certainly think about it, won't we, Alex.'

'Sure.' He threaded his arm about her waist. 'And if Sophie should pursue the idea of flying we won't stop her.'

His folks gone, Adelia pressed her cheek against his back, the sexy siren of a moment ago is wilting. 'Thank God for you,' she whispered. 'If you weren't here they'd run rings round me.'

They would too. When it comes to her daughter Adelia is a veritable tiger but wrapped up as his family are in their own difficulties, Maurice and Sarah at odds and his parents not much better, she can't rely on their support.

The General is crazy about Adelia but still smarting from the troubles of '48 Ellen maintains distance. As for his sister there's talk of separation, Maurice spending time at the clinic and Sarah seen about town with a certain pilot.

Adelia never looked better yet now-and-then wanders the house in conversation with moonlight. Maybe Alex should do as Maurice suggests and accept her eccentricities. Chatting with Joe Petowski is not a regular occurrence, it happens mainly when she's anxious.

Wednesday night after a visit from Sam Jentzen he woke to find the bed empty. First port of call is the attic. She converted it to a sitting room and whenever on nocturnal walkabout that's where you'll find her.

She's there now knitting, her shoulders bare, a ravishing Madame Desfarges.

'Come on, honey, you'll get cold,' he took her by the hand.

'Just a minute, Colonel Bogey,' she said falling into forgotten verbal habits. 'I want to finish this row.' She cast off the remains of a sock and then handed it to him. 'These are for when you leave on Sunday.'

As far as he knows he's not going anywhere Sunday. He's three days to get his affairs in order, not that he needs three, winter of '49 he devised a stratagem securing his affairs. Depending, as it does, on the cooperation of another it's a difficult plan to execute, hard on those involved, harder still on himself for if it goes belly-up it will leave a slur on his name for generations to come.

At such a time he gets a hint of how it must've been for others in her life. But for Korea he would've left things alone but had to be certain if worst comes to worst she will be in good hands.

Thursday, he sent a cable to Paris, buzzing it through in private pouch. It might not read like a plea for help yet the man who receives it will know it to be so.

~

Saturday evening they sat in the Orangery, Adelia looking through seed catalogues. 'That piece of land behind the gazebo would make a marvellous Italian garden. We could lay terraces and dig in Persian and English ramblers.'

'Do you ever think about going back to England?'

'No. Why do you ask?'

'I was recalling a conversation we had and wondering if you felt the same.'

She put the catalogue aside. 'What's going on? You've been like this all week, wandering about the house like you've lost your favourite toy.'

Alex shrugged. She wants to know why her husband is casting lingering looks at the home and the people he loves. What can he say? Should he lean over and in his best Baby Rourke RAF drawl say, *'sorry, old girl, but I've left you homeless!'*

'What is that awful noise?' Adelia went to the window.

Alex's hair stood on end. 'It's a Huey, a helicopter.

'So it is.'

He didn't go out to receive them. You don't invite the devil in.

Mrs Brock came through. 'There's a Captain Macintyre to see you, sir.'

He went into the hall. 'Hi Jamie. What's new?' James Macintyre grimaced. 'The drop's been brought forward. We leave 0600 hours tomorrow.'

~

Jamie gone he sat grinding a hole through the bottom of his cup.

Adelia couldn't stand it. 'Who was that chap with sinister eyes?'

'Sinister eyes? You make Macintyre sound like an extra in a B movie.'

'He looks like an extra in a B movie. And why the helicopter? That was even more B movie. Couldn't he have called or phoned? '

Alex shrugged. 'That's Jamie. He's an Aussie and thinks he's Errol Flynn.'

'I don't like him and I don't like helicopters chewing up the lawn.'

'Jamie's okay once you get to know him.'

'I don't want to know him, not if he makes you this miserable.'

She cleared the dishes, the suspense and half-eaten food making her sick.

Hot water gushed out the tap making marks on the silk shirt.

'Damn shirt shows every mark,' she muttered, reaching for her apron.

His hand closed over hers. 'Leave it for Mrs Brock in the morning.'

She tugged at the apron. 'I'll do it. I need to do something.'

'I said leave it! You look all in.'

Their fingers locked into the cloth. The apron stretched. Darkly stormy she gazed at him. Then, heart banging, she walked away.

He's leaving and doesn't want to tell!

Overwhelmed by nausea, she ran up to her bathroom. She is pregnant, her breasts heavy and tender and the need to clean every room in the house.

It would be wonderful to tell Alex but how can she now he's leaving.

Every night this week he was in Sophie's room. Adelia could almost hear the shutter clicking. Ordinary people go on holiday and take a Box Brownie so they can look back and remember. He is going away but not on holiday.

He tapped on the door. 'You okay in there?'

'Go away.'

He opened the door. 'You look bloody terrible!.'

'Bloody terrible? That's a nice thing to say to your wi....'

She slid off the toilet onto the floor.

When she came to she was in his arms in their bed. The lights were off and he'd pulled the eiderdown over them. And there in the dark he told her.

'I'm leaving for Korea 0600 hours tomorrow.'

'When do you think you'll be back?'

'I don't know.'

Carefully she slid out of his arms and stood unbuttoning her shirt.

He switched on the light. 'You want help with that?'

'It's okay,' she said. 'I can manage.'

Then he is in front of her a wide expanse of chest blocking her view. The sight of him stripped her fingers of the little power they had. She fumbled and he took over. 'I like this shirt,' he said. 'It's a great colour. You were wearing something like this the day I found you. You spoke of my eyes, how they reminded you of Sophie. It was the best, and worst, day of my life.'

'What a horrible time you've had. I'm so sorry.'

'Don't be. I wouldn't swap a second.'

He undid the rest of the buttons and started on her underwear, rolling down her stockings his hands warm on her legs.

Downstairs the radio is playing, muted hum of conversation rising up the stairs. The clock ticked, her heart beat and time honed down to a precious collection of sights and sounds. Lamplight shone on his hair, a scattering of strands like salt on a wintry road. His lashes feathered on his cheeks, lines corner of his eyes deepening in concentration.

The thought that she might lose him sank through her senses like curare.

Air touched her breasts cooling her skin. He gazed at her and her spirit swelled with pride. What a man, she thought. Even in the face of danger you take your time. He stripped and stood, hands on his hips, in a proprietary gesture. 'I get a kick from thinking all this is mine.'

'And that is right,' she whispered. 'I am all yours.'

Hands closed about her waist, warm lips pressed into her right breast. Like the softest silk his mouth moved in a slow circle about her nipple. He bent his head trailing his mouth along the valley of her chest, his lips ascribing the same lingering circle to her left breast. She quivered, her nipples hardening in response. When he sucked, she drew him close, harbouring a bittersweet secret. But the thought of the morning assailed her.

'What's the matter? Is that not good?'

'Yes, it's good. It's always good.'

Dearest, darling, she held him, telling the things he liked to hear. How happy he had made her, how his presence lit her life like a beacon and how that beacon burned bright in their daughter. She didn't mention the baby. There'll be no talk of that, no celebration with the bottle of champagne hidden in the kitchen drawer. One child is enough for a soldier to worry about.

Stretching to his full height he smiled quizzically. 'Your body feels real tender. Is there something you want to tell me?'

'No.' Suddenly she was on the edge of panic. 'Only that I love you.'

He lifted her into his arms. 'Don't be scared. It's going to be all right.'

She was scared, fear pressed against her as a mountain presses on the land.

Patting and stroking, her hands raced over him. Until this moment she thought she knew him. Now he's going away. The shoulders so straight and square will leave. His long back and flat belly would leave. His neck and stubborn chin, darkling dovetails of hair back of his head, infinitely precious, those too would leave. God knows what would return. Maybe a tin box!

'Alex!' she stuttered. 'I want to tell you what's in my heart.'

He touched her lips. 'It can't be done. Believe me I've tried.'

'I must. I love you with all my heart and soul and you have to know.'

'Come on now.' He flattened his hands against her breasts as though to hold her together. 'No falling apart. It wouldn't be fair until I've had my loving.'

He drew her pants down over her hips. 'Very pretty but they've served their purpose. My appetite is about as wet at they come.'

A tear slid down her cheek. She brushed it away. 'It's only a snivel,' she muttered. 'It'll go in a minute.' But the snivel ran amuck.

'Don't!' He crushed her to him. 'Don't or you'll get me going. I don't want to leave but I've been given a second chance and I'm hanged if I'll be ungrateful.'

'Oh don't talk like that!'

Alex gazed into her panic-stricken eyes. 'Hey,' he chided softly. 'I can't have you looking red-eyed and puffy. I'm going to put loving in the place of pain.'

He carried her to the bed, muscles cording and quivering in her body. Every pain touched him. Every jangled nerve was his nerve.

Moving rapidly down her body he kissed her sweet womanhood. She tasted of everything he loved. She was wisteria from the walls of his home, the fighter, the homemaker, the digger of earth and wielder of magic. She was mysterious woman, the tender mother of his daughter. She was luxurious sex, the scent of their mutual desire. Tonight there was a new taste, sorrow.

Sorrow came back on his tongue. He probed deeper but pleasure was elusive. The thought of the morrow was robbing them both.

'Please,' he muttered against her. 'Try for me.'

0600 hours came between them.

He pushed between her thighs and rolling on his back took her with him. She clung like a limpet, arms and legs about him and eyes tightly closed. Desire raced through him. Without breaking contact he swivelled on his knees and bunching his muscles thrust inside her. Silently her head recoiled. He thrust again. Again she recoiled, a mantra rising in the air. 'I won't let you go,' she whispered. 'I shall take you into myself and keep you forever.'

~

At 0500 he woke and reaching out shut off the alarm.

She was asleep, her fingers looped through the band on his shorts. Gently, he extricated her fingers. He dressed and went to Sophie's room.

She was awake. 'Hello Daddy.'

'Hello sweet-pea.'

'You going away?'

'For a while.'

'Can I write to you?'

'Uh-huh. Give them to Mommy to post.' He bent and kissed her. 'Love you.'

'Love you too.'

Downstairs he went, Rosie and Willow following, their tails hanging low and ears crushed knowing this to be no ordinary farewell.

A last reconnoitre of the house, checking doors and windows, though Christ knows why because if harm is to come to his family it will be invited in.

In the sitting room he drew the drapes, his reflection in the glass.

A stranger stared back, a tall man in a hooded Parka and heavy boots and wraps and laces, the trappings of the modern soldier.

This last year he's grown used to a civilian way of life. Loved and beloved he's forgotten how it feels to step back inside the Camera. For all the armour and guns he can't do the one thing he wants, and that is to protect his family.

He paused in zipping his bag a lace scarf and pair of woollen socks added overnight. Seen as unnecessary he should remove both but hasn't the heart.

He thought about the cable sent to Paris. Then Click, his guard is down and he is recalling his first visit to the Mill, Bobby Rourke telling of his love for a woman, how he did wrong to bring her to the States, that she was ill and needed someone to look after her. '*Someone who'll be there when things get rough, a mean sonofabitch who won't let anybody push her around.*'

At the time Bobby was referring to Alex; now he's hoping if push comes to shove another mean sonofabitch will do the same.

Chapter Twenty-Seven
Anyone There?
September 1950.

Yesterday at the Anti-Natal clinic a nurse recalled her own
pregnancy. 'I'll never forget it! Nauseous all the time and
ugly stretch marks, I was glad when it was over!'

Adelia can't remember Sophie's birth but if it was
anything like this, Hunter Junior, the invisible swell,
causing her to throw up every morning with an aversion to
most foods plus the urgent need to pee twenty-four seven
she's glad it's a blank.

Once again she's on the loo and Frank tapping on the
bathroom door.

'Phone, Mizz Hunter!'

'Okay, thank you.' She flushed to toilet. 'Do try not to
get pregnant, Frank,' she said, washing her hands. 'It plays
havoc with your social calendar.'

'I'll bear that in mind.'

She unhooked the phone. 'Hello.' There was a click,
Frank replacing the downstairs phone, and then the long
distance back buzz. Her heart leapt.

'Darling! Is that you?'

'Mizz Hunter?'

Her shoulders sagged. Of course it's not Alex! When he's away on army business all messages are relayed back via an American source.

'Mizz Hunter?'

'Yes,' she said, dully. 'This is she.'

'May I speak with Colonel Hunter?'

'The Colonel is away on business. Can I help?'

A pause and then, 'thank you no. I'm sorry to have troubled you.'

The connection was broken.

'Damn nuisance,' she stepped under the shower. 'Five in the morning? How thoughtless is that? You'd think people would call at a reasonable hour.'

Showered, she went through the closet trying to find a shirt with a little give in the material. These days she lives in dungarees everything else too snug. So who was that calling? Clearly not an army man, they would know Alex is away.

America is at war with North Korea. Rolling tanks and men with grim expressions it's all you see on the newsreels. Fearing for Alex she called Bill. He said not to worry, a storm in a tea-cup it'll be over in no time.

She persisted. 'But what about Alex? He's there as part of an Advisory Group?'

Bill lost his temper. 'UN peace-keeping my ass! We both know what he does and it ain't peaceful. I'm hoping this will turn out to be small fry but yes or no Alex is a soldier and you know what soldiers do.' Bounced back into the Hunter world of take-it-on-the-chin she stopped asking questions. It's not as if she didn't know the nature of her husband's business and phone call or not it's pointless to pursue it.

Dressed and ready for the day, a basket of flowers from the garden, she wheeled her bicycle from the garage. Frank was polishing the cars.

'You off to pay your respects to the Captain?'

'I am. Anything you need while I'm out?'

'Nothing, thanks.'

'We are collecting Sophie around six?'

'Sure enough.'

'Frank?' she paused. 'Why aren't you with Alex? You're usually part of his team.'

'I am.' He sloshed water over the wheels.

'So why are you here?'

'He asked me to stay and look after his girls.'

'Of course he did! And thank you, Frank, his girls are grateful.' She mounted the bike. 'The person on the phone, did you know him?'

He shook out the wash leather. 'It was the Guvnor's friend, the sculptor.'

~

Gates to the Mill were locked, the house shuttered and bolted. Adelia propped the bike against the wall. The bicycle is a gift from Ellen. 'I remember that other old thing you used to ride,' she said. 'Sophie's too grown now for a thing like that but I see no reason why you and Junior can't enjoy fresh air.'

A nice gesture but so out of common for her mother-in-law Adelia smells a rat. This will be about Sophie and the

Royal Ballet and Ellen working undercover contacting Old Girl networks and pulling strings.

Adelia smiled grimly. *She thinks I don't know what she's up to. Sophie's not good at keeping secrets and news of auditions for the Royal Ballet to be held in Richmond can hardly be kept secret. We'll go to the auditions but that's all. Right now giving serious thought to my little girl living away from home is more than I can bear.*

Basket in hand she ducked through a gap in the hedge. *The roses aren't good this year, black-spot and mildew spoiling the hardiest variety. So it's chrysanthemums for Bobby, autumn colors of yellow and amber.* She thought to do a little weeding and brought a trowel but someone has already tidied under the spruce.

'Oh!'

A sculpture of a Golden Eagle hovers over Bobby's grave. Wings outstretched, the bird rides the wind, talons unsheathed and argent eyes raking the sky.

There's an inscription base of the plinth: '*Age shall not wither them nor the years condemn, at the going down of the sun and in the morning, we will remember them.*'

The gate clanged. 'It's you again.'

Bobby's mother has arrived.

Adelia carried on placing the flowers. 'Yes, it's me again.'

'What you brought this time?'

'Chrysanthemum.'

'I hope you'll clear up later. They stink when they're dead.'

'They do rather.' Adelia picked up her basket. 'I must be going.'

'Is it you left that bird?'

'No.'

'It shouldn't be here. Nobody asked my permission. Did they ask you?'

'Why would they? I have no jurisdiction over matters here.'

'That's right 'cos it ain't your house no more...not that it was in the first place.'

'Good day, Mrs Rourke.'

'So you gonna leave it here?'

'It's not mine to move.'

'Well, somebody's got to and it ain't gonna be me. I got my back to think of and that thing looks heavy.'

'That *thing* is a lovely *thing*.' Adelia couldn't help making the point. 'Your son being a pilot during the war I imagine he would appreciate it.'

'It's a piece of trash and should be moved.'

'I'm sure if you feel that way about it, it can be moved. You probably need to speak to the donor.'

'Donor?'

'The sculptor.'

Mrs Rourke tossed her head. 'If'n your talkin' about Gabe Templar as thinks he's Lord almighty these days swishin' about the world gettin' his picture in the paper consortin' with heathens and the like I wouldn't soil my lips.'

Adelia smiled. She couldn't help it, the righteous attitude, the cherries bobbing on the hat and contempt for thousands of dollars of unique statuary was too funny.

It was a mistake to smile. A fire burns in Mrs Rourke's bosom that time and distance will never quench. 'What you grinnin' at? It was you put my poor boy into the ground, you and your dirty dealin's.'

'Dirty dealings?'

'Yes, dirty dealin's!' Mrs Rourke nodded. 'I dare say you've forgotten about that, you and that Gabe's secret rendezvousing.'

Adelia walked away.

'That's a handy memory you got,' Mrs Rourke shouted. 'It leaves out the bits you don't like, lets you to sit in your fancy house with your fancy Colonel and think fancy thoughts. I wouldn't mind a memory like that. Real handy! But it don't change what you did and it don't change what you are, first and last a whore!'

~

Adelia and her mother-in-law are collecting Sophie from ballet class.

'There she is! Cooee, Sophie!' Ellen called. 'We're over here!'

Ballet shoes in hand Sophie ran toward them. 'Guess what, Nana?'

'What sweet-pea?'

'We're doing 'Nutcracker' for this year's concert and guess what again?'

'I've no idea.'

'I'm to be Clara!'

'No! Oh, Sophie, that's wonderful! Isn't it wonderful, mommy?'

'Yes, it is.'

Sophie flapped her hands excitedly. 'And today there was a famous Russian dancer over with the Royal Ballet taking barre exercises. She asked my name, where I lived and had I been dancing long and would it be alright to speak with you, Mummy.'

'Why would she want to do that?'

'I think it's about Bennington.'

'Bennington?'

'The dance school in Vermont! The lady said Nana knew all about it.'

Still chattering excitedly Sophie climbed up front with Frank. Adelia settled in a seat and waited. It didn't take long.

'I suppose you think I've jumped the gun.'

'Now why would I think that, Ellen?'

'Because you always think I'm trying to undermine you when it's not that at all. I was talking to my friend Sylvia. You know her. You met at 'Giselle' last term. Tall, elegant PBK Bryn Mawr in furs? No? Well, she's a friend of Betty Rappaport, who is on the Bennington Board of Trustees. And she said we should…'

Adelia knows about Bennington and the ballet school close by, she read the reports Frank gathered. Both the school and the college have an excellent reputation but it means Sophie staying as a boarder. This is Ellen playing a long game, all that about London and the Royal Ballet when she was always steering toward another school.

'But this is in Vermont?'

'Yes.'

'It's so far away!'

'It's not so far. Modern travel, planes and fast cars, I'm sure, Frank, would be only too happy to run Sophie to and fro. Isn't that right?'

'Yes, m'm.'

Adelia glared at him in the mirror. 'It means boarding out.'

'Yes but only during the week. She'll be home weekends. It's not like London, thousands of miles away. It's just down the road.'

'I'll have to speak to Alex.'

'Alex is not here. You can't speak to him. You must speak for yourself and if it's to be the right school you can't waste time. The problem is you come from a small country and apt to measure distance in tens of miles rather than thousands.'

'It needs to be discussed! I see little enough of her as it is, and I don't know why you're pushing this! Vermont will affect you and the General too. Going there you wouldn't see so much of her. Is that what you want?'

'What I want is beside the point. Surely it's more what we *all* want.'

'And what do we *all* want?'

'The best for Sophie, education wise.'

Three weeks later Ellen Hunter can relax *education-wise*. Sophie is enrolled in the private school attached to Bennington where for a week she will mingle with other children and decide if that's what she wants to do.

Sophie will want it, it was always the dance.

To be fair it is an excellent school. You've only to meet other students to know she'll be part of a unique program. 'This will be her dorm,' Adelia is shown round. 'And this is her bed.' The tutor waved an elegant arm. 'As you see by the décor our girls have their own ideas. As long as it's clean and within the bounds of decency we leave it with them. We aim to encourage individuality. Self-exploration in our branch of the Arts is a must, don't you agree?'

'Bye, darling.' Adelia got into the car. 'If you're worried you've only to call.'

'I shall be fine.' Sophie smiled. 'You will take care, won't you, darling Mummy?'

A meeting with the vice-principal, a preppy lady formerly from Cheltenham, Gloucestershire, and Sophie's English accent is back with a vengeance, every vowel and consonant sharp as a whip. Living among the hypnotic Southern drawl Adelia fought tooth and nail to hang onto her 'Britishness' as Ellen calls it. Everything changing, precious people vanishing from the earth, she must hold onto something.

'Better take this.' Sophie passed the black-cat purse. 'It's a little young for me.'

Slender and beautiful, and with her hair pulled back from her face suddenly so grown, she ran up the steps without a backward glance.

'She'll be okay,' said Frank, pulling out of the drive. 'Don't need to worry about Miss Sophie. She's a chip off the old block.'

Adelia hugged the black cat purse. 'I know,' she said, 'But it doesn't make it any easier. In fact, being so like her father means I miss her more.'

'Got her daddy's eyes, hasn't she, ma'am.'

'Yes and his memory. The other day she was playing cards with her granddad and beat him hollow. Do you know how she did it?'

'She memorized cards that had gone before.'

'Every blessed one.'

Frank grinned. 'That's one of the Guvnor's tricks, spotting cards. He could clean out a Vegas blackjack table in no time at all.'

'Alex played cards in Las Vegas?'

Frank ducked his head. 'Did I mention Las Vegas? I could have sworn I was talking about some other place.'

They travelled on. At the intersection he glanced in the mirror. 'Will you need to stop off on the way, Mizz Hunter, the baby and all?'

'I'm fine at the moment, thank you. He, or she, seems to be having a nap.'

She gazed out the window but saw very little. There's been a call from Sam Jentzen. There were concerns, he said, could he stop by the house later.

Concerns? One word and fear, which until then was always in the background, surges to the surface. I mean, if a four-star General is concerned then so is she.

~

Tuesday she was in the attic scraping walls when a door slammed downstairs.

'Hello?' Adelia hung over the banister. 'Anyone there?'

Silence and a branch of wisteria tapping the window. She went back to the endless task of stripping wallpaper.

Hard work, the walls padded with endless layers from Regency stripe to Edwardian roses, it keeps her busy.

The house is so quiet! Sophie not here and Mrs Brock only doing two afternoons a week the place is forsaken. She switched on the radio.

'.. *UN troops coming under heavy mortar fire at all positions....*'

She switched it off again.

The phone rang, General Jentzen asking if she'd be home today. 'Of course,' she said. 'Where else would I be?'

She doesn't care for the man, he and his minions always the cause of helicopters on the lawn, and of bags being packed and goodbyes being said, her mouth stinging from the kiss when the giver thinks there may not be another.

Naturally, Alex coming home is always wonderful. The door will slam, a kit bag drops to the floor, and booted feet pound the stairs.

'*Where are my girls!*'

'What?' Scraping knife upraised she froze. 'Is someone there?'

Ridiculous! She needs to stop being silly. Oh, but damn General Jentzen, and damn Ellen, and damn me for giving in!

'You won't regret it,' Ellen was jubilant. 'A couple of years tuition with Madame Kolesnikova and she'll be ready for the Royal Ballet.'

'So, you do intend for her to go further afield!'

'Why not?' she'd retorted. 'The best should have the best and as you very well know the Royal Ballet is the best.'

'Why is your mother like this?' Adelia asked Sarah.

'Because it's what she wanted,' said Sarah. 'Before she met Pa she was a dancer and a very good one.'

The auditions and phone calls made sense then. What you can't do you teach.

'Rosie! What are you doing?' The dog is in Sophie's room making a heck of a fuss. Adelia went in. 'Why are you barking!'

Rosie is another restless wanderer. She paces from Sophie's bedroom to the nursery and back. Now she is staring at the wall, tail wagging madly.

'What are you looking at?' Adelia stroked her. 'There's nothing there, sweetie, only ballet posters. And please don't tell me you're another balletomane. Two in the family is quite sufficient.'

It was rather sweet, the dog missing Sophie, but after a while when the barking changed to an unhappy whining Adelia dragged her downstairs. This great barn of an empty house is trouble enough without Rosie adding to it.

Yes, damn the war and damn Ruby Rourke and her awful letter.

It arrived early post yesterday, the notepaper smelling of liquorish.

'*I dare say you won't like me doing this,*' she wrote, '*but you with a memory thing and people telling lies about my boy you need to know the truth.*'

Her letter seemed oddly low-key. It told of an affair between Adelia and Gabriel Templar, listing dates and times of meetings of 'illicit roundevous', though how the woman knew dates and times is a mystery.

The mystery was solved second post this morning when another envelope popped through the door. '*I forgot this, pages from my boy's diary.*'

Here was a revelation, Adelia reading of a woman she neither knew nor liked, a cheap tart, according to the diary, who swanked about in furs while playing Bobby for a fool. True or not she threw it in the bin.

~

Lights drawing in and the wall-paper comes away like cross-sections of a tree. It makes her sad to see it. People lived in this house before. Flesh and blood, they laughed and loved. They had lives. Now they are forgotten.

These days the man Gabriel Templar is a celebrity. He lives in Paris, his picture in the Times Friday, an article about St Jude's, the promise of a statue.

What's this? She is down to the plaster and what appears to be a mural. Faded and damaged by time and the stripper, but yes, a painting of a ship tossing on the ocean and, of all things, the White Cliffs of Dover.

'Oh look,' she whispered. 'I'm not the first English person to live here.'

It seemed to her then that Alex was with her gazing at the mural.

'Uh-huh, and if things don't work out right, Korea-wise, and Sophie gets into the Royal Ballet, you can always go back.'

'I wouldn't want to. There is no home without you.'

She thought about the letter and what Mrs Rourke said, that Bobby died because of Adelia. God, she is so lonely and with no Alex to hold her close saying, 'baby, it wasn't like that. You did care for him.'

'Then why did he kill himself?'

'I heard he crashed the plane to avoid killing the dog. It makes sense. It's what the Bobby Rourke I once knew would've done.'

'Is that true or are you saying that to make me feel better.'

'I am saying it to make you feel better yet it remains true.'

'I do love you.' She reached up to kiss him. 'Who was it told you about Biffer?'

'My back-up man, Gabriel Templar.'

Pop! A mirage vanished.

For one wonderful moment it truly felt as though Alex were here but in fact there's only Rosie whining and a patch of sunlight on the wall.

~

When the General finally arrived he wasn't alone.

Adelia was with her father-in-law in the nursery hanging curtains.

Cars pulled into the drive, army staff cars and Doctor Feldstein's Masarati.

There was a huddled confab in the drive and Jacob glancing at the window.

Her heart stopped. 'No,' she whispered. 'Please no.'

'What is it?' Bill was down the ladder his face reflecting her pallor.

Unable to answer she stood hands bracing her belly. If I don't move, she thought, if I stand absolutely still then these men and their serious faces will vanish.

Bill Hunter knew differently. Forage cap off, he ran his fingers through his hair.

'It's my boy,' he said.

The doorbell rang. A wall of shiny shoes and somber faces, Mrs Brock ushered them in. Adelia's gaze fastened on Gabriel Templar and the dressing bag over his arm. The last time she saw this man was at Bobby's funeral when he looked like a Rodeo rider. Now he is elegant in dark pinstripe, a gold fob watch and black leather boots so polished she can see her face in them.

She recognized the dressing bag. 'What are you doing with that coat?'

'The Colonel left it with me.'

'What do you mean left? Left as in accidentally left? The Colonel has total recall. He couldn't forget if he tried.'

'He told me to give this to you if anythin' happened.'

'And has something happened?' How unkind she was, how hostile! But damn it all why make it easy? If she has to suffer then this man must do the same.

'There's talk of boats being sunk.'

'And my husband?'

'Missing, Mizz Hunter,' interjected General Jentzen.

'Presumed dead,' muttered another.

At those words Bill groaned, a small broken sound, the way poor Biffer whined when he died. Adelia pulled Bill to her. Stiff and unbending, he fought every inch of the way and then his hand touched her swelling stomach and he was still.

Missing maybe, but dead no! She won't accept it as she won't accept the coat.

'You can take that away and bring it back the day you bring my husband back.'

She would have said more but the man fell.

Pole-axed, Gabriel Templar stretched his long length on the floor.

'Poor young man.' Mrs Brock was on her knees beside him patting his face.

Adelia, heart slashed in two, was unable to move.

The men moved him to a sofa where he lay, face empty of expression.

'Is he dead?' said Mrs Brock.

'No,' said Jacob, 'out cold.'

Adelia had no time for any of it. Holding onto Bill, one supporting the other, she could only stand and breathe, beyond that the world was silent.

Gabriel Templar came round, pulled a length of twine from his hair and sat with his head in his hands. It was Bill who went to him, hands shaking.

'What is it, son?' he said. 'What made you fall? Was it something you saw?'

Beyond seeking an answer to pain Adelia didn't understood why he said it.

'I'm split in two.'

'Split in two?'

Gabriel shook his head.

'Are you sick, man?' said Jacob, impatient.

Again he shook his head.

'Are you in pain?'

'Yeah, I am,' he said, his gaze fastened on Adelia. 'But it's not my pain.'

'No,' she said. 'It's mine.'

Chapter Twenty-Eight
Vanishing Breed
North Korea.

The old woman gave him away. She saw him under the wagon. Her eyes widening heralding a scream Alex put his finger to his lips 'Hush, mama-san,' he whispered. 'You do not see me. I am *dokkaebi*. I am invisible.'

It was worth a shot but never a small guy, among the people this side of the 38th parallel he is a giant.

'Yowl!'

The old woman woke the village with screaming. Mouths open showing rotten stumps of teeth they came at him with sticks. Nothing to them, he could've crunched a couple of heads and be gone, but he was weary and the idea of crunching heads didn't suit. So he dropped his arms and let them come.

The Kunsan operation was fucked from the start. Their unit under attack and no returning fire they lost three raiders in as many minutes. The focus was the infiltration of Incheon Harbour in advance of a major assault. They were to use rubber boats. That no one knew of tides and tidal currents resulted in men shot to pieces in the shallows. Some got away. But for Macintyre's decision to drag Tom Farrell from the drink others might also have escaped.

He shouldn't have been there. Until a dumb ass UN General suggested him good for morale his job was purveyor of peace under the blanket of UN Advisors - which meant tracking from village to village, watching men kill and being killed, and from a battle zone to a communal grave, digging children out of a ditch, their doll-like faces serene in death.

Now a prisoner of the North Koreans he and Jamie Macintyre and Tom Farrell are aboard a cattle-train bound for the Interior. Guards went through their pockets, various items, a photograph of Adelia among them, vanishing into one guy's pocket. It was then Macintyre tried messing with the guard and got a kick in the head for his troubles.

Alex was not amused. 'Chrissakes Jamie,' he whispered.

'You gotta have a giggle,' says Jamie. 'If you can't laugh life's not worth living.'

'Sure laugh, but keep it down or you won't have a life to live.'

The train rattled on, Alex furious knowing he shouldn't have brought the photograph. Frank Bates got that shot the night they took Sophie to see *Giselle*. 'There was a guy hawking a camera outside the theatre,' said Frank. 'He took pictures of Mrs Hunter and Sophie. I relieved him of the film.'

Fall of '43 Franklin Washington Bates, Company Chaplain as he was then, went over the side of a Landing Craft. Alex went in after and slipping a rope round the mammoth neck hauled him to the shallows. Later the Padre, as Bates was known, invalided out. He reappeared later in Group minus the dog collar and fiercely loyal to the

Guvnor. 'Stay with my girls. Keep them safe,' was his last order.

Tom Farrell shuffled closer. 'Sorry about the snap-shot,' he said. 'They took one of mine. It was a nice one too, Mary in the garden the day the boys were born.'

Alex nodded. 'Simon and Sebastian, born during a raid, 1800 hours, 8th May 1942.'

Tom rolled his eyes. 'Good grief, Ash, you and your memory!'

'Yeah,' he nodded wryly. 'Me and my memory.'

'That was the week the local church and our house flattened. Luckily for us Mary was in the Cottage Hospital being delivered of twins. Your family still in Virginia?'

'Yes, thank God.'

'Thank God, indeed! They'll be safe there, nothing too troublesome.'

Inside the steel manacles Alex crossed his fingers. 'Nothing too troublesome.'

Encouraged by bayonets, they are out the train and on foot. Some of the guys are wounded, Macintyre a bloodied head and Farrell suffering from dysentery. Apart from old scars opening up on his hands Alex is okay so he and an RUR instructor chivvy the others along. From what they've seen no one must fall by the wayside and live.

~

Three days later having been shunted from camp to camp they are on the match again. There is no obvious bravado. They are all too weary. Even Macintyre is subdued.

They march in silence. It is hard to be *hors de combat* early in the game. Hardest of all is the lack of footwear, Alex's boots stolen at the first camp. Now all he has is socks wound about with a scarf, elite army issue footwear courtesy of an army wife.

They march to another camp with another set of guards. So far this lot don't have too many bugs up their asses; relaxed you might say apart from a John Wayne Kiddie-Captain with the AK-47 who's already marked Macintyre's card.

Though quieter, Jamie is still being an arse. He can't keep his mouth shut, must test the guards, all the while drawing attention to himself and the rest of the prisoners.

'What's troubling him?' said Tom.

'He's just being Jamie.'

'Maybe he's thinking he should've left me to drown.'

'He's an Aussie. He's not thinking anything.'

Tom smiled. 'Where were you going when the photograph was taken?'

'My Pa had tickets for *Giselle*. A gloomy piece but we enjoyed it, especially Sophie.'

'Sees herself as a ballerina, does she?'

'That or a test pilot.'

'Goodness me! We breed them fine these days. Mary and I used to go to the ballet. Nowadays I can't manage it. Crowds you know. I can't take them as I used to.'

'Sure. It's why I bought our house. At the time I had specific reasons for wanting it. Privacy was top of my list, privacy and security, the Eyrie is all of that.'

'I like the name. It conjures images of dark Yorkshire moors.'

Thinking of home, the pink tiled roof, sunlight on the orangery, and ice-blue wisteria on the south wall, Alex stumbled and fell. 'I don't know about Yorkshire moors,' he struggled to his feet. 'More a Suffolk vicarage.'

'Oh no, really?' Tom was horrified. 'Ice cold sheets and abysmal plumbing? How dreadful! And here was me thinking to visit.'

'It's okay. I'm not that much of a Spartan I forgo creature comforts. As for visiting, you, Mary, and the boys, are welcome at my Vicarage any time.'

'I'll keep you to that.'

Major Tom Farrell is an agency man. Linguistics expert on loan to Group he and Alex were together in '46. Interned in a German POW camp, thin to the point of emaciation, Tom survived the war. Now God help him he's back where he started.

'Bless you, Tom.'

'For what?'

'Trying to boost my spirits.'

'To be honest I was trying to boost my own.' Tom sagged against a tree stump, cords of withered musculature in his neck manipulating his jaw. 'Poor Mary! We'd just got over the last lot, the twins beginning to see their Pa as something other than a bogeyman.'

'It's tough.'

'How old is your little girl?'

'Seven last birthday. I missed her early years. I had hoped never to miss another.'

'Never mind, there's always Christmas, *Away in a Manger* and all that. I love Christmas. Is there anything like a kiddie's carol concert for making a grown man weep?'

Alex couldn't answer. Not so long ago he dug infants from a grave and helped take them to their silent mothers. Then he went back to dig out the fathers. Throughout it all he'd remained dry-eyed; Christmas and Carol concerts is another world.

~

Third day in succession they were dragged from the hut to listen to bullshit lectures. '*You have been duped by fellow officers! Learn the truth! Accept re-education! Adhere to lenient policy and you will be shown mercy!*'

According to an interpreter they are part of a Lenient Policy re-education program, solitary confinement, beatings and enforced marches, the withholding of mail and medical aid the not so lenient punishment for non-co-operation.

'*All officers are required to attend re-education classes. Bad behaviour, noises and laughter is forbidden. Violators guilty of such acts will be disciplined.*'

Tom Farrell had had enough. Quaking with cold, his lips blue he turned to Macintyre. 'I say, Cuthbert, old chap! What is your opinion of this Lenient Policy?'

'I think it's twaddle, Claude, old bean,' says Macintyre.

'What say we forswear these proceedings?'

'I think that a very good idea.'

'May I interest you in a waltz, Cuthbert?'

'Charmed, Claude'

'After you then, Cuthbert.'

'No, Claude, old bean, after you!'

Fool or heroes, Alex can't decide. Tom takes his chances. His stint with Montmorency, the invisible bulldog, should go down in history as courage under fire. Every day, a piece of string tied to his wrist, he takes Monty for a walk. Three times he strolls around the perimeter pausing now and then to let Monty take a piss. Final stop is outside the commissar's hooch where, judging by the expression on Tom's face, the invisible dog takes a long and a very smelly dump.

Then there's table tennis. Lop! Lop! Back and forth Tom and Jamie pat invisible bats against equally invisible balls. As usual, the loony Brits are in on the act, queuing at the wires, heads turning left and right in unison, applauding and ramping up the absurd. 'I say, well played, Cuthbert!' and 'Jolly good shot, Claude!'

The first time they pulled that stunt the guards stood open mouthed, their heads turning left and right following nothing. They soon learning what was going on and though still baffled know they are mocked.

This *Cuthbert and Claude* pantomime is their party piece.

Here they go again, Jamie, the Aussie muscle, and Tom, the Oxford academic.

Macintyre bowed. 'Ready when you are, Claude?'

Tom holds out his threadbare jacket, curtseys then away they go waltzing to the 'Blue Danube', musical accompaniment supplied by the Brits via paper-combs and whistles. Round and round, everyone, even the guards are smiling. Then the Commandant takes offence and the guards are onto them - wood thudding bone.

Locked as he is in the Hole, squatting handcuffed in a narrow bunker, punishment for not heeding the Lenient

Policy, Alex didn't see the last entertainment but heard it and had he tears would've wept.

Silly bastards, he thought. The thing is Tom is ill and likely dying and may see this as his way out and ever the gent elects to leave with humour.

Three days Alex has been in the Hole. He squints through the slot trying to gauge time by the position of the sun while wondering whether he'll be fed.

Mouth to slot ratio, the guards slopping in rice, he's pretty much mastered feeding time even to the grains stuck to the sides.

'See the world in a grain of rice?' he mutters. 'Who said that, William Blake? No, that was flower or something, wasn't it?'

'Hey Camera!' a voice calls from an adjacent box, the Marine Corps Sergeant. 'Is that you talkin' to yourself again?'

'Naturally! How else can I ensure an intelligent reply?'

'You're full of shit.'

'I know.' Alex taps on the side of the bunker. 'So they've got you in now?'

'Seems like it.'

'You been a bad boy, Sergeant?'

'Yes, sir, Colonel, sir!'

'Tut-tut. Go to the back of the class.'

Alex is struggling to hold it together. Shut away from the rest, six foot plus jammed into a tiny chicken coop, if he could think beyond the pain he might figure a way out.

'You thinkin' of runnin' again?'

'It has crossed my mind.'

'Forget it. Save your energy and figure another way out.'

'What way is that?'

'The one I told you about, lettin' go of your body.'

'I have been thinking about that but can't see how it works.'

'That's 'cos' you haven't tried.'

Alex has lost count of how long he's been in the Hole this time around. According to the Camp Commissar it's his own fault. He doesn't have to be locked up. If the Colonel were to behave he could be free at the drop of a hat.

'You here many weeks now, Colonel, sir. You are a forgotten man.' The KG2 Camp Commissar has excellent English. 'I was many years missionary boy.'

Is Alex surprised that a missionary boy can string a man to a beam, arms behind his back, toes touching the ground, his body balanced between points of agony for five long hours and when finally cut down is told, 'we see you at class, Colonel? Talk on lenient policy and third movement of Beethoven's Fifth.'

The first month it was cakes and ale, a US Army Colonel a prize worth keeping. But as days went on and he declined to attend class, and was three times found beyond the perimeter, invitations were of a different kind, the commissar saying if he was found on the wrong side of the wire again a man from every hut would be shot; 'to encourage dishonourable action is unbecoming of officer.'

When Alex replied that the duty of an American officer is to resist the enemy no matter the threat, he was again conducted to the Hole.

The Yank Marine warned him. 'The commissar's gunnin' for you. He don't mean you to get out alive. The only way you're comin' out of this with your ass intact is to withdraw from your physical body.'

'And how do I do that?'

'Die from the toes up, Ash Hunter. Do it right and you'll leave pain behind.'

The Marine said it was a yogic technique he'd learned from a friend. 'Once you get it it's like riding a bike. You ride a bike?' Alex said he didn't but his wife did. Few men get mail here. That there is mail getting through is obvious, the Commissar talking of wives decorating an attic and a daughter attending a dance academy in Vermont.

~

They let him out for ten minutes and then came again.

'Look out!' Macintyre is on his feet. 'Bastards are coming again!'

The guards led him away.

'Steady the Buffs,' croaked Tom.

'Keep your head down, mate!' shouts Macintyre.

'Semper Fi, Ash!' hissed the Marine.

That Marine! Lightning flashing and thunder rolling, he arrived middle of a storm like an Old Testament prophet, fatigues cut to ribbons and hair tied with twine. Nobody knows who he is or where he came from or what kind of man he is. You can't pin him down! First he's here and then over there, beyond being made of rubber he is an ordinary guy, cussing and covered with lice like the rest.

The guards give him wide berth. They say he's a Djinn.

Alex asked why they were afraid.

The Marine smiled. 'They think I'm a figment of your imagination.'

Figment or not, next time in the Hole - knowing it was literally do-or-die - Alex did as suggested and closing his eyes willed life from his body.

Cold, hungry and gut-sick with dysentery, it was easier than he thought. His feet were the first to go. Bit-by-bit an icy torpor rolled up his body and where once was cracked and bleeding flesh there is nothing. That nothing was so welcome he redoubled his efforts until eventually there was no pain and no Alexander Hunter, only a light-bulb for a brain which he switched off.

Tom Farrell died that night. Alex was in the Hole when it happened and yet saw it all as if under a spotlight - what's more Tom knew he was there.

'Hello, Ash, old fellow, you out the Hole? Tell Mary I died easy, will you, please,' he panted. 'Don't tell her the truth.'

'Don't you worry.' The Yank Marine had him in his arms, rocking him like a baby. 'Ash will tell her one day.'

'My boys,' Tom began to weep, tears tracking through grime.

'Rest in peace, ' said the Marine. 'Your boys will grow up tall and strong and make you proud.'

'How will I rest in peace when there's no corpse to bury?'

'You'll be okay. Sleep now, someone's come to take you home.'

'Oh yes!' Tom smiled through his tears. 'It's my mother.'

A burst of light and he was gone.

The Marine laid Tom down and then turned to Alex. 'I see you made it.'

Bang! Alex was back in his body and in agony, blood rushing to cramped limbs. The guards brought him out but something must have happened to spook them because next morning they heaped a pile of rice in his dish.

'Yankee tiger eat good,' they said. 'No make slant-eyed bastards crazy.'

Back in the hut Alex asked about the Marine, what did the guards do to him?

Macintyre frowned. 'What Marine?'

Alex couldn't believe it. Why had no one else seen him? It's true their whispered conversations went on in the Hole but surely someone saw him. Time went on and Alex had to face the fact, no one saw him because there was no one to see. Still he thinks on it. Didn't the guards make the sign of the evil eye when he approached? The following day as Alex was brought in to see the Commissar a couple of guards turned away warding off the devil.

Then he understood. It was him they feared. He was the Djinn.

~

Being some kind of evil spirit didn't stop the Commissar. A creative man, he liked to work up close and personal. What he could do with a nail file and patience is beyond belief. He came with the guards.

'Good morning, Colonel. How are you today?'

'Fuck's sake!' Macintyre erupted. 'Leave the bloody bloke alone!'

Alex staggered to his feet. 'Forget it, Jamie.'

'I can't!' Jamie was up and swinging. 'This fucking moron wants to kill you.'

They tied Alex to the spar. The Commissar sat filing his nails and reading the 'Shanghai News.' Several glasses of sake later he filed Alex's nails.

Zzz-zuz, a plane saw buzzing, back and forth over three fingers of his left hand, blood frothing and a white space for a wedding band.

He was out and away at the first drop. For a while, pain reduced to a whine, he seemed to hover above his body. Then he was watching his mother. Ellen was reading a letter. She was weeping, a handkerchief pressed to her mouth.

Unable to bear her sorrow he flipped away to the nursery. Rosie, the dog, ran in and began barking. Then Willow, good old cat rescued from the wild, began turning circles, purring and kneading the blanket.

She seemed able to see Alex as did Rosie who went into begging crouch.

He would've stroked her but his fingers passed through air.

It was Adelia he was desperate to see. The Will and what he'd done with it occupied his mind. The way he'd left things, clauses and rigmarole, she'd never forgive him. Then the door opened and in she came.

Bang! A wave of love sent him crashing back to his body and to the hooch where the Commissar was sweating. They dragged him to the Hole. A bird pecking stray rice brought him round. Such pain! If this is what it can do, split the body from the soul, then the process may operate in reverse. During the war he felt Adelia to be his guardian angel keeping him company. Not wanting her near this filthy place he prayed God deny her entrance. 'Keep her out, Lord! It would break her heart to see it.'

He prayed with great fervor but with little hope. In the winter of '46, in Berlin, he decapitated a man, removing the head from body in the manner of slicing the top off an egg. That God should hear and answer a prayer from the man who did that is beyond comprehension.

He must have passed out. Next he knows it's pitch black. He's still in the Hole but the top is loose and Pappy Frobisher is telling him it's time to get up.

'Come on, son,' he was saying. 'Time you were leaving.'

'Okay, Pappy,' he muttered. 'I'm coming.'

It was hard but Alex made it onto his knees. A fly landed on his hand, what was left of it. He twitched it away. So tired, so very tired, he couldn't move.

'You got two choices, son,' then said Pappy. 'You can let that little weasel run you ragged or you can get up on your hind legs and walk.'

Pappy Frobisher had no time for malingerers.

Alex got up and walked.

The moon was so bright he had to cover his eyes. There was a kerfuffle going on, a lot of shouting, US prisoners out in the compound and what sounded like a riot going on down by the latrine.

Men were scuffling and swearing and the Brits in the other compound making a howling din. 'Bastards!' they were shouting. 'Leave him alone!'

Alex drew nearer and saw the Kiddy-Captain, the KG2's bum boy, standing over the latrine prodding a bundle of rags with a pointed stick.

The bundle of rags rolled.

Oh my Lord!

It was Jamie Macintyre.

Intent on hooking a rosary from Jamie's broken fingers the kid stabbed again. Jab! Jab! He poked the body, pushing it down in the shit and slime.

That rosary! The first time he saw Jamie praying he laughed. Jamie had shrugged. 'It's insurance against old age, mate, a short life and a swift end.'

Shouting and gesticulating prisoners crowd the latrine. The guards are jumpy, no one watching out for a crippled Colonel. As for the Captain, he was having fun, and didn't care about an AK-47 propped against an oil drum.

Jamie's body rolled over, his bruised and bloodied gaze fastened on Alex.

'Kill me,' said his eyes. 'Be a mate. Give me my miracle.'

Alex picked up the AK-47 and shot Jamie. Then he locked, loaded and fired again, the Captain falling, his mouth an Oh of surprise.

Then boom, it is Alex's turn to fall, the thud-thud of a fifty caliber machine gun echoing in his ears. There's mortar fire and what sounds like an Allied raid on the compound, men and guards alike scattering and planes swooping.

Well, what do you know? Relief is here.

Alex closed his eyes. Pappy Frobisher is right - it is time to go.

Book Three
Where there's a
Will

Chapter Twenty-Nine
Dying Hard
Summer 1953

When the stairs creaked Adelia woke. Colonel Alexander S
Hunter might be able to wriggle pass enemy encampment.
He might crawl by machine gun placements in silence yet in
five years of marriage he hasn't been able to bypass the
Eyrie security, a creaky stair, third from the top, giving him
a way.

Listening to various sounds, the snap of a buckle as he
pulled off his pants, the click and spin of the barrel of a gun,
a key grating in the lock as the gun was stored away, and
then a watch being wound, zusa-zusa, the scratching as he
pushed his fingers through his hair, she is tempted to yell,
'What in God's name are you doing? Get into bed this
minute! I've been lying here worrying about you for
hours!' Yet she was glad to have him home and so said
nothing.

Once in bed he dragged her close, hands about her
breasts the rough texture of his palms snagging the
nightgown. Cussing under his breath, he rolled her about
tossing the gown into the darkness. The top sheet followed.
When the Colonel is home and hungry for love he won't be
hampered.

Eyes tight shut and lips spread in a smile she stretched.
Down came a hand over her mouth. 'It's the bogeyman,'
he whispered. 'If you want to be thoroughly loved, Mrs
Hunter, don't peek. But then if you want to be a kill-joy
open your eyes and I'll vanish in a puff of smoke.'

Adelia raised her arms, 'I know this is a horrible
nightmare but because I'm British and have a stiff upper lip
I shall grin and bear it. Carry on, Colonel Bogey. If you
need assistance don't hesitate to say.'

A rumbling rippling through his hands into her body he
laughed. 'No assistance needed. Lie back and think of
England.'

She opened her mouth to tell him how much she loved
him but he was upon her like a tiger dragging her up against
his chest his mouth on hers.

Oh, the blessed man! Until he was here kissing her she
hadn't known how much she'd missed him, from top to toe
the ache bordering on pain.

Heat surged between them. Within seconds she was
covered in sweat.

'Alex?' she whispered. 'Where have you been? You're
soaking wet.'

Down her body he moved, a heat wave moving with
him. When his lips curled about her nipple she cried out
twining her hands in his hair trying to hold him still. In
moments like these he has no time for gentility. Neither
would he allow her to be passive needing her pleasure as
much as his own. Fierce, tender but insistent, he knew her
body and understood the caresses that delighted.

'I've missed you so much,' she said, her eyelids trembling with the need to open. 'Let me open my eyes and look at you.'

'No, baby.' His hands came about her face, his palms over her eyes. 'Be with me here in the darkness. Don't let me go.'

'I'll never let you go.' Her arms tightened fiercely about him. 'Never.'

He lay across her with the smell of foul water. His skin felt muddy! And his hair wasn't soft and springy as remembered it was stiff and matted with dirt.

'I thought you were never coming back. I thought you'd forgotten me.'

'I'd sooner die.' Gently, he kissed her. 'Sorry, I have to go.'

'Go?'

'Got to go. I'll always love you...always...always.' He was leaving, his body becoming less under her hands, dissolving even as she opened her eyes.

'Alex!' she screamed and woke up.

She was kneeling on her haunches in the bed holding nothing in her arms but the cold morning air. It was a dream, a vile mocking dream.

No need to look at the clock to know the time. Two minutes past four, given the time delay it is the exact time her husband went off the radar.

'Sorry, ma'am,' the army told her. 'He went missing beyond the demilitarised zone. A distress call did go out but recovery forces were engaged elsewhere. '

When in despair she asked why the demilitarised zone the reply was perfunctory. 'He was doing what all soldiers are prepared to do. He was giving his life for his country.'

There was a tapping on her door, Frank Bates. 'You okay?'

'The dream again.'

'I guessed as much.'

She gazed out of the window. The sky was strips of navy-blue velvet edged with coral, the Mill tower visible through the trees sheathed in darkness. She used to live in that house, not that she remembers it. A block of time is missing to her, the summer of '42 to the New Year of '49 shrouded in forgetting.

In 1953 the Mill has a new name. Paradise, gossips call it. Absurd! If people are to be believed life in that house was far from heavenly, and the new owner is never there, travelling far and wide, he must feel the same.

She stood under the shower feeling as though God reached into her brain during the night removing a fuse. Early this morning she was treated to another instalment of When Johnnie Comes Marching Home. Terrible dream it always leaves her drained and memories of the day in September rekindled.

They came, or rather Gabriel Templar came to tell her Alex was missing. She was cruel that day. They deserved it. They lost the best man that ever lived, a man who honoured his parents and who adored his wife and child...maybe.

'Missing, Mizz Hunter,' they said. 'Presumed dead.'

She'd wanted to die, to sink in the ground. Gabriel Templar beat her to it. Eyes rolling, he fell. When asked why he said her pain knocked him out.

'Anything we can do?' General Jentzen asked. 'Any help we can give?'

'I'll be all right,' she'd replied. 'My husband left me amply provided.'

At the time she referred to the babe in her belly, Timothy William Hunter, a legacy of love. Financial security was the last thing on her mind yet as her husband's Will was to prove she was less secure than imagined.

Behind her in Alex's dressing room the little brass clock chimed seven. She padded along to the nursery breathing in a wonderful baby smell. Timothy Alexander William George Hunter, Tag, his Gramps calls him, sleeps on his belly, his backside a quilted hillock and his thumb wedged firmly in his mouth.

Two and a half years old he is his sister's pride and joy, his Grandpappy's reason for living, and his mother's sanity. What Timmy might have been to his father no one will know since he left never knowing he had a son.

A photograph stands on the dresser. Taken on their wedding day it is out of focus, the judge's wife juggling with a camera. Adelia gazed at Alex's blurred smile. 'I thought you loved me. What did I do to make you hurt me so?'

She threw open a window. Sunlight blazed in. A breeze blew open the curtains, jiggled the clockwork mobile, causing teddy bears to sing and dance.

'Cup of tea?'

'Thank you, Frank.'

'Soon as you're done with breakfast I'll load up the van.'

'Okay.' She yawned. 'It was midnight yesterday before I finished the last wreath but I am pleased with the lilies and think the Senator's wife will be.'

Other than her children and Bill Hunter, Frank Bates is the best legacy the Colonel could have left. Business partner and friend, he was also an intimate part of Alex's life thus he is extra beloved.

Timmy is awake. Black curls ruffled and eyes the colour of early morning sky, how like his father he is. 'Up, Mummy,' he said.

'It's too early. Why don't you go back to sleep?'

'No! Up!' Timmy's conversational skills are determinedly shorthand.

She lifted him out of the cot as the door to Sophie's room opened, Rosie meandering out, oiling her smiling waggy way into the passage.

'Dog!' Arms outstretched Timmy fell, knocking air from Rosie's lungs.

It's as well we've a big dog. Biffer wouldn't have withstood the rigors.

In the Eyrie things are either up or down. Biffer ate rat poison December '49. Alex left for Korea late July 1950. The General had a heart attack in November '50. Timmy was born February '51, and the first reading of the Last Will and Testament of Colonel Alexander Hunter read on the 4th July.

Kapow! Another defeat for the British!

Tag under her arm like a parcel she made her way downstairs, Rosie on her heels, a gentle bitch who follows

Timmy during the day yet out of loyalty sleeps on Sophie's bed while she's at school. Timmy lies down to rest with a bald teddy bear and a well-sucked blanket. Sophie takes the 'Aviator News,' ballet slippers, and a scuffed cat-shaped purse. Adelia retires with a couple of lovingly preserved pillows and a copy of the 'Funeral Director's Handbook.'

At breakfast Rosie has a bowl of 'Doggobix', and for Timmy, who adores the rusk-like texture, a single 'Bix.' Ellen Hunter disapproves of her grandson eating dog biscuits. He likes them and has the constitution of a lion.

Over the years family feeling toward Adelia has vacillated. Ellen dotes on Sophie. That she's allowed to dote keeps things on an even keel. Sarah and Maurice have troubles of their own. Their sons, David and Peter, beanstalks with acne, are regular visitors. The tightest relationship is between Adelia and her father-in-law.

The heart attack of 1950 softened Bill Hunter. These days he spends most of his time at the Eyrie. Proud of her achievements at the New Valley Rest, and baffled by the terms of his son's Will, he is Adelia's staunchest ally. When her face appeared on the cover of *Time* magazine he was first to buy a copy.

'Down, Mummy! Out and in garden.'

'Bath first.' She sliced oranges feeding them into the juicer. 'When Mrs B comes and you've had your breakfast you can go in the garden. Mummy has to go out today and so Gramps is coming extra early.'

'Gramps!' He wiggled his fingers excitedly.

'Yes. You two can spoil one another.' Adelia gazed at her son and thought how hard it is for Ellen and the

General mourning their son, especially when pallbearers bore only the weight of family sorrow and the US flag.

No corpse, thus no interment, the service was of thanksgiving. So many uniforms that day the church was flags of many nations. Afterward when they took their leave, gloved hands closing over her own, she heard the same phrase. 'Ash was a big man with a big heart. We shan't see his like again.

~

Prompt at ten the side door clanged, the General for his morning Jasmine tea and hot buttered scone. 'Anybody about?'

'Up here, Bill!'

He poked a bunch of freesias round the dressing room door. 'I was passing the florists and thought my favourite daughter-in-law might care for these.'

'Lovely.' She gave him a kiss. 'Sit. Soon as I've finished I'll make tea.'

'Where is everybody?'

'Timmy's with Frank dropping wreaths at the parlour. Sophie's at Sue's.'

'When is she due back to the college?'

'Oh, they've a fortnight yet to play around.'

A powerful body out of place amid blue-sprigged chintz he flopped on the chaise. 'Is ballet to be her full-time education now?'

'It would seem so.'

'Do you mind her being away?'

'Of course! I miss her like crazy.'

Summer 1950 saw commencement of battle for Big School. Ellen Hunter fired the first round. She'd a friend who was principal at Bennington oughtn't Sophie to be enrolled? Alex settled the argument. After his folks went home Adelia hugged him. 'But for you they'd run rings round me.'

Grief bowed Adelia but didn't break her. It's true Sophie attends Bennington, it's also true mother and daughter send away for the Aviator News.

When changing the beds she wraps Alex's pillows in towels and fearful of losing contact keeps them in a drawer during the day.

Oh but here it is! Grief taking her unawares she crouched over the pillows.

'You're having a blue day?'

'A bit.'

The General pulled a pipe from his pocket. 'That'll be the Will playing on your mind. Don't know why we needed three separate readings. One was plenty.'

'I thought you'd given up smoking.'

'I have. This is a comforter for a senile baby. Like you I got that darn piece of paper on my mind. I should go with you tomorrow.'

'Thank you, Bill. I'm just glad you can be here for Timmy. To be honest I don't know what I'd do without you.'

'You'd be okay. There's plenty others lining up to take my place. I called last night but you were out with your doctor friend.'

'You don't like Jacob.'

He shrugged. 'He's a bit too smooth for my liking.'

Adelia was only partly listening. Going through her daily ritual she un-stoppered a bottle of cologne and breathing in the scent touched the stopper to her wrists, left and right. Then she passed his brushes through her hair, once, twice, three times. After that she tested the blade on his cutthroat razor, the chased-silver handle warm in her hand, recalling how he'd shave in the shower, a mirror propped on the soap-tray and water running down his long back.

One, two, three! She touched every item three times, telling herself that if she did this every day, if she kept the faith then maybe one day...

The mirror on the dresser reflected her frown of concentration.

Bill watched. What a beauty with her silver-gilt hair. Her eyes! Dark emerald, lashes long and black and her mouth full and soft, she's a beautiful woman who has forgotten she is beautiful. 'You oughta get rid of that stuff,' he said sharply.

Her hands moving like she's blind, he didn't like her doing it.

'Take it to the Salvation Army. Hanging onto his gear won't bring him back.'

'I can't part with any of it. Not while there's hope.'

It was on Bill's tongue to say what hope but he couldn't bear to say it.

Downstairs, anxiety chewing away, he followed her from room to room. 'So what about this Feldstein character? You got an arrangement with him?'

'No arrangement. We have fun.'

'Fun doesn't last.'

'Jacob adores Timmy. They get on well.'

'That's cosy but he doesn't come here to say howdy to a child. He comes to see you.' The telephone started to ring. 'See, you've got them ringing twenty-four seven, especially since you've had your face on the front of *Time*.'

Adelia picked up the phone.

'Hello beautiful.'

'Hello Jacob. We were just talking about you.'

'Who is we, male or female?'

'Decidedly male,' she said smiling at Bill.

'I'd better mind my manners then. Look, Delia, this legal business tomorrow? I'm in Richmond most of the morning. You want me to pick you up?'

'If it wouldn't be putting you out.'

'Spending time with you is hardly putting myself out.'

Bill was at the window with Alex's field glasses about his neck. 'There was a time he wanted to be an ornithologist. I was set on him following Pappy Frobisher. Maybe if I'd let him do what he wanted he'd still be here.'

'Your son had a strong sense of identity. I'm sure if he had really wanted to study birds he would.'

'Kind of you, daughter, to say so, but I'm not sure.' Bill gazed up at the hand-painted ceiling. 'Look at this house! Look at the work he put into it, night and day busting a gut. I didn't appreciate it. I thought he was chasing rainbows. I was wrong. I was wrong about a lot of things.' He turned to face Adelia. 'One thing I'm not wrong about. He worshipped the ground you trod.'

Mute, she returned his gaze.

'I guess what he did makes it seem like he didn't care. The problem is you don't know what he went through to get you back. The stuff that Rourke character put him through, the lies and the beating he took.'

'Beating?' Adelia went cold. 'What beating?'

'Forget it! Ancient history, I shouldn't have mentioned it,' said Bill. 'Forget what I said but don't forget he loved you. You and Sophie are what he lived for. This Will business is all wrong. Alex was a wealthy feller. George Frobisher was major bucks. Even with a trust fund you'd be comfortable. So what was he thinking of? The way he's tied you up makes it seem he didn't trust you.'

'Perhaps he didn't,' said Adelia, buttering scones. 'I have a poor track record.'

'That wasn't your fault. You'd got the amnesia business and were saddled with Bobby Rourke. And see what *that* fool did with his money!'

'Don't get upset. I'm quite able to take care of myself. Frank and I have the New Valley up and running. The past is water under the bridge.'

'But is it? Maybe that Culpepper has more tricks up his sleeve. Maybe I should come with you, leave Tag with Mrs Whosis and spit in his eye.'

'Scone?'

'The doctor says I gotta go on a diet.' He gazed at the scones, his craggy face so pained she put her arms about him.

'Don't worry. It will turn out fine.'

'I do worry. If Alex had felt more secure about me and his mother's affections he wouldn't have left you hog-tied.'

'I don't feel hog-tied. I'm no longer troubled by amnesia. The children are fine. You take care of Timmy.

When Sophie's of age she'll be a wealthy young woman. As for money, the funeral business pays its way.'

'You and that Bates!' The General shook his head. 'When you first said you'd bought the funeral parlour your ma-in-law but blew a gasket. She thought it unfeminine, you and that dark-eyed Sue messing with corpses.'

Adelia smiled. 'I don't mess with corpses. I'm only a figure-head.'

'Some figurehead! How many proposals did you get in the post today?'

'A few but not necessarily for marriage. Is Ellen still blowing a gasket?'

'Couldn't rightly say,' he demurred. 'You managing the Senator, if that goes as I think it will you'll have half of Virginia sashaying along behind.'

'Orders are mounting.'

'How are you coping with all the cars?'

'We have a man to manage that. Frank does the rigs. I do the flowers and a little facial corrective work. Sue is the main attraction.'

'I saw last week's do. Blue blazes that was some spectacle! I don't mind telling you when those rigs rolled by, the flowers, the horses and the rustle of skirts, every hair on my head stood up.'

He bit into a scone. 'You ever thought of going back to England?'

'Do you think I should?'

'Hell no! I'm only thinking ahead. I wouldn't want you to go. You're a good girl,' he said gruffly. 'I couldn't wish for a sweeter daughter. But you need to think ahead. A boy needs a father. With my dodgy heart I won't last forever.'

'Yes you will.'

'I'd like to if only for your sake. Considering the trouble you've had, memory-wise, I'd sooner see a strong male beside you.'

'I'm in no rush. As for my illness, if I can survive Korea without losing it, *memory wise*, then I can survive anything.'

'Stubborn little thing, aren't you?'

"Fraid so.'

'Sophie and Tag both got a stubborn streak a mile wide.'

'They take after their grandfather.'

He laughed. 'That Feldstein character told me he thought you cured of the amnesia. He reckoned losing Alex cleared the decks.'

'He told me the same.'

'Korea was a goddamn waste! He was happy. He had you and Sophie and would've had Tag. Why couldn't he live to enjoy it?' Bill cleared his throat. 'That sculptor guy Rourke left money to? Does he disturb your peace of mind?'

'You mean do I remember my ex-lover?'

She didn't remember her supposed affair with Gabriel Templar. Then in the fall of 1950 Mrs Rourke sent a letter. That was the end of any peace of mind.

'I don't remember and neither do I want to.'

'Can't say I blame you. However you look at it the men in your life have mighty peculiar ways of showing devotion.'

'Indeed. Recurring amnesia can be a blessing as well as a curse.'

He flinched 'Does that mean you'd sooner forget my boy?'

'Forget Alex?' She thought of last night's dream. 'I'd sooner die.'

~

Adelia phoned the driving instructor for another lesson. Would he pick her up, let her drive to the New Valley Rest and collect her later.

The gentlemen of the Rest were arriving with a client. Smart in dark jackets and pinstripes they wheeled a metal gurney up a ramp into the treatment room. Frank was already busy in white coveralls and rubber apron.

'Is there anything I can do?' said Adelia tying back her hair.

'If you've finished with the flowers there's number six.'

'I'll get started.' Number six is a woman in her late sixties or so the town had been led to believe. 'She's actually in her seventies,' said Adelia reading the death certificate. 'Still never mind. We'll do our best.'

Hooking up a stool back of the client's head, she opened up her box of tricks. No one receives preferential treatment, not even the senator, yet this client, an elderly lady with an unhappy face, will be treated with particular care.

'Be good in there!' Frank shouted. 'Don't be giving her a clown's nose or anything foolish! We don't want any malpractice suits.'

'I'll be good.'

Adelia worked the brush in the pot. Amnesia has its droll side. Had she remembered the woman presently on the gurney she might be tempted to paint her nose canary yellow or insert a daffodil where the sun didn't shine; happily Ruby Iolanthe Rourke raised nothing in her mind save regret.

~

Friday is Mill day. Adelia likes going via Richmond Road and the Wild Life Park to watch giraffes nodding through the trees and to listen to the lion's throaty call. The park was built on the site of an airfield, the con-tower and outlying buildings replaced by metal enclosures and encircled by an electrified fence. From there she usually cycles to the Mill and Bobby and Biffer.

Poor Biffer! He had a rotten life. Alex wanted the dog buried in the garden but Sophie wept. 'Biffer loved Daddy Bobby. They'll be happy together.' They came, the three of them, fearful of being caught, to bury Biffer under the spruce.

If it wasn't for the cross you wouldn't know it a grave, and if you didn't know it a grave you might think an eagle had landed. A beautiful thing it has the words carved on the underbelly, *'Age shall not wither them.'*

Under the spruce is rich in loam. Everything grows here, even bulbs the gofers gnaw. Adelia comes ready to tidy the grave. A fortnight ago she came to trim the Gloire de Guilan. Mrs Ruby Rourke, now passed, stood behind her.

'Those roses ain't yours to cut.'

'I'm sure they won't be missed.'

'I don't know why you come here week after week.'

'I like keeping the grave tidy.'

'Why when you don't remember him?' Mrs Rourke seemed genuinely puzzled. 'You might as well put flowers on a stranger's tomb.'

'Possibly, but I feel it's the least I can do.'

'Ain't nobody takin' care of my grave when I'm gone. Nobody cares for me now. Ain't no one gonna bother when I'm six-foot under.'

'I'm sure somebody will care.'

'Bobby left you nothing. What d'you expect to get from this?'

'I don't expect to get anything.'

'Is it right you still don't remember me?'

'I'm afraid I don't.'

'That letter I sent some time back I was only tryin' to tell the truth.'

'The truth is always good to know.'

'I don't suppose you remember the other feller, him as is troublin' my boy's grave with rubbishy bits of wood.'

Gabriel Templar is the talk of the artistic world. With the Paris exhibition in the Tuileries his reputation is sky-high. There are whispers of a work commissioned by the Guggenheim Museum. That being so it's likely this 'rubbishy bit of wood' is worth tens of thousands of pounds.

That day Ruby called out. 'Will you put flowers on my grave?'

She might do it. At least she's not putting flowers on Alex's grave.

It was Sue Ryland who prompted the New Valley Funeral Parlour.

It was after the first reading of the will.

Staggering shell-shocked from Daniel Culpepper's office, having learned she was tied and bound, Adelia and Frank stood at the Parlour window.

Frank asked what she was going to do. 'I don't know,' she'd gazed at the 'for sale' sign. 'Maybe I'll buy this place.' Sue Ryland, unaware of a crisis, overheard them talking and that evening approached for a loan.

'I guess you think I've a nerve askin',' she'd said, dark eyes searching.

'Not at all,' said Adelia recalling a time she asked Alex for a loan.

It was Frank drawn to Sue who suggested a partnership. Between them they bought the Parlour and the shop next door, gutting all and raising the New Valley Rest. They offered an individual service; should the family require a particular theme for the ceremony, or favourite colour or standard, they would oblige, the finest pomp and ceremony plus a dash of spice.

Business was brisk especially for horse-drawn rigs. Their first client was a local businessman who loved the Hunt. Female funeral directors are a novelty, female mutes more so, especially if the raven haired mute wears tight cream britches and leads a pack of hounds as the advance guard.

In the fall of '51 Emiline March died followed a week later by her beloved sister. Both ladies elected to be buried by the New Valley.

Lemon and lavender were colours of choice, rosebuds and baby's breath wreaths, lemon palls with white cockades in the gentlemen's hats and lemon balloons floating from the rigs. Sue was stunning in a white tuxedo and Adelia ethereal in lilac velvet.

Time magazine sent a reporter, an article entitled '*Modern American woman*,' Adelia's picture set between Mrs Dwight D Eisenhower and Betty Grable.

When interviewed she was asked what her husband – a hero missing in action and Holder of the Medal - would have thought of her enterprise. She kept her head. 'My husband was an innovative man. Some of his ideas were surprisingly novel. I'm sure he would appreciate our little scheme.'

~

'Right, Mrs Hunter! No right!' The instructor slammed the brakes.

Adelia is at the wheel of a car and yet again confused by road markings.

'I'm awfully sorry,' she said, flustered. 'Is that your right or mine?'

The instructor mopped his brow. 'There is only one right to an American road, as there is only one left.'

'I ought to give up,' she says downcast. 'I'm never going to be good at this.'

'Indeed you will be. You're a natural with an automobile. You just need to remember driving in America isn't the same as in Britain.'

'You're very patient.'

'Not at all, ma'am!' The instructor blushed (he lives every week looking forward this one hour) 'You are my star pupil.'

They set off back down the avenue, the open-top filled with sunshine. On the way back they passed the Nature Reserve people spilling out of the gates.

'They've made a lot of changes here,' said the instructor.

'So I believe.'

'I bring my boy most Sundays. They do exhibition stuff, some guy flying eagles. It used to be an airbase run by an Irish feller called O'Rourke. Apparently, he got roasted one night and crash-landed his own runway. The feller that owns it now is a millionaire. Spends his time with playboys in foreign lands, so they say.'

Adelia was silent. She couldn't have contributed anything half so dramatic.

They pulled into the Eyrie. Sophie ran to meet her, a delicate spindle-legged beauty with braces on her teeth. 'Sue's here! Can I play with Becky?'

'Have you done your homework?'

'Uh-huh, and I've practised my *entrechat* and *pas de chat* fifty times.'

'Is there mail?'

'Yes, but nothing from Daddy.'

'Perhaps you shouldn't...!' Unable to say what she ought to say Adelia bit her lip. 'Just keep writing and I'll keep sending. If Daddy is able to answer he will.'

Reassured, Sophie danced away.

Ellen Hunter came from the Orangery with Timmy in her arms. She passed him over. 'Don't you think it's time you stopped the letter-writing charade?'

'You think writing to her father a charade?'

'Adelia please! You know very well what I mean. It's one thing to encourage the child to hope, quite another to cherish a hopeless dream.'

'I can no more tell her to stop than I can tell myself.'

'You ought to prepare her for the worst.'

'Sophie knows the worst. She's doing what we all do - hoping for the best.'

'I suppose you know what you're doing.'

Sue Ryland sat on the table swinging her legs. 'How did the lesson go?'

'It would help if I knew my right from my left. What about you?'

'I got that new vet over to look at Sorrow's ear. He says it's nothing more than hayseed. A good-looking boy he can fix my fetlock any time.'

Adelia laughed. 'And the wreaths? Did you like them?'

'I did. You should leave the stiffs to me and Frank and make wedding posies instead. Don't you think she'd make a great florist, Mizz Ellen?'

'Anything would be an improvement on funeral directing.'

'Oh, la-di-dah!' Sue turned to Adelia. 'That guy from _Time_ called again. He wanted to know if you and him could get together.'

'What did you tell him?'

'I told him you wouldn't but I would.'

Sophie rushed in. 'It's Becky's birthday tomorrow. Can she stay over?'

'I don't see why not.'

'I've an idea,' says Ellen. 'Why don't you and Becky and Timmy stay over with Gramps and me? We could have a barbeque and watch TV.'

That night Adelia read Sophie's letter. '*Dear Daddy, I twisted my ankle today doing fouette en tournant. A very tricky step!!! Timmy is well but inclined to throw up. Last Thursday he swallowed a button. Mummy had to take him to the doctors. I am practising my French. Mamselle thinks I have a good ear. I don't know why Becky can't get it. All you have to do is listen. Mummy and Jacob took me and Tag to see Peter Pan. I liked Wendy. She is English like me and Mummy. Davy and Petey are coming at the weekend. We're going on a picnic...*'

'Oh dear!' Ellen isn't alone in her concerns. Sophie's letters are chatty gossip. Three years yet she writes as though her father would walk through the door.

At first not knowing what to do Adelia sent the letters to Sam Jentzen. He made a suggestion. 'We got a lot of lonely boys and girls stationed out there in Korea with no folks of their own. I'll send Sophie's letters to them. If the Colonel is alive he may get one of them, if not the kids can share 'em.

So the letters went out and in return Sophie receives return mail from serving men and women in Korea but so far nothing more.

The telephone rang. 'Hello, Adelia. What kind of day have you had?'

'Middling, Jacob, how about you?'

'Friday looks promising. I'm dining at the Carlton with a ravishing blonde. Next week the same ravishing blonde accompanies me to hear Tosca.'

'You managed to get seats?'

'I did. You are coming?'

'If I can get a baby-sitter.'

'If you can't, can I come baby-sit you?'

'That rather depends on what I find at the lawyers.'

'Me and my bed are awful lonely.'

'Likewise.'

~

Adelia retired to bed. Soon a familiar scent comforted her heart.

Before long he was beside her, strength and passion faint yet still there.

Darling, Alex, her life and her love!

Spring of '51 she attended a memorial service for Major Tom Farrell and Captain James Macintyre, their remains latterly recovered from Korea and brought to Arlington. During the service James Macintyre's mother spoke with Adelia, saying how her son adored Alex. 'He said the Colonel was a good man.'

'*Is* a good man, Mrs Macintyre,' she'd replied.

Mrs Macintyre had smiled. 'That's right, my dear. Keep the faith.'

Adelia hugged the pillows and kept the faith.

Chapter Thirty
Angel in Paris

The stewardess smiled. '*Champagne, Monsieur?*'

'*Non, merci, Mamselle. Je vais avoir un jus de fruit et une Paris Match.*'

Gabriel gazed out of the window. What a sight! Below the ground was a checkerboard of green and browns, of valleys and oceans. To his right are acres of blue sky, and to his left more acres, and beneath him the world!

Heading back to Paris after a meeting at the Guggenheim, Gabriel recalls the first time he sat in one of these. During the war whole battalions of Marines were ferried aboard these giant carriers. Packed aboard a troop ship he was only happy when his feet touched land, or so he thought until that first flight.

'*Paris Match, m'sieur.*'

'*Merci.*'

The stewardess smiled. Gabriel blushed. Four years of living with the lingo and still he's stiff as a board. French is a sweet language. You can do pretty much what you want with it. When he's with kids from the school it's second nature. One-to-one he sounds like he's quoting the phrase book, 'French for Idiots.'

'*Et votre jus, m'sieur.*'

Gabriel couldn't help but smile. Fruit juice at thirty thousand feet and a paper whosis to stand it on!? He's doing what eagles are born to do defy gravity.

Back in '49, thrilled as he is now, Gabriel had laughed. A guy across the aisle laughed with him. High on first-class travel is how he met Charles Beaufort. A thin fellow in tweed jacket, leather patches on his elbows, Charles was sipping tea from a china cup. 'Is this your first time?' he said, British and proud of it.

'It sure is,' Gabriel had leaned into him. 'I thought I was gonna be nervous, but how can you be nervous when there's all of that below.'

'My sentiments exactly.' He offered Gabriel a cup of tea. 'I see you're reading Captain Fordyce's book on the plight of the Bengal tiger.'

Gabriel said he got it from the library and how he didn't like what the hunters were doing and that back home he had a place for wounded critters.

That's how it went between them. Released by his crazy situation, a man of property, dollars falling from his pockets, this and every other sky the limit, he opened up his heart to a stranger, told of his animals in the pen, of his passion for carving, and of his love of a woman.

Imagine it, Gabe Templar, murdering ex-con sitting with an ageing British aristocrat sipping China tea and swapping heartache! 'We need reserves where animals can live in safety,' says Charles, an accent so sharp Gabe could've planed oak with it. 'We need cash and we need land. But people aren't interested. They think Nature will go on ad infinitum.'

'I got land,' says Gabriel. 'If you know of anyone wantin' to make use of it they'd be more than welcome.'

With nothing to lose, talking to a man he was never likely to see again, he told of Bobby Rourke's bequest, how he was left thousands of dollars and hundreds of acres of land and didn't know what to do with either.

'I know that area of Virginia well,' said Charles Beaufort. 'It would make a fine conservation area.'

'Then do it!' Gabriel opened his arms. 'Take it and use it.'

'This is an idea we need to discuss in depth, Mister...?'

'Templar. Gabriel Templar.'

They shook hands, the guy giving him a business card. 'Perhaps when you get to your destination you might give me a call. I'm lecturing at the Sorbonne this week and then back home to Suffolk on Friday.'

Suffolk! That did it for Gabriel. 'I had a friend who lived there. She said it was a real pretty place.'

'It is. If you're ever in the area I'd be happy to show you just how pretty. Give me a call or drop by. The address is on the card. Ask for the Abbey.'

That day Gabriel slid the card in his pocket. Though probably never getting to England he would give the guy a call and put Bobby's bequest to good use.

Airports are hellish places. Carried along with the mass, folks scrambling for trolleys, that first trip was a nightmare. Daniel Culpepper had arranged for a guy to meet him, Gabriel was to 'look for a guy with a board and your name on it.'

He'd collected his bag and was waiting in arrivals when up pops a little guy in uniform. 'Pardon, M'sieur. His Lordship wishes to know if you require a lift.'

Next he knows he's in a limousine, a crest on the door and a flag flying. It turns out Charles Beaufort is a famous naturalist who writes books on ancient languages and tribal customs – he's also related to the King of England.

Gabriel offered the land and acquired an illustrious partner, sponsors appearing overnight, business consortiums vying to provide machinery and manpower. In less than a year the Reserve was up and running. It was Charles who bought into the idea and it is Charles, good friend that he is, arranged for Gabriel to go that first time on Safari to Kenya.

Kenya! There are times looking back when he has to pinch himself, Gabe Templar, the town loon sitting under the stars eating smoked Yak and drinking tsampa tea. At that time hopes and dreams revolved around the love for one woman and the need to carve. It was no use thinking of love, as it is no use planning a future, his world going crazy - Paris, Charles Beaufort, and a priest called Sebastian Kline changing everything.

Bobby Rourke made education the point of his bequest. He didn't specify which and where but since Paris was mentioned - and about as far away from Fredericksburg as a man could get - it became the chosen city.

Though Father Sebastian's way of teaching was hardly traditional, L'Ecole de St Denis brought sight to the blind in more ways than one.

It took time to appreciate the bequest. Resentful of being shoved around, and ashamed of his shortcomings,

Gabriel mooched the streets. 'Why do this to me, Bobby Rourke? You should've killed me while you were alive instead of punishin' me from hell.'

Until Paris he didn't know lonely. The noise, the automobiles and busy sidewalks overwhelmed him. Struck dumb by fast-talking Parisians and their close-knit society he longed for home. Conscious of wood and shapes that only needed his fingers to bust out he yearned to carve. He missed Ma and the zillion stars of a Virginia sky. Most of all he missed Adelia.

People say it's better to have loved than never loved. Don't believe it! All his life he loved that girl. She was the beating of his heart. Now his heart is silent. The silence is nothing to do with her being married - though knowledge of that burns his soul. It is her forgetting him.

'Do you know how it makes me feel?' he tried telling Charles Beaufort. 'I'm empty, a fish that's been gutted, nothin' left but skin and scales.'

Gabe was drunk the night he said that - drunk with a Lord, and drunk as a lord - him who'd never let a beer touch his lips was out of his scull on absinthe.

He woke next day tucked up in a truckle bed in Charles's apartment.

'I'm sorry,' he'd said, knuckling his eyes. 'I don't know what came over me.'

'I do,' said Charles. 'It's grief, the food of the soul.'

'If that's what it is I don't want to eat no more.'

'You have no choice. It's why we're here.'

'What to be unlucky in love?'

'No, to appreciate the difference.'

Lord Charles Beaufort is on the board of governors at the St Denis. It was he suggested Gabe leave the Sorbonne and instead become caretaker and odd-job man at the school and for payment tutorials with the director, Father Kline and fun with the kids. Now, four years on, he has respect for Baudelaire, a love of Paris and a passion for Auguste Rodin.

The museum at the *Rue de Varenne* is a well-worn track. He spends hours staring at the statuary wondering how mortal man could achieve such beauty. Though his first love will always be Cellini, the book, Adelia's birthday present never far from his side, Rodin is the ideal.

Fr Sebastian passes his hands over the cool marble. 'It's about symmetry,' he says, his fingers conjuring visions of their own. Gabriel's favourite is The Kiss, the hand on the woman's thigh, gentle yet hungry, he knows how that feels.

Slowly but surely Paris became his city and *Le Francais,* the language of Kings. He got a loft in *St-Germain des Pres*: with so much in the bank he could've got a bigger apartment but likes being in the heart of things, seeing the rich Parisian life, the odd-balls on the sidewalk and the lovers holding hands. Working for the school is no different to home. He fixes handrails and ramps for wheelchairs. He fries fish and unblocks sinks and all the while gaining a passable Left-Bank patois, kids lending their slang to *le Yankee blond.*

In the evening he unblocks his head giving life to wood and stone. One day, between the rough and the smooth, and with help from Charles Beaufort, he acquired a little symmetry of his own, a way of thinking, comfortable in denim or cashmere, happy to eat in the commissary or dine at the Ritz.

He is M'sieur Gabriel, the guy from Virginia, sculptor, man and friend.

One day chatting over a bowl of Bouillabaisse in the Latin Quarter Gabriel saw he was never dumb, he was only waiting. The kids in the school ain't dumb either, they're blind. And he's not here in Paris to spend Bobby's dough and read Baudelaire. He's here to learn a lesson in love and to pass it on.

Anger still abides, he regrets killing Pa and the years spent in the Pen yet knows that but for those things he wouldn't be here. People along the way, Bobby and his sharp tongue, Pariss Island and girls with points and pouts, are markers. He's been given a second chance yet there's a price to pay for Savile Row suits and a Cartier watch -the loss of his Other Self.

Gabriel asked Charles if he'd ever thought himself as more than one man.

'What do you mean?'

'I'm split in two, that I own one half of me and someone else the rest.'

'Oh, I know that one,' said Charles. 'It's called marriage. I own a tiny sliver of me. My wife, my son, and daughters have the majority share.'

Seeing him joking Gabriel left it. He couldn't explain other than to say he'd travelled thousands of miles but had lost a precious gift along the way.

'You need to unwind,' says Charles. 'You are too much inside your head. There's a chap here in Paris I go to.'

Sanjay Patel lives above a strip-joint. He is old and tiny but a tough guy. Pariss Island has nothing on him. He slaps Gabe around, stomps on his back, piles hot stones on his chest while massaging his scalp with a wire brush and always giggling! On the tenth visit he stopped giggling long enough to teach his student how to walk on the wild side, out-of-body travelling he called it.

Six months and a millennium later Gabriel saw the stars from a whole new angle. Bobby used to say it's about recognising the enemy. Sanjay Patel says the opposite, 'it's about recognising angels.'

~

Gabriel took a week out of schedule and flew home to Virginia.

Ma was waiting at the airport. 'How long you stayin'?'

'Not long. Me and Charles are thinkin' of goin' to Egypt.'

'What, travellin' again? You sure you ain't turnin' native.'

Then followed the usual question and answer session, Ma asks if he's met anyone nice. He asks how're things at the Eyrie. She says why do you want to know and when he doesn't respond loses her temper, why can't he be happy with a French girl, at least then she'd go to her grave knowing him settled.

An hour and she's still yelling. 'I don't know why you don't let go. What's so special about her? Okay, she's good lookin' but beauty is as beauty does!'

She's goes on so long Gabriel can't sit still. 'It's not the way she looks,' he argues. 'It's about who we are, she bein' part of me and me part of her!'

Ma goes crazy. 'Foolish talk! This is that Indian thing, sittin' with your knees crossed and your fool head in the clouds? You need to come down to earth and quit with this hoo-doo rubbish!'

He grins. 'Hoo-doo?'

'You know what I mean, the business of twin souls.'

His grin died. 'You don't need to worry about that anymore.'

'Why's that?'

'My twin soul up and left me flat.'

That afternoon he took the airfield road. The Reserve keeps growing. They've a new primate house and a glasshouse for reptiles plus acres of scrubland for wild cats to roam free. The plan is to build a movie theatre. They are open seven days a week and with admission prices kept to minimum scores of people flock in.

'Everybody's talkin' about it,' says Ma. 'It's even been on the newsreels.'

Gabriel sat for a while watching crowds pass through the turnstile, a brass plaque hanging over the gates with the words, *'For the Few.'*

It gave him a good feeling and a sense of a certain ex-flier breathing down his neck. 'What's this, old sport, Gabriel's Ark?'

'No, Bobby. It's yours.'

~

Back home he mucked out the stables and groomed the horses. From there he went to the barn. It's under the tarpaulin, the oldest and trickiest piece. He was a kid when he found this hunk of wood. Soft pliant Lime brought down by gales, he knew its beauty and dragged it home rather than see it rot.

Years it's been under wraps, the pony that pulled it long gone. Now the wood is like the man seasoned and subtle. At first he would stare thinking it more wild beast than a plant. Month by month, year after year, he's toyed with it, flexing a knife without an idea of what might be growing beneath his hands.

Slowly, painfully, the tree gave birth, an indescribable being heaving into the light. Father Sebastian believes the sculpture to be the Hand of God.

It could be as Pa said 'the work of the devil.' It's dragged on long enough and as yet is faceless and fighting for life in the way a newborn foal fights.

Sebastian Kline, a blind Jesuit priest, is the driving force behind the Templar work. Gabriel is reluctant to exhibit thinking his stuff not good enough. Then in '52 after an exhibition in the Tuileries Sebastian came to Fredericksburg.

A bloodhound sniffing, he paced the barn. He got to the Lime tree and stopped, hands upraised as though about to walk into glass. He was ages stroking the thing, long fingers feathering muscle and sinew seeing what eyes could not.

'The Lord sent you to do this, Gabriel,' he said, 'it's why you were born.'

The piece is destined for the Guggenheim. Though thrilled Gabriel is anxious, a voice in his head saying the piece was promised elsewhere.

He set to, his tools as he left them wrapped in cloth and razor sharp. Selecting a chisel he began to shave the wood. An hour passed and another. Ma set a tray on the bench. He worked on, light in the window changing hue as night approached. A face is emerging - rising cheekbones sharpening under the chisel.

Eyes are evolving and a mouth at times human and then again not.

Day passed into evening, fingers blistering he works on. Thoughts came and went of Paris and the Tuileries, Charles and a proposed trip to Kilimanjaro, Ma here alone in Virginia and ever the undercurrent Adelia.

It was late when he stopped. An armchair stood in the corner oozing stuffing where mice made a nest. Exhausted, he dropped into the chair, starlight shining through the window. It was on a night like this Hunter went down.

Since receiving Hunter's cable plea for help he's been waiting.

Winter of '49 they made the deal. Hunter called him 'Oblige me, Templar. Meet me at the Lincoln Memorial.' They met at the Lincoln Memorial, Hunter in army greatcoat, his hands in his pockets and his mouth grim.

'I need you to be my best man.' That's what he said.

At first Gabriel was insulted, thinking it a cruel joke, Hunter asking him to stand at their wedding. Then he saw he was referring to a fail-safe partner to fall back on in dangerous situations, a Marine tactic as well as the Army.

'I know it's asking a lot,' says Hunter, 'but if we don't do this she'll be at the mercy of every sneak-thief.'

Gabriel didn't like the way it would look folks seeing it as betrayal.

'You don't need to tell me,' Hunter had grated. 'I know how it will look, but I can't worry about that and neither can you. We can only make her safe.'

'Sooner or later there'll be somebody. You can't keep bees from honey.'

'It's not the bees I'm worried about,' says Hunter. 'It's the rats.'

'There are good guys out there as well as bad.'

'Yeah and not so long ago she was almost throttled by one of them. Bobby was all kinds of idiot but no killer. Her illness and his weakness made him so.'

'For the love of God!' They argued until Hunter lost his temper. 'I thought you cared for her. I was wrong. You're a fair-weather guy. You talk a good talk but when the chips are down we don't see your ass for dust.'

On and on until worn down by the truth of it Gabriel agreed.

In the fall of 1950 he slept in this chair and heard booming surf and saw men bayoneted in the shallows and knew a loss.

It was then his heart faltered, a quickening in his chest like a bird preparing to leave the nest. The Big Bang came later wʰ   wyer called.

          ction came via Culpepper, if worst came
          vas to give the greatcoat to Adelia. 'It
          annot.'

Then that snake-hip shrink Feldstein phoned. 'Colonel Hunter's missing. We're off to see his widow. You're to accompany us, though given your history I think it wrong, today's bad news being good news for you.'

A murder of military crows they went to the Eyrie. Face ashen, she came to the door. Gabriel thought she would faint but it was he who fainted.

Bang! His heart stopped and never truly started again.

Gutted from breast to balls as a fisherman fillets a trout, down he went, the link between him and Adelia severed. That day God put a concrete wall between them and it didn't matter what she felt he didn't feel it with her. She could weep and his eyes would be dry. She could return to England he wouldn't know. There had been a parting, something good and beautiful is gone, and the ordinary Gabe left behind to succeed in worldly business while his shining self, the One that nested within - the Healer and Lover of Mankind – flown away for places unknown.

There was silence, a dull ache, and yesterday's scars. One winter's Eve he went to bed a fit man but woke in agony, his back lacerated from shoulder to hip as though a burning brand dashed across his spine.

Ma said it was hives, Sebastian Kline stigmata. Gabriel sees it the marks of Cain. Now there's to be a final reading of the Will and the scars bleed.

A while ago he and Charles Beaufort went on safari to Kenya. You'd think that the miles between Adelia and him would lessen pain. If anything the loss under the starry sky was keener. He wishes he could let go. Life would be easier if he did. He's had the odd date, Parisian girls, brilliant and sassy. Living in the city helps, honking horns and street traders shouting their wares, noise acting as a baffle. At night he throws open the windows letting the hubbub in. He couldn't do that in Kenya, endless stars and space afford no barrier for the soul.

That last night in Kenya a Maasai warrior spoke to Gabriel. Charles translated. 'He says you are a warrior from beyond the stars and that you wear a disguise.'

'What does he mean disguise?'

The Maasai let fly another speech.

'He says you wear human skin in order to observe.'

'What am I observin'?'

'Life.' The warrior made chopping movements with his hands. 'He says, 'you are two beings, one is of fire, the other of darkness, and that as with the sun and moon one wakes while the other sleeps.'

'Which part of me is here now?'

'The warrior asks what do you see in the sky.'

Gabriel tipped back his head. 'Stars and a solitary moon.'

'He says you are the solitary moon.'

There was more talk, Charles struggling to translate. 'I don't know whether I've got this right but I think he says your other self sleeps to live. Your sun, which I feel is a separate being, hides behind the earth waiting to be born.''

It was weird and kinda amusing but not amusing when the guy suddenly spat in Gabriel's face. Charles grabbed his arm. 'Don't be offended. To be spat upon like that is a compliment. He honours you.'

The Maasai began to dance. Eyes like smoke-filled caverns and feet on springs, he leapt up and down. Other warriors joined in until there was a circle of waving plumes. On and on, Gabriel's head filled with visions of endless grassland and creatures running free. The leaping stopped. The warrior made a speech and all jogged away into the night.

'One last thing,' said Charles. 'The chief says your other self won't return until you help set him free.'

'Him free?' Gabriel was puzzled. 'Male?'

Charles had nodded. 'Yes, him. And one last word, your sun won't rise until you've kept your promise.'

'And who have I promised?'

'A goddess made of wood.'

Chapter Thirty-One
Landlord

The morning brought the third and final reading of the will.
Adelia dressed for the occasion, a black moiré suit, fitted
jacket and pencil skirt, patent killer heels, a white linen
shirt, a black silk matador hat, and a gorgeous pair of ice-
grey elbow length suede gloves. Ivory skin, emerald eyes
and poppy-red lipstick, think Maiko Geisha on a painted
Japanese screen and you'd find Adelia.

There was another with Daniel in the office. Half hidden
behind an aspidistra - the severe cut of his suit, white linen
shirt and black tie contrasting with a mane of shining hair,
Gabriel Templar, Paul Revere by way of Savile Row.

Face empty of expression he got to his feet.

Daniel hurried forward. 'I think you know Mr
Templar.'

They shook hands - Adelia resisting the need to wipe
hers. She sat and so did he one elegant leg crossed over the
other. 'I understand you're to officiate at Senator Cole's
internment,' said Daniel all a-twitter. 'That's quite a
coup.'

'Indeed.'

'That's good, very good.' Ill at ease he shuffled papers
and then clearing his throat segued from friend to lawyer.

'Once again we're dealing with this unfortunate business, the third and final reading of the late Colonel Hunter's Will. Let us hope we can proceed without too much delay on either…'

'Excuse me, Daniel,' said Adelia. 'Might I ask if Mister Templar's presence here is a legal requirement?'

'It is.'

'Ah,' she nodded. 'I wondered at this feeling of *déjà vu*. Could it be he is a beneficiary in my husband's Will?'

'Beneficiary?' Daniel pursed his lips. 'One might call it that.'

'*Déjà vu* indeed, Mister Templar.'

Gabriel Templar rose, made a half bow and sat down again.

'Perhaps I should clarify the situation. Mr Templar is present at the reading because under the terms of your late husband's Will he is required to be here.'

'Daniel,' said Adelia teeth on edge. 'Do not refer to the Colonel as late. I understand the military terminology used to describe my husband's situation is 'missing in action.' I know the word late to be perfectly correct when dealing with a person's demise, but late and missing do not mean the same thing. By all means refer to Colonel Hunter as missing but if you say late I shan't be able to stay. Do you understand?'

'I do and I apologise for employing the term. I shall endeavour not to use it again. Very well then, if I may continue, the terms of Colonel Alexander Hunter's Last Will and Testament set out certain…'

She hadn't finished. 'And while on the subject of correctness I must say I would've appreciated prior knowledge of Mister Templar's presence, though having said that I'm not altogether surprised to see him. Were he to be absent from a legal contretemps involving me and mine I would be more surprised.'

More paper shuffling and more coughing.

'Carry on, Daniel,' she said, reigning back anger. 'I shan't be doing anything too outrageous.'

'Very well.' He pushed the papers aside. 'As you know only too well much of this is old ground over which we've travelled at varying times. In order to save time and pain might I suggest we stick to essentials?'

'By all means.' It is warm, Adelia's clothes sticking to her. She would've preferred to roll up her sleeves but felt the gesture might precipitate the carrying out of an innermost desire, namely to box Gabriel Templar's ears.

Daniel pressed ahead. 'The Colonel first came to me in the winter of '49. He was anxious for your safety and for your daughter. He wanted you to be secure. He wanted you never to have to worry again. He wanted...wanted...'

Wanted...wanted...She gazed out of the window. She's heard it all before. The first reading was clear in her head; a phone call from the Pentagon, the bodies of US Servicemen recovered from Korea but Alex not among them. 'Surely that gives us hope?' she'd said. Bill's answering nod was reserved. A soldier, he knew behind every official line a story waited to be told. A reading of the Will followed shortly after, bequests to the family, gifts to Frank Bates and the rest of the staff. That part of the business concluded and the room cleared save for Adelia and senior Hunters Daniel resumed. Ten minutes in Bill is on his feet. 'Of course the house belongs to Mrs Hunter junior! It's her husband's estate.'

Alex had sold the ground under her feet and the roof from over her head. She could stay in the Eyrie, eat fruit off the trees, sleep in the bed, grow old and die, but the house wouldn't be hers.

All was entailed in a Trust so legally binding as to be Houdini-proof. There was a generous monthly allowance, a sum most housekeepers would be thrilled to earn, but then most housekeepers earn their keep by cooking and cleaning. Their duties don't usually include the master's bed.

'You slipped up,' she muttered. 'A whore worth her salt knows the going rate.'

Daniel was looking at her. 'Did you say something?'

'Nothing worth repeating. Is the end in sight?'

'I can stop any time you like.'

'Then do' she said. 'Forget the legal verbiage. Tell me in plain English what this document means.'

'Very well! There are three beneficiaries in the final Will. Your daughter inherits the sum of five hundred thousand dollars, her inheritance in the form of a trust and under governance and management of this office until she comes of age, or until such time she makes personal representation to her legal guardian. You, Mrs Hunter, inherit an equal sum.'

There was more, Daniel's expression said so. 'There is a third beneficiary, Mr Gabriel H Templar inherits a third equal share.'

'And the Eyrie?'

'Ah, that's where it gets rather tricky.'

'Oh do tell about tricky!' she said. 'I never knew what the word meant til now.'

'Well, it is complicated but the nub, the gist…!'

'Daniel!'

'I'm sorry but I know how this must sound and I am trying to spare your feelings. The money and house are inextricably linked. All three have an equal share of money and all three an equal share of the house. Once all conditions of the Will are met you can do what you want with the money. But the house stays under joint ownership. You can't give away a share of the house any more than you can deny access to another beneficiary.'

'You mean this man can take up residence in my home?'

'Yes.'

'And I can't stop him?'

'No.'

'What if I decide I can't be party to this?'

'Then the money, your daughter's included, goes into a holding zone.'

'And the house?'

'If Gabriel is precluded from a share then nobody gets a share.'

'You mean my children and I would have to move out?'

'It would seem to be the answer.'

'It's the only answer. I couldn't share my life and my children with a stranger, especially not a man who calls his house Paradise. He might end up calling mine Purgatory or something equally vile.'

Gabriel Templar frowned. 'Excuse me?'

'The Mill? I understand you call it Paradise.'

'I don't own the Mill.'

'Oh! Well, even so I couldn't share my home with you. I don't know how my husband thought I could. As for paying my way I run a successful business. I don't need to beg from anyone. It is a great deal of money but we don't need it. Sophie has a substantial inheritance. If moving out is what it takes so be it.'

Daniel sighed. 'Would it were that simple! As an adult you have a right to do what you want but where the children are concerned this document initiates procedures that prevent you taking such a step. From now on any decision affecting Timmy and Sophie must be agreed via this office.'

'How can that be? Where Timmy is concerned my husband never knew him.'

'He might not have known in specifics but he was a soldier and planned for that eventuality. Therefore, as of today, and until they come of age, there is another beside you who has a legal interest in your children's future.'

'Oh surely not!'

The silence in the room was so thick, a dollop of cream, and like humble pie, she could have eaten it. She turned. 'Did he make you guardian?'

'He did.' Gabriel Templar was on his feet.

'And you agreed to it?'

'I agreed because he asked.'

'But it's wrong, you foisting yourself on me and my daughter!'

'I've no wish to foist myself on anyone. I'm as hassled as you.'

'How are you? I can't believe Alex aimed a pistol at your head.'

'Then you don't know your husband! The Colonel was good at aimin' pistols. He could tell you what you should do and feel in a couple of sentences.'

She sprang to her feet. 'How dare you tell me I don't know my husband!'

'Please!' begged Daniel. 'This isn't helping. Adelia, I'm sure when you consider the implications you'll see that this is meant with the best of intentions. '

'Isn't that what the road to hell is paved with?'

'Surely you can see this is tied to your mental condition.'

'My mental condition?' Adelia's heart stopped cold. 'My husband said I had a mental condition? '

Daniel rearranged the items on his desk. 'Not in so many words, but can't you hear what I hear when I read this, the fears of a man who is trying to protect his beloved from the more dishonest of the world?'

'Do you call stealing my home honest?'

'I'm sorry but I can't allow that to go unchallenged. I've been dealing with Mr Templar for years and can say, hand on heart, he is an honest man.'

Gabriel Templar held up his hand. 'Thank you Daniel but I don't need defendin'. If I were in Mrs Hunter's shoes I'd feel the same way.'

Adelia's eyes flashed. 'You have no idea of the way I feel. And you've a damn nerve to suggest you do. What do you want with my house? '

'I don't want your house. I don't want the money either but if I don't accept it then neither you nor Sophie will get what's yours.'

The telephone rang. Daniel picked it up. 'A message from Doctor Feldstein? There is an emergency at the hospital. He won't be able to take you home.'

'That's all right,' she made for the door. 'I'll take a cab. It's yet another example men not living up to their word.'

'Don't leave like this!' Daniel ran after her. 'You can challenge this! It would be tough to fight it but you could.'

'I'm not challenging anything. If this is what he wanted, if the man I adored thought so little of me who am I to deny him.'

'Your husband loved you,' said Gabriel.

'How do you know? Did he tell you so?'

'He didn't have to.'

'His deeds don't match his words! And when I think about it didn't you once say the same of Bobby Rourke? Wasn't he another of my ardent suitors? For God's sake! She pushed the door. 'If this is love give me the other kind.'

~

She stood on the street for ten minutes or more trying to find a cab but there was none. Then a low silver coupe rolled up. He leaned out. 'There's a veteran's parade. You won't get a cab. If you need a lift...'

'It's fine, thank you,' she said, stiffly. 'I wouldn't want to trouble you.'

'It's no trouble.'

She thought of what was ahead, the struggle through traffic and shrugged. She wouldn't cut her nose to spite her face not even for this man.

'You could drop me at the funeral parlour.'

He reached across locking the door.

She leapt away from his touch.

'It's okay,' he said. 'I didn't want you falling out.'

'I shan't be doing that.' She clenched her fists. 'I'm not suicidal. Not yet!'

Tight with rage she sat gazing out of the window. Why did you do this Alex? Couldn't you trust me to take care of our children? And what about the years before you found me? Wasn't I a good mother then?

Sadly she doesn't know how good. Life in Suffolk and early days at Virginia, like her love affair with this man, lay hidden under a blanket of forgetfulness.

In a poisonous codicil to a letter Mrs Rourke intimated a squalid affair. '*The whole town knew about you two. You ought to be ashamed, sleeping around with every Tom, Dick, and Harry, while my boy was dying for love of you.*'

The letter had shocked her yet while she had the confidence of Alex the writings of a lonely old woman could be borne. Now she's not sure of anything. If Alex thought her an unfit mother she might be everything the town said.

'You were never that.'

She turned to stare. 'I beg your pardon!'

'You were never anythin' but kind.' He pushed a pair of dark glasses over his nose. 'I've been thinkin' why the Colonel would have separate readings.'

'I don't want to talk about it.'

'Maybe you don't but I'm gonna say what I think. Him and me fought different wars. I was in the Pacific he was in the European Theatre. Different people yet when it comes to carin' for loved ones our fears would be the same. We'd want them cared for but wouldn't want it hasty.'

'I don't follow.'

'It's in the missing presumed dead. The military love words but there are situations in war that can't be covered by words. When I was in the Corps I heard of Japanese soldiers who kept fightin' never knowin' the war was over. When they came home they were strangers, kids grown and wives moved on.'

'Are you trying to say my husband might be a prisoner on some far-flung Pacific island because if you are you're not exactly helping.'

'I'm suggestin' the Colonel was tryin' to give you, and himself, three years grace.'

'I see. And now that those three years are up and he's not here am I to assume the time of grace is over and declare him officially dead?'

'Okay.' Frustrated, he pushed his fingers through his hair. 'You've made up your mind about the situation. I won't say no more.'

The car pulled up outside the funeral parlour. Gabriel switched off the engine and sat looking at smart grey awnings and shining plate glass.

Adelia looked with him. Frank has been busy, the decorative waggonette in the window stripped and polished, the wheels oiled and the crystal glass shining. Wreaths were laid inside purple lilac shimmering against the white.

'You bought the place next door?' Gabriel queried.

'We needed space for another rig.'

'From what I hear you got high society makin' use of it.'

'Grief cuts across social boundaries. Our motto is, "grace and dignity at a reasonable cost". We try to give the grieving client the best we can.'

'I thought I did that when I owned the place.'

'I'm sure you did, however you're a wealthy man now and don't have the bother of customer satisfaction.'

He didn't speak. Adelia knew she was being unpardonably rude and that he was incredibly forbearing but still she couldn't let it go. Damn him to hell, she thought, and his natural grace, how can he know these things?

'How do you know these things about my Alex?'

'I don't. I'm an ex-Marine who thinks like a Marine.'

She gazed at him taking in the broad shoulders, deeply tanned skin and sun-bleached hair. Gossip says he's a Johnny-come-lately ex-jail bird turned successful artist who took Bobby Rourke's derelict flying club and turned it into a Nature Reserve. He jets about the world, climbs mountains and treks deserts. Sahib, they call him in the Hawaiian Bar.

But what was he to her? Forget Mrs Rourke's letter. According to May Templar, his mother, he and Adelia shared more than sexual favours; companion and friend they supported one another through thick and thin.

'Inseparable,' she overheard her say. 'Heart and soul, you couldn't put a knife between them.'

Now it seems her heart and soul is her landlord. And if that isn't enough she's spellbound by his presence, every nerve singing.

'Don't you think it odd that once again you're on the acquisitive end of my life and loves?' she said hoarsely. 'Not too many years ago another man was reducing my circumstances while leaving you a sizeable testament of good faith. What is it about you that makes men want to cover you in gold?'

'You're mighty cruel.'

'I know and I'll be sorry tomorrow but right now all I can think is I loved my husband and you stole him away. What were you to him?'

'A necessity.'

'A wealthy necessity now I would have said.'

He whipped off the glasses. 'You think this is wealth!' he said, his eyes dark and stormy. 'You talkin' to me like I'm dirt?'

'I don't know what to think.'

'I'll tell you what I think! I think you didn't know your husband. If you did you'd understand why a man like Ash would go to such lengths to secure peace of mind. I think he took a gamble when he went to Korea concocting this Will trusting you to know and believe in his purpose. What's more I think he'd turn in his grave today feelin' you were lettin' him and yourself down.'

'How dare you talk to me this way!'

'I dare because I'm the one put my name to this! And because when he asked me to do it he laid down pride expectin' me to do the same. If you had half an understandin' of what went on that time you'd see it but you're so caught up in your own pain you haven't considered anyone else.'

'Don't you lecture me!' Adelia scrambled out of the car. 'I am in pain but it's not the house or money that hurts me. It's you! I hate the way Alex took you into his confidence. I hate the way he relied on your good sense rather than mine. I hate that in his last dealings on earth he turned to you rather than me.'

She slammed the door. 'And I hate the idea that you and I were lovers!'

~

Jacob swung into the Parlour parking bay.

'I've come to take you to lunch.'

'I couldn't eat a thing.'

'Then come to my apartment for a sherry and feet up.' They drove to his apartment by the river. 'So how did it go? Not too many shocks I hope.'

'No more than last time.'

'If you feel you've been given a bad deal I've a friend who can help out.'

'No thanks. I've had enough of lawyers to last me a lifetime. Besides, I'm learning to live with my impoverished state.'

'It's not your future alone in jeopardy. It's the children's. This friend of mine is a sharp blade. If there is a legal flaw he'll find it.'

'I couldn't do it, not to Bill. He doesn't deserve that kind of censure.'

'Would there be censure?'

'Not of him perhaps but of his son. Must we talk about it?'

'My lips are sealed. The offer's there if you need it. Excuse me a minute while I check my service.'

Adelia watched him go. She won't tell no matter how he probes. It's too painful for her to comprehend, let alone a stranger.

How odd! All this time and still she sees Jacob as a stranger. He should be more. He is good to her and the children but with her hopes so fixed on Alex she hasn't been able to bridge the gap.

A master of patience, Jacob calls with invitations to a gallery or show. She rarely accepts. It isn't that she doesn't like him. It's that he sees her as a challenge and that makes her wary. Moreover, she thinks if she were once to let down her guard he would prove controlling. She's had enough of controlling men consequently this is a rare visit to his apartment.

He returned with glasses of chilled wine and a warm smile.

'Is this a ruse, Doctor? Are you inviting me up to see your etchings?'

'Could be, although I do have etchings as you're about to witness.' He drew her to a room overlooking the river pointing out various paintings hanging from the walls. 'This is a Modigliani.' He looped his arm about her waist. And this is a Sisley.'

'Are they real?'

'The Sisley is real.'

'How can you tell the difference?'

'There's no comparison.' He turned his eyes darkly magnetic. 'No matter how brilliant a fake it can't come near the real thing. You ought to know that since you've kept me dangling for that reason.'

She gazed at him. 'I have never lied to you, Jacob and I've never given false hope. There has only ever been Alex.'

'Only?' he queried, eyebrows raised.

Recalling Gabriel Templar's hands on the wheel of his car and the way those hands had made her feel Adelia gritted her teeth. 'Yes.'

Jacob emptied his glass. 'Alex is dead. Once you accept that you can start to live again.'

'I am living.'

'You're biding your time waiting for a miracle.'

'Miracles have been known to happen.'

'Yes and pigs to fly! Another drink?'

'I don't think so. It's late and I'd better be getting back.'

'It's only three-thirty and the General's minding the store.'

'I don't like taking advantage.'

'He won't mind. He loves you and the kids. As for taking advantage?' he whispered, his thumbs caressing the base of her neck, 'why don't you take advantage of what's on offer here?'

'Oh that is good,' she closed.

'Of course it is. Come! Sit down.' She sat on the piano stool. He stood behind her working his fingers through her hair. It felt good. His hands are warm and today more than any other she needs to be close to someone.

'Relax,' he said. Adelia closed her eyes. He unbuttoned her collar, his thumbs working her collarbone and then into the valley of her chest easing his fingertips under her brassiere, stroking the rise of her breasts.

'Jacob?'

'Let it happen. It's good.'

It was good. She arched her back and his hands were about her breasts moulding and working the flesh. He eased the shirt over her shoulders and knelt by the stool caressing her nipples and sending chills down her spine.

A fire was building in the pit of her stomach, an ache that needed to be relieved. His hand was working under her skirt, touching her knees and then her thighs, fingers searching. Yes, she thought, holding onto the sides of the stool spreading her knees, allowing him access. Please do it.

He was drawing her pants aside, easing his fingers inside and she was wet, hungry for release. 'Yes,' she whispered, closing her eyes and dreaming of Alex. It was Alex who loved her and Alex who caressed her.

'Do it!'

He was sucking her nipples, his fingers more urgent, and she was aching.

'More, darling,' she groaned. 'Make it happen.'

Then his mouth was on hers. Pleasure emptied away.

She wiped her mouth. 'Sorry, Jacob, I can't.'

He was furious. 'Oh well,' he pushed back his hair. 'I guess it's an improvement on last time you were here. I didn't get to hold your coat.'

'I'm sorry.'

'So you should be. What d'you think we're doing here? I'm a man not a puppet. If you aren't prepared to give as good as you get don't tease.'

'So is it love you want?'

He shrugged. 'Nice but not mandatory, you either want me or you don't.'

Adelia stared at his face, the strangely exotic colouring, thick brown hair and dark eyes. Everyone likes Jacob Feldstein. He is bright and witty and funny and smart. But he's not Alex.

'I'd better go.'

'You'd better. I'll get my keys.'

'Don't bother I'll call a cab.'

'I may be a fake. I may be unacceptable to you. I may even be a sore loser but I'm not a heel.' He opened the door. 'I'll look forward to *Tosca,* that's if you haven't found someone else to pass the time.'

The cab pulled out of the drive. Adelia inserted her key. No sign of Timmy. The General will have taken him out. She closed the door and turned.

'Oh my God!'

Alex was everywhere, memories of him running at her honking like a gaggle of geese wanting to be fed. From the moment she saw his jacket back of the chair he was coming at her, in the wisteria at the window, in the French cigarettes he smoked and the scent of his cologne. His heart was beating in the ticking of the clock and the rattle of the central heating. He was everywhere, in every room, clambering over familiar objects, rushing, running, scrambling to touch, to kiss, to hold...!

'No!' She slammed her hands over her ears. 'For pity's sake stop!'

Weary, she climbed the stairs to the bedroom and closed the curtains.

She took the phone off the hook and lay on the bed. The scent of him was in the bedroom lingering in the pillows. She put the pillows out on the landing and closed the door - you can have too much of a good thing.

Chapter Thirty-Two
Golden Eagles

'I'm going to have to take the load off for a couple of minutes,' said Bill, puffing. 'You go on ahead. Me and Tag will sit awhile.'

'We'll all rest.' Adelia spread a rug on the ground. 'Sophie, you and Becky take Timmy for an ice cream. Then we'll look at the sea-lions.'

She was unpacking the basket when a woman approached.

'Say Miss, can I have your autograph?'

'Autograph?'

'You are the gal from *Time* magazine, aren't you?' said the woman. 'The one who does the fancy movie-star funerals?'

Adelia shook her head. 'I think you've mistaken me for someone else.'

The woman walked away.

'Adelia Hunter.' Bill tutted. 'Is that any way to treat your public?'

'Probably not, but these days I don't get to spend a great deal of time with you and so I'm making the most of it.' She looked at him, not liking his colour. 'And you need to take a holiday.'

'I'm doing okay. The doctor's pleased with me.'

No he's not, she thought! He's worried as are we all.

Tuesday Bill collapsed at the golf club. Blood pressure sky-high and unstable heart rhythms, he spent the week in CCU on a heart monitor.

Now everybody is on tenterhooks.

'Sam Jentzen called last night,' he chewed on his spectacles. 'He reckons most of US POWs are home now. There may be a few deep in the interior. They're looking but it'll take time to find them.'

'Then there's still hope.'

'Uh-huh, except time is the one thing I don't have.'

Adelia made no comment. Hope is best left unspoken.

'You missed a wing-ding of an interment last week,' she said, trying to cheer him up. 'Carriages, a gospel choir, flowers coming out of our ears and free booze all around.'

'You don't say! Who were you burying, Harry S Truman?'

'Somebody much more important...Ruby Rourke.'

He gave a great snort of laughter. 'You are kidding me!'

'I am not. I was asked to help. Needless to say I did my best.' She laid a hand on her heart: "Blessed are the peacemakers for they shall be called the children of God.'

'Hah! I do not believe it! How come she had you officiating?'

'It was in her Will, along with a banker's draft for flowers to be placed on her grave in perpetuity, plus, a long list of what she wanted and how she wanted it from fuchsia pink wreaths to the scattering of rose petals.'

'Ye gods! Some nerve after what she did.'

'I don't remember what she did.'

'It's as well you don't.' He shook his head. 'Ruby Iolanthe Cropper gone? Well, I'll be dammed!'

'You won't be damned. You'll be in a much better place.'

He grinned. 'Doing what?'

'Baby-sitting cherubs for a start,' she said, Timmy and the girls running toward them. 'Making sure they don't get up to mischief.'

'That would suit me fine.' He patted her hand. 'But I should tell you I shan't be availing myself of your services precious though they are. The army will carry me home, then that honour will at least be accorded one Hunter.'

Adelia kissed him. 'Dearest Bill! Talking of cherubs...'

'Gramps!' Timmy jumped on him. 'Dere's a man wid wings.'

Sophie licked an ice cream. 'Falcons and things.'

'Let's go watch,' said the General, taking Timmy in his arms. 'If I'm to be airborne I could use some advice.'

~

The falconer had his back to them yet even from thirty yards Adelia knew him as did Sophie. 'It's Uncle Gabriel.'

This isn't the polished business tycoon. In natural surroundings, booted feet planted deep in the earth and birds overhead, he is a different man.

Adelia folded her arms over her breast. If she could've got by without revealing the contents of the Will to the family she would but Daniel was explicit. 'You're obliged to inform them of any new changes.' The latest news did nothing for Bill's blood pressure neither did it further her relationship with Ellen and Sarah, both thinking if a son and a worthy brother saw fit to publically humiliate his wife he must have cause. Bill, bless him, stayed true

'To think a son of mine would leave a share of his wife and kids to another man! That guy!' he muttered. 'What kind of a rag tag is he? His clothes! That's Tag's inheritance he's got on his back.'

'To be fair he hasn't touched a penny, nor for that matter have I.'

'Neither will you! I'll see you in rags before I let you take a dime. No need to worry. Ellen's sorted Sophie. I've seen to you and Tag. Nobody's going to put my grandson's nose out of joint.' He shook his head. 'I mean, what is it about? Can't be about money, his Zoo turning cartwheels. I can't stand to look at him! See his hair! What is he some kind of hobo?'

This was no hobo. Casual in corduroy riding britches and polo shirt he looked well. It's the long hair that gives a *laissez-faire* appearance.

'I went by the Mill the other day,' said Bill. 'The chimney was belching smoke like it hadn't been lit in years. They say he sold it in '49.'

'To whom?'

'No one knows. I hear his mother works for you these days.'

'I wouldn't say work.' Adelia's smile took the sting from the words. 'More like uses the New Valley for market forum dishing tea and scandal.'

'Don't you find that tricky?'

'I am learning to live with it. May Templar hates being idle and the Parlour gives her plenty to do.'

'And Templar's designs on you?'

'He doesn't have designs on me.'

'Baloney! The feller's crazy about you.'

'I don't know how you can say that after what happened.'

'I say it because it's true. I saw his face when we came in. The fellow's in love with you. I'm not so old I don't remember how it felt.'

An eagle flew out of the blue sky with mighty talons outstretched. Down came the bird, the thud as it landed on the leather gauntlet echoing about the field. 'Oh!' Adelia winced. As the bird landed so Gabriel stretched, his shirt parting company with jodhpurs to reveal ugly scars circling his back.

Sophie ran toward her. 'See that, Mummy? He looks into the sun?'

'Golden Eagles can do that,' said Bill. But both Sophie and Adelia knew it wasn't the eagle that stared into the sun. It was the man.

~

'Mrs Brock, have you seen Willow?'

'No, mum. He hasn't been around all day.'

'Was he here yesterday? I don't recall seeing him.'

The cat's gone yet again! What on earth's wrong with it? One minute you can't shift it from the hearth the next it's nowhere to be found.

Adelia is in a rush. It's *Tosca*! Jacob is calling at six but will find everything behind hand, Timmy with toothache,

Willow disappearing and Frank thinking of quitting! To top
that the Black Widow dream is back with a vengeance!

She woke in the night terrified because where before she
was getting ready for a funeral, this time she was throwing
a rose into an open grave. Then she could see inside the
coffin except it was a bunker and Alex crouched inside.

In the dream she shouted. 'I know you're in there
Alexander Stonewall Hunter and I'm coming to get you so
don't think you can hide!'

Screaming with rage, she leapt into the grave. The
bunker opened and a tin soldier popped out, a pistol aimed
at her breast. She slapped the tin-soldier. It fell only for
another to take his place. Wham! Wham! A rifle range, she
fought tin soldiers throughout the night.

The worst of it was Alex's face was hanging on every
soldier.

She woke shouting. Why dream such a thing? And why
would her beloved husband get between her and salvation?
Is his grave so hard to vacate?

~

They were late getting to the theatre. Jacob is furious.
'We've missed the first Act. Box or no they won't let us in
until intermission.'

'I'm sorry,' she said. 'Timmy had toothache. I wasn't
going to leave him.'

'Those two? You really do let them rule the roost.'

'I wanted to be sure.'

'They had their grandmother fussing over them. They
didn't need you.'

The car pulled into the parking zone. The valet opened the door.

'See? Full House!' Jacob pointed to a notice board. 'Once in a lifetime this production comes to Virginia and I miss it on account of a toothache.'

Adelia swept through the foyer kicking the train of her gown out of the way. For two pins she'd tell him what he could do with his blessed *Tosca*.

Jacob is impatient with the children. He talks to them but at a distance.

Hiking her skirts, she climbed the staircase, mirrors replicating the polished ivory of her shoulders. 'Fabulous gown.' Jacob patted her bottom. 'You and your derriere make up for your tardiness.'

Adelia made straight for the bar. Two glasses of wine later she breathed out, what with Timmy fractious and Frank leaving she's worn out.

'But why Frank?' she'd asked askance.

'It's Sue,' he'd replied. 'I can't be around her if she don't want me.'

Adelia knew they were lovers. She also knew Sue hankered for more.

'What will you do?'

'As much I love you and the kids I'm gonna have to strike out on my own.'

'Must you? You know I'll back you in anything you want to do but don't go now, not with this Templar business hanging over us?'

Frank sighed. 'I promised the Guvnor. Wait for me, he said, take care of my girls until I'm home. I was glad to do it because you were needy and I love him. Then Sue came along and I figured I'd got my reward. But you know how it is, ma'am. She wants me but don't want my colour.'

'I'm so sorry.'

'You'll be okay. The Colonel is my friend. I trust his judgement. If he put that Marine in back-up position he knew what he was doing.'

~

Intermission they took their drinks to the mezzanine floor wandering through a watercolour exhibition. Adelia stood sipping her drink and thinking of Timmy. People came through from the bar, a tall, dark-haired naval officer among them. In the muted light he could've been Alex, same quick agility swerving away from a waitress with an overloaded tray.

It didn't matter where she looked he was there. A man touched an easel and it could've been his hand, same broad palm and long fingers. Someone laughed the same husky chuckle and her heart leapt. Is there nowhere in the world she can go to get away from the past?

Turning a corner she came face to face with Gabriel Templar. Instincts were to cut him dead but Frank's words rang in her head, if a close friend like Frank is able to trust Alex's judgement why can't she?

She opened her mouth to speak but he passed by.

Jacob leaned close. 'I see Templar's here. Get the jacket? Savile Row and Paris, it's amazing what money can do.'

'He has style, born with it I would have said.'

'Well, if anyone knows about that it's you. You two were close. Alex tried shielding you from gossip but it was a longstanding arrangement, very Anglo Saxon, sex in the tool-shed among spanners and ball-cocks.'

'You make it sound tawdry.'

'I meant to make it sound exciting.'

Adelia sighed. Why are we here, she thought? We don't even like one another. 'I suppose that's your thing,' she said sourly, 'psychoanalytical sex among the Rorschach Tests.'

'Less psychoanalysis and more of the sex!' He opened a box of raspberry truffles sliding one between her lips. 'Let me know when you're up for it.'

~

Gabriel was with a group of business men, sponsors of the Kilimanjaro trip who wanted to buy him out of the Reserve. They are talking about Tosca, comparing Puccini to Wagner. Gabriel finds Wagner hard going. Charles Beaufort once suggested a weekend in Bayreuth, a serious affair, asses on wooden benches and doors to the hall locked so no one could leave they were stuck inside for three hours. He would've liked to close his eyes and let the music speak for itself but the benches wouldn't let him. They were worse than the kiddie seats at the Christmas concert.

'Hah!' He smiled at the memory and across the way Adelia smiled.

Whoah! Heart thrashing he sat back. Is this a sign of pack ice melting?

A guy nudged his arm. 'Have you thought any more about our proposal?'

'Sorry?'

The guy switched to the business of the day, trying to persuade Gabriel to sell his share of the Reserve. It's okay, Mister, he thought, you don't need to try. As far as I'm concerned it's a done deal.

He will sell and then he's out of Virginia and on the way to Suffolk, him and Ma taking a cottage on the Beaufort Estate.

Ma can't wait. She met the Beaufort daughters when they visited the park, Julia and Clare, English roses with blue eyes and clear skin. Now she looks at the future and sees blue-eyed grandchildren.

Bored with the opera, she sighs. 'Gabe, pass me that box of candy.'

A couple of minutes later, 'I can't understand a word of this.'

'That's because it's in Italian.'

'Eyetalian! How am I supposed to understand if they sing in a foreign language? Oh look! There's Delia and that doctor!' She waved and Adelia waved back. 'See that gal?' says Ma to one of the guys. 'There was a time when I thought she might be my daughter-in-law.'

'Tough luck, Gabe, missing out on a true Southern belle,' said a guy.

'She's not one of ours,' said Ma. 'She's British. She came over in '46 with her baby. Her first feller died so she up and married a soldier. Now he's dead and she's a widow again, poor gal.'

'But not for long,' said the first guy, 'not if her escort and half the male auditorium has anything to do with it.'

The curtain rose. Gabriel tried concentrating but could only gaze across the auditorium. In a dark gown with her hair piled on her head against the blue velvet cushiony backdrop she is a priceless jewel in a velvet box yet fingers looped through her necklace she isn't comfortable.

Feldstein watches her like a hawk. Gabriel doesn't care for him. Whenever they run into one another the guy goes out of his way to be sassy.

Last week Gabriel swung a deal getting a couple of aging tigers away from a decrepit European Zoo. Part of the team transporting animals to the Reserve he was leaving the DA's office when up comes Feldstein. 'If it isn't Tarzan,' he said, checking price tags on Gabriel's clothes. 'You're quite the adventurer these days, must be quite a change from digging graves.'

Gabriel watched him walk away that day with Hunter whispering in his head: *'It's not the bees I'm worried about. It's the rats!'*

~

Jacob is pissed off. Three years he's worked this claim supporting her and the kids. Now with the Will completed and certainty of Ash Hunter's death he was sure of a reward. But no, the sculptor is where it's going.

'You really have treated me like shit.'

She turned. 'I beg your pardon?'

'I said, you've treated me badly.'

'I'm sorry. I thought we could've had more.'

'We could have had everything if you'd let go of ancient history.'

'Are you saying my husband is ancient history?'

'No, I'm not, though why you hold onto a memory that's stripped you of house and home and made you pawn to another man is beyond me.'

'You've been listening at keyholes, Jacob.'

'Maybe I have but don't change the subject. I'm not saying your husband is history. The history you cling to and have these three years is anything but ancient. It's alive and sitting across the way only waiting for the nod.'

'I am fond of you, Jacob, but we want different things. It's possible I could have been more honest. But you're wrong about Alex. Everything he did was for me and my children. I should've known that and trusted him.'

Catching up her gown, she pushed back the chair and left the box.

'Excuse me!' Gabriel was on his feet and out through the curtains.

She was hurrying round the corridor toward him. They met midway.

'Mister Templar,' she said panting. 'I wonder if you're not too busy you might drop by the house tomorrow.'

'Any particular time?'

'Possibly around four?'

'Four will be fine.'

Having delivered her message she went back the way she came. 'A splendid Tosca, don't you think, if a little muscular!'

On his way back to the box he paused to adjust his tie and saw in the mirror the ghost of a guy in RAF uniform who smiled and said, 'all you need in life is a haircut, a shit-load of money and a beautiful girl on your arm.'

Gabriel has the money. Now he needs a haircut.

~

1355 hours he was on the doorstep. It was like coming home, the Eyrie wrapping about him in a shawl. She met him at the door and walked round introducing him to the cook and the gardener, Frank Bates he knew from an ache in his jaw. For a moment he thought he was being given the Grand Tour before being offered the house but she was being Adelia.

'Mister Templar? You've cut your hair!'

'I thought it was time.'

'It's very becoming.'

'It feels kinda draughty.'

'Do you think the crew-cut will dent your Sahib image?'

'I hope not.' He grinned. 'I worked on it long enough.'

'Can I touch?' said Sophie. 'It feels like a soft brush.'

'Can I?' asked Timmy.

Adelia lifted Timmy and he patted Gabriel's hair. 'This is Timothy Alexander, or Tag, as he's known to his friends.'

'Hi, Tag. How you doin'?'

Timmy pushed into Gabriel's arms. 'You look like my Daddy.'

'How can you know, sweetie?' said Adelia. 'You've never seen your Daddy.'

'Yeth I have,' Timmy protested. 'He reads a story every night.'

'And he kisses me,' said Sophie.

'He's a busy Daddy then. Shall I take Timmy, he fidgets rather.'

'It's okay,' said Gabriel. 'I like the feel of him.'

Adelia couldn't keep her eyes off him. With short hair he was a blonde version of Alex. They could have been brothers. 'Thank you for coming,' she said awkwardly. 'I would've understood if you'd stayed away.'

'I couldn't have stayed away.'

'I'm so sorry for the things I said. I realise now you were only trying to carry out his wishes.' Then aware of the children listening she changed the subject. 'Would you care for something stronger than tea?'

'I don't drink.'

'Oh! That must set you apart in the playboy stakes.'

'I wouldn't know about playboys.'

'Aren't you part of the in-crowd then, the international set?'

'Do I look like I'm part of the in-crowd?'

The silence was broken by the scratching of Sophie's pencil. 'Uncle Gabriel? I'm writing a letter to Daddy. Would you like to hear it?'

'Sure.'

'Dear Daddy, we heard on Nana's new TV you'll be home soon, so me and Becky and Tag are making a surprise. It's a concert. I'm to dance the Sugar Plum Fairy, Becky's throwing her baton, Rosie will play dead and Tag's going to sing. He's not very good yet. He's only little...that's as far as I've got.'

'That's fine,' said Adelia. 'Put it in an envelope and I'll post it.'

They went through to the sitting room, the distance between them closing.

'I understand from your mother you've travelled the world.'

'That's Ma exaggeratin'.'

'She said you spend a lot of time in Paris. What were you doing there, apart from creating beautiful statues?'

'Learnin' to read and write mostly. Okay, maybe not so much learning. I already had the best teacher. Let's say I was beginnin' again.'

'How brave of you.'

He blushed. 'You think so?'

The telephone rang. 'Excuse me. Hello Bill, are you all right?...have you?...don't despair. Things may still turn out right...Yes, I'll tell them...'

'That was Gramps. You're to leave early tomorrow for a trip to the Bay. Perhaps you'd better get your things ready. Take Timmy with you, love.'

They didn't want to go and swarmed over Gabriel, Sophie in tears.

Adelia sighed. 'Sophie is finding it hard.'

'She's missin' her Pa.'

'We're all missing him.'

'Is there no news?'

'No, but we're not giving up hope. Mister Templar, I asked to speak to you because last night I saw how awkward this is for you. That day in Daniel's office I said dreadful things. I hope you'll be able to forgive me.'

'There's nothin' to forgive. Maybe the Colonel could have done somethin' less restrictive but he was scared for you.'

'Was he?' Tears filled her eyes, Bill Hunter's latest communiqué adding to the misery, the war department having issued the final list of US POWs due to be released, Alex's name not among them.

'He was tryin' to protect you the best way he knew.'

'And he chose you to do it? He must've thought a great deal of you.'

'It wasn't so much what he felt for me. It was what I feel for you.'

He pushed an envelope toward her.

'What is this?'

'I sold the Nature Reserve. This is money I owe you.'

'I can't take this!'

'It's yours and the children's.' He pushed away from the chair. 'I agreed to do this for the Colonel because at the time you were ill. You're not ill. You are strong. You don't need a stranglehold on your life and nor do I.'

'And the guardianship of Timmy and Sophie, is that a stranglehold?'

'Lookin' after your babes could never hurt me.'

'Does that mean you're willing to stay their guardian?'

'If you, and they, would like me to.'

'I would like it and I'm certain they will. I'll take the money providing you take half. I'm sure my husband never intended you to feel badly about it.'

'The Colonel meant for you to be loved by those that love you.'

'Thank you for saying that.'

'I gotta be goin'. I got chores to do. Maybe Sophie and Tag would like to come over some tine to see the baby rhino?'

'They'd love it. And so would I.'

~

Adelia's going through Alex's closet packing his things into a cardboard box.

Bill is right, they need to go.

One-by-one she went through the closet drawers finding rare and wonderful things like a book on birds, a score of Bach cantatas and an anthology of poems by Walt Whitman.

A wooden chest held mementoes of childhood, army memorabilia mostly, yet every now and then there was a glimpse of the man, and the boy, she never knew.

There were letters from his paternal grandfather, George Frobisher, drawings Alex had made, sketches of plants and animals. There was a dog's collar, the name Sherbet engraved on the clasp. There was a BSA badge, a photograph album, mostly group shots of men in military school, Bobby Rourke among them looking so young and carefree.

It was when she found a pair Sophie's socks wrapped in tissue that the things went back into the chest. Too much! It was breaking her heart.

Chapter Thirty-Three
Debt Repaid

News of Frank's imminent departure flashed through the wires several buyers showing an interest in the New Valley Rest, Gabriel Templar among them.

He called the Eyrie with an offer. Adelia was sitting on the chaise pulling on her stockings. 'Are you sure you want to be involved with all that again?'

'I wouldn't want it to go to waste not after the work you put in. You brought a whole new dimension to the plantin' business.' He laughed. 'And with coverage from *Time* it would be crazy to pass up the chance of makin' all that money.'

There was a sticky pause, neither sure they were able to joke about circumstances surrounding money. The moment passed. All was safe again.

'We're burying the Senator today. If you've nothing better to do perhaps you'd like to pop along later this evening for a celebration supper.'

'What are you celebratin'?'

'How about you and me being friends?'

Adelia replaced the phone. The radio is playing, the broadcaster talking about the end of the war and how UN prisoners are being exchanged. She listened with no real expectation. It was as Bill said, they would have heard by now.

She redialled. 'Ellen, Sophie's got a thanksgiving service for the end of the war tomorrow. If Bill wants his morning free for bowling I can collect them.'

'So you've picked up a car.'

'Yes, but nothing too sporty. I would have adored a coupe like Sarah's but carrying all Sophie's bits and pieces thought best to stick with a saloon.'

'Must be a great relief being able to drive.'

'It's wonderful! Bye, then, must dash.'

'Hang on a minute?' said Ellen. 'I want to thank you for the way you've been with Bill. I know he's not the easiest of men, downright cussed at times. But he does love you and you have shown great kindness toward him. To be honest, I don't think he would've got so far without you and the kids.'

'Oh Ellen!'

'That's all, honey. Just that and to say I'm thinking of you at this time.'

Adelia was stunned. Kind words from Ellen are gold dust. Tonight when everybody's gone she'll cherish the moment. Right now she's the Senator to bury.

~

Two forty-five and they were running late. She hurried to the prep room where Sue sat beside the open casket. 'What's the problem?'

'The Senator's not ready.'

'Oh dear.'

'He's hanging on. He feels he hasn't had his full three score and ten.'

Sue Ryland has definite opinions about the deceased's readiness to embark upon a last journey. Most times it's okay to close the coffin, when not she pulls up a stool and sits encouraging the troubled soul to move on. Adelia is content to wait; so many eccentricities of her own she can afford to show patience with Sue's.

Ten minutes and they are ready to roll. It is to be a colourful affair, the Senator's wife left specific instructions. 'Chubby lived and died a happy, vulgar, man. Bring out the best!' The Senator was a racing man with roots in Donegal thus the predominant colour is Shamrock Green. Four matched bays pull the rig and cream coloured lilies pile high about a green velvet pall. Frank and Hiram sport Derby hats and green cockades while gentlemen ushers, dapper in black frockcoats and buff coloured britches, escort the Senator's wife and daughters aboard a second rig.

The horse's tails and manes are plaited with green ribbon. Sue is a knock-out in emerald green jacket, cream britches and a black stock, leather high-tops, a silk opera hat, kid gloves and a silver-topped cane completing her outfit.

Adelia wears a nineteenth-century hunting ensemble, long skirts over a showy stretch of white petticoat, a fitted velvet jacket, white lace jabot and Tricorne hat with veil. On her arm she carries a basket of yellow crocus bulbs, give-away tokens in memory of the deceased.

Frank pilots the first rig with Lemuel alongside fairly bursting with pride. Hiram drives the following rig, Levi, his second son, beside him. Sunlight shines on the harnesses, bells jingle and horses toss their heads. A band assembles. A couple of toots on a horn, a slide on the trombone, a crack of a whip, and off they go.

The gates swing open and out rolls the first rig - Sue's luscious cleavage leading the way. The second rolls with Adelia out front and a footman bringing up the rear.

They swing onto the main road to the popping of flash bulbs. A crowd has gathered, scores of people line the route and children run alongside.

Adelia knows this to be her final foray into New Valley Vaudeville. She refused Gabriel's offer to buy into the business. Another public washing of their particular set of laundry is more than anyone can stand.

The procession turned into the Avenue, people joining the mourners and singing along with the band, the funeral taking on a carnival atmosphere.

They passed the Hunter residence. Bill is by the gate. He looks tired yet is smiling. Ellen and the children are beside him, Sophie and Timmy wiggling their fingers in unobtrusive waves. On they roll toward the hill and the climb toward St Jude's and there waiting beneath the pine trees is the Lone Ranger.

Spectacular in black frockcoat and silver waistcoat Gabriel tipped his hat.

'Afternoon, ma'am.'

'Good morning.' She passed a camellia for his buttonhole. 'You look like you should be wearing a mask and a cape.'

'And you look like a Riverboat Gambling Queen.'

~

Gabriel sat at the back of the church stifling a smile. He didn't know what to make of it all. When he owned the Parlour his plantings were carried out in grim solemnity. The idea of balloons and Riverboat Gambling Queens never occurred to him. Judging by the expressions on the faces of today's congregation it hadn't occurred to them either.

Adelia crossed the nave to genuflect before the altar petticoats kicked out in a flurry of lace. Yeah, thought Gabriel, make the most of it. The fashion for carnival never lasts. A year on and it'll be black Cadillacs and misery.

How things change, a couple of years and everything topsy-turvy. One day he and Ma haven't a pot to piss in then they've a house in Richmond, an apartment in Paris, and maybe a cottage in Suffolk. What Good Fairy waved her wand?

The Good Fairy is gazing about the church, her eyes troubled.

He won't stay long. Though she smiled and made space for him she'd sooner he wasn't there. Charles Beaufort is right. 'Careful, Gabe,' he said, when he phoned with the news. 'If she's the woman I think she is you'll need the patience of Job to coax her from her grief.'

It all feels unreal. The last time Gabriel sat in this church it was awash with roses and glittering candles and Bobby Rourke's baloney. The Senator goes with orchids, Yeats' poetry, and 'Danny Boy' sung by a choir.

'The summer's gone and all the flowers are dying,
Tis you, tis you must go, and I must bide.'

The music soothing Gabriel closed his eyes. He's tired. He didn't sleep a wink last night and woke this morning with his back on fire. More lines, he looked in the mirror and saw how they fanned up and out like bleached veins in a leaf.

'Bug's wings,' is how Ma put it. 'Like you gonna bust out as Jiminy Cricket.'

The scars set Gabriel's teeth on edge, arriving in the dead of night and whispering of God's displeasure, he connects them with Alex Hunter.

Throughout that last reading of the Will Gabriel sat with his hand in his pocket holding onto dynamite, a letter in his fist addressed to, '*My dear wife.*'

Years the letter has stayed in Hunter's coat. It's a heavy envelope, the accompanying note says, '*this letter explains my actions. Make sure she gets it, Templar. Not only will it exonerate me I'm hoping it will vindicate you.*'

Hunter read from the letter that day at the Monument in '49, no great orator yet that simple plea from the heart gave Gabriel the courage to play his part.

'I w*onder if by now you have recovered the early years in Virginia. I do sincerely hope so. To forget even a moment of life, my dear wife, would be a great loss.*

My hope is that in reading this you'll understand a little more and learn of another, who, though perhaps still forgotten, loves you as I love you.

I trust Gabriel Templar as I trust a brother and can show no greater testimony to that trust than leaving this in his care. Read it, beloved baby, and know I have loved you all of my life and shall continue to love you long after my death.'

A couple of lines yet what power. Gabriel will never forget the way Hunter sat cradling the letter in his hands and struggling with the words, his hope that one day she would say, it's alright, Darling Alex, I understand.

Gabriel was angry that day in Washington. He was angry in the lawyer's office, Daniel Culpepper yawing away and her green eyes ripping everyone to shreds. He wanted to toss the letter in her lap and yell, 'read that, for Chrissakes! Then we can all get some peace!'

The letter was never meant to stay with the lawyer. Like the coat it was meant to be given when the military called. The plan went belly-up. She put an arm-lock on it. 'I don't want it,' she said. 'Return it to me when you return my husband.'

The letter weighs heavy in his pocket, especially now when things seem more hopeful, her faith in her husband and his carrier pigeon restored.

She must read it. She must! Because until it rests in her hands Alex Hunter is never going to rest and bug's wings will keep growing.

~

The Senator planted in a goodly manner his wife offered a spray of orchids.

'Please take these, Mrs Hunter. You sent my Chubby off in style.'

Adelia is glad it's over. As always on such occasions she observes all through the gaze of a funeral director, more concerned with draping the pall than the tears of the bereaved. Today she finds it hard distancing herself from sorrow. Perhaps it was the way things were carried out, poignant songs and the Senator's wife's delight in her Chubby. The Senator's daughters, beautiful women with strong American faces wept yet with a certainty that all was right under heaven.

Their love and faith touched Adelia. She felt for Ellen! To bury one's child is terrible yet to be ignorant of their fate more so. Day after day, night after night, Adelia drives herself crazy pondering the manner of Alex's death. She tiptoes toward the idea, hovers on the edge of hideous possibilities - what might have happened, what terrors, what pain - and rushes away unable to bear it.

It was too raw. Too now! Too forever!

All throughout the service she felt as though she was being observed, or under surveillance a better description, eyes following her every move. It was happening now in the cemetery, the Senator's casket lowered into the ground.

The New Valley puts on a show that gives the congregation licence to stare. It's pointless selling tickets for the front row if you don't want an audience yet the eyes that follow her today don't count wreaths on the coffin, or scrutinize the widow's tears, or look at Sue and wonder if she's wearing a bra. These eyes pierced figured velvet, ripping Adelia's bodice and her heart to open view.

~

The mourners are leaving, the last wreath placed on the grave. 'Still here?' said Adelia to Gabriel. 'I thought you might have got bored and gone home.'

He smiled. 'I can think of plenty words that apply to the New Valley Rest but boring ain't one of them.'

'It is a bit of a thing, isn't it?'

'It's a spectacle, I grant you that.'

'But not your cup of tea?'

'No, not mine. I have a leanin' toward Earl Grey.'

They fell in step. Photographers gathered about the cemetery gates pushing and shoving trying to get the best picture for tomorrow's review.

'Watch out,' said she, conscious of flash guns popping. 'The press are here.'

He shrugged. 'That's okay. It'll be you they're after not me.'

'Doesn't a world famous sculptor rate a profile in *Time* magazine?'

'Sure, but I don't see anyone of that description here today.'

'You are a very modest man, Mister Templar.'

'And you are a very beautiful woman, Mrs Hunter.'

'Here you are, ma'am.' Frank passed the last crocus basket down from the rig.

'Excuse me, Gabriel.' Adelia shook out her skirts. 'I need to get busy. Perhaps we could meet at the house for supper?'

'Sure thing. I'm lookin' forward to it.'

The band started up again. She took her place behind the first wagon. Off they went again starting down the long incline toward town.

Adelia is weary, the hem of her skirt dragging in the dust.

People are taking photographs calling out her name.

'Delia!' they shout. 'Mizz Hunter! Look this way, will you?'

Hands reach out for the crocus. Head down, trying to balance the basket and at the same time hold up her skirt she passes bulbs this way and that.

A man's hand reaches out from the mass. She proffers a bulb.

He takes it, his fingertips brushing the palm of her hand like a kiss.

Startled, she turned to see who it was, and tripped on her skirt.

The hand flashed to her elbow to support her. By the time she'd regained her balance her saviour had been swallowed up in the mob.

Weary, she moved on. It was a hot day, dust rising off the wheels.

She raised her veil to wipe her eyes and a photographer called out.

'Over here, Mizz Hunter!'

She looked up.

A camera flashed.

And she saw Alex.

She dropped the basket.

'What's wrong?' Gabriel came out of nowhere.

'I saw Alex.'

'Alex?'

'Yes!'

She ran, pushing through the crowd, elbowing her way into the thick of it, kicking and shoving. *He is here! I saw him! He was wearing dark glasses!*

People closed in about her, smiling, patting her arm, saying what a great funeral, and does she like it in the States and had she ever thought of being in the movies?

'Let me by!' She ran up and down searching. 'Please let me by!' At length, panting and closed in by the crowd, she leant against a tree, every bit of energy drained.

Gabriel took her arm. 'Do you want me to look?'

'No,' she said. 'It wasn't him. How could it be? He is dead.'

The rigs were moving away wheels squeaking.

A few remaining crocus bulbs lay crushed in the dust.

Trembling, she bent to gather them.

Gabriel crouched beside her. 'I'll give you a hand.'

Oh, she thought, I've done this before. I've knelt in dust and this man with his long tanned fingers knelt beside me.

A door creaked open. It hovered midway between open and closed and then slowly slid shut.

'Come on.' He helped her to her feet. 'I'll take you home.'

Chapter Thirty-Four
Wooden Tears

There was no one home at the Eyrie. 'Will you come up with me?' she said.

They climbed the stairs to the attic sitting room.

Adelia sat on the chaise. 'I really did think it was Alex.'

'It's warm out there.' Gabriel crouched before her. 'Maybe you got overheated.'

She gazed at him. He had petals in his hair. She reached out to brush them away and a door opened memories unfolding in 3-D picture post-cards.

St Faith's and the air-raid in '42. She remembers coming to Virginia, the Reception centre and the Marine that came to meet her. She remembers Bobby's wounded face. Bobby trying to kill her! Bobby dying! A life of yesterday merged with today, the good, bad, and the mundane, and shining through a thread of solid gold - this man.

'Gabriel,' she said, softly. 'Gabriel, darling.'

Instantly he knew. He caught her hand. 'You've got it back! Hallelujah!'

She lay against him and he rocked back and forth.

'Kiss me, Gabriel.'

Hands gentle about her face, he kissed her.

'Will you make love to me here in our room?'

'If that's what you want.'

No questions, no hesitating he spread his jacket on the floor the way he used to.

He took off his shirt, scars on his back the marks of a whip.

Eyes heavy with tears she watched. Naked he undressed her holding her hand so she might step out of the skirt, always respectful of her clothes and her body.

She lay on his jacket. He kissed her, his mouth sweet and his kisses tender.

They didn't speak, only gazed at one another lashes feathering their cheeks. Her orgasm came slowly and deeply, a wrenching pleasure that was also a bittersweet pain. He went to withdraw but her fingers spread on his shoulder. 'Stay,' she whispered.

Uncertain, old habits hard to break, he hesitated. She put her arm about him, pressing down. Groaning, he moved again, powerful muscles in his back straining down.

'I love you,' he said.

'I know.'

~

Lazarus returning from the dead, Gabriel left the Eyrie a new man. For the first time in his life he is free but he doesn't kid himself. Everything he has, carving skills, friends, his home in Paris and in the States, his health and pleasure all spring from one woman.

Head on her breast, she held him. Her fingertips brushed the scars on his back but she didn't ask how he got them, the moment not for questioning.

'I love you,' he'd said.

'I know,' she said. But it's all she said.

When he got home Ma was at the door.

'She got her memory back.'

'Oh my Lord! And does she know who you are?'

'She knows.'

'And does she know the nonsense she's put you through? Does she realise what a catch you are and how much better you could do for yourself?'

'I'll never do better than her.'

'Maybe not but it won't do harm to be humbled a little.'

He stepped under the shower. Thirty minutes they were together, more fulfilling than former meetings of old and more worrying - her kisses feeling like adieu.

Water ran down his chest turning his skin mahogany. Tense, muscles tight, he waited for the pain that would follow when hot water hit the scars.

There was nothing, just water running down his back.

His back is clear. The bug's wings, the puckered mass that looked as though someone had taken a cat o' nine tails to him had gone.

Baffled, he gazed in the mirror. Again a thought crept into his head. This is about Alex Hunter. Father Sebastian thought the scars were a scourge. Charles Beaufort disagreed. 'This is no Christian rite. This is older. It may well be the scapegoat principle, the belief that one man can take on the sins of another.'

Ma was in the doorway. 'Your back's clear.'

'Seems that way.'

Gabriel took a sweater from the closet. A cellophane bag quivered - Hunter's coat, a reminder of unfulfilled promises. He picked up the car keys and ran.

'Be careful, son!' Ma yelled. 'She's still a widow. Don't expect too much.'

Gabriel doesn't have expectations. His hope is that he will be seen as an artist in his own right, living breathing flesh and blood and not a substitute for a dead man.

Needing to get back to the Eyrie he put his foot on the gas. In the back he's got toys for the kids, a giraffe for Sophie, and a toy train for Timmy. He has scored his initials in the wood and was going to joke about it: 'Careful of them pieces,' he was going to say. 'One day they might be worth somethin'.'

Anxious, excited, he swung the car onto the road and found to his surprise that instead of heading for the Eyrie he is turning toward the church on the hill.

It's cold in St Jude's and dark, candles on the altar and a red lamp glowing indicating the Presence of the Host.

There's restoration going on here scaffolding set-up to the walls. This afternoon the metal poles was an early Irish Christmas tree, green balloons tied to planks. Now it's a tubular crucifix. Only the martyred Christ is missing.

Apart from a guy in the organ loft tuning the pipes Gabriel is alone.

He sat scrunched up in a pew, collar round his ears and hands in his pockets.

Once upon a time he knew Adelia. They had an open telephone line, her thoughts and feelings as bright and clear to him as stars in the sky. Their intimacy used to delight and scare him. At the same time it made him resentful, seeing himself the town loon and murderer, not the guy who lives in Paris, buddy to a Lord.

Earlier Adelia teased him about being famous. His stuff is getting known yet where she's concerned he's still the guy who sat in a pew, her furs swirling about his knees.

Truth is he'll always be the guy who shared a bible with her - ex-con, itinerant grave-digger - as he'll always be the guy that's going to lose her.

Last year he went to a play with Father Sebastian -Left Bank kids smoking pot and talking bullshit about a guy called Damocles who couldn't see how tricky life could be until a sword suspended from a single hair was hung over his head.

Bullshit it was yet Gabriel sees that sword hanging over his head. Every time the guy in the organ loft stokes the bellows air rolls down the length of the church and the sword swings. He sighed. 'What do you want from me Hunter?' he mutters. 'I done everythin' you wanted. Ain't that enough?'

Frustrated, he walks to the altar and stands looking at the Angel of the Annunciation. The statues are in poor shape, the Angel's wings infested with beetle and the Madonna's face so worn She looks like a ventriloquist's dummy.

The organist is playing the organ. Gabriel didn't recognise the piece but thought it might be a Bach chorale, words to the poem he used to read:

'Rise up, my love, my fair one, and come away. For lo the winter is past and the rain is over and gone!'

It is bitter cold in the church, condensation on the Madonna's face, her painted eyes heavy with tears. Gabriel reached out to wipe them away and the Sword fell.

The church door blasted open. A gust of wind blew down the central aisle whirling sorrow and joy, dust and leaves and yesterday's confetti before it.

A voice whispered in his ear, 'Semper fi, Gabriel.'

'Oh Jesu!' Then he remembers Bobby's funeral and a promise made in this church, '*take this love away and I'll carve you an angel that'll outlive the church!*'

Click! Click! A telephone is being reconnected, a line re-established.

The wooden Goddess answered his prayer. He'll never have Adelia for his wife.

She is already married.

~

Adelia was waiting for Gabriel. The cook was saying goodnight.

'Mrs B, do you have the correct time?'

'It's eleven-thirty.'

'No sign of Willow, I suppose.'

'Nu-huh! I put his fish out but he didn't take it.'

This will be the fourth night in a row the cat hasn't come home. Willow was Alex's cat and ever a stray coming and going as it pleased. Maybe I should get a pup, she thought, another Biffer, dear little dog whose sole purpose in life is to love.

Now with memory returned her life with Bobby Rourke takes on new meaning. Where before with only gossip and poison-pen letters to go by she tended to regard him the martyred hero and herself a scheming whore, she now sees life at the Mill as more complex. That Gabriel emerges a devoted lover and friend is no surprise. That she should think him capable of deceit her shame. The greatest revelation is Alex.

Until a few hours ago he was two men, the shy Major of '42 and the strong and forceful Colonel of latter times. Today another man was revealed, a composite of the two. Meeting her in Virginia he was hurt and angry yet loved her enough to crawl through pig muck to learn the truth. In '48, at Sophie's Ballet Concert, he was kicked and punched, yet, honour written through him like the legend in Blackpool Rock, he took it all. Asked why he said he owed it to Bobby. 'He saved your life.'

So many memories and with every memory gained his loss is the greater.

'Hey, Delia?' Sue strolled in. 'Me and Frank are off now.'

'Is everything all right now between you two?'

'It's as alright as it's gonna be.' Sue perched on the table. 'Did you see the thing in the paper about Gabe and his milord settin' up a Park in Britain?'

'I read it.'

'D'you think he's likely to go live there?'

'Possibly.'

'You and the kids goin' with him?'

'No.'

'I guess you're still thinkin' on your man. D'you reckon there's much hope?'

'There's always hope.'

'What about you and that Jacob?'

'I don't love Jacob.'

'Do you have to be in love to have fun?'

'I think I do.'

'Were you in love with Baby Rourke?'

'Not according to Ruby.'

'Ah, what did she know! There are women like Ruby everywhere, your mother-in-law for one. They're always chasin' misery sayin' you should stick by the rules and be unhappy. I say if it feels good and it don't hurt nobody then do it!'

'You are a modern woman, Sue.'

'I'm as old as the Blue Mountains. If I care for a man I don't need a piece of paper tellin' me it's right. I don't need to be in love neither nor him love me.'

'We're two different people.'

'Difference is you're not willing to bend. You won't have sex with a man unless you love him. I ain't so picky. Gabe doesn't love me but if he were to ask I'd go for it.'

'But what good would it do?'

'What good?' Sue stared. 'You ask me that? And you the woman he's been chasin' for years?' She stubbed her cigarette and strode away. 'God knew what he was doin' when he gave you amnesia. Only a silly bitch would forget the love of an angel.'

Adelia watched her leave. She said nothing. What's the point? Sue is moving on. Frank had driven his last rig. Timmy will be in nursery school soon and Sophie is to audition for the Royal Ballet School in London. All things must end, even grief.

Her love for Alex was the bedrock of her life. Today a ray of hope pushed through the rock like a bean-shoot. The shoot had a name, Gabriel. But it's too late. Too much harm has been done to too many people. They can never be together, and if, after their moment of love here in the attic there is a price to pay, so be it.

~

It's one o clock. Gabriel isn't coming. Restless, she paced up and down. The house is quiet without the children, every other sound amplified, the clicks and bumps of electrical switches, mice in the egg house and birds shifting under the eaves.

Alex's field glasses hang over the stair post. As always he is in the air, the scent of his cologne and in the distinctive smell of French cigarettes.

There he is walking through the arch, a tennis shoe in his hand: '*That dog's been chewing my shoe again. Look after him, Sophie, or he'll have to go...*'

She walked along the gallery and he's there the night she saw them dancing to the radio, Sophie a high-stepping pony and her father an adoring war-horse. 'One, *two, three, one, two...watch out for your toes, sweet-pea! One, two, three...*'

Every step Adelia takes is a trap. She will leave, go to England. But how could she, when he's here in this house. She leaned against the wall. 'I miss you.'

The echo whispered with her...*miss you!...miss you!*'

That night she dreamt she was on a train filled with travellers. Ruby Rourke in a pink frock and hat with roses sat in the corner. 'You look nice,' Adelia said. She nodded.

'I ain't been to this place before. I thought I'd better push the boat out.'

The train rolled on. It came to Adelia that though she's alive and dreaming other people on the train are dead. They didn't seem to mind. The train pulled into a station. Bill was on the platform, in uniform medal ribbons on his chest.

He pulled on the door handle wanting to get on board. 'Not yet, Bill,' she held the handle from the other side. 'I need you to stay with me.'

He kept wrenching as Adelia fought to keep the door shut. Then a flight of cherubs flew out of the sky and hung on the handle with him, fluttering and cooing. She was about to let go when a hand came down over hers, the fingers mangled.

'Hold on, Dad,' said a voice. 'I'm on my way.'

She slept again and dreamed she was in the Mill tower staring through the open door. Bobby was pollinating lilies, Biffer curled up beside him.

'Hi, honey.' He looked up and smiled. 'How you doin'?'

'I'm all right. Have you seen Alex in your travels?'

'I've seen him.'

'Is he at rest?'

'Does he look like he's at rest?'

Then she saw the same metal bunker and Alex a caged animal!

'No!' she screamed. 'I won't have it!' And as before jumped into the grave and began clawing at the bunker until a pin hole appeared.

Digging her fingers into the hole she pulled.

Boom! A Jack-in-the-Box sprang out, a painted smile and empty eyes.

She woke and afraid to go back to sleep reached for the phone. It was off the hook and must have been so all night. She thought to phone Gabriel. But then no! One mustn't make use of a person just because he's there.

There were two people she could call. One would bring love and faithfulness. The other would bring desire thus cancelling out the former.

The phone was picked up. 'Will you come?'

She waited. A car was coming up the drive, headlights shining.

She opened the door. Jacob came in closing the door behind him.

She led him to the attic. Once inside she let her robe fall to the floor.

'Let it be as you want,' she said.

~

It was late when Gabriel knocked on the door. He passed Alex's greatcoat.

'I brought this.'

Jacob came out of the kitchen, a piece of toast in one hand and cup of coffee in the other. But for a flattening of the lips Gabriel's expression didn't change.

'There's a letter in the pocket,' he said. 'You need to read it.'

'Thank you.'

'And you need to put the phone back on the hook.'

'I will.' She closed the door.

Jacob smiled. 'That's one fellow you won't be seeing again.'

'Yes,' she said. 'And you're another.'

She took the coat upstairs and laid it on the bed. Hearing the front door slam she went under the shower scrubbing Jacob, and a debt, from her skin.

Why the coat now? What's so important it can't wait until morning?

She stripped the dressing bag away. There was a letter and a jeweller's box in the pocket. The box contained the Medal and a single row of pearls.

'No!' She pushed it all back into the pocket. 'No last words.'

She was dressing when the phone rang.

It was Ellen. 'I've been trying to get hold of you. Bill's had stroke and been taken into the Veteran's. Please come! They don't think he's going to make it.'

~

'What have they said?'

Ellen was in the foyer. Fragile, a tiny bird, she collapsed against Adelia. 'He's had a massive stroke and is paralysed down his left side. It's awful! To see a man like Bill struck down like this is more than I can bear.'

Adelia led her to a seat. 'Is Sarah with you?'

'She's in Florida with that pilot. I left a message with their service; hopefully they'll get here in time.'

'So you're here on your own?'

'A friend came with me in the ambulance.'

'And the children? Are they with the housekeeper?'

'Uh-huh. Petey and David are over so they're all in one bag.'

'Who's in there with him now?'

'Well, the doctor and the nurse and the wires and things.'

'Can I go in and see him?'

'Oh sure! He's only just come round but he is looking for you. I have to rest a minute. There's so much going on I'm finding it hard.'

'Of course! What room is he in?'

'He's in twenty-eight.'

Adelia turned to go but Ellen called her back, a handkerchief pressed to her mouth, as though holding her lips together. 'Honey?' she said tremulously. 'Something wonderful has happened. We haven't told him yet because we weren't sure his dear old heart would stand it. But it is wonderful. Truly, truly wonderful!'

Puzzled, doubting the wonder of the situation, Adelia hurried away. She'd thrown an overnight bag in the car, phoned Sue and dropped the keys at Mrs Brock's. She didn't see Jacob leave and was glad of it. If there was a debt it's paid.

She tapped on the door. A young nurse was fixing a band about Bill's wrist.

'Is it okay to come in?'

'Sure, you can. The gentleman's with the doctor.'

'Gentleman?'

'Uh-huh, the one waiting to see General Hunter.'

Adelia closed the door. Oh Bill! A bloom of waxy sweat on his face he was trussed up in a ratty hospital gown, drips to his arm, a catheter to his genitals and a bib about his neck, yet in amongst the paraphernalia he is still there, eyes watchful.

'Hello, sweetie.' She kissed him then tossed the bib into a wastebasket.

Saliva dribbling from the side of his mouth, he mumbled something.

'I got these at Bergdorf's.' Trying not to weep she held up a pair of pyjamas. 'They were to be for Christmas but we'll bring that forward.'

He slid sideways. The nurse propped him up.

'I've brought Jasmine tea,' said Adelia. 'It is his favourite.'

'You could put it in a beaker?'

Adelia unscrewed the top, but shaking, spilled the tea. 'Sorry,' she said, mopping the table. 'I'm a bit dithery.'

'It's okay. I'd feel the same way if it was my Pa.'

Eyes closing in satisfaction, Bill slurped the tea.

'He enjoyed that, ma'am.' The nurse mopped his chin, tidied up, and then put the buzzer by Adelia's hand. 'Buzz if you need me.'

'I will.' She sighed, all energy gone. Knowing him unable to reply she didn't bother with questions, simply sat holding his hand and talking of Sophie and Timmy. No mention of England she talked of the future, and in every hope included Bill.

'Timmy's down for the Academy so when you're well we'll go to the outfitter's and see what he needs.'

The door behind her opened.

Bill jerked convulsively and started to weep.

'Oh, darling, don't cry,' she said, wiping his eyes.

He wasn't looking at her. Mouth open and with great gasping sobs, he was gazing over her shoulder and trying to hold out his arms.

Adelia's heart stopped. She knew who it was he saw.

Then she was moving aside and letting him through and Alex was by the bed, scooping his father up in his arms, his dark head against Bill's grey head.

'Dad,' he is crying. 'Oh Dad!'

Chapter Thirty-Five
Black Widow

Sunlight shone on a brilliant array of medals. The escort waited for the hearse to arrive. Eight men of similar size and build gathered in the porch, best greens, buzz cuts and strong jaws, the army's finest come to do honour to a soldier.

Alex passed his cap to Frank. Frank saluted smartly and marched away.

It only seems a minute ago, thought Alex, since I stood here waiting to carry Bobby to his grave. Now I escort my father.

The General died two am Tuesday morning. Alex and Adelia were with him. One moment he was awake, his gaze fixed on a beaker of Jasmine tea, and by ten he was gone, his hand closing about a drawing Tag made for him.

It is as it should be. William George Sherman Hunter would not want to be a bedridden cripple. They'd had three days of grace, Sarah, Maurice and the boys kept the morning vigil, Ellen the afternoon, and in the evening, and throughout the night, it was Adelia or Alex, their hands linked across the bed.

Despite the General's illness a lot of healing went on in the room, no need for words only the touch of hand and

the uncontrollable need to kiss to make sure it was real and
not a dream.

It was Gabriel Templar who discovered Alex. Having
got the call from Culpepper about his father, Alex was on
the point of leaving for the hospital.

The light was on in the Mill tower, and like a moth to a
flame, or a magnet to trouble Templar was drawn in. He
came pounding up the stairs and stood at the door
resignation on his face. 'She said she saw you. I didn't want
to believe her.'

Alex was sorry for him. By being alive he had blown a
man's dream apart.

'She wasn't meant to see me. I wasn't quick enough.'

Templar had scanned the room seen the bed-roll and
neatly folded blankets, and Willow, the cat, sitting in the
window.

'You've been livin' here.'

'Uh-huh. I bought it in '49 when I drew up the Will.'
Alex had zipped up his bag the sound screeching through
the empty building.

'Sure you did! You're a great tactician. It's what you do
best, Army, occupy the high ground.'

'I wouldn't say high ground more a neutral zone.'

Templar had stood gazing about. 'Where are you
goin'?'

'My father's had a stroke. He's in the Veteran's.'

'Does she know?'

'I only knew myself a moment ago when Culpepper
phoned.'

'That man again!' In a perfectly understandable burst of frustration Templar had spat on the floor. 'He's into everythin'!'

'It would seem so.' Alex slipped dark glasses over his nose.

'What's with the shades?'

'I have trouble tolerating bright lights. Excuse me.' He'd swung a bag over his shoulder. 'Scat, Willow!' Shooing the cat before him he made for the stairs.

'How are you gettin' there?'

'A cab, I guess.'

'I'll give you a lift.'

'Aren't you expected elsewhere?'

'I can make a call.'

'Help yourself.'

Templar dialled, punching out an all too familiar number. 'The line's engaged. I'll try further along the way.'

Alex didn't ask why the guy needed to phone the Eyrie. He knew the comings and goings of that house.

They took the highway out of town and then a question and answer dialogue that fooled no one. 'You look pretty beat up, Colonel.'

'Yes.'

'How long have you been back?'

'I landed on American soil a fortnight ago.'

'And you didn't tell anybody?'

'I was in no fit state.'

'Everyone's been goin' crazy.'

'Didn't look like that earlier.'

'If you mean me and Adelia there's nothin' happenin' there. You made sure of that when you drew up that Will.'

'I did it to safeguard her.'

'*Merde! Ne me prenez pour un imbécile*! You did it to safeguard yourself! If anythin' was gonna stop her carin' for me it was obligation.'

'You underestimate Adelia.'

'I underestimate nothin'. You knew what you were doin' when you put that thing together. You had us bound and tied like the hogs she used to raise.'

'You're confusing me with some other guy. It would take a Machiavellian brain to come up with a scheme like that. I'm only a simple soldier.'

'Simple soldier my ass! They don't call you the Camera for nothing.'

'Actually, no one calls me that anymore. As of last week and me returning to the military fold, my given title, not that it signifies, is Brigadier General.'

'Jesu! You are one scary man.'

'If I am anything at all Jesu has everything to do with it!'

'Why are you pissed at me when I've done everythin' you wanted?'

'I'm not pissed with anyone. I'm bone weary. All I want to do is see my father and then go home to sleep.'

'So go do it. There ain't no one gonna stop you. '

'I'm not sure I can go home. I don't know I have the right.'

For a while there was silence. 'You look like shit,' then said Templar. 'Why don't you close your eyes and get some rest?'

Alex had wanted to sleep but aware of dreams he'd encounter he preferred to talk, to try to describe what happened at Incheon, the debacle and his capture, but half a dozen words, and lulled by windscreen wipers and the warmth of the car slept.

The moment he closed his eyes the nightmares began. He was back in a military hospital. The Korean doctor, correction, the interrogator, was reading Sophie's letter. *'Dear Daddy, yesterday was my ballet midi exam. Miss Kolesnikova chose a piece called 'Pavan for a dead Princess.' The examiner said I showed great promise. Christmas was quiet. We went to Nana's. Mommy stayed home with Tag. Davy lost a tooth fighting with Pete. I kissed him and made it better. Mummy and me and Timmy think about you all the time.'*

Love and kisses from your daughter, Sophie.

PS. Willow keeps looking for you. I told him you'll be home next Christmas.'

That letter! For two years it was the wellspring of life and almost the cause of his death. Faded and tattered, it arrived in the summer of '51 via the blood-spattered pocket of one Corporal Powers, a Sapper from Kent.

Camp 2 shared resources, every man throwing what he had into the middle and there it was, a scrap of hope among fag ends and worn razor blades.

Bemused, Alex had stared. He'd know that handwriting anywhere. He couldn't believe it. All this time behind the 38th and not once getting mail and now there's this letter from his daughter in the hands of a stranger.

He'd stuttered. 'This was written by my daughter.'

'Your daughter?' says the Sapper.

'Yes, my daughter, Sophie.'

'Then it's all yours, cock.'

'How come it's in your pocket?'

The Sapper shrugged. 'Same way it's came to yours a gift from God.'

An FBI investigator thought the letter a possible breach of security. A polite, but puzzled Korean interrogator thought it a tool of Western propaganda.

'Please to tell, Colonel, sir, what is this document?'

'It is a letter from my daughter.'

'To whom is the letter written?'

'To me, her father.'

'Why the signatures?'

At that point Alex would retrieve the letter and smile. Who wouldn't? It had been passed from line-to-line and from hand-to-hand. Even in the POW camp amid the dirt and degradation - folded and refolded, blood-spattered and worn - it shone like a beacon. His daughter's words were enough yet add to that the hundred-and-one postscripts, sketches and kisses from the pencil stubs of serving men and women behind the lines, many of them now dead or missing, and it is a sacred paean, a love song from a child to her father.

Click! The Camera would note every initial and sketch filing away information for future use when hopefully he might be able to help. Then he would pass the letter back to the interrogator, and, repeating the same old litany, name, rank, and service number suggest the signatories wished his daughter well.

'But who are they?'

'I do not know.'

'They are US personnel.'

'Well, there you go then.'

'What are these drawings? What do they represent? What about this one?' The interrogator indicated a miniscule drawing of a jar-head with a Mohawk haircut, an arrow pointing to a rainbow drawn on the side of his head.

'What are these symbols?'

'A rainbow and an arrow.'

'What do they mean?'

'I haven't a clue, but would suggest they're from the Wizard of Oz.'

'The wizard of oss? What is that?'

'A US movie.'

'A movie? Hollywood?'

'Affirmative. Hooray for Hollywood.'

'But why is it there?'

'I couldn't tell you.'

'And this...and this...and...?' The interrogator pointed to other drawings.

'They all seem to be good wishes sent to my daughter.'

'Why would US troops wish your daughter well?'

'You would prefer they wish her harm?'

Pit-pat, back and forth, inane question followed by an inane reply.

Back home in the USA Agent Forbes, an FBI investigator, went through a similar rigmarole.

'It was General Jentzen came up with the idea of sending your kiddie's letter out to folks across the 38th.'

'So I believe.'

'How do you reckon your interrogators saw it?

'They were bemused.'

'Bemused?'

'Yes, puzzled by the various words and images.'

'They thought it subterfuge?'

'Maybe.'

'They didn't think it was the GI guys and gals being kinda cute and sweet?'

'I don't know what they thought.'

'I guess they don't think US military has a heart.'

'Does the US military have a heart?'

Offended by the little quip the G-man wrote a couple of lines in his notebook and then left the room. Alex was pissed with the whole goddamn business. Cold War hysteria running rife, he anticipated a prolonged debriefing but this three day proctologist probe of his spotless military ass is not to be believed. Sure, the days is interspersed with trips to a VIP lounge and tots of bourbon but it still comes down to this, he's in a room not much bigger than a cell and questioned about everything from his thoughts on Ike to when he took his last dump. Then he is left alone for periods of time while being observed through a two-way mirror.

Fuck that for a game of tin soldiers. He didn't survive three years behind enemy lines to sweat it out in his own country.

~

A week later and the Agent still at it: 'So, Colonel…excuse me…*General*, you described how Major Farrell died, dysentery, I think you said. You also spoke of Captain James Macintyre, the Australian national, who you say you shot.'

'I did say that.'

'Because he was…let me look at my notes, "…dying in a latrine.'

'Affirmative.'

'He was dead when you fired the rifle?'

'Probably.'

'You're not sure?'

'Not a hundred percent.'

'You say you shot the Captain with an AK-47 taken from an aggressor.'

'I didn't take it from anyone. It was lying on the ground.'

'Lying on the ground?'

'Probably.'

'You don't seem sure.'

'I'm not.'

'How can you not be? You're the Camera, the man with the know-how. Mister Memory. How can you not be sure of anything?'

It was at that point that Alex wanted to treat the guy to a little wall-to-wall counselling. A battered army fist connecting with that flabby jaw would have felt good. Chicken shit desk jockey! Where's he been the last three years, sitting on the tidy side trying to get a man to say things he didn't want to say! If a US Colonel, a Ranger, a Holder of the Medal, wasn't going to bend for the Commissar missionary-boy, he's not going to bend for this prick.

The camp Commissar is long gone, blown to buggery by a US medium bomber. That was the sound Alex heard when going to ground, a raid on the compound. Three

POWs wounded and the jail and the wooden boxes, and the Hole and the commissar blown to Hell. Alex surfaced to a scorched groove in his head and a new Commissar with a broom sweeping real clean.

Suffice it to say he was up for a beating. The Kiddie-Captain dead, there would have been a lynching but for a change of command. After the ritual beating Alex was thrown onto another train heading for the Yalu River. By then he was pretty sick, his back ripped to the bone and his right hand infected.

'I see by the medical notes,' the G-Man again, 'you've lost the use of your right hand.'

'It says that? I lost the use of my right hand?'

'It says, "lacerations to the palm and three fingers of right hand amputated.'

'Nah, I don't think so.' Alex removed the glove and waggled the three fore-shortened fingers. 'Do they look amputated to you?'

'No, sir, they don't. They look pretty damn painful though.'

'They were pretty damn painful.'

'So, you still got your fingers but were transferred to a military hospital?'

The guy was getting on Alex's nerves. Why this waste of time when there are things he needed to do and people he is desperate to see.

'Fucking moron!'

'I beg your pardon?'

'Golly gee, I must stop doing that.'

'Doing what General?'

'Cussing. My wife can't abide swearing. I guess I learned bad habits while I was away. I better quit or she'll be washing my mouth with soap.'

'Ah, yes, your wife. It's that we don't understand, your decision to keep your freedom under wraps. Why would you do that? All that time away from your family, why the blanket of silence. It is your right to do so! Lord knows, what you've been through. But having met Mrs Hunter, I confess I wouldn't be able to exercise such self control.'

'I doubt you would.'

'So why the need to stay away?'

It was a fair question. Why did you stay away Ash? Weren't you being cruel to everyone you knew and loved? His answer to that is that it's a million times more cruel to send a crazy man back among their midst.

'After all, Agent Forbes, isn't this what our little chats are about? It's why we're gathered here, you wanting to know if I still walk the Company Line. That I haven't turned turtle and become a danger to his family, or more importantly, a traitor to his country?'

At least the Agent hadn't the gall to blush.

'Why do you think you stayed away,' he's back to it. 'Did you doubt your ability to pick up family life? You suffered at the hands of a brutal regime, not just your hand. I understand you were beaten more than once.'

'Affirmative.'

'And for days at a time you were often incarcerated in the...what is it...the bunker?'

'The Hole.'

'And beaten more than once?'

'I think we've established that.'

'How do you feel about that?'

'How do I feel about what?'

'How d'you feel about being beaten? You were a Colonel, the full bird, a professional soldier respected by men under your command, a holder of the Medal, and some little slant-eyed little nip is jerking you around.'

Slant-eyed nip!

Alex keeps hearing those words. They're neither right nor true. Before taken prisoner he fought alongside ROK soldiers who laid down their lives for their country. Ko-trai, an excellent scout, took a bullet that was meant for Tom Farrell. The world turns and an idiot trashes a continent.

'To backtrack, was Captain James Macintyre dead when you shot him?'

Alex shrugged.

'And after you shot him you were taken back to camp and beaten.'

'What is it with you?' Alex queried, mildly. 'You like the idea of a man beaten so bad blood pools at his feet? You like hearing of flesh torn away in strips.'

It was a couple of guards. They didn't want to, he could tell by their faces. To them he was a Djinn, an evil spirit able to be in two places at once. They were afraid for their souls, which meant they beat that much harder.

The pain was indescribable. He needed no help from a ghostly Marine. He was his own ghost, a gaunt man in filthy skivvies hovering above a nursery. God, he'll never forget it! There was a baby in a cot. In this out-of-body dream he leaned over the cot and the baby chuckled.

Alex could see the baby and hear it gurgling. He could weep too, his baby son in sympathy, tiny hands like anxious sea anemones. The child's tears brought mommy, love-light streaming from her eyes. Such was the intensity of feeling his spirit was drawn back to his body and to the Commissar saying, 'cease beating and return the Colonel his footwear.'

In those days his footwear was a pair of matted socks. US army boots are a prize. The first camp took everything, the scarf he squirreled away to bind his socks leaving an inch square to lie down at nights breathing her scent.

After the bombing raid on KG2 he was moved to a different camp. Eat, sleep, shit, an animal in a funk hole, so long as he lay on his stomach he could manage the pain in his back, the same with his head , a thick scull having saved his bacon. His hand, however, was badly infected.

At night he would squeeze as much pus as he could from the finger-stumps but try as he might he got sick and getting sicker prompted phantoms.

'*You've gotta get help, Colonel.*' Voices would tease and plead.

'Semper fi, Sergeant.'

'*You're sick, sonny. Your fingers are about to drop off.*'

'I'm managing Pappy.'

'*You're not managing, brother in-law. You need to go on sick call.*'

'Don't make me laugh, Maurice. This is a butcher's shop not Johns Hopkins.'

'*Please, Ash! Ask for help even if you have to beg.*'

'A Colonel of the US army does not beg.'

'*Dumb ass! Rank hath privilege but not where gangrene is concerned.*'

'I must sleep…Alexander S Hunter…Colonel…Eighth Army…under article 17…Geneva Convention…claim the right to remain silent…'

'*Alex! Darling! I implore you! Ask for help!*'

That was the voice that did it. In the middle of raging sickness she knelt beside him and wiping his brow with red chiffon begged him to seek help.

Friday and Agent Forbes's still sweating it out. 'You went on sick call.'

'I asked to go on sick call.'

'And the Koreans agreed?'

'To my everlasting surprise.'

'You were taken to a military field hospital. How were you treated?'

'Pretty well, thanks for asking.'

'You received medical care.'

'I did.'

'Do you remember what?'

'Maggots.'

'Maggots?'

'Maggots! Basically, they let a fly, or in my case flies, land on the infected area. The flies lay eggs, the egg turns into maggots, the maggots eat dead flesh.'

'Sounds primitive.'

'Primitive is as primitive does.'

'Your account of time spent at the hospital is vague. Do you remember what drugs you might have had?'

'You mean Benzedrine, LSD, and all that other mind-bending Psy-war crap you keep going on about? Is that the drugs you're referring to?'

'Do you recall being given such drugs?'

'I don't remember much of anything. I was out my scull convinced I could see and hear all manner of weird shit, like people and dead dogs.'

Mind-benders he did not need. His mind was throwing a party. Face down on a bed, he couldn't move for pain and couldn't sleep for men moaning. He could feel maggots under the bandages, *hear* them chomping his flesh. Minutes, hours, days, passed. He wasn't sure he could be bothered any more. Then the Marine sat by his bed. 'Wanna go walk-about, Ash? Find a better memory?'

He didn't care. 'Knock yourself out.'

Alex went into a coma and found he and the Marine were outside the Eyrie gazing through the window at a Christmas tree. 'What are we doing here?'

'We've come to say goodbye to an old friend.'

They were looking at the sitting room where Sophie sat crunched up on the carpet with Biffer in her arms. They were back in time watching a dog die.

'Why did you bring me back to this? I can't stand to see my girls cry.'

'They aren't the only ones cryin'.'

Sure enough, there through the window was the real life flesh and blood Alexander Stonewall Hunter with tears in his eyes.

'This is one hell of a dream.'

'It's no dream. Watch!'

He watched and saw Biffer die and then another Biffer roll out of Sophie's arms. The dog, a pup, happy as a clam, bounced across the carpet and leapt out through the window, glass melting and reforming behind. Next, he's warm and furry in Alex's arms, a wet tongue licking his face. Then someone whistled and a voice called, 'Here, Biff! Come on, old sport!'

The dog was gone, tail wagging, and heading toward the Mill.

'It was Bobby Rourke calling the dog, Agent Forbes. A dead man called and the dog went. So what do you make of that? Christmas trees, a ghostly Marine, dead dogs and a dead USAF ace? Vague enough for you?'

'I've heard similar reports. From what I've read of the files a great many men went through psychotic experiences. The enemy has its ways.'

'Affirmative.'

'If I may say so, General Hunter, you've come through remarkably well.'

'I'm mending.'

'Yes, sir, considering the mental and physical torture, your hand, the solitary confinement, the beatings, you are in good shape.'

Alex pursed his lips. 'Good shape?'

'Yes, sir.

'What am I hearing, Agent Forbes?'

'Hearing, sir?'

'I believe I am hearing uncertainty.'

'No, sir.'

'Yes Sir! I hear it and have been hearing it since touching base. It goes something like this, "considering what you went through, mental and physical torture, blah-blah…you're in good shape. In fact, General, you're in remarkable shape! And ought you to be in such a good shape?" That's what I hear.'

'Not a bit of it.'

'Oh, yes, every bit.' Alex got to his feet. 'I was one of the last to get through. I left a lot of good men, friends and colleagues behind. Some will be brought home. Many will have to stay put, known unto God alone.'

He hung his jacket on the chair. 'Fourteen days I've been back in the Land of the Free. Fourteen days fielding impertinent questions - I won't say interrogation. Interrogation of a soldier in the US Army suggests cause for concern.'

He unclipped the field scarf. 'As I said, I'm one of the lucky ones. I got two arms, two feet, two eyes, and am relatively sound of mind. A couple of minutes with men like you, Agent Forbes, and I realise sound and sane isn't what you want. You don't want living POWs. You prefer us to be dead.'

By this time the Agent is backing away.

'Dead is dead in a metal crib, and no cause for concern.' Alex popped his cufflinks and set them on the table. 'Then again I could be wrong. Three years behind the 38th makes a man a tad cynical.' Taking his time he unbuttoned his shirt. 'Dead is perhaps extreme. I reckon you'd settle for me drooling and being wheeled about in one of those dinky little sicky-chairs.'

'Not at all, sir,' the Agent is anxious now. 'You're high, wide, and handsome, testament to an army man.'

Alex isn't angry. He's disappointed. He had thought better of his country.

A mirror occupied the left-hand wall. Calmly he flipped his shirttails and turned his back, the glass reflecting scored and roughened skin.

'Is this okay for you?' he said. 'Will this badge of courage and what it means suffice? Am I an honest man, Agent Forbes, and loyal to my country, a soldier worthy of the name? Or will only a cross and nails satisfy you?'

Chapter Thirty-Six
Lime Tree

So…that was Korea. What happened there as subject matter, especially where his loving wife is concerned, is done. Not that Alex thinks she can't handle it; her ability to roll with the punches amazed and shamed his. From the Mill tower he'd watch her drive by with his children in the back of the sedan, Sophie, a perfect tin-type of her mother, and Timothy Alexander William George, his beloved son.

'Thank you for my children,' he said the first night home.

God, he's proud of her. Such confidence and strength, she's all a man could ask of a mother and a woman. Look at the funeral business and the success she made of that. He caught the Senator's funeral and the old woman the week before.

If anything showed strength of character it was Ruby Rourke's funeral, Adelia carrying out the woman's wishes. Maurice is right, don't mess with perfection.

Adelia asked how he managed Korea with a photographic memory. Did the Camera make life more difficult? Recalling the men who died, some beaten to death, some hanged, and those who turned their faces to the wall, he said it helped remembering home. She thinks he's a hero. He prefers not to think about it.

It's hard letting go. Nights are bad. He wakes shouting. Medics prefer a guy not to shout. They don't pin medals on men who shout especially Generals.

Well, here's one General who's not ashamed to shout.

Templar asked when Alex planned on telling the family. He said he planned calling Adelia that night but got the call from Culpepper.

'So how come nobody knew you was alive?'

'We were always being moved about.'

'You had weeks to let your folks know.'

Here in the light of day it does seem a crazy plan but, a beast in a cage, Alex needed to know he couldn't do harm. It didn't matter what medics said. He had to be his own judge and jury. Had he thought he was less than one hundred percent he would have stayed MIA and Templar winning the lottery.

In the spring of '52 attitudes in Korea underwent a change. There was a shift in military strategy. Slowly, size and rank stopped being a scourge and became useful. In some bizarre way Alex had acquired a reputation to the inmates and the Koreans.

He was *Mogwai*, a Devil Lord, and apparently the one to go to if help was needed. Over the weeks, beatings and punishment only a wink away, he used his reputation to parley for aid. Behind the battle-front diplomacy was at work, peace talks being held and negotiations between Super Powers meant medical aid and a reduction of physical force. He never saw the Marine Sergeant again. Memories of him are ambiguous, sometimes taking the face and form of another, maybe even Tom Farrell or the crazy Aussie, Macintyre. When thinking of home the Djinn might be Adelia, or Sophie's letter to daddy, with its myriad doodles and messages. More often than not he associates Gabriel Templar with the guy but no doubt that was the Will playing on his mind.

It was a dangerous time. Thinking back, what with the Hole and the beatings the guards could've killed him at any time yet here he is alive and but for the loss of fingers pretty much in one piece. The weirdest thing, the codicil, if you like -and the piece of Intel that sticks most in Agent's Forbes mind- is the shooting of Macintyre.

With the bombing raid on KG2 the remains of Tom Farrell and Jamie Macintyre were passed back along the line, it was propaganda, the US raid held responsible for their deaths. Here's the weird thing, the post-mortem revealed Tom died from a combination of beriberi, malnutrition and former hurts from back in the '40s when he was POW in Germany. Jamie Macintyre died from multiple stab wounds.

That's it, multiple stab wounds. Not a single bullet wound, no AK-47 real or otherwise shot Jamie which is odd when you think about it.

Alex's right hand has limited capability. His left is good but not yet ready for a 45. From a physical point of view he's not a great catch. That the military continue to pay him a stipend is now more to do with the Camera viewing distant horizons.

As of yesterday he processes a thread of activity alongside a branch of the USAF SERE project. Search, Evasion, Resistance and Escape is a project close to his heart. Since his escape from Italy certain aspects of life gathered under the SERE code are known to him. The job has high-spots and low. Other than that, it's as a former USAF Ace pilot would say, 'SSDD: Same shit, different day.'

~

'Escort shun!'

The hearse arrived, a black Buick rolling through the gates, the flag, Old Glory, blooming through glittering glass. The committal ceremony takes place at the graveside where the family wait. Chairs are set out and wreaths about the grave. Alex took his place, the casket is hoisted up, three paces forward and three left. Accompanying Top Brass shuffle into position, a beat of a solitary drum, the tread of boots, and the General, God rest his soul, is on his way.

Nails digging, Ellen clutches Adelia's hand. Unaware of pain Adelia watches the casket and the leading bearer. How wonderful he is, how upright and strong! Thank God he is home!

They gather at the grave, family right and Top Brass left. Ellen is in the middle, Sarah, Maurice and the boys on her right. Adelia is left with Timmy and Sophie. She hadn't wanted Timmy there but a chip off the Hunter block he would come.

Sophie has taken the loss badly. Only her father's presence soothes her.

'You don't have to come to the funeral, Sweet Pea. Gramps wouldn't expect it.'

'He would, Daddy.'

She's right. Bill would expect them to be at his funeral, as he would expect the Army Top Brass in spades. 'It's my right,' he would say. 'I've earned it.'

Adelia misses him. She depended on Bill's strong grip on life and complete lack of falsity. He left a gap that only his son could fill.

Lord! The moment Alex appeared in the hospital! It took her by the throat and rendered her speechless. 'What's the matter, baby?' he'd said, hoarsely. 'Cat got your tongue?' She'd gazed at him, thoughts running through her head, he's lost weight and his hair is sprinkled with grey and his skin pale. Other hurts, terrible hurts, his hand and his back were later revealed.

Paralysed with joy she was only able to stare. Alex waited, a pulse quivering at the corner of his mouth. Bill waited with him, his faded blue eyes round like a child.

'Do you still love me?'

'Yes.'

'Do you still want me to be with you?'

'Yes!'

'And do you forgive me?'

'There's nothing to forgive. You came home.'

~

The escort carried the casket to the grave lowering it onto a wooden platform. When Ellen shuddered Adelia took her hand. Sarah is remotely soignée in a silk suit, her hair bobbed and shining. A whisper circulates. She's dropped Sam Jentzen's son. No more talk of divorce. Maurice looks as he always looks, a wise owl, spectacles on the end of his nose and furrow between his brows. He catches Adelia's eye and makes a sympathetic moue.

Someone's missing. She's looking for Bill, expecting him to come round the corner, a forage cap on his head and a putter under his arm. '*That caddy don't know a niblick from a hole in the ground*.'

That's okay. Sooner or later she will see him. 'You don't believe in that twaddle, do you?' he would say. 'It's horse feathers! When you're dead, you're dead. Nobody's ever come back to tell us different.'

She didn't argue. You didn't argue with Bill. Yet it was on the tip of her tongue to say that quite apart from her living husband there is a soldier who every evening around seven sits in the Orangery. He sits, smokes a cigar, and then fades quietly away, a trail of smoke lingering. Joe Petowski, God-Father to all. Then there are the misty shapes that when the moon is high float about the attic bedroom. And Bobby and Biffer who many say can be seen in the glass greenhouse at the Mill.

The Eyrie is filled with energy. Only the other day she heard Sophie in close conversation with a peony. Timmy frequently talks of his best friend, the 'man wid de wings'. Perhaps it's as well the house is on the market.

'Fire!' A volley of shots rang through the air, making her jump and sending birds hurling into the sky. A solitary bugler up on the hillside plays, 'Taps.'

The flag is folded and quartered into a neat pack of sorrow.

Alex marches toward his mother. He halts before her and salutes offering the flag and his country's thanks for the life of the General.

Ellen shakes her head: 'It's for Adelia. She was good to him.'

Adelia accepted the flag. Alex saluted, and then must salute again because Timmy's on his feet, stiff and proud in little grey shorts, his hand in sharp salute.

'Hello Daddy,' he said.

Alex lifted him into his arms. 'Hello Son.'

'I've been waiting for you.'

'And I have been waiting for you.'

Later that evening, the children abed and Alex driving Ellen to her sister's Adelia sat alone in the house. She'd written to Sue saying they were going to Europe for a while and that she wouldn't return to the 'New Valley.' She thanked Sue for her friendship and asked her to think of Adelia's share of the business as her own to sell or keep as she chose. She wrote a letter to May Templar saying the Eyrie was on the market and that they would probably move closer to Ellen. No letter for Gabriel. She had nothing to say. He was alive in her and always would be.

It has been a long, sad day. Her hat weighed heavy, a nice hat, she almost lost it in a snowstorm at Bobby's funeral. A man caught it and hung it on an angel's finger.

She unzipped her frock and hung it beside Alex's greatcoat. A slender woman in black underwear, a single strand of pearls about the throat, she took the letter from the greatcoat pocket and was about to open it when a door downstairs slammed.

Footsteps sounded on the stairs. Alex entered the bedroom. Chest heaving, he reached back locking the door. No special haste. Methodical, deliberate, with the same purpose he does everything in life, he stripped his clothes.

Flattening his palm, 'stay put', he showered. Soon he was back naked but for shorts his hair a shining skull cap. He took the letter and laid it on the dresser.

'You won't need that.'

Tears filled her eyes but fearful of losing sight even for a second she dashed them away. Worries went through her head. He's lost weight. He's pale as though he's been living underground. He is terribly hurt! Oh, poor hand! Poor back!

Bridge of his nose creasing, he frowned. Knowing he hated to see her cry she bit back tears. She wanted to speak but nothing worked, not her legs, nor her vocal chords, only her hands rising to soothe the shadows under his eyes.

'You want something to do with those?' he said. 'Give them to me. I'll put them where they'll make us both feel better.'

He slid her hands down his shorts closing her fingers about his erect penis.

'Ah yes.' He closed his eyes. 'Thank you, Lord Jesus, for bringing me home.'

For a while he stayed thus and then his hands rose wiping away her tears. Tilting her chin his mouth descended. As he kissed her his penis jerked wetting her hands with a light semen spray. 'Sorry about that,' he whispered. 'But it's been a heck of a long time and that is the effect your kisses have on me.'

Huffing, puffing, her heart too full to speak, she gazed at him.

'What's the matter, sweetheart? That mangy Willow still got your tongue?'

'Alex,' she needed truth between them. 'There's something I need to tell you.'

He kissed her eyes. 'There's nothing you need tell me.'

'I must! I have to tell you that the other day I…we…Gabriel…!'

'No,' he spoke against her lips. 'There's nothing, I repeat, nothing you need tell me other than you love me. Do you love me?'

'You know I do.'

'Then that's all I'll ever need to know.'

She never did learn what was in the letter. The next day it was gone.

~

They're back from Italy staying at Sarah's. She lives in New York now, an apartment in Manhattan. The Parkers are divorced, all hope of reconciliation gone.

Alex and Tag are killing time seeing the sights. The womenfolk are on a shopping spree and then to meet up with Luke Jentzen, Sarah's latest amour.

After three months of being dragged from one Continental boutique to the next by his wife and daughter Alex chose not to go, besides, he is fond of Maurice Parker and finds the split painful. Taking tea with Sarah's new lover is too rich for his blood maybe in time but not yet.

'Maybe but not yet,' is what he was hearing from an old friend. Frank Bates is holding on to the funeral business. Adelia is out and so is Sue, who in the space of a couple of months met and married an oil-rich Texan and gone to raise hell in Calvary. Now with Sue leaving and the hiring of Beth, the nanny to Timmy and coming baby, Frank's interest in Virginia is rekindled.

With a couple of hours to kill Alex thought to swing by the Guggenheim and see what all the fuss is about. Templar's latest statue was unveiled a week ago. It's on loan to the museum and from there to be shipped back to Fredericksburg and St Jude's, the church on the hill.

News is they had to hire a crane, the roof coming off Templar's barn.

Art critics are calling the statue the New Kiss and the sculptor the New Rodin. Broadsheets carry serious stories about it. While in Rome Alex saw the headlines in *Time* but not wanting to disturb Adelia in early pregnancy stayed mute.

A catalogue from the foyer, and Timmy on a tight rein, he strolled through the lower galleries.

'Daddy can we go to de zoo?' said Timmy, bored.

'If we get time.'

'Gramps and I went to de Zoo. Dey had eagles and tings.'

'*Th*ings, Timmy.'

'*Th*ings. Eagles and *th*ings.'

'Good boy.'

Basking in his father's approval, Timmy became expansive. 'I see eagles all *th*e time, Daddy. *Th*ey fly up and down my room.'

'Maybe you'll be a pilot when you get bigger.'

'Not me! I'm going to be Captain Marvel and fly *th*rough walls.'

'Daddy had a friend that was a flier during the war. He was a brave man.'

'You're a brave man, daddy. Mommy says so.'

'Does she?'

'Look, Daddy! *Th*ere's *th*e man wi*th* wings!'

Templar was by the archway talking to a heavyset guy whose face Alex recognised as patron of the arts and big name in Manhattan society.

Calm, a simple cotton jacket and nice pair of leather loafers, Templar looked well. His hair is growing again switching his collar.

Alex was about to move on when he saw the statue.

'Christ!' he muttered, stopped in his tracks. It was immense. Small wonder they needed a crane! It must have been worked in two sections. No one, not even Templar could have lifted that!

'Christ,' he said again, and began walking toward it.

A colossal angel grew out of a tree. One booted foot poised in the air, the other trapped in the wood, she hovered, shoulders hunched and muscles straining as though to leap from the tree required effort, such effort wings have been damaged in the process.

Click! Click! Click! Alex stared and stared.

The Angel is locked in battle dragging a man from the bole of a tree. He, the man, is barely visible. You can see part of his head, his shoulders, and his right hand. The Angel's gaze is fixed on Heaven. Fingers splayed, her left hand snatches at space while her right arm is thrown behind, her fist closing in the man's hair. Her face is barely human yet to the men who love her infinitely known, cheekbones that slant upward, eyes and brows on a rising plane, neat pointed ears and a delicate nose. No robes for this angel, she wears dungarees, a strap floating loose, her left breast exposed.

'Look at her hair!' A bystander gasped. 'It's alive!'

It is the hair you remember. Electric, curling and alive, a thousand, thousand separate strands it flies about her face with a life-force of its own.

Animals curl about the base of the tree, a fox, a pig and a curly haired dog, a leash coiled in a circle. Cherubic faces emerge from the bark, sheaves of wheat, fruit and flowers, all spill from around the bole! Stars and moons and planets, birds, bees and everything that lives amassed about her feet.

Back of a vaulted arch, it couldn't have been better sited. Wood golden in colour and backdrop a rich dark blue, the Angel appears to be flying in a midnight sky.

It is beautiful and tortuous. Every sinew cracks. Every strand of hair shines. There's dust on the angel's boots and softness on her skin. The dog pants and the bees buzz. It's a world, a Universe, a paean to the Creator, and yet the Angel has but one purpose - and that is the man. She brings him Life, drags him into Being, and yet looking at the statue you can't say who gives life to whom.

'Mummy!'

'No, Timmy!'

Timmy is running, pushing through the mass of people about the statue.

He hops over the rope barrier and stands pressed against the base of the statue, his arms outstretched and eyes closed.

'You can't go in there, young man!' shouted a custodian.

'Yes, he can,' said Templar.

You can see why a child would want to do that. Alex wouldn't have minded laying his cheek against that Angel, resting on pure goodness.

He stared at the face but could not speak. There were no words.

He stood so long Timmy got bored and pulled on his hand.

'Can we go to *the* zoo?'

'A minute, Son, I want to have a word with Mr Templar.'

He walked over. Templar straightened, a look on his face that Alex had seen before, half anticipating and half aloof.

'Has she seen this?' Alex asked.

'Would she recognise herself?'

'Never in a million years.'

'That's what I thought.'

'It's breathtaking. It must have taken a hell of a lot of work.'

Templar ducked his head. 'I'm not sure about the wings. It was never my plan to carve them but you know how it is with these things. They take over.'

Alex didn't know. A concept, a skill like that, is beyond his understanding.

In Italy he wrote to Templar via Culpepper. Since Daniel made it clear the guy neither wanted nor needed a dime of the Hunter estate no mention was made of money. Guardianship of the children was the subject matter. A letter returned the same week, Gabriel would be pleased to remain the children's guardian. No mention was made of Adelia yet there is a situation, a pregnancy that has to be of interest to Templar, Alex can't let that pass by unspoken.

He folded the catalogue. 'We've been looking at houses and think we've found the right place. It's not as close to my mother as hoped but has a great view of the Sound. We're going to be busy for the next couple of months, aren't we, Timmy, painting and decorating?'

Timmy nodded. 'Mommy's giving me a new baby brother.'

'Or sister,' said Alex.

'No,' said Timmy firmly, 'brother.'

'Anyway, we're very happy about the baby. What with the General passing and Korea it's not been the best of time for anyone. We see this newcomer as a gift and are all real grateful. We thank God for the chance and plan to give this little girl, or boy, as Timmy seems to want to insist, the very best we can.'

Templar smiled. 'That's good to know.'

The smile told Alex his news was not so new, that where Adelia is concerned the man would always be light-years ahead.

'I heard this was going to Fredericksburg?'

'One of them, yeah.'

'You got another like this?'

'I got one the Madonna would prefer.'

'You are a talented man.'

They stood looking at the Angel.

'Have you given this a name?'

'The museum wanted to call it the Second Annunciation but I couldn't go with that, not with a name like mine.'

'I guess not!' Alex grinned. 'The Press would have had a field day. I can see the headlines, "Gabriel blows his own trumpet!'

'Ma would've got a kick from it but it would've killed me.'

'Maybe you should change your name to Ralph or something.'

'It would be less of a problem than livin' up to an Archangel.'

'I imagine it's not easy. The wings must be hell on the cashmere.'

'It has been known.'

'So what are you calling the statue?'

'I don't know. The papers have come up with all manner of stuff, none of it open to print. My tutor, Father Sebastian, says over time it'll probably be known as Reluctant Angels. It's a good name but thinkin' of my own life I'm goin' with A Second Chance.' He smiled. 'Do you need me to tell you why?'

'Nu-huh.' Alex shook his head.

They stood in silence, the past, present, and future flowing about them.

Alex offered his hand. 'It's good to see you.'

'Likewise.'

'What will you do now?' he said.

Templar shrugged. 'I don't know. I guess unless a miracle happens I'll go on being the sculptor and town loon. Seen any good miracles lately?'

Alex rested his chin on the top of Timmy's head. 'Yes.'

Perfidia
by
Dodie Hamilton
(extract)

Prologue
Ritual

Sophie tied up her hair, scraping it way off her face and into a high ponytail. She didn't want it flapping in her eyes. When you're going on a date there's nothing more annoying than hair in your eyes.

Okay, that's done, now for the lips. She hunted through the make-up box searching for the lipstick. Not just any lipstick! No soggy pinks or maudlin mauves, but the reddest, brassiest, Woolworth's Counter rouge a lèvres she can find the one she borrowed from Lola, the exotic dancer at the New Revue the one she keeps for such an occasion a run around the Great Park.

Three times applied and blotted her mouth is now seriously red. Not a Coco the Clown mouth! No, luscious and inviting lips, the way she likes it when dancing. Several coats of jet black mascara, her lashes curled, combed and swept to flutter like bat's wings.

A last slick of gloss possibly?

'Easy with that,' drawls a voice from the dressing room. 'You'll be passin' the wild cat enclosure. We got Bengal tigers today. It's hours before feedin' time. Needless to say they're pretty upset. I don't want them seein' all that juicy red meat and leapin' the wires, at least not until I've tripled your life insurance.'

'Funny,' said Sophie and continued glossing.

This nightly touch of the theatrical must be carried out in a manner befitting a ritual, with gravity and care, because for God's sake it is a grave situation! No one, not even the man standing through there will ever know how grave.

Grey cotton vest and leggings, Nike running shoes, a loose sweater tied about her waist in case of rain, and it usually does rain this time of night, it's hardly most glamorous outfit. Sophie doesn't care. It's practical, an essential stage of the ritual and has been so for twelve years.

'You ready to go?' the voice calls, casual yet as ever so very concerned.

'I'm ready.'

'Then I guess you'd better go.'

She pushes open the doors to stand for a moment on the veranda overlooking the Italian Gardens. It is a beautiful night, the stars silver filigree and the moon a great copper disc hanging low on the horizon.

A great wail of sadness, silent yet audible to all, passes over her heart. Why must it be like this? Why like so many pieces of jigsaw am I spread over and about this world? There is no reply from the house, only the clink of cufflinks in a box and the rustle of a linen shirt dropped into the laundry basket.

Come on, Sophie, she urged. Get on with it. There'll be no rest in this house until you're back again.

Down stairs she ran, along the corridor, and out through the Great Hall, down the passage, through the brick pantry and out a side door and under the loggia.

Pausing, she listens. It's so quiet, no one stirring, not a dog barking or a mouse squeaking.

She ran out onto the Mound, the dew heavy on the grass and her shoes kicking up water. She'll run twice round the Park. If he's there waiting they will meet. If not, if he's forgotten or moved on or if it truly is as she is told he is no more than a dream in her head then she'll return. She'll shower and sleep. The sun will rise and another day, and another life, will begin.

Printed in Poland
by Amazon Fulfillment
Poland Sp. z o.o., Wrocław